PRAISE FOR COOPERATIVE LIVES

GRAND PRIZE FINALIST—2019 SHELF UNBOUND
BEST INDIE BOOK COMPETITION

CATEGORY WINNER (LITERARY FICTION) & GRAND PRIZE
SHORT LIST—2019 MILLENNIUM BOOK AWARD

WINNER IN GENERAL FICTION
2019-20 READER VIEWS LITERARY AWARDS

WINNER IN FICTION
2020 BOOK EXCELLENCE AWARDS

GOLD MEDAL IN CONTEMPORARY FICTION
2019 LITERARY CLASSICS INT. BOOK AWARDS

WINNER—2019-20 JACK EADON MEMORIAL AWARD FOR
BEST BOOK IN CONTEMPORARY DRAMA

WINNER—2019-20 AUTHOR MARKETING NETWORK
AWARD FOR BEST FICTION DÉBUT

REVIEWER'S CHOICE AWARD
2019 FEATHERED QUILL BOOK AWARDS

SILVER MEDAL IN ADULT FICTION
2019 WISHING SHELF BOOK AWARDS

SILVER MEDAL, BEST FIRST BOOK
2020 INDEPENDENT PUBLISHER BOOK AWARDS

SEMI-FINALIST—2019 SOMERSET BOOK AWARDS

"Finegan's luscious novel *Cooperative Lives* follows characters whose lives change when they are brought into close proximity with each other through a series of coincidences, accidents, and international espionage... The story moves forward and backward in time with ease, teasing forth details and offering clues about a deeper underlying story and tangled interconnections... [It is] tempting to turn pages at a rapid speed, but masterful prose, marked by evocative phrasing and apt metaphors, encourages savoring each exquisite sentence and its imagery... Ambitious and sophisticated, *Cooperative Lives* is a diverse and gorgeous tapestry of character studies and is a pure delight to read."

Wendy Hinman, Foreword Clarion Reviews (5 stars)

"Written with all the passion and flourish of a love letter yet with all the calculation and clockwork of a crime novel, Finegan's novel is a fascinating slice-of-life that rings true even as it attempts the fantastic."
Michael Radon, US Review of Books (Recommended)

"[Finegan is] a master of the slow reveal. At first, the profusion of minute details about his characters' lives feels gratuitous, yet the voluminous threads eventually weave together to show how these wretched and paranoid characters became the lost and broken people they are today... Contemporary fiction fans will be enthralled by the tragic lives of upscale Manhattanites in this tale of espionage, corruption, and infidelity."
BookLife Reviews (Publishers Weekly)

"Happenstance, serendipity and luck dominate as the lives of characters crash against one another like pinballs in Patrick Finegan's *Cooperative Lives*. A novel that perfectly captures the unscripted events and coincidence of real life, where you can do your utmost best, and it's never quite good enough... A powerful, chic and evocative read, *Cooperative Lives* proves a superb début for Finegan and a must-read for discerning readers of top-notch literary fiction. It is recommended without reservation."
BookViral Reviews

"Incredibly evocative... [I]t is in his characterisations where Finegan really excels... [E]ach person is given a distinct voice and identity, making it not only easy to work out who is speaking, but also makes the reader genuinely care about these characters. The reader is able to see both sides of a situation and can empathise with the people in it, becoming impartial observers in a way... *Cooperative Lives* begins quite slowly but gradually builds momentum to a shocking climax... Maybe not one for those who like their novels fast-paced, but *Cooperative Lives* is a well-written, character-driven thriller which will keep readers hooked." *Lou Harrell, Reedsy Discovery (Loved it! 🥇)*

"A deliciously rich, intricate plot... The story has everything I look for in a fiction novel; espionage, intrigue, tension, corruption and a fantastic display of real human behavior... Overall, this is a perfect example of character interaction and development."
Lesley Jones for Readers' Favorite (5 stars)

"A reader expects so much more from literary fiction than from its less culturally evolved siblings. And not just in the quality of writing. One expects more depth, more complexity, more resonance, more beauty. One expects, and deserves, a novel like *Cooperative Lives*... [I]f you are looking for a book to savor, to appreciate the writing as much as the story line and plot, to satisfy your love for words as much as existential observations or distractions, look no further."

Joel R. Dennstedt, Independent Book Reviews (5 stars)

"An intricate and intriguing tale with a lot of plot twists and details hidden in plain sight... The people in this story are well-drawn, each with their own fully-developed personality – and their individual personality quirks together drive the plot, demonstrating the author's gift for truly elegant plot design. This is the sort of book that rewards, indeed perhaps requires, reading more than once in order to catch all the little details and plot points one may miss on a casual reading... *Cooperative Lives* is a complicated but beautifully engineered book, with its intertwined secrets, interacting lives, and the carefully-woven story that emerges from them."

Catherine Langrehr, Indie Reader

"A true testament of pure literary creative skill that casts a huge shadow over all things that have come before in the genre... With heart-stopping revelations that the reader simply will not see coming and the most detailed character development that could ever find its way into literature, this is a novel to be savored and revisited again and again in the future."

Entrada Book Reviews

"The changes in point of view are often abrupt, but the reader who follows from person to person, lie to lie, and secret to secret will find themselves at the heart of a dark web that stretches well beyond the building to a case that almost seems ripped from the headlines of the late 2000s and early 2010s when this story takes place. While the author describes this work as extremely recent historical fiction, this character-driven story is most definitely a work of exquisite literary fiction that uses the exploration of its characters to drive the narrative."

Chanticleer Book Reviews (5 stars)

"Finegan gives each character, however minor, heft, with backstories and quirks that deepen the plot, as well as exploring varying facets of the human condition... [He] is a gifted wordsmith, crafting sentences that are rich and multilayered, which propels the story along beyond the intricacies of the plot... A rare work of literary fiction that also shines as a mystery and a thriller, *Cooperative Lives* offers a brilliant exposé on the shattered nature of modern lives."

Self-Publishing Review

"There is a nostalgic feel to the work, despite it only being set a few short years ago, one which gives it the grandeur of the past at the same time as dealing with the real human issues of present daily life... A must-read for fans of unique literary character study."

K.C. Finn, Reviewer's Bookwatch

"A gripping, character-driven novel and a literary work of art... Set in New York only a few years ago, it is a story written with a gold-tipped pen; a story full of complex characters, many, if not all of them, inherently imperfect and distrustful of others... Do I recommend this book? Yes, absolutely! If you enjoy a 'thoughtful' tale, the sort of story that keeps you guessing, a story populated with well-constructed characters, then this is for you."   *Wishing Shelf Book Reviews (5 stars)*

"An intricately plotted, well-written tale. Finegan's style is clean and straightforward. His characters are imperfect and easily relatable people who experience the peaks and valleys that inform all lives... Strong on both character and plot, it's most likely to be enjoyed by readers drawn to intelligent writing."   *Blue Ink Review*

"Finegan writes with authority and grace... [He] avoids clichéd stereotypes for his fascinating cast of characters, with each exhibiting strengths and weaknesses as they navigate the ins and outs of their daily lives – their layers of armor stripped away until there's nothing left but raw emotion fed by love, hate, and the subtleties in between... [A] masterfully written work of literary fiction, *Cooperative Lives* gives readers an incisive look at ordinary people being blindsided by the uglier side of life, and does so with beautifully evocative prose."

The Independent Review of Books

"This book is elegant and intriguing. The characters are complex and the prose flows seamlessly. I found myself falling deeper and deeper into a black hole of suspense the more I read. *Cooperative Lives* is an exquisitely thrilling read!"   *Literary Titan*

"With a generous helping of plot twists and well fleshed-out characters, this book is an intricate study in the forces of human nature. The story is skillfully woven together to create intricate layers of intrigue that will keep readers enthralled clear through to the unexpected conclusion."

Literary Classics Reviews (5 stars)

"*Cooperative Lives* takes an intriguing look at the intersecting lives of the residents of a Manhattan Coop. The multitude of personalities weave a complete story told in alternating points of view, rolling backward and forward in time, and tie the apparently unconnected neighbors in unexpected ways."   *Bradley Allen, Manhattan Book Review*

"Filled with twisty turns, shocking revelations, and provocative portrayals of institutionalized power inequities, *Cooperative Lives* is a precisely engineered cautionary tale that entertains."

Cardyn Brooks, InD'tale Magazine

Cooperative Lives

COOPERATIVE LIVES

a novel by

PATRICK FINEGAN

TWO SKATES PUBLISHING
JERSEY CITY, NJ

© Patrick Finegan, 2019

PUBLISHER'S CATALOGING-IN-PUBLICATION DATA
Names: Finegan, Patrick, author.
Title: Cooperative lives : a novel / by Patrick Finegan.
Description: Jersey City, NY: Two Skates Publishing LLC, 2019.

ISBN:	IngramSpark HC:	978-1-7339025-2-6
	IngramSpark PB:	978-1-7339025-0-2
	IngramSpark ePub:	978-1-7339025-1-9
	Kindle Press PB:	978-1-0908936-3-5
	Kindle Press ePub:	978-1-7339025-3-3

Subjects: LCSH Apartment houses, Cooperative--
New York (N.Y.)--Fiction. | Manhattan (New York, N.Y.)--Fiction. |
New York (N.Y.) -- Social life and customs -- Fiction. |
New York (N.Y.)--Fiction. | Spy stories. | Suspense fiction. |
BISAC FICTION / General | FICTION / Literary | FICTION / Suspense.
Classification: LCC PS3606.I53375 C66 2019 | DDC 813.6--dc23

Two Skates Publishing LLC, One Harborside Place, Jersey City, NJ 07311
www.twoskates.com

Printed in the United States of America
1 3 5 8 3

for Dorene

PREFACE

It is perhaps unorthodox to declare a story which transpired 6-8 years ago in the country's largest metropolis historical fiction but labelling it otherwise would be a deception. The election of a bilious talk show host to the world's highest office, the NSA-sponsored surveillance, cataloging and storage of millions of Americans' phone logs and recordings, the petulant, self-imposed withdrawal of Great Britain from the EU, the global contagion of anti-immigrant nationalism – no pundit could have predicted these developments in 2013. And no one would have believed him.

I intended this book as a work of contemporary fiction. It described, I think accurately, the city and world I lived in. Just six years have elapsed since its completion, but I might as well have described ancient China. The world and New York City of 2013 no longer exist. I hereby present, for better or worse, the world's most contemporary historical novel.

THE CHARACTERS

THE RESIDENTS

M/M Ezra & Allison Pfouts 14P

M/M Sheldon & Marian Willis Vogel......................................14N

M/M Gerald & Mildred Whiting Błaszczyk...........................13N

Nelson Foster, co-op chairman.. 10E

Randall Dykeman, resident manager...9N

M/M John B. & Susan McDonald Roberts 8B

Melissa Roberts, daughter 8B

M/M George C. & Hanife Kaplan Wallace 7H

Alya Wallace, daughter..7H

M/M Sanford Hotchkiss.. 6E

THE RELATIVES

Enis McDonald...................................... mother of Susan Roberts

Eleanor Roberts................................ elder sister of John Roberts

Steven Roberts .... elder brother of John Roberts

Charles & Evelyn Wallace ....parents of George Wallace

Marcia Wasserman.................................... ex-wife of John Roberts

Muriel Vogel..sister of Sheldon Vogel

Helen Vogel..daughter of M/M Vogel

THE STAFF

Randall Dykeman .... managing agent

John Dibolo... concierge

Emanuel Torres .... night concierge

Robert Faulk.. daytime doorman

Truman Firth... superintendent

THE DOCTORS

Dr. Rajit Kher	hematology, NYL
Dr. Lester Martinez	ER, St. Luke's Roosevelt
Dr. Hubert Simmons	psychiatry, St. Luke's Roosevelt
Dr. Rebecca Steiner	pediatric oncology, NYL
Dr. Abigail Weinstein	ER, Renown

THE LAWYERS

Catherine Fallis	Fallis & Son, Esqs.
Andrew Fallis	Fallis & Son, Esqs.
Denise Stojanovska. legal assistant	Fallis & Son, Esqs.
Morton Williams, Esq.	M. Williams, Esqs.

THE SUITS

Dr. Gürhan Erdoğan	President, NYL Health Systems
L. Sanford Hotchkiss	Chief Counsel, NYL
Stuart Chu	Director IT, NYL
Andrea Lyden	Director IT, NYL

THE SUITORS

Stanley Hochstabler	insurance, squash

THE PRESS

Meryl Scott Rupert	Fox 5 News

THE AGENTS

Geoffrey Błaszczyk	CIA
Jill Fitzgerald Kroll	FBI
Marja	unknown

Part I:

The Lives

Chapter 1

The hand flickered then vanished – the void suffused by a momentary blue afterimage. Foot commuters massed into the intersection and motorized ones lurched against them. There was no mistaking the simultaneous cue – neither the darkened red orb nor the burn-in of the remonstrating hand. Fenders were thumped, oaths sworn, and heeled and wheeled travelers scuffled for possession of the asphalt.

THURSDAY EVENING, SEPTEMBER 13, 2012

present day

Wallace edged the bucket out from under the faucet and lowered it into the shower stall. He bent over for the next bucket then proceeded to fill three more. He stubbed his toe against the toilet and nearly crippled himself against the door as he exited. Power outage, no telling how long it would last. Wallace groped his way down the corridor past the guest bedroom into the kitchen.

Wallace knew from the Big One in 1977 the tap would cease flowing within the hour as the last drops from the rooftop tank were drained. The beer would continue flowing, however, at the sidewalk cafes until sunrise or until the marooned hoofed home to the outer boroughs, fought their way through the bus lines, or climbed dark staircases to their hermetically-sealed, steaming-hot apartments, thinking they could take a cold shower, hop in bed and call in sick if the lights returned after their night of bacchanalia.

They would not get to the shower part. Their awakening would come sooner, the moment they made their way from the foyer to the bathroom to relieve themselves. A sharp croak and dry silence would follow the flush. And then where would they go? In a dry toilet, a modern-day chamber pot they could neither lift nor empty from the window? Wallace shuddered. The

memory of 1977 was nauseating. This time, Wallace had it covered for four days if he flushed sparingly, perhaps five.

How long would this one last? There was no way to tell, no
one to call. Wallace terminated landline service the day she
moved out. It was such a waste – $70 a month in fees and taxes
just to maintain a 212 dial tone. How many years had they paid
for that? At least seven after becoming hooked on mobile. The
cordless units were ugly, expensive relics – museum pieces from
a pre-cellular age. The same phone company that sold them the
data plan assured them they would be grateful during a power
failure for maintaining landline service, never mind they did not
own a traditional handset. They switched to cordless units which,
as they learned from incessant beeping, drained power swiftly.

For whatever reason, she bought the phone company's pitch.
He did not. Now she was gone, and so was his phone. His Blackberry was useless. Well, not useless, just incommunicado. He
could play Brick Breaker, consult his PDA, and whip out a light-
ning-fast photo editor. But he could not make calls, Shazam the
elevator music, or post angry diatribes on Facebook. More pressing, he could not access the Internet. The cell towers slept with
the city.

Wallace felt his way about the kitchen, groped above the refrigerator and in the pantry for pitchers and vases then filled each
at the kitchen sink. Next, he filled the bar glasses and lined them
in a row along the counter. He grabbed cling wrap and a saucer
and edged his way to the guest bathroom. "You can never have
enough water," he intoned. Crouching down, he latched the bathtub drain, placed a sheet of cling wrap over it, then secured the
seal with the saucer. He turned on the faucet. He'd be the only
clean person in New York. "Clean-smelling," he emended.

Wallace peered into the guest bedroom. He visualized the lavender walls and coral drapes but saw only a slate expanse. The air
was torpid, asphyxiating. Wallace pulled the door shut, absorbing
its vibration as a soft, mournful tremor. Perspiration dampened

the flashback: a college course in thermal dynamics. AC dissipation, ten degrees per hour – he somehow wrung out the equation. So many thoughts were shapeless, but not this one. Curious how the quantitative stuff returned so easily. But power outages? Too many variables. Wallace could scarcely deflect them. Resolving them was unimaginable. A mere hour had elapsed, yet the heat and humidity pervaded his home as freely as a spent marriage or disease.

Wallace returned to the kitchen. He inspected the collection of pastas, cereal and canned goods with a flashlight, then verified the range still worked and pilot lights were lit. "Natural gas. Score one for fracking."

He opened the refrigerator and tried without success to wedge the milk, butter, boneless thighs and yogurt into the freezer. "She never defrosted it … ever!" She never used it. Wallace estimated the accumulated permafrost at 70-80 liters – enough to fill a small bathtub or solemnize the iceberg between them – the one that wouldn't thaw, not with a thousand blackouts. Wallace emptied the produce bins onto an upper shelf and spread towels and newspapers around the base. He would be considerate to his neighbor downstairs, even if the ones upstairs were not. *Click, click, click.* He still flinched at the tap of heels against un-carpeted marble. *Drip.* And smelt dampness weeping through his ceiling.

Wallace leaned against the counter. The urgency abated. He would not go hungry or die from thirst. He would not suffer the stench and humiliation of a toilet that would not flush. The other discomforts he could endure.

He placed a flashlight next to the oven, checked the bag of double-A batteries in the refrigerator and powered down his cell phone. He decided to venture outside.

∞∞

Wallace lived alone. His wife left him four months earlier. She said he was a jerk, so demanding that living with him was impossible. Everything had to be just this way or that. If things were not exactly the way he wanted them, he threw a tantrum like a baby. Well, if Wallace was inflexible, his wife was a slob – tossing her shoes everywhere, piling clothes on chairs, cluttering every bureau and surface with junk or objects of no importance to Wallace. One by one, she encroached on his closets. His clothing was confined to a small bureau and plastic bin under the bed, next to the one for his cranium. She and Wallace were utterly incompatible. He could scarcely remember how they met. How did they ever fall in love?

Wallace shuddered. He remembered how they met. He remembered how they fell in love, and how everything fell apart. Hanni left before Wallace lost his job, his second one, the one as CTO of NYL Health Systems.

"It's a wonder they hired you at all. Always brooding, always on the defensive. I can't believe they put up with you so long." The voice was Hanni's, but it was pointless to argue with voicemail. Return calls were routed to her lawyer.

What did it matter? She was a cheat. The segregated possessions under the bed consoled him. They at least were boxed and unspoiled.

Miraculously, Wallace kept possession of the apartment until it sold, which could happen any moment, or perhaps not happen for a year. The market was fickle, more so because of the "improvements" she insisted upon over the years. The Pierre Deux furnishings and chintz drapes were dated, the all-granite baths neo-Soviet, the Tiffany lighting Victorian, and the electronic telecommunication and security system brazenly futuristic. A buyer would have to remodel everything or share the peculiar eclectic tastes of his ex. Or be like him, amazingly tolerant despite being an inflexible sputtering volcano. "The slightest perceived insult can set me off, but an epic $37,000 tile failure?" His hands swept over the glistening pate and corona – the one he refused to shave clean. "She's right. I'm impossible."

Wallace grabbed the flashlight from the stove and headed to the bedroom. He passed the foyer on the way, removing a key card from the device next to the door and shook his head, "I live in a damned hotel. What buyer would want this?"

He ran his fingers along the neatly made bed. Under the duvet lay identically sized hospital corners, as primly turned as the flag on his father's coffin. Or his brothers'. Just another veil of order; all so thin.

Wallace pocketed a wallet and, pausing a second, reached into the bedside bureau for an envelope. He counted nine twenties, some tens and several ones and felt relieved. Credit card readers and ATMs stood dormant, so his two hundred thirty-six dollars were precious. Wallace stuffed forty into his pocket and returned the rest to his bureau.

He fetched shoes from the closet, turned off the spigot in the tub, and pulled the apartment door shut behind him. Using the flashlight, he found his way to the stairwell and descended six flights to the lobby. Thank heaven they were outbid on 19A; 7H was just fine.

An aside to the doorman camouflaged his anxiety. "It looks crazy out there." He flushed at his own remark. "Crazy" was unartful, even for Wallace. He hastened, "Have you heard anything?"

"It *is* crazy. Everyone's gone *nuts*, as if it's Mardi Gras. My sister's watching live from Chicago on CNN. She says it's dark from Philly to Boston. Something about grid failure. Ten-to-one some *lunatic* goes on a rampage."

Wallace interjected. "Any word when they'll restore power?"

"They aren't saying. Repair crews can't go anywhere. The streetlights are out and every car in the state seems to be at this intersection. Only they're not. They're at the next intersection and the next, all the way to the Lincoln Tunnel and up to the

Bronx. These guys won't get home before four. They're *psycho!* They'd be better off having dinner and a beer."

Wallace nodded assent. How else could he respond? Confession? It hadn't helped him before. He stepped outside. A curtain of buildings dissolved into blackness above him. The Seventh Avenue proscenium stretched to his right – a pastiche of honking horns, giddy tourists, stranded commuters and snarled automobiles gleaming in each other's headlights. Candlelit tables fronted bars that never previously served in the open. All the seats were taken. Glasses clinked, people giggled, and the pavement trembled with the beat of a subwoofer. Wallace ploughed on to the grocer.

Wallace did not patronize the grocer often. It was overpriced and the produce frequently bruised. He preferred the supermarket at mid-block and Whole Foods at the Time-Warner Center, but knew from experience they would be shut, conserving cold air as best they could, squeezing perishables into their freezers. He wasn't even sure what he would buy. Actually, he just wanted to browse, to persuade himself he had covered his bases, not forgotten anything important.

The store was packed. Wallace wedged his way inside and observed midst the flickering cell phones and strategically placed candles that the salad bar and bread shelf were empty. As were the snack shelves and beer pantry. Surprisingly, there were still a few bottles of Poland Spring. Wallace paused, taking mental stock of his inventory, then pushed onward. The thought of bottled water disturbed him even during a blackout. It was the principle of the thing, he told Hanni. "Paying for a resource that flows free from the tap, shipping it from Fiji, creating all that garbage; surely you can find an attractive water bottle."

"Oh, I just reuse the ones I buy," she replied.

"Until you buy the next one," he thought, "which is usually at the next corner."

He returned to the front of the grocer and his gaze climbed to the shelf above the cashier. It was still there, the Carnation powdered milk he purchased during the 18-hour teaser in 2003 and returned the following morning.

He was proud of the purchase at the time. With it, his family could dine properly for days. He mixed a batch the moment he got home, serving it with grilled hot dogs and sauerkraut. But the milk was sour, undrinkable. The next morning, he discovered why. Microscopic mealworms, thousands of them, nested in the box but were invisible by candlelight. When was the last time the grocer sold a box of powdered milk? Wallace grew up with it, but that was in the sixties. The "sell by" date on the box was January 1983. And it was still there today, back on the shelf.

A woman followed his gaze upward, pushed in front of him and shouted, "The powdered milk, please!" Wallace smiled and squeezed his way outside.

He decided to treat himself to a beer. He strode east on 58th Street, a quieter street than Seventh Avenue, 57th Street or Central Park South, and found a seat near the window. Even here, off the beaten track, there was a buzz of excitement, of the exotic, but Wallace found it comforting – a break from the stress of his dwindling bank account, waning unemployment benefits and nonexistent social life. Hanni would never let him stay in the apartment if she thought he would bring someone home, her own indiscretions notwithstanding. She reckoned accurately. Wallace didn't know any women, not well that is. Besides, he needed time to regain his footing. Even Hanni understood support obligations were worthless if he was so disoriented he babbled gibberish. Solicitous, calculating Hanni, she knew her ex-husband was a loser.

But not tonight, he exulted. Tonight, he was master and commander, the man whose much ridiculed compulsion to microanalyze and plan, plan, plan actually paid off. He chuckled. How was Hanni handling this? He half expected a call. "Then again, she's probably out with his ex-boss. Such grand fun!"

Wallace ordered a draft. It was warm, sticky, but somehow perfect for the occasion. A couple from Rome tried to involve him in their conversation – idle chatter about this once-in-a-life-time Bohemian experience. Wallace smiled amiably and agreed. "Wait until they return to their hotel," he reflected. "Definitely Bohemian and definitely a trip to remember." Wallace thought about his soft bed, stocked kitchen and water reserves and ordered another beer.

The Italian couple paid their bill and left. They were gone almost an hour when Wallace noticed the small plastic bag under the table. It was nearly invisible in the candlelight. He emptied the contents on the table. Souvenirs: several postcards, an "I love New York" refrigerator magnet, and a Statue of Liberty pen. He could not recall the couple's name or their hotel. He was certain, in fact, they had not volunteered their names. Neither had he. After all, this was New York, even during the bonhomie of a blackout. The couple paid in cash; that much he remembered. Tonight, everyone paid in cash.

Wallace leafed through the postcards but saw no use for them. He spread them on the table, a sightseer's tableau, and watched in embarrassment as spilt beer seeped up and deformed the images. He did not expect them to be so absorbent. Wallace glanced about furtively, gathered the cards into a limp stack, and set them on the edge of the table near the wall. He pretended nothing had happened.

Wallace inspected the pen. It was kitschy but reminded him of Hanni. He would use it the next time she made him sign something. She made him sign so many things. She would have a riposte, of course. She always did, but Lady Liberty's blank stare would be his reply. "This is what I think of your overweening wit. It's base metal, a worthless imitation of real intellect and taste. Where do I sign?"

The magnet spoke truth too. Wallace *did* love New York, even if he hated his life. He heard someone at the far end of the bar shout, "She's driving me crazy," so he raised his glass and concurred, "Hear, hear!" then wiped foam from his lips with his sleeve. Wallace shoved the pen and magnet into his pocket and rummaged among the trinkets for his money. He ordered another beer.

Wallace returned home two hours later, a couple dollars in his pocket and wobbly. The night concierge stood his post, dutiful even in darkness. "Good evening, Mr. Wallace."

"Hello, Manny. Do you know whether the mail was sorted?"

"It should be. The lights didn't go out until late. Let me check." The concierge stepped back from the candlelight and disappeared into an office behind the desk. He reappeared with a small bundle. "Here you go, Mr. Wallace. Have a pleasant evening."

Wallace marveled at the building's antiquated postal system. Tenants were still assigned cubbies in an office behind the front desk, rather than mailboxes with keys. Despite a $6 million makeover of the common areas, tenants still asked for their mail in person, sorted by hand each afternoon by the concierge. And when tenants left on vacation, the concierge bundled the mail neatly as it accumulated, and discreetly slipped the bundles into the apartments when they outgrew the cubbies. Some tenants left a key in their cubby expressly for that purpose, and for bringing up packages and dry cleaning. Not Wallace. He was on indefinite vacation, right here in Gotham Central. He toted his own packages and dry cleaning.

Hanni adored the co-op's "personal touch" but Wallace considered it pretentious extravagance. "Why can't the postman sort the mail? It's *his* job. You'd think they'd put a bank of mailboxes in when they renovated. Instead, we're paying for a full-time doorman just so the concierge can hide in the back and sort mail."

"You're hopeless," she sighed. "That's what makes this building special."

"Thank you, Manny. You have a nice evening, too." Wallace cradled the bundle under his arm and opened the door to the stairwell.

Where had they unearthed so many candles? Large incense candles were positioned at every landing and on many of the steps. No one stores this many candles, he thought, not here in New York where every inch of closet space is rationed. "They must have looted Bed Bath & Beyond."

He recalled how terrible the looting was in 1977, his second summer in New York. He recalled the riots. He dreaded stepping outside back then. "Everyone is so amiable tonight, so chipper," he thought, "as if this is just one big frolic. But what happens tomorrow or the day after if the lights are still out? It won't be candles they're after."

Wallace's chest heaved as he reached the seventh floor. He congratulated himself for buying 7H and not 19A, as if the decision were his and not the other buyer's. He cursed himself, though, for letting himself go to seed. He should not have let her get to him that way. It was time to move on, just as she had.

He sat on the top step for a moment, catching his breath, then leafed through the bundle in his hand. Two catalogs, a bank statement, assorted junk mail and a postcard. Chicago skyline. Wallace flipped it over and held it near the candle. He did not need to inspect the handwriting. He knew it was Hanni's.

"Spending a few days with my sister. Forgot to tell you – the broker found a buyer. We're looking at a closing date of…"

Wallace shoved the postcard back into the bundle and rose to his feet. He could read it later; right now he needed to urinate. He fumbled at the front door for his wallet and the Statue of Liberty fell to the floor. Wallace's flashlight dimmed considerably. "C'mon man," he admonished himself. "I need to piss."

Wallace pulled the key card out of his wallet then froze. The walls spun around him and he struggled to gulp back the whoosh of sour beer from his belly. Nausea swept over him. Wallace steadied himself against the door but his arm trembled. He lowered the card into the slot. A red light twinkled. Access denied. He tried again. Same result. He pulled the "I love New York" magnet from his pocket and thrust it down the hall.

What was Hanni doing now? Laughing. He remembered he consented to the high-tech security outlay because, as she reminded him, he could no longer complain about keys jangling against his side as he jogged… as he jogged… as he charged down the stairs, two at a time, lunged park-wards into the darkness, reached what he sensed was a bench, retched on his shoes, then relieved himself while still unzipping his fly. A hoarse whisper rose from the bench, "Eeww, gross! Let's get outta here," and a second voice murmured assent.

Wallace groped around in vain for the water fountain he swore he'd once seen and nearly crippled himself against a bench. He cursed his clumsiness then lowered himself to the bench's edge. Reflux burned his mouth and throat, the sweet, sickly stench of regurgitated beer clawed at his nostrils and he felt the surface of his teeth dissolving. Wallace recalled those last few bottles of Poland Spring, the ones he left for another customer. "You can never have enough water," he intoned.

There were so many electronic door locks to choose from – keypads, palm readers, touch-screen patterns, proximity cards. Hanni chose magnetic key cards because they were slim, cheap, and could be operated while intoxicated, something she considered crucial. They were prone on occasion to de-magnetize, but he kept copies at the gym and his office. He no longer had an office and his gym membership expired.

Wallace sat on the bench and brooded. He spent the night gazing at where his building should have been, taking mental stock of the water, bath and ample provisions awaiting him … once he found a locksmith. A flash threatened rain, but the rumble ebbed and Wallace heard only the muffled honk of frustrated drivers. A slim crescent moon rose before dawn above the

Sherry-Netherland Hotel, a soft pink scythe on the still-black horizon. He managed a smile. Hanni's moon. For the first time in months, his mind was serene … and alone. The wretched taste and odor cleared the remnant wisps of fog. "Yes, Robert," he murmured, "It *is* crazy *out there*."

Chapter 2

The figure wavered uncertainly, but 175 joules steadied its fulgent limbs. Was it a moth? Dust in his eye? Wallace felt sure the walker reawakened and winked at him. But a hand reached forth and swept the illusion aside. It flashed fifteen times and the city returned to schedule.

SATURDAY MORNING, OCTOBER 13, 2012

"Whoa, not yet!" The man clutched his daughter and lurched back onto the sidewalk. A taxi brushed his gym bag as it veered from the center median into the turn lane and jarred the curb, defying the plainly visible white stripes between the lanes, the white illuminated stick figure beckoning from across the crosswalk, and the patrol car idling on the opposite corner. A mass of tourists, dog walkers and locals sprawled onto the intersection, then dispersed westward toward Columbus Circle and northward into the park. A hansom cab picked its way through the crowd.

Artisans' Gate, the corner of Central Park South and Seventh Avenue, was a tricky intersection. Swarms of harried New Yorkers and inobservant tourists ensured traffic signals were flagrantly disobeyed. Drivers interpreted red lights as extended yellows and pedestrians lingered between lanes long after and before the lights changed. It was a natural conflict, the order of things in an intensely urban environment.

The conflict intensified when the city severed Broadway into uptown and downtown segments at Times Square. Overnight, Seventh Avenue became the preferred conduit for vehicles that otherwise thronged down Broadway. They converged there along the edge of the park, Central Park South, dozens per minute, from the Upper East Side, Upper West Side, and Queensboro Bridge, bringing noise, fume and confusion.

Jack and Melissa glanced back at the balcony. She wasn't watching. Not today.

"That was close," remarked Melissa, maneuvering through the rush of cyclists and joggers circuiting the inner perimeter of the park. Along these park "Drives," traffic rules meant less than they did on 59th Street. It was tacitly understood: pelotons could roar through stop signals; cyclists could pedal against oncoming traffic; and skaters could zigzag in and out of the jogging lanes. The police had other priorities. To cope with the onslaught of self- and gas-propelled vehicles, or just because that is how they were, runners projected a hardened don't-mess-with-me attitude, especially toward pedestrians, the only group lower down the food chain.

"Sure was," agreed Jack.

Foot travelers entered Central Park's crosswalks at their peril, even when the walk man beckoned. Jack kept an eye peeled for cyclists and skaters but seldom glanced at the signal. Few did. At least he wasn't texting.

"Let's take the lower section. Not as much wind." He watched his daughter dash to the small meadow short of Heckscher Playground.

Jack could not fathom how octogenarians with their pocket-size pooches managed. Most got as far as the benches inside the gate. But there were still plenty of stooped figures towed into the park's interior by their leashed charges. One such figure stepped onto the lawn with her Yorkshire terrier, hesitated, then moved further down the path alongside the playground. The woman had steeled herself against careening cyclists, skaters and taxicabs, but was unprepared to engage a twelve-year-old girl with a racquet, even if she was standing in her favorite dog patch.

Jack recalled the morning after signal patterns were modified to handle the spillover from Broadway. He wheeled Susan to the balcony upon hearing a woman sobbing on the street below. A crowd gathered at the athletic club across the street and traffic inched its way around the cab that came full stop after making a left turn from the westbound lane. The driver stood near the cab, its door ajar, his gaze cast downward. A passenger fidgeted in the rear of the taxi. And an old, nattily dressed woman lay on her side in the intersection wailing inconsolably as she cradled what might have been a West Highland terrier. The scene played out for twenty minutes before the crowd dispersed, the woman was led back into her building by some neighbors, and the police conferred with the driver.

Neither Jack nor Susan recognized the woman. They lived here how many years? Fifteen? And yet they still only knew a handful of neighbors by name. But to not even recognize her? It seemed appalling to not remember seeing her face or the small dog that was taken from her. He was conditioned like every New Yorker to look down in the elevator, to not meet a stranger's gaze in the subway, to avoid eye contact unless absolutely necessary. But his neighbors? "Do I really tune everyone out when I pass through the lobby? Or stare right through them?" Jack knew the answer. Except for the doorman, Jack did not even recognize those who helped the woman inside, although a checkered blazer was definitely familiar. He had seen the blazer before, many times in fact, just not the head it supported.

"It was a Maltese, honey, not a Westie," was Susan's lone contribution. Jack nodded and wheeled her back into the apartment.

"Thwop." Jack lofted the shuttlecock into a smooth upward arc. "Thwop." Melissa returned it with a swift overhand flick. "Thwop." Jack thrust his arm across his body and backhanded the volley. "Thwip." His daughter nicked the bird off the edge of the racquet and Jack lunged forward to flick it skyward. "Thwop." Melissa delivered a decisive blow and the bird caromed off his forehead.

Jack massaged the point of impact. "You're supposed to hit the birdie over the net, even if it's a pretend net."

"I *did*. I pretended it was a small net."

Jack grinned and arched the shuttlecock high over the imaginary net.

Melissa began playing badminton in the summer with a $2 set she purchased at the "A Dollar More" store in Chinatown. For years there had been a Dollar Store on Mulberry Street just south of Canal. Then A Dollar More sprang up across the street and, within weeks, Dollar Store was no more.

Melissa bought the set because she hung out after school with a classmate who lived on Bayard Street, a block from A Dollar More. The friend grew up playing badminton the way Jack grew up playing sandlot baseball. Melissa could outrun and out-endure any boy in her class but could not swat a shuttlecock to save her life, until she spent $2 of her own money at A Dollar More and dragged her father into the park for hours of clandestine practice, just so she could out-duel a classmate. She succeeded, and then some, as she did with anything athletic. She was his wife's daughter.

It was Susan, 17 years his junior, a former FSU track star, who always seized the competitive "let's go play" baton. But Susan decided on impulse in April to join a friend in Squaw Valley for spring skiing, her first ski trip in years, then insisted for her first run on ripping down a craggy, shaded chute on the west face of KT-22. Alone. She lost control within seconds and, six months later, was still ruing the misadventure.

So Melissa asked "Dad" to help with serves and volleys. Dad agreed because he had time, plenty of time. The implosion of Dewey & LeBoeuf in May was the closing act on a career that began auspiciously at the University of Chicago and Brown & Wood, but took a turn for the worse in the 1980s. Jack moved from Brown & Wood to the legal bowels of Drexel, Burnham & Lambert, thinking investment banking was a better fit, returned to securities underwriting at Brobeck, Phleger & Harrison, and finished unceremoniously at Dewey & LeBoeuf. Three esteemed firms, three abrupt dissolutions, three black marks on a résumé that would otherwise impress almost anyone. Try as he might, he could not shake the stigma of one who, notwithstanding his non-management role, worked almost exclusively at giants that failed. Jack looked forward to these daily sessions with Melissa. They were considerably cheaper than therapy.

In early September, *The Wall Street Journal* illustrated the cover of its "Greater New York" section with a map of Central Park, marking every sport a reporter witnessed during a single day canvassing the park. Right there at the bottom of the map, below Heckscher playground, was a sketch of a father and daughter playing badminton, although "sketch" is perhaps generous. They were glyphs. Their raised racquets could have read "Walk" and "Don't Walk." The paper didn't name or interview anyone, but Jack and his daughter identified themselves immediately. They were the only badminton-playing duo in south Central Park. Jack tucked the *Journal* in his desk – something he could reminisce about when Melissa was grown. It was one of the few pleasant mementos from his otherwise disappointing year.

Crossing 59th Street from the park side to return home was easier. The turn lanes drained down Seventh Avenue, not up, so oncoming drivers could spot pedestrians exiting the park, even if they themselves ran the light. But there was still confusion. Turn lanes now opened and closed for the minute *after* the cross-town lanes turned red, reversing decades of convention – of opening and closing *before* the cross-town ones.

Inevitably, someone in the cross-town lane revved their engine and lurched forward just as the turn-lane vehicles halted and the pedestrians rushed into the crosswalk. Today it wasn't an engine. It was an old bay pulling a carriage that responded to a gentle flick of the reins and nearly trampled Jack and Melissa in the process. The duo skittered out from the encroaching legs and advanced toward their building. The horse thrust back its head, shook its mane and snorted. The hand flashed agreement.

∽⤫∾

"We're back. What's for breakfast?"

"You'll have to ask Daddy. I'm paying the bills."

"Anything interesting?" Jack inquired.

"Maybe. You received a call from Stanley Hochstabler. We can discuss that later," parent-speak, they all understood, for, "when Melissa is not listening."

Hochstabler was their life insurance agent, the only person who had ever sold Jack anything by phone. Jack could not remember why he hadn't hung up immediately; it was so long ago. But he did not. Within minutes it became evident Stan was an alumnus of FSU, just like his wife, who began working life as a flight attendant on the very same long-defunct airline as she did. But Stan was considerably older than Susan, almost Jack's age, and lived alone in Boston.

Stan somehow won his attention. The result was $4 million in term life insurance for twenty years at approximately $4,500 per year, a mere tenth what they paid annually for medical, dental and disability insurance, and one fortieth what they paid on their mortgage. Jack did not bother calculating how it stacked up against alimony. The premium was rounding error on his then-outsize annual distribution from Brobeck Phleger & Harrison. And Stanley reminded him, should he die, his new wife would not have to sell the apartment to pay off the mortgage. Stanley sold comfort and Jack craved it. Jack sensed, in hindsight, he was an easy mark.

Jack paid the life insurance premium for sixteen years yet was, actuarially speaking, very much alive. Stanley was probably calling to sell him a whole life conversion.

Jack selected a mixing bowl, prepared the pancake batter and set it aside. He emptied the can of hash on a preheated skillet. The hash recoiled, splattering the wall, floor and appliances. Jack lurched backward and chided himself for not wearing sleeves. He poured grits into a boiling pot of water, secured the lid, and adjusted the burner to low. He heated another skillet and poured batter into three pre-greased molds. Bubbles percolated up and popped like his reclusive, late brother's acne. Jack extricated the molds and flipped the pancakes. He stared down at Yoda, Darth Vader and an unnamed storm trooper. They gazed back blankly. The way his brother did. In San Francisco.

Jack cleaned the molds and prepared a second batch. "Look," his daughter said later as she selected two Yodas and two Vaders, "The Clone Wars!"

"Take no prisoners," Susan commanded, and the three consumed their breakfast.

Jack did everything now, or so it seemed. He managed breakfast, schlepped Melissa to school, shopped daily for groceries, sat downstairs for hours with the laundry, and prepared dinner. Susan still paid the bills, but the rest was on Jack. He hadn't realized until the accident and Dewey's failure how little time a "mom" actually had to herself. If he wasn't tending chores, he was accompanying Melissa to 6 am skating sessions, reviewing homework, bathing Susan, dressing Susan, or wheeling her to the doctor. He crawled into bed most evenings before Melissa.

It was not as if Jack were new to toil. He worked hard at Dewey and like a dog at Brobeck and Drexel, but so had legions of others. They were conjoined at the hip, part of the greater machine, rewarded handsomely for their indenture. They spent most of their days and evenings seated, growing fat and graying but convinced they would provide well for their families, buy a dream house somewhere, and retire early to enjoy it. Jack sighed at how little "retirement" had bought him – neither a dream house nor income security nor time to enjoy it. Except he did enjoy it – in a way. Tending to his wife and daughter was calming, comforting, even if his financial situation was not. He was beginning to understand what "quality time" meant. It wasn't what he imagined it to be during those long nights at the printers, poring line-by-line over each new page of a prospectus.

The deep recurring blare of a rig's air horn drew Jack to the window. A policeman was issuing citations to three pedicabs parked illegally along Seventh Avenue at the corner. Another officer stood in the street, motioning aside two pedicabs whose drivers foresaw the predicament and were pedaling furiously into the intersection to avoid citation. Together, the vehicles and officers blocked the turn lanes, and a crowd of pedestrians spurned the flashing hand.

Jack cleared the table and sat beside his wife. Melissa retreated to her room to play on her iPad.

"You need to transfer money into the core account. Our balance is down to twenty-four hundred," his wife began.

Jack nodded. They maintained a portfolio of mutual funds and CDs but kept little in cash. This cost them dearly during the financial crisis, but the damage was done. "How much do we need to get through October?"

"Twenty thousand. Twenty-three to be safe."

Jack knew better than to object. Tuition at Brierley, the $2 million mortgage, medical insurance, skating lessons and ice time, his continuing obligation to Marcia – he knew instinctively it added up. He also knew they were burning through principal. With decent market conditions, he could count on $13,000-14,000 per month in investment income, but times were uncertain, and the past few months had been a roller coaster. In addition, he accrued $4,600 each month from the Pension Benefit Guarantee Corporation, which assumed only partially what vested when he worked at Brobeck and then Dewey. Plus, there was the matter of the claw-back, a pall the bankruptcy trustee cast over those misfortunate enough to have partnered at Dewey & LeBoeuf. The magnitude was unresolved, but it was likely to be large. His family wasn't treading water. It was sinking – slowly, but it was sinking.

"Okay. I'll transfer funds on Monday."

"There's another thing. Hochstabler says you have to convert the insurance policies this year if you want to qualify for whole life without a medical review."

Jack postponed the decision each year for the previous six, ever since Stanley began calling again. The last time they spoke, a conversion of even one of the million-dollar policies would have cost seventy-eight hundred dollars annually. Jack had resolved to convert just two of the policies and let the others lapse. If he died, Susan would collect enough to repay the mortgage and she and Melissa could live comfortably off investment income and his pension. Jack postponed conversion because he wagered the life market would continue to soften. The economy was moribund; Europe was in shambles. And no one was racing to buy life insurance. It was a buyer's market, provided you had the income to afford it. But conditions had changed. He was jobless.

"That's a lot of money," he replied. "We're trying to reduce overhead, not increase it."

"But what if you die suddenly? Think about Melissa. You're 58. Your father died at 60. Your brother died at 39!"

Jack's voice softened. "Sweetie, I'm not going to die. My brother died of … in unusual circumstances. And my father … he smoked. Besides, they weren't really…" He tried a different tack, "What I mean is, I'm just overhead. No one wants a superannuated underwriting attorney. The deals aren't there. Or they're handled by much younger lawyers."

He continued, "I'm retired, not as planned, but nothing ever goes according to plan. We just have to roll with the punches and, right now, we should not be purchasing lottery tickets."

"But what if we won the lottery? Wouldn't that be great? Then all our problems would be solved."

Jack smiled wanly and put his hand on Susan's shoulder.

"Oh, I didn't mean that!" she inserted, suddenly embarrassed. "I just mean, well, why shouldn't we play the lottery if the price is right? You've paid in all these years. Why let the policies lapse if we could somehow recover all you lost at Brobeck and LeBoeuf? What's it to Liberty or Prudential?"

She had a point, but he did not like the idea of being worth more dead than alive.

"Let me run some numbers. I'll call Stanley on Monday to get more information. Would that be okay?"

Susan's brow smoothed, furrowed slightly, then straightened. "I'm meeting Hannah for drinks at the Ballfield Café. She's checking up on me. Want to join us?"

"No, but I'll wheel you over. Melissa and I can do some blading and check out the action on the Mall. The leaves are really starting to color."

Hanife Wallace, or was it Kaplan, was the former neighbor who, upon leaving her apartment and husband, invited Susan on a ski trip to, in her words, "catch up." Jack found their meetings awkward. Hannah must have too, and not just because of The Accident. Why else would she fuss and fawn over Susan more than Jack ever could, dodging substantive conversation? Perhaps if … no, their meetings would still be awkward. There was still The Divorce.

The Wallaces were previously their neighbors, real neighbors, the kind you knew by name and befriended. But she moved out – no idea where, just out. She yammered about staying off the grid – no postal address, no email, just a cell phone that kept changing. Susan considered it delightful; Jack considered it suspicious. But Susan took sides, as friends evidently must after a divorce, and Susan determined unilaterally that her family would ally with Hannah. Husband George, "Wally" to his friends, might just as well be deceased.

Almost deceased. Jack still greeted George as Wally when they chanced upon each other in the lobby, but that seldom occurred.

They did not have "date nights" anymore at their respective dining tables after putting their girls to bed. They did not hang out together at the rink, watching their girls practice spins. And they did not bring their girls to the next theater installment of *Harry Potter* or *Twilight*.

Jack caught himself. It had been fifteen months since the Wallace girl died. It happened so suddenly: the illness; chemotherapy; hair loss; surgery; death. Hannah left Wally within days. It was as if she couldn't stand the familiar mannerisms or features. Jack flew with the family to the funeral but had not exchanged more than a handful of words with Wally since. Jack sensed any conversation would be awkward.

"Hey Jack, how's it going?"

"Great! Lost my job, up to my eyeballs in debt, and my wife's answer to our prayers is a $4 million bounty on my head. How are you doing?"

"Couldn't be better. My daughter's dead, my wife detests me, and I locked myself out of my apartment during the blackout. What's to complain?"

Jack heard about Wally's misadventure from Manny, the night concierge. Actually, everyone heard about Wally's misadventure. No one came out and said it, but George "Please-don't-call-me-George-Wallace" Wallace was the laughingstock of his cooperative, perhaps the city. Who in their right mind would install electronic security in a high-rise doorman building, a building so secure you could not activate your own elevator buttons? That privilege was reserved for the elevator attendant or, if he took a break, the concierge electronically from behind his desk. There were cameras in the lobby, elevators and entranceways. And there was a palm print scanner at the garage entrance. To the best of Jack's knowledge, no tenant ever lost anything because of a breaking and entering. Yet George *Wally* Wallace installed an electronic card reader, perhaps to show off his IT expertise. He did something with corporate security and computers; Jack was sure they discussed his work. Or maybe he was just crazy.

"When did you agree to meet?" Jack asked.

"Hannah said she'd call around noon, but I'd like to say three. I don't want to start drinking earlier. She gave me her new number."

A chorus of sirens interrupted their conversation. Two dozen flashing squad cars made their way leisurely westward along 59th Street.

"Tickets to Tatzu Nishi's 'Living Room'?" Jack inquired jokingly.

Susan responded blankly.

Jack washed the dishes, then inspected the pantry. They needed milk, OJ, Ben & Jerry's – the essentials – and something for dinner. He poked his head into Melissa's room. "I'm running to Associated. Want anything?"

"No thanks," came the reply. She was past the stage when Mint Milanos or Lorna Doones would make her day. Now she needed a shopping spree along Prince Street or carte blanche at the Apple Store, but she was mature enough to sense circumstances had changed. Maybe she did want the Mint Milanos after all. Maybe she was just doing her part to rein in the family budget.

Jack grabbed a jacket and left the apartment. He walked westward along 58th Street until he reached the firehouse, glanced to his right, then crossed the street. He knew instinctively this was the safest place to cross – midblock on a one-way street with good line-of-sight.

Jack recalled reading aloud to his wife the results of New York's first-ever Pedestrian Safety Report, published by the Department of Transportation during the summer. He was trying to rationalize why he did not, as Melissa's role model, wait dutifully at every corner for the light to change or cross only in marked crosswalks.

Serious pedestrian crashes were about two-thirds deadlier on major street corridors than on smaller local streets. The most dangerous corners for pedestrians were those that allowed left turns through or past opposing traffic, and midblock crossings on small, one-way streets were statistically safer than crossing at the corner. Not mentioned in the report: the number of babies and toddlers in strollers whose parents used them as shields as they parried forth in traffic, parents who dared drivers to hit their children, perhaps hoping to sue afterward and "win the lottery." Jack encountered a parent like this nearly every time he rented a car and wondered aloud what it must be like growing up with parents who regard their children as a fungible, albeit pricey, commodity. "What's the deal? Do they have inventory at home, so they can afford to lose one? I don't get it."

"Calm down, dear. They're just in a hurry," was Susan's reply.

Jack knew he could die any minute from a heart attack, from the crane overhead on 57th Street, from collapsing scaffolding along the sidewalk next door, from a slip in the stairwell, but he would never be one of Manhattan's 155 annual pedestrian fatalities. Sure, the streets were chaotic. They were intense. But you just had to remain alert. He drilled the lesson into his daughter. No texting or calling while moving, no jaywalking without careful assessment. Use common sense.

Jack returned home with "the essentials" and fresh salmon. He'd bake it under a bed of chopped basil, tomatoes and black olives, and serve it with wild rice and steamed broccoli. He could have dinner on the table in 50 minutes. He brought his daughter a bag of Mint Milanos.

Susan was still poring over the bank statements when he returned. It was pointless to intrude. The budget did not add up and he knew it. Besides, he knew she would revisit the topic when they were in bed, when he had no place to hide, when she could talk freely about insurance and "winning the lottery."

❧❧

Jack and Melissa sat on the curb outside their building, strapping on their inline skates and fitting their wrist pads. Susan waited in the wheelchair. They hung the gym bag with their shoes on the chair's handle and edged their way to the corner. Mid-Saturday afternoon, early autumn – traffic was heavy and the park teemed with activity.

They made their way to the café without incident, greeted Hannah, and agreed to return for a drink in an hour. Susan told them to take their time.

Jack maintained a love-hate relationship with inline skates. He loved their mobility and meager demand on storage space, but hated their braking, hated it intensely. His previous pair screwed a block of rubber to the back of the right heel. His new pair didn't bother. Most of the time, Jack barreled along and held his breath. If he had to stop short, he would drag a blade and, more often than not, be spun around wildly. He had his share of road rash and once banged the pavement so hard he vomited, but was out there again today, just so he could enjoy "quality time" with his daughter.

Thankfully, the day's activities were muted. They stuck to the Mall, joined in the skate dancing beyond the northeast corner of Sheep Meadow, and wove their way around the benches fronting the band shell. The Mall's promenade had been "repaved" during renovation with sand and gravel, so Jack and Melissa kept to the side paths. They made their way to the rear of the Loeb Boathouse, bought cones, and finished them near the Margarita Delacorte Memorial. Melissa considered climbing the mushroom to sit aside Alice and the dormouse, but the skates posed a hurdle. Besides, the other children were younger. Melissa's days of romping about Wonderland were over.

Father and daughter arrived safely at the Ballfield Café at 4:30. They waited for an elderly couple to leave, then seized the vacant chairs and brought them to Susan's side. Jack positioned his chair so he could gaze beyond the base paths to the Time Warner Center and the buildings lining 59th Street. His own balcony hid just below tree line. He grabbed the sack from Susan's wheelchair and handed Melissa her sneakers.

"Welcome back. Did you two have fun?" Jack winced at the question. Hannah had a way of making him feel she was addressing a child. In fairness, she was this time, but her gaze was fixed on him.

"Busy out there," he replied. "I thought the holidays were over."

"Not for the Europeans. They're always on holiday."

Jack ordered a beer for himself and a Push Pop for his daughter. Melissa fawned over the assembly of canines in the café, including the one-eyed pinscher at the neighboring woman's feet. She inquired when she might have one of her own, but Jack waited for Susan to answer.

"In a year or two, honey, when you're old enough to walk it at night. I'm in a wheelchair and Dad has his business trips. It wouldn't be fair to the dog, making him hold it all night."

Melissa giggled. "Dad doesn't have any business trips. He's not working."

Hannah arched her brow and changed the subject. "Susan and I have been discussing suing the hospital and pediatrician for malpractice. She says they should have diagnosed the disease earlier."

Jack winced slightly but said nothing. He would speak with Susan later. Hannah continued.

"Listen, Darling. You're a lawyer. Susan's right. What else am I supposed to do? Wally is broke, hasn't worked in a year, and the apartment won't fetch more than two million. I know. That's the latest offer. I'll be lucky to net six hundred after the brokers, government and Wally get their share. How's anyone supposed to live on that?"

"You have a job," Jack offered meekly.

"Listen Silly, I'm just an event coordinator, not a high-priced lawyer. The companies I work with are under all sorts of pressure, a microscope. Right now, big corporate bashes are as popular as Ebola."

Jack tried to steer the conversation to the premise of the case, not its imagined payoff. "You brought Alya to the doctor the moment she couldn't finish her program. You thought it was an asthma attack. I was at the rink, remember?"

"That's not the point!" she steamed. "That doctor gave her a clean bill of health just three months earlier. He signed a statement for her school. She was probably just as sick then. And then the hospital…"

It was Jack's turn to change the subject. "Wally isn't working?"

"You've got that straight. My good-for-nothing ex-husband. With security breaches happening everywhere every day, you'd think he'd be indispensable – the guy who designs and maintains network safeguards. But with all his droning about firewalls, firewalls, firewalls, someone decided it was easier to fire Wallace."

Hannah seemed pleased with the pun.

So that was it. Wally could not provide for her in style, so some poor pediatrician, his malpractice carrier actually, would have to provide for her instead. Except that it would not be the pediatrician or the carrier. It would be Jack and Susan and others like them. Life insurance seemed cheap because health insurance was so expensive. And kept getting more so. The truth was it was all expensive. There was no way to make ends meet. So Alya, her memory actually, was just a tool. It was all about leveraging the dead. He wanted to ask how forsaking a fixed address, phone service and email account promoted her event planning business, but Melissa interrupted.

"Look, Mom, they posted a picture of Rachel's dog! And Coach Ryan's!"

It was true. The café was the leash-friendliest place in Manhattan. A corkboard was festooned with dozens of photos of dogs, each the pet of a patron. There was even a communal water bowl at the entrance.

Two years back, guests inquired why the café could not also display photos of their kids. So for a summer the café did. Melissa's photo was there, as was Alya's. The three adults must each have remembered this; they fell silent.

The silence lasted several seconds. A cyclist skidded onto his side, narrowly averting the small poodle that scampered out of the café to greet an incoming terrier. The poodle's owner rushed outside, scooped her up, glowered disapprovingly at the cyclist, then returned to her chair, facing it toward the back. The cyclist sat on the ground for a second, shook his head, glowered back, then raised himself and moved on. No one said a word. No one lent a hand. Everyone went back to their conversation.

Jack paid the check, hoisted the skates over his shoulder, and wheeled Susan to the café's exit. They bade Hannah "Good afternoon," and started back toward Seventh Avenue.

"Hannah agrees with me. She says it would be foolish to let the policies expire."

"You talked to Hannah about my life insurance policies?" Jack was incredulous.

"Of course, Silly. Hannah's on her own, now. She was helping me get perspective."

Jack simmered. Hanife Wallace was always affable, always refined, but everything about her irritated him. And now he had to settle for "Silly" instead of "Honey" or "Dear." How long would that last? Until, he figured, he sacrificed another month's overhead to extend the $4 million bounty on his head. Jack frowned but said nothing.

Melissa winked conspiratorially and took over the wheelchair. She swerved Susan left and right through the crowds, whooping with laughter as she and Susan skirted one near collision after another, using the waning daylight to conjure up the hairpin turns of Monaco and the jerky motion of the Cyclone.

Jack settled himself against a boulder and gazed at the browning foliage, tinged gold and rust and highlighted by the burgundy of sumacs. He wondered whether Melissa would ever know the vibrant reds and yellows that were commonplace when she was a baby. Verticillium Wilt had infested the park and wiped out nearly every maple. Another fungus, Anthracnose, had years earlier decimated the elms and dogwoods. But Maple Wilt was especially insidious. Autumn colors now spanned the spectrum from ochre to brown. Jack wondered whether Melissa would regard the photos they took when she was a baby as digitally enhanced, as artificial products of some downloaded app.

How do you insure against something like this, he thought? Who do you sue to bring the colors back? How do you bet on earthly decay and retire in comfort? Jack had drafted contracts to hedge nearly everything. But he lost a naked wager on lifetime employment, suffered steep losses in the market, and watched with somber dismay as the world around him decayed. This was not the legacy he dreamt of leaving his child. Melissa trotted back to his side. Susan wheeled herself determinedly. Both were flushed and breathing heavily.

"We almost squished a squirrel. Good thing he had reflexes." The words could have been Susan's or Melissa's; they befit both.

"Shall we head back?"

The sky was bright but the streets had darkened. The buildings cast long shadows against the park. Cars, bikes, pedestrians – they blurred together. The tempo accelerated. Rental bikes had to be returned. Out-of-towners needed to find parking. Evening activities beckoned. There was a throng of pedestrians at the Seventh Avenue exit and a crush of vehicles along 59th Street. Even the walk figure seemed impatient.

Susan maneuvered herself to the curb so she could make a beeline for the graded portion on the opposite corner. Jack held Melissa's hand, a few paces back, separated from Susan by the bodies of joggers, tourists, parents and children. The cross-town signal turned red and the crowd edged from the park exit midway across 59th Street. Vehicles in the westbound lane continued turning south on Seventh Avenue. The crosstown signal changed, the vehicles slowed, and the crowd pushed into the eastbound lane, Susan at the fore. *A sudden foreboding – Jack flung the paddle aside and lurched forward, frigid water crashing upon him.* He shouted for Susan to wait but his words scarcely pierced the throng. *She plunged overboard and the raft catapulted him backward. Indescribable cold enveloped him. Disorientation, paralysis, the realization of being pinned against a boulder – the raft plus the crushing force of the long winter's snowmelt.* The eastbound turn signal was still green and an M7 bus swerved into the lane. *He knew he was just inches from the surface. Inches. The raft broke free and he grabbed the rigging, hauling his head above the water, gasping for air.* The bus blared its horn and tires screeched as the driver tried to round the corner more tightly. *He screamed her name but the water was deafening. The raft churned about roughly, then surged through a narrow channel.* Jack heard a thump and the dismayed cry of half a dozen pedestrians. The voice at the end of his arm shrieked, "Mommy!"

The bus slowed to a crawl as it straightened southward along Seventh Avenue. Jack could see the driver's blanched face framed in the left side mirror. *What have I done?* The crowd hesitated then dispersed at the curb, some continuing south along Seventh Avenue, some heading east or west along Central Park South. An old man in a checkered blazer wheeled Susan to the corner. *The river widened abruptly, and a boy dragged himself aboard.*

"That was close, young lady. Good thing I caught hold of your chair."

Susan was ashen. As ashen as Jack. He rushed forward to console her. "Are you all right?"

She nodded dumbly.

45 years older but just as helpless. Jack clasped the old man's hand, but the man withdrew it quickly.

"I can't thank you enough. You live here, I know. I see you all the time." Jack corrected himself mentally. "Actually, I see your jacket all the time. I don't think I've ever noticed your face."

"Sheldon Vogel. 14N. And you …"

"I'm sorry," he stammered. "Jack Roberts, 8B, front elevator, and here are Susan and Melissa."

Sheldon bowed slightly to Susan and Melissa.

Jack struggled for something to say. He was still on the raft, rubbing his arms for warmth, fumbling to regain composure. Jack was the consummate mingler but couldn't converse with the person who just saved his wife's life. Surely something more than, "Thank you."

He studied Mr. Vogel's face beseechingly. It betrayed some stubble but was otherwise meticulously groomed. The teeth were perfect, probably dentures, and the white mat above his brow might have been a hair piece. He wore lightly tinted wire-frame glasses and smelled faintly of shaving cream, despite the stubble. The man reminded him of Ray Walston, the actor who portrayed *My Favorite Martian* on television in the 1960s. Only this Ray Walston had flushed cheeks, a perspiring forehead, and small, greenish-gray eyes, not the fuzzy black-and-white flicker of his childhood RCA. The man was massaging his right shoulder.

Melissa blurted out something extraordinary. "Thank you, Mr. Vogel, for saving my mother's life. You are a very good man."

The man started. "Well, uh…"

"Yes, of course I am, and you are a good woman for saying so!" he said, regaining his composure. "Now I want you to watch your *sister* more carefully," he said with a sidelong wink at Mr. Roberts. "The way she speeds around, she's liable to get a ticket."

Melissa laughed at the sheer preposterousness of confusing her mother for her sister, not at the man's joke about the ticket. Even Melissa knew police only ticketed taxis, pedicabs and other liveries. Everyone else could speed or swerve as they pleased.

The man shifted his stance in evident discomfort. "Won't you excuse me? I forgot something inside." He turned to go, hesitated, then turned back. His voice was deliberate. "Be careful, Mrs. Roberts. I've seen some terrible accidents at this corner."

The man brushed past Robert, the doorman, and disappeared into the building. Jack noticed he was shaking.

Chapter 3

Five seconds. Just five seconds before the hand scooped up the stooped figure and pulsed down from fifteen. He was sure the letters W-A-L-K had lingered longer. Pedestrians penalized again. Why did they make the figure look so feeble — the city's ode to scoliosis? He had utterly no chance of crossing in time.

SATURDAY AFTERNOON, OCTOBER 13, 2012

Sheldon undid the tie and peeled the shirt off his right shoulder. His ribs ached. His elbow throbbed. The arm hung numbly at his side. He shifted his stance to inspect the back of his shoulder in the mirror. The swelling wasn't visible, but

he knew it was there, pressing against the impression left moments ago by the M7 bus. It was a matter of minutes before the arm would stiffen and be immobilized by pain. It wasn't broken and the shoulder wasn't dislocated but they hurt like hell. He struggled out of his undershirt to inspect his torso.

He was sure the ribs were unbroken — cracked perhaps, but not broken. He was able to vomit, then cough out the sour remnants of his lunch without collapsing from pain. Still, they had been compressed rather hard. It was remarkable he could still breathe, that he wasn't gasping like he had when he stepped last week in front of a bounding retriever. The dog should have been leashed. So should the wheelchair. But why stop there? He could have been hit by any number of objects; his reflexes just were not what they used to be.

Sheldon's ribcage would stiffen along with his arm, perhaps even his neck. He felt a twinge but ignored it. By evening his side would be dark purple, an inky vessel for a thousand broken capillaries. And by Wednesday, his side would become a splotch of red, blue and yellow, fading eventually into a bilious, fleshy slab.

Marian would know what to do, but Marian was dead – killed by the hospital, just as the hospital killed his daughter, Helen, and his sister, Muriel. He was not going to the hospital and was not going to see a doctor. He was not going to see anyone. He was going to wait out the pain until he could move his side again. And then maybe, just maybe, he would see a doctor, but not in a hospital!

Marian spent her last few years in a wheelchair, the last few before NYL killed her. Sheldon knew you couldn't yank back against a moving chair. The momentum was too strong. So he pushed Mrs. Roberts forward, as hard as he could, and she accelerated in bewilderment to a place of relative safety. No one noticed when the bus brushed off the old man in the checkered blazer. No one noticed his gut swallow the chair's handlebar then cough it free. No one noticed when he staggered, regained his footing, and walked with a deliberate, seemingly dignified air to the wheelchair, then rested his arms against the handles. All eyes were glued to the wheelchair and its stunned occupant.

Sheldon picked his blazer and undershirt up from the floor and laid them carefully on the bedside chair, the one he occupied as sentry when Marian was going through treatment. He ran his hand through the thick, white crop and scratched his scalp. He and Marian shared a small one-bedroom apartment off the back elevator. His work desk and credenza were in the corner by the window. The window faced an apartment forty feet away on the opposite side of the well so the drapes were drawn.

It was always dark in the bedroom now that Marian was gone. The apartment was the most he and Marian could afford, but they regarded it as cozy, and Sheldon's business benefited from the cachet of a Central Park South address. He was not just a money manager; he was a money manager on Central Park South with neighbors who were the *Who's Who* of American theater and ballet. There were many fitful months, but they invariably paid the rent, and when the tenants voted in the early eighties to incorporate, Sheldon and Marian pooled their respective savings. There were times when they scarcely ate, but they always paid the maintenance and spoke endlessly of cashing out their now wildly over-priced shoe box to buy a "real" home in Oneonta. It was too late now. Marian had her plot in Oneonta, but Sheldon wasn't ready to share it.

Sheldon knew they had invested wisely. He noted ruefully that it was his *only* wise investment, then reminded himself it was not really *his* investment. It was Marian who yearned to see the trees, birds and grass, to feel closer to the farmstead she left behind when she volunteered as a nurse at the end of the Korean War. Central Park was her answer. Sheldon wanted to live in the Bronx, close to his beloved Yankees, close to those who spoke with a proper accent.

Marian swayed his perspective on Manhattan, even moderated his accent. People said he sounded like Jerry Orbach. "Good thing you haven't heard me sing," he replied, until Marian reminded him that no one remembered El Gallo and *The Fantasticks*. They were referring to his role in *Law and Order*, in which, Marian assured him, Mr. Orbach never sang.

Well, Sheldon remembered *The Fantasticks* just fine. He remembered it like yesterday. It was the fall of 1959. Eisenhower was President. Sheldon had spent three years in the Reserves but never shipped out. It was peacetime and the country was brimming with youth, hope and, so it seemed, prosperity.

Sheldon helped his father lay tile in the washrooms at a nursing home in Brooklyn, studying accounting during the evenings at Baruch College. It took two weeks' needling from his father and, because his father could not keep a secret, his sister, mother and next-door neighbor to muster the courage to ask the ash-blond nursing assistant on a date. Had she not worn a badge broadcasting her name, Sheldon would never have found the nerve. Somehow, the badge made it easier, not quite an invitation, but almost. He spent hours rehearsing the syllables, "Marian Willis."

It turned out Marian already had a boyfriend and she was four years older than Sheldon. But Marian did not forget him and looked him up the following May when her then-boyfriend moved on.

Sheldon's attempt to impress her was *The Fantasticks*, an off-Broadway musical that opened that month to generally positive reviews at the Sullivan Street Playhouse in Greenwich Village. The price was right, the show was new, and it was in the Village, Sheldon's way of intimating he was "cool."

Sheldon's heart stopped when he entered the theater. The playhouse was a black, subterranean room, not larger than his family's living room, furnished with perhaps 100 seats surrounding a tiny raised platform with a couple shabby curtains. A harp and piano were wedged to the side. The props, what few there were, were cardboard. Sheldon felt Marian would never forgive him. She would walk out on him right there, on the banks of this River Styx.

Marian did not walk out. She leaned her seated body against his, second row right, peered up as El Gallo stepped forward to introduce the story of two feuding families and the clandestine love of Matt and Luisa, and began to sing "Try to Remember." She fell in love. Sheldon was already in love. They married in September.

Right now, Sheldon needed to think. He was aching from pain but his head ached more. It ached for a week. Everything was electronic now. You did not phone in your orders. You entered them the efficient way, the automated way, the instantaneous way – online over the computer. The irreversible way.

It seemed so innocent. He wasn't steering the client toward some dubious penny-stock investment. He hadn't exchanged insider information with some mucky muck at Goldman. He hadn't entrusted funds with Madoff, as so many of his neighbors had done. And he hadn't bet $11.5 billion on sovereign debt like MF Global. Sheldon Vogel prided himself on his integrity, his conscientious stewardship of other people's money. There was never a hint of impropriety. Sheldon valued that reputation.

The irony was, Sheldon Vogel's integrity was never in question. His record spoke for itself. Sheldon's idea of research was to pore over newspaper clippings and trade journals and run crude calculations in Excel, congratulating himself when his intuition paid off, vowing to work harder when it did not. In the end, he chose stocks that, taken together, unwittingly resembled the Dow Jones Industrials. Sheldon Vogel's integrity was never in question, just his returns. They were like his sister Muriel's blood tests, the ones taken three months before she died – unremarkable.

Sheldon's clients came and went. But his mainstays, the ones who enabled Marian and Sheldon to scrape by, were local affiliates of Actors' Equity and the Theatre Musicians Association. Both organizations doled out responsibility for managing portions of their pension funds to individual money managers, who in turn made investment decisions and charged annual fees for their services. Sheldon managed the life savings of actors and musicians and took this responsibility seriously.

Sheldon held on to just three clients after Marian died, the two pension funds plus a trust fund he managed, in his words to Marian, "as a favor" – a favor Sheldon now wished he had forsaken.

The trust beneficiary was his next-door neighbor, Allison Pfouts, whose husband, Ezra, passed away in October, 2003. Sheldon and Marian had been the Pfouts' neighbors since moving into the building in 1971. They ran into the Pfouts in the elevator, in the laundry room, at the garbage chute and at the annual stockholders' meeting after the building became a cooperative, but that was the extent of their familiarity. Sheldon could not recall a single instance of stepping into the Pfouts' apartment or of the Pfouts stepping into theirs. Until October 3, 2003, that is, when Ezra Pfouts summoned Mrs. Pfouts and the attending nurse closer to his bedside and whispered his dying words, "Don't worry, Allie. I've arranged everything. Sheldon Vogel will take care of you."

Sheldon and Marian were summoned in late October to the reading of Mr. Pfouts' will. Before commencing, the attorney made a point of recounting Mr. Pfouts' last words, pausing for theatrical effect, as if that final nuncupative declaration was Ezra Pfouts' actual will and testament.

Sheldon and Marian were struck dumb. At first, they feared Mrs. Pfouts was indigent and thereafter entrusted to their care. Worse, they feared Mrs. Pfouts would move in with them. Silently, they wondered if it would be bad form to rise up and dash for the door.

The lawyer continued, "I shall now read the will."

What Mr. Pfouts meant was Sheldon Vogel was appointed manager and financial fiduciary of a trust fund set up to provide for Mrs. Pfouts, assuming Mr. Vogel wanted the business. What made the bequest peculiar was that the asset allocation guidelines were particularized in the trust's charter. The charter prescribed a certain perpetual mix of cash, fixed income securities and equity. It also directed that certain portions of the stock holdings be allocated to certain industries. The fund manager's job was to calculate the portfolio's actual allocation after each year's market activity and bring the portfolio back into alignment. He would be free to choose between individual securities in a designated industry, but the industry allocations and aggregate allocations between cash, stock and bonds were not discretionary. In return for fulfilling these guidelines, the fund manager would earn 1.8 percent per year – take it or leave it. The securities were worth $1,687,366 as of the date of the reading. Sheldon glanced at Marian for reassurance then took it.

Monday evening, Sheldon began rebalancing the trust fund's portfolio, the same way he rebalanced the portfolio for nearly a decade. Before going to bed, Sheldon logged into the custodial account of the Pfouts trust and placed sell orders for 240 shares of Merck and 400 shares of Pfizer to reduce the client's percentage exposure to pharmaceuticals. The trades would clear by the close of business, Tuesday. He also executed buy orders for Cisco and Intel, reduced the portfolio's reliance on several REITs, shut off the computer, kissed the portrait of Marian Vogel on the forehead, and went to bed.

The zero key stuck when he entered the sell order for Merck. Or his fingers shook. Or he wasn't paying attention. One fact was certain. He did not read the transaction confirmations and must have clicked through the short sale confirmation. He sold 24,000 shares of Merck instead of 240 – 23,400 more than the trust held, and therefore borrowed the remainder on margin from the trust's broker. To compound matters, Merck's share price rose with the market. Merck was up $3.80 by the close of business Wednesday, so his loss on sale was already $88,920. And there were still two more days before he had to deliver the securities.

Sheldon was bewildered when he logged into the account on Thursday morning. He saw the error instantly but had no idea what to do. For the first time in his life, he was deeply afraid.

Sheldon's father died on December 31, 1961 from a massive coronary – not celebrating the December 29th birth of his only grandchild, Helen, nor Sheldon's pending graduation from Baruch College, but rather the arrival at New City Stadium in Green Bay, Wisconsin, of the New York Giants for the 29th National Football League championship game against the Packers. Sheldon was still with Marian and Helen at the hospital, and Muriel was helping the elder Mrs. Vogel in the kitchen. She brought her father a beer. He did not reach forward to take it.

Muriel shook her father, rushed to the kitchen and returned with her mother. Mrs. Vogel also shook her husband, hesitated, then brought the beer back to the kitchen. She rummaged through a drawer for a stopper then placed the corked bottle in the refrigerator. "I guess we should call the police," she announced matter-of-factly. Her husband was already bagged and carted to the morgue before Sheldon returned home from the hospital.

Mrs. Vogel put her grief in perspective. "God decides when it's time for us to enter this world and leave. He took your father while the Giants were still winners. If God were angry with him, he would have taken him at the end of the game." The Giants lost 37-0. Mrs. Vogel knew; her husband made it to Heaven. She gave Sheldon the open beer from the fridge. They wished each other "Happy New Year."

❧

$88,920 and counting. Mrs. Vogel would have known what to do. So would his wife, Marian, the younger Mrs. Vogel. He wondered whether Bank of America already alerted Mrs. Pfouts to the short sale. Of course not, he thought, this is chicken scratch. But to me? To the trust?

Sheldon decided to cut his losses. He consulted the Excel worksheet he updated on Monday evening. He typed 100,000 in a blank cell then divided it in another cell by the portfolio's aggregate value as of the close of business Monday, $1,544,878.73. The result was 0.06473. Rounding up, Sheldon placed orders electronically to sell 6.5 percent of each security in the Pfouts estate. This would accommodate the asset allocation requirements of the trust while freeing enough capital to close out the short sale. Several hours later, after verifying the trades had gone through, Sheldon unwound the trust's short position. To his relief, Merck's share price had retreated forty cents from the previous day's close, so the trust's total loss, inclusive of commissions and borrowing costs, was just $87,631.

Just. Sheldon felt miserable. $87,631 was $27,631 more than Allison Pfouts withdrew each year to supplement her social security income. It was enough to pay for three of her semiannual cruises and was a substantial percentage of her principal. The loss would come to light. It had to.

Sheldon doubted whether Mrs. Pfouts would pore over next month's statement. She might, but the market these days was volatile. The Dow ratcheted up or down by a percentage or more seemingly daily. A 6.5 percent decline would not seem outlandish, especially if masked somewhat by the market's actual upward movement.

What worried Sheldon was how the loss would be characterized, as a short-term capital loss rather than a long-term one. Allison's accountant, her lawyer in fact, would catch the discrepancy immediately. It would not take long before she detected the trades Sheldon made to cover his tracks. And then what? Sheldon saw his world unraveling. It was just a typo, a really big typo, but it felt like fraud.

❧

Marian gave up nursing to devote full time to her family. It was unthinkable in 1961 to do otherwise. So she and Sheldon lived in the family apartment on Grand Concourse and 138th Street. The arrangement was temporary, of course. Sheldon would soon be working.

Nine years and three careers later, they moved into an apartment in Hell's Kitchen opposite the parking lot that paved over the debris from the original Madison Square Garden. Accounting was a bust. Sheldon fumbled with numbers. So, he sold life insurance for a while and would have continued had the insurance carrier survived. But he had the misfortune of hitching his wagon to Equity Funding Corporation of America, a company whose executives cooked the books by fabricating policies and policy holders. When news of the scandal broke, Sheldon threw in the towel. The policies he sold to the guys from the Service and to Marian's friends from nursing school were worthless; and the annuity income Sheldon and Marian banked on from policy renewals evaporated, as did many of their friendships.

Sheldon resolved to insulate himself from the misdeeds of others and, more important, get closer to the money. He hung out a shingle and became a money manager. To improve his connections and cachet, he and Marian moved to Central Park South.

❧

Sheldon rummaged through the bottom drawer of his dresser. He knew it was there, forsaken but not forgotten. He gave up smoking for good on his twentieth anniversary and pushed the last remaining pack to the back of the drawer, just in case he should relapse, as he so often had. But this last time he did not, and the cigarettes lay there untouched for thirty-one years.

Sheldon found the unopened pack among the sweaters his wife bought and so neatly folded. He could not remember the last time he wore one. He preferred his blazer and, when it was colder, long underwear and a parka. Sweaters itched, especially the ones Marian picked out for him, so there they lay, neatly folded, nestled in front of a pack of cigarettes. Sheldon fetched a matchbook from the kitchen counter and plodded into the bathroom. He opened a small window that faced into the well and seated himself on the lid of the toilet. His side ached. He leaned left against the pedestal sink, fumbled with the packet, and slipped off its wrapper.

Sheldon thought about the times he stationed himself on the bench inside the park, the bench that now bore Marian's name, savoring a cigarette in peace. He could not smoke inside, not as long as Marian lived, and by the time she died, Sheldon had long lost the urge.

The truth is, Sheldon never "savored" his cigarettes. He endured them. He took slowly to tobacco while he was in the Service, more out of boredom than compulsion. And when he left the Service he resolved to quit. But quitting was hard, devilishly so, so he did not. He cast the pack aside for a week or two, especially when he went on vacation or neared an anniversary, then bummed one from the superintendent or the handyman and the cycle began anew. Until his twentieth anniversary, when his wife's persistent cough was diagnosed as early-stage lung cancer.

Lung cancer! Marian never smoked. She hated it. But Muriel had; her father-in-law had. And Sheldon had. He gave up smoking for good.

Marian loved the park, as did Sheldon. His one frivolity, his one spendthrift allowance after she died was to dedicate a bench to her, courtesy of a $7,500 donation to the Central Park Conservancy.

Sheldon went this afternoon to Marian's bench to think, beseeching her for guidance, for a sign. The sign, if it came, was hidden among the torrent of people scurrying past. Sheldon rose in resignation then pushed a wheelchair away from a veering bus as he returned to the building.

Sheldon searched the medicine cabinet for the mixed jar of Percocet and Vicodin that Marian bequeathed him when she died. Marian also left him bottles of Prednisone, Levamisol, Gefitinib and half a dozen dietary supplements, but right now he was grateful for the Percocet. He placed two tablets in his mouth and washed them down with a cup of water. He glanced at the vial of Prednisone, the anti-inflammatory steroid prescribed during Marian's chemotherapy. "Not yet," he thought. "If I ruptured something, I want my doctor to see it." He did not want to wind up like his sister, Muriel, one of three hundred thousand names chiseled into gravestones at Woodlawn Cemetery in the Bronx just because he took a steroid to reduce swelling and hid the problem. That's why her oncologist was too late. "For Christ's sake," he said, swearing in his wife's religion. He did not dare swear in his own. "The orthopedist worked for the same damned hospital!"

He reseated himself and examined the packet of cigarettes. The label surprised him.

Sheldon expected to see "Chesterfields," the cigarettes Rod Serling so often inveigled him to try while he and Marian watched

The Twilight Zone. Instead, submitted for his consideration was a packet of "Old Gold," a brand he regarded, even in 1961, as matronly. He doubted whether either brand was still marketed or even distributed in the United States. Overseas, perhaps.

"I shouldn't have removed the wrapper," he thought. "They might have been worth something."

Sheldon recalled the slogan and chuckled, "Not a Cough in a Carload." "Right," he thought. "They're all dead."

⊰⊱

Muriel died within two weeks of diagnosis. The stomach cancer had progressed to her bones and liver. There was nothing to do but say good-bye. That was 1992. The previous year, Local 32BJ of the Service Employees International Union went on strike. Muriel lost her doormen. So did Marian and Sheldon. Sheldon volunteered as concierge and mail sorter, a terrific opportunity to sniff about and meet his neighbors. Marian kept him company. By the twelfth and final day of the strike, Sheldon knew which money managers and brokers corresponded with which tenants, when each tenant came and went, and who they entertained as guests.

Together, Marian and Sheldon networked like pros and were soon on a first-name basis with every tenant in the building. Sheldon's client list improved measurably. When negotiators narrowly averted a second strike nineteen years later, Marian and Sheldon sighed collectively, and facetiously blamed their weakening economic situation on the agreeableness "nowadays" of doormen and landlords. "Landlords used to be tough!" Sheldon railed.

"And doormen had spines!" rasped Marian, before coughing up spittle and sipping from the cup Sheldon held for her. He mumbled something about the IV, diverting her attention as tears welled within his lids and dripped in cadence with the bag.

The strike was harder on his sister, Muriel. She lived alone in the family apartment on 138th Street in the Bronx. The neighborhood had changed. The apartment was still located conveniently next to the downtown 4 and 5 express trains, but that was its only enduring virtue. Muriel did not want to commune with her neighbors, and she fell out with Marian – steadfastly refusing to say why. Well, that was her problem. Marian never hurt a fly.

Muriel only ventured outside during the daylight. She double bolted her door during the evenings and seldom opened the windows. But she still had to bring trash to the basement. She tripped on the last flight of stairs on the twelfth and final day of the strike. Her back ached horribly and she gave up working. She wore a brace, sought regular help from a chiropractor, even tried acupuncture. The pain only worsened.

Her doctor sent her to a specialist at NYL North. The orthopedist prescribed painkillers to ease the pain and steroids to reduce the inflammation. The steroid might have been prednisone. Sheldon could not remember. The orthopedist monitored her x-rays, modified the medications, took blood samples, and prescribed all manner of physical therapy. Sheldon had to accompany her; Muriel threw a fit if he suggested Marian.

It took eight months to detect the real problem, cancer in the bones. The assigned oncologist never stood a chance. He seemed embarrassed to deliver the diagnosis. The orthopedist offered his written condolences after the funeral, including his card in the event Sheldon or his "lovely wife" should ever require his services. He read somewhere that the oncologist had been promoted to president. Cardigan? Mulligan? Born again? Never again.

෯෯

Sheldon ran the bath. The water would relax his muscles, lessen the stiffness. It was all Marian would have prescribed, that and a good night's sleep. "The world will seem brighter in the morning," Marian would say. Except Sheldon knew it would not be. The Pfouts Estate subterfuge gnawed at him, mocked his imagined ethics, promising to fester like his aching side into a sore that was too extensive and ugly to hide. Why did he race to cover the trade? Why had he not just come clean and promised to make it up? Because he could not. He did not have enough liquid capital.

Sheldon brushed his teeth. They were good teeth, just three fillings, straight, strong and white. Sheldon's uncle was a dentist, and the dentist's niece and nephew were his best patients. Sheldon started at the image in the mirror. His lips were parted wide on the right to make room for the brush. The teeth glistened and foam dripped from the corner of his jaw. For a moment, it was the crazed sneer of a con man, a beast who gorged on unsuspecting investors, then picked clean their remains with an Oral-B toothbrush and Crest Multicare. The beast would reappear in the morning and the following one. Sheldon could bluster his way through life, disguised behind his good-natured smile and checkered blazer, but the creature in the mirror would bare its virile sneer every morning and someday betray him. "Oh Lord, what have I done?"

Sheldon struggled with the brush. His right arm throbbed, and his left arm was clumsy. He could not floss, just rinsed with Listerine and spat.

Sheldon disrobed and set himself carefully in the bath. The water was warm, womblike. Sheldon breathed deeply, slid lower, and rested his head against the ledge just left of the spigot. The water massaged his shoulder. He was still thinking about his teeth, his near-perfect set, and what little they bought him. "A man is only as handsome as his soul," Marian would say, and the dispirited Sheldon concurred. Marian always knew what to say.

He gazed absently at the pile of clothing on the toilet seat, at the packet of cigarettes on top, and then, almost imperceptibly, curled his lips into a smile. A moment passed and his smile broadened into the toothy grin of a child whose first at-bat is a home run. "Thank you, Marian. Thank you, God. One of you is looking out for me." The sign was there all along, in plain view, ever since he rummaged among the sweaters. He knew the sign was from Marian, not God. But he acknowledged God, just to be respectful.

Marian had not worn much jewelry after her first two bouts with cancer, just her half-carat solitaire, wedding band and occasionally a pair of hoop earrings. So her jewelry chest was shoved to the back of a closet, not surprising in a city like New York where living space is precious. But the chest was not empty. It was chock full of love's tender offerings, offerings that, even absent his fair Norman maiden, were worth their weight in "Old Gold."

Sheldon was not rich, but he never considered himself poor. And he loved Marian more than he could ever express in words. For their first twenty anniversaries, first twenty Decembers, first twenty Mother's Days and first twenty birthdays together, Sheldon gave Marian jewelry – diamond earrings, a pearl necklace, an emerald brooch – whatever Sheldon thought would catch her fancy. Marian inevitably protested, but just as inevitably relented. A buddy from the Service had a stall on West 48th Street in the Diamond District, so Sheldon paid close to wholesale.

Sheldon thought about the contents of the jewelry box. Marian's real fondness was not for diamonds or pearls, but for charm bracelets and sturdy, elaborate settings – the kind that commanded $1,730 an ounce in today's market. Old Gold, indeed!

The Percocet began to take effect. Sheldon relaxed. He imagined his battered body beginning to mend. Sheldon bathed himself thoroughly but would cleanse his soul in the morning.

He would call Mrs. Pfouts and her attorney to his apartment, explain how a keyboard malfunction (he would omit the possibility of user error) caused a sizable capital drain that he quickly detected, plugged and just as quickly resolved to remedy at his own expense. If Allison and her attorney agreed to keep everything private, he would immediately indemnify the fund for all losses, interest and fees incurred as a result of the errant trade and would, as a gesture of good will, halve this year's annual commission.

To be safe, he would enlist Mr. Roberts to accompany him. How could he refuse? He just saved his wife's life.

Sheldon knew the man in 8B was a lawyer. He knew the occupation of every tenant-owner in the cooperative. That was his job, sizing up incomes, sizing up opportunities. Sheldon needed a witness tomorrow and knew John Roberts would fill in nicely. He might even persuade him to draft the paperwork, lend it an air of legal gravitas. That would impress Mrs. Pfouts, perhaps even her attorney.

Sheldon imagined he was reclining on Marian's bench in the park. The warm water was sunshine on his brow and a gentle breeze against his shoulder; the blue tiles were the glistening windows of the Time Warner Center above the trees, and his legs were pathways that forked deep into the park and westward toward Columbus Circle.

Sheldon reflected on the many times he sat there after Marian died, wondering when he too would share a plot in Oneonta. Most days, he just idled. He had no one to nurse, no one to care for, no one to appreciate his gentle soul. So, it withered like the autumn leaves, until his mind was a vacant lot, a wintry expanse pining for spring but resigned to a long, dreary winter.

Sheldon could live to ninety. His mother had. Or he could die tomorrow. He had outlived his wife, his sister and his daughter. Putting aside his penchant for unintended contact sports, he was as healthy as an ox. But his mind was weary. Life had become tedious. He longed for Marian.

"Well, old girl," he thought, "You bailed me out again" – the Percocet, the gold, the path to forgiveness and redemption. The Vogel family's God was not big on forgiveness or redemption, but Marian's was, and Sheldon revered Marian above anyone else, including the Vogel family God.

Sheldon hummed a strain from his favorite musical, and his pitch-perfect baritone echoed off the bathroom tiles like a choir of voices at the Met, or at a modest basement theater in Greenwich Village. The words mirrored those on Marian's bench. "Deep in December it's nice to remember without the hurt the heart is hollow." Sheldon blessed Marian again and knew someday soon he would follow.

Chapter 4

"We used to live at the corner of Walk and Don't Walk. I don't know anymore. It's too symbolic, too Southern. Didn't they start this in Little Rock? The last thing I need is to obey another white man."

Silence.

"It was a joke, honey, a joke!"

TUESDAY AFTERNOON, APRIL 3, 2012

Susan feathered the clutch, shifted into third, then swerved right off First Street up the Bay Bridge ramp to Oakland. Traffic was light on Interstate 80, not yet choked by the crush of afternoon commuters.

6 months ago

present day

Susan adjusted the mirror. The Embarcadero and the tip of two P30 Race Carvers framed the top of her face. She decided it was youthful enough, despite the miscarriages and late-term abortion. She delivered Melissa, of course, but Melissa could entertain herself with Daddy. Susan was determined to rip Lake Tahoe, both on and off the slopes, and to party as if there were no tomorrow, because tomorrow loomed ever closer, ever drearier, ever bleaker.

A steel gray Z4 pulled alongside to pass then slowed for a better look. The driver peered over his shades, gave her an approving nod, then roared past. Susan smiled. The nod validated her decision.

She made the decision after her "surprise" birthday party in March. Jack reserved the back room of Trattoria Dell'Arte, a restaurant decorated by wall-sized fragments of faux statuary – a colossal marble nose out front, Amazonian breasts in the foyer. In attendance was the usual stable of neighbors, Brierley parents, and business associates.

Melissa was instructed to bring Susan directly to the restaurant after skating. The pretext was a visit to the nearby ATM for morning ice time and lesson fees. Jack could approach from the other direction as if returning from the office. He could suggest dinner or an aperitif and they would enter.

Jack's office was in the Calyon Building, the Crédit Lyonnais Building to his office mates and the J.C. Penney Building to his contemporaries. There were large revolving doors out front for the many companies that leased space, rechristened the building after themselves, and just as quickly vacated. The building stood catty-corner from the Museum of Modern Art on Sixth Avenue and 53rd Street. Its owner commissioned the sculptor Jack Dine to define the plaza in front with its own decorative statuary – three crude, oversized headless bronzes of the Venus de Milo. Susan wondered whether Jack's choice of Trattoria Dell'Arte was mere coincidence or fixation with monstrously large female body parts. She stood an inch taller than Jack, that much was true, but doubted whether size entered his calculus. The restaurant was just close, convenient and familiar. Jack always opted for the familiar.

The three rendezvoused precisely as Jack connived, and he persuaded Susan against protest to step inside for a celebratory drink. Her birthday was not until Thursday, but he had been called to London on business and would have to catch the 9:40 red eye from JFK; or so he said. "I'll make this up to you, sweetie, I promise, but right now I would like to buy the loveliest forty-year-old in New York City a glass of champagne."

"I'm thirty-nine!" she protested.

"Right," he admitted, rather solicitously. "I have just enough time to buy the loveliest young woman in New York City a glass of Roederer *Grands Crus*."

"Dad's right," Melissa added, "You look gorgeous."

Gorgeous? She wore gray sweatpants, a lavender tank top and a garnet-red Seminoles hoodie under the Burberry Brit double-breasted trench coat and chestnut Hunter boots. Her hair was pulled back in a loose bun and her skin was clammy with perspiration. Her running shoes were stuffed in her handbag.

She squeezed in a workout at the Reebok Sports Club while Melissa practiced at Wollman Rink, but had to dash twelve hundred meters from 67th Street and Columbus Avenue to pick Melissa up on time – cumbersome in boots and a trench coat, even for a long-forgotten track star. Susan scarcely felt gorgeous but nevertheless assented.

⇜⇝

Susan surveyed the rearview mirror. She wore loose-fitting jeans and her garnet-red hoodie. A pair of Oakley Flak Jackets shaded her eyes. Her hair fluttered wildly. The open-air convertible was a must. So was manual transmission. She searched an hour online before locating a company that still rented stick shifts, settling on a powder blue Mazda MX-5 two-seater with six-speed manual transmission. She shifted into fifth, veered around a blue Super Shuttle van and emerald town car, then punched the gas and watched the vehicles shrivel behind her.

A Camry cowered in front, then a pickup truck. She breezed past an eighties-era Dodge Charger – much nicer than the one she drove in college, a 1984 model handed down by her mother. The garnet red finish gleamed, and a gold stripe ran down its middle. School colors – like her hoodie.

Susan hadn't seen a Duster in years. Or was it a Shelby? Ten years ago, she would have known the difference. But no one drove in New York City. So, she stopped paying attention. To a lot of things. Cars aged slower in Northern California, she thought. The winters were kinder, and the air was cleaner.

Would cleaner air and kinder winters have slowed her husband's aging? Unlikely. Besides, Brobeck was a California firm. Jack's office was on Broadway near Times Square, but he spent weeks at a time in San Francisco. His daily exercise consisted of trotting to and from home and the office on 50th Street or hailing a cab to JFK. He invariably returned on a red eye, appeared briefly for a shower, then hustled to 50th Street to start the cycle anew.

All those dotcoms he helped bring public. Where was their cloud-based application to peel back the years, to make his infant daughter more than a JPEG image on his Blackberry, to bring back the suave heartthrob she married? Buried among the ashes of those dotcoms, just as Brobeck was, just as most of their 401-K investments were. No, you did not age slower in California, but the reminders of your past did.

She glimpsed Spear Street Tower, the former global headquarters of Brobeck Phleger & Harrison, before ascending to the freeway. For how many lawyers was that a memorial? And the turbocharged Charger she passed, was that hers? It seemed so strong, sleek, independent, but she entrusted the keys sixteen years earlier to another driver. God, how she wanted them back!

Sixteen years she defined herself in terms of her husband, and now her daughter. Was there anything left to call her own? Did people ever remark, "Oh, he's Susan McDonald's husband," or, "Melissa is going to be a star, just like her mother?" Or if she wore her varsity jacket, would people instead inquire, "Oh, did Jack go there?"

It had been ages since Susan drove a stick shift, ages since she sat behind the wheel. Jack always drove during trips to the Hamptons and now that they were watching the budget, their daughter's occasional commute to competitions. Hard-working, conscientious Jack. Jack came to a complete stop at stop signs. Jack drove within a hair of the speed limit – 35 miles per hour if the sign said 30, 70 if the sign said 65. And Jack always passed on the left, even when the right lane was open, and the two remaining lanes were straddled by an old biddy in a 1980s Impala. Jack played it safe, just as he played it safe on her birthday.

∂∽∂

The trattoria's bar was in the front. Uneasiness crept over Susan as the maître d' led them to the back. "Surprise!" everyone shouted and then crowded her for a hug and kiss beside the cheek. The attention was suffocating. "What did Jack think," she fumed silently, "that I sit at home in Dolce and Gabbana, all showered, coiffed and perfumed, just so I can fetch my daughter from the rink and put dinner on the table? How would he feel if I cornered him in his Garmin Sharp bib shorts, belly protruding from his matching cycling jersey, and dragged him stinking and perspiring to a surprise retirement party?" Susan smiled graciously, but inwardly yearned to scream.

Retirement party? Was her husband really that old? Many of his contemporaries had already left the law, taken up travel or settled in the country. Had Jack begun at Dewey Ballantine after law school, he most certainly would have cashed in his pension by now. It surely would have been large enough. "It's a young man's game," Jack would remark, presumably to his shadow, while he loosened his tie after an evening of contracting. Melissa was in general already asleep. Jack would deliberate silently for a moment, shoulders hunched, chest sagging – torn between his nerves' desire for four fingers of Don Julio tequila and the pressure to assuage the presumed needs of his much younger spouse.

Gently, nobly perhaps, Jack would straighten his shoulders, reach forward to caress Susan's cheek, and whisper something about saving his appetite for morning. Then he would slink into the bathroom for his Levitra, hang up his clothes, slip into bed, and perform his marital duty – if not passionately, at least urgently. Jack then rolled onto his back exhausted, struggled mightily to attend to her briefings about Melissa, and fell deeply into sleep.

How many times had this scene played out, year after year? Sixteen years? More tired performances than *A Chorus Line*. It was hard to imagine how she endured it.

Susan hated herself for detesting him. He was such a rare package when they met – debonair, sharply dressed, attentive in bed. He was a real gentleman, and, until recently, in no need of

Levitra. Their first date was at Windows on the World, 106 stories above Manhattan, followed by an evening of dancing at The Rainbow Room. Jack knew how to waltz, how to foxtrot. He moved effortlessly from one tempo to the next, quite literally sweeping Susan off her feet. He did not address Susan as Susie Mack, as her college friends and fellow flight attendants did. He insisted on "Ms. McDonald" and only reluctantly assented to "Susan." She did not hold it against him that he loathed rap and floundered at disco, falling behind the tempo. Her contemporaries were worse. Or they were lechers. Jack most certainly was not.

Besides, Jack did not advertise his age. Sure, he asked the town car driver that second evening to take them to the RCA Building, but even David Letterman joked about the building's reincarnation as the GE Building. And who could blame him for calling the Sony Center the AT&T Building? Its ornamental Chippendale roof so closely resembled a telephone cradle that any other name seemed absurd. It was not until Jack secured tickets to a Knicks-Bulls game at the "*new*" Madison Square Garden that Susan resolved to investigate. She did not ask him directly; she consulted an online directory of lawyers to learn when he was admitted to practice law. 1979, the year she entered third grade. Susan recalled another David Letterman punch line, "Joey Buttafuoco!" Definitely creepy, but Susan reasoned she was no Amy Fisher, that Jack looked considerably younger than his age, and he most certainly was not a lecher.

It took three weeks' prodding before Jack invited Susan to his apartment, a spacious one-bedroom unit in a black glass high-rise on the corner of 66th Street and Second Avenue. The front door opened to a sunken living room with sweeping views of Midtown Manhattan. The floor was tiled in black onyx. Centered against the living room window was an ebony Bösendorfer on an artificial zebra carpet.

Black lacquered furniture with cream-colored cushions framed the sunken seating area. A kitchenette was visible to the right of the foyer, together with a corridor that led presumably to the bedroom. Recessed lighting bathed the piano. The city sparkled below.

"Do you play?" Susan inquired, stunned by the opulence.

Susan subleased a small ramshackle apartment with three flight attendants in Hell's Kitchen. She spent as little time there as possible. The kitchen was a narrow counter at the end of a tiny living room overlooking a parking lot. The bedroom was a windowless cell, just large enough for two twin-sized beds. The living room held the other two beds. One of them was Susan's. Inexpensive rust brown carpeting covered decrepit floorboards; posters from the Met were stapled to the walls; and a Seminoles pennant hung over Susan's bed. The bathroom reeked from toilet overflow that had never been thoroughly cleaned, and the tub and wash basin backed up regularly. Most of the yellow one-inch tiles were broken. Paint peeled from the ceilings. The refrigerator stank of sour milk and the cupboard was infested with cockroaches. Mice fought for remnants of late-night pizza while the occupants slept.

"A bit," he responded. He led her into the well, hesitated, then helped her onto the piano. She giggled but refrained from laughing uncontrollably because he seated himself solemnly at the keyboard, raised the lid, and proceeded to play – fluidly, emotionally.

"That's lovely. What's it called?"

"'Rhapsody in Blue.' By Gershwin."

"Idiot!" thought Susan. This was not the first time she scolded herself. "All right, Bozo, why don't you ask him what you're sitting on?"

Jack read her mind. "It all sounds the same, really. I mean there's so much of it. Thousands of struggling songwriters, each reworking the same themes, the same eighty-eight keys, for as long as people have been selling music. It's amazing anyone produces anything different anymore."

"I just happen to like Gershwin," he added, "and Porter." And with that he segued into the crisp opening staccato of "Night and Day." Susan asked him to sing the lyrics but he could not. His voice cracked and he stumbled with the keys, so he proffered her the book and played from memory. Susan hummed the melody, but she took the opportunity while he was sleeping to jot down the lyrics, the final stanza of which she remembered to this day.

"I think of you night and day, day and night under the hide of me. There's an oh such a hungry yearning inside of me, and this torment won't be through till you let me spend my life making love to you, day and night, night and day." And like the tick, tick, tock of the stately clock, Jack kept that vow, even if it meant foregoing his favorite tequila, and imbibing lately on Levitra.

Susan saw the exit for Napa but continued driving east on I-80. Her mind lingered for a moment, drifting back to when they were dating. Susan had just turned 24, but Jack was ensconced in meetings that week in San Francisco. Susan caught a standby flight Friday morning. Jack met her at the gate in a collared shirt, gray trousers and navy-blue blazer. He took command of her wheelie and led her to the curb. A black town car pulled up and escorted them to the short-term parking area where Jack had parked his Taurus rental car. Susan remembered her coworkers' reaction the following Tuesday. "He reserved a limousine to take you from baggage claim to the parking lot?" Susan was as incredulous as they were, but inwardly she was proud. Jack exuded class.

Jack took the exit for Napa, remarking he had discovered a quaint restaurant overlooking the valley. They would be just in time for tea. Susan knew not to ask how Jack discovered the restaurant. His previous marriage was off limits. Susan also knew they did not drive to Napa for tea. So they chatted about wine. That was a safe subject, one which animated them for nearly an hour.

They drove along the eastern edge of the valley then turned right at the sign for Rutherford Vineyards. He conversed freely about his love for certain varietals and the vineyards that dotted the valley. He obviously knew the way. They paused above a small parking area at the top of the hill. The valley stretched before them, much narrower than it seemed along Route 128 below. Pale green and yellow swathes marked the vineyards, divided into top and bottom halves by a faint dusty road. Coastal redwoods and pines framed their sides and blanketed the mountains on the horizon.

Susan cupped her hands above her eyes. The sun hung low on the horizon but still blinded her. Beyond the narrow parking area stood the silhouette of a one-story Mediterranean-style villa that, she surmised, harbored a second or third story further down the mountain. Jack edged the Taurus down to the building. The valet greeted them, "Welcome to Auberge du Soleil," and handed Jack a claim check.

The pair dined on the balcony, nestled against the railing, taking in the valley and a spectacular sunset. An eagle soared overhead. Another circled in the distance. The sun dipped below the horizon and its oven-like warmth gave way to evening chill. Jack stood, draped his jacket over Susan's shoulders, then reseated himself. Susan finished her bacon-wrapped veal and used a bread stick to scoop the last morsel of orange mascarpone and polenta onto her fork. A couple rose from the next table and reentered the building. "That's Ted Danson," Susan whispered breathlessly. "I love *Cheers.*"

Jack nodded. "And Mary Steenburgen. From *Melvin and Howard.*" Susan did not know who Melvin and Howard were, so Jack expressed his gratitude for pointing out Ted Danson. "I worked like a fiend during the eighties; missed nearly every episode of *Cheers.* I'm glad you pointed him out. Steenburgen was married for years to Malcolm McDowell. That's probably why I recognized her."

"Oh," Susan responded. "Who's he?"

"Another actor," replied Jack gently. Susan wondered whether Jack was being evasive or just did not know anything more about Malcolm McDowell. He did work really long hours. "Danson is a lucky man," Jack added, "an, oh, lucky man."

"Yes," agreed Susan, hesitating. "They did a wonderful job casting *Cheers*."

Jack paid the check and escorted Susan through the building into the courtyard, then left toward their vehicle. "The valet has your keys," Susan reminded him.

Jack nodded but directed her past the car to a path that curved around the building. Cut into the hillside below the restaurant were a number of terraces, each sheltering a small Mediterranean cottage, or maison. Jack found a terrace and maison to his liking, produced a key, and opened the door. Susan's luggage stood inside the door, nestled against Jack's. "I hope this is okay," he inquired. Yes, it was okay. It was perfect. Everything was perfect.

❧❦

Susan pitched left then right around a cluster of tractor trailers that blocked the lanes. The interstate beyond Sacramento became steeper. The rigs battled one another for the clear, open road, but wound up cluttering the lanes to do so. Susan veered narrowly around the right side of a Safeway tractor, then swerved tightly around the white tractor trailer to her left. The speedometer flitted with ninety, but the sports car gripped the road securely.

"Slalom," thought Susan.

Susan loved the exhilaration of flying down groomers, testing her knees against moguls, then pushing her reflexes in the steep, craggy chutes off KT-22. Susan congratulated herself for renting the Miata. "I'm enjoying this much more than some five-star cottage tucked into a hillside," she insisted, blinking back a tear.

"Damn wind," she added, glancing in the mirror at her fluttering hair. Susan kept the needle in the low eighties, determined to outrun Jack's shadow.

ࣞ∼ঌ

Susan packed and boarded the plane the day after Hannah called. She needed to get away – immediately. Neither Jack nor Melissa protested.

Hannah told her not to expect luxury. "It's cheap digs, darling. Can't afford the Ritz or even Motel 6, but I'll leave the light on for you." Hannah chuckled at her joke. Susan was silent. "You know, Tom Bodett? National Public Radio? Oh, never mind. The place is clean, cozy and by the lake. At least it was ten years ago. We'll have a whale of fun."

Susan knew there were no whales in Lake Tahoe, but assured Hannah, yes, they would have fun. She strained to hear desperation in Hannah's voice. Remorse. Anything. Hannah lost her only child. She discarded her husband of fourteen years and, as far as Susan knew, no longer managed conventions for the hospital. "Joyously emancipated" was surely a euphemism. Susan shrugged. Either way, the trip was Hannah's, not hers. Nothing was hers.

She tried raising the top when she reached Donner Pass. The roads were clear, but the clouds closed in around her and it was freezing. She pulled over at the exit for Donner Lake.

That was when Susan learned why Jack rented full-size sedans when he skied, even when he traveled alone. He could lay the skis down between the seats. The positioning wasn't elegant, but he always found a way. Susan found a way at the rental shop. She wedged a ski into the floorboard on either side of the passenger seat, then reclined the seat fully so that the tips peaked up like goal posts. But now she could not raise the top. She opened the trunk, reached into a large suitcase, and pulled out gloves and a ski jacket – a black quilted Bogner with fur trim. She considered driving all week with the top down but wondered how she would cope with snow. The thought of shoveling the car's interior made her laugh. She resolved to find a shop in Truckee. Someone would know what to do.

It was drizzling lightly when she exited Interstate 80 in Truckee. She found a service station and described her predicament to the attendant. He began to chuckle. He was still chuckling when he set her on her way, skis duct-taped securely to a trunk-mounted vintage bicycle rack. The man salvaged the rack from a wrecked Ford Tempo the previous summer and wagered he could resell it later. Later came sooner than he expected.

The attendant charged Susan two hundred dollars cash, inclusive of installation and accessories. Accessories included a roll of duct tape, a bungee cord, an old sponge, a bar of soap and a box cutter. The man rubbed the top of the skis with soap before taping their tips to the bicycle rack. He then secured the tails of the skis to the back of the roof with the bungee cord and duct tape. He taped the sponge under the skis where they made contact with the car. Before mounting the rack, he emptied the trunk unceremoniously, throwing a boot bag and suitcase on the passenger seat. He explained using the trunk might be a "hassle," but if she was expecting company, "the fella can cozy up with the luggage" or remove and remount "the contraption" himself.

Rain began pelting the MX-5 when it crossed the Truckee River onto Route 267, a narrow mountain highway that wound through twelve miles of dense pine forest to Kings Beach a couple miles west of the Nevada border. Susan decelerated to see but resolved not to let rain dampen her enthusiasm. She had glimpsed Boreal Mountain Resort at the top of Donner Pass and now passed the turnoff for the Resort at Northstar. Cars were still filing out of the lot. Conditions were fine near the peak, Susan was sure. Six minutes later she began the descent to Kings Beach and, on cue, the rain subsided.

The afternoon sun burnt a hole through the clouds, bathing the lake in a glorious, iridescent glow. Susan's mother would have regarded it as a sign from the Lord. She would have reached for her hymnal. Susan did not have patience for the hallelujah crowd. It was just the sun's rays penetrating an opening in the firmament, but her heart beat faster and she felt like rejoicing.

Susan flipped on the radio. It was off since Vacaville. The stations kept drifting in and out of range; there were too many hills for decent reception. Plus, she had the top down most of the way; the wind and traffic were deafening. So she drove to Lake Tahoe without music. She pushed the "scan" button to find a station.

Susan cringed at the strength of the signal. "It is sin that stands in the way of salvation; it is by sin that man is liable to condemnation and ruin!" Susan reached for the volume. "But there is hope for pardon…." Susan switched it off.

"Jesus fucking Christ! Even in Lake Tahoe. Lord deliver us from preachers selling salvation."

Susan resolved to download a playlist to her cell phone the moment she returned home, if she returned home. She was increasingly undecided. "And no fucking choir music! Or George Fucking Gershwin." She hesitated before adding, "Or Cole Fucking Porter," but she did not sound convinced. She mouthed the lyrics she jotted down so many years earlier.

"Why is it so that this hunger for you follows wherever I go? In the roaring traffic's boom, in the silence of my lonely room, I think of you day and night, night and day…." Tears welled in her eyes. She removed the Oakleys to dry the tears with her sleeve.

The afternoon sun hung low above the shore. It burned another hole in the clouds and bored into her eyes. She braked as she neared the end of the descent, then veered right onto 28, the two-lane road that rimmed the northern shore of the lake. The lake shimmered brilliantly, and Susan winced.

She barely heard the screech. The impact was instantaneous, a glancing blow to her fender that spun her through the bike lane into the undergrowth lining the road. A red four-by-four blared insistently as it swerved from the opposite direction around a careening Pathfinder. The arctic blue sport utility vehicle regained control and slowed twenty yards ahead, pulling to the side.

Susan sat back, dazed. She was uninjured. She got out of the car to inspect the damage. The fender was mangled. It hung down and pressed against the tire. The gnarled metal reminded her of the sculptures she saw that month at a museum near her daughter's school. Melissa had an after-school art assignment there; otherwise, Susan would never have stepped foot in the Guggenheim. Old people staring at paint splotches; she much preferred artwork about real subjects.

The sculpture she remembered was by John Chamberlain. Actually, all the sculptures were by Chamberlain. The Guggenheim ran a retrospective of his work – hulking sheets of automotive steel crushed into menacing forms. "Jeez," she muttered, inspecting her fender. "Now you're an artist. I hope you feel inspired."

The wheel looked okay. The hood was not buckled and she saw nothing to suggest damage to the engine. The rental car company would love this. And of course she would have to explain the accident to Jack. She dreaded that, not because he would scold her. He would never do that, which was part of the problem. No, he would show concern, grave concern for her, exclusively for her, not the car. And he would manage her more closely, tightening the leash a bit further, just as he had for sixteen years.

Her thoughts veered back to an art opening at the Museum of Modern Art. Susan was four months pregnant. She and Jack were engaged. Jack pointed out one of the guests – Judy Collins, a thin, modestly-dressed woman with graying brown ponytail and small, wire-framed glasses.

"Who's she?" Susan recalled asking.

"A folk singer, very popular when I was in college," Jack responded.

Susan watched as guests slowed, glanced back, then whispered to one another as they passed her. Some circled back to introduce themselves. The atmosphere was respectful, as if the guests had crossed paths with the Queen. Ms. Collins was obviously more interesting than the paintings, thought Susan. In fact, everything was more interesting than the paintings – the guests, the hors d'oeuvres, the wine.

A crushed fender reminded her of the works of John Chamberlain; the grime on the windshield reminded her of an art opening at MOMA. Susan could not fathom why Jack frittered money away on such events. If he wanted to glimpse a childhood idol, he should have treated her to a Rolling Stones concert. That she would have understood.

Susan leafed through CDs of Judy Collins the following day at Tower Records. The wistful blue-eyed figure on the jewel box was familiar yet scarcely resembled the aging schoolteacher she met at the museum. Where had she seen her before? Susan brought a compact disc to the kiosk at the end of the aisle and fitted a pair of headphones. The voice restored her memory. She listened rapturously in her youth … to *Sesame Street*.

Susan never mentioned her research to Jack but found it curious that her fiancé fixated during college on a woman who sang to Muppets. Thank goodness he had matured beyond that.

Susan declined further invitations to art openings. Jack attended them alone. He did, however, treat her to a marvelous dinner after the MOMA exhibition in a townhouse across the street where, Jack explained, the one-time Vice President of the United States, then 70 years old, died having sex with his 25-year-old aide. Susan loved the story. Jack agreed it was the right way to go, "although Happy was not exactly happy." Happy was his wife. Susan loved that part, too. Who would name their child Happy?

Jack and Susan did not have a chance to name their first child. Susan entered a triathlon two weeks after the art opening, withdrew from the bicycle portion with cramps then miscarried. Susan was distressed but Jack was devastated. They would try again, she consoled him, and they did. But she sensed anxiety beneath his supportive facade. She felt tethered. Susan resumed training immediately, if only to get outside.

☙❧

A young woman, a teenager actually, stomped over from the Pathfinder. "Damn it, there's a stop sign. Can't you see? You're supposed to stop before you turn." She was crying. "If I hadn't swerved into the other lane I would have killed you." Susan did not correct her. No, she could not see. The sun blinded her, but that was beside the point. She should have stopped before turning the corner, especially because she could not see. She was grateful the girl swerved. She was grateful the oncoming truck had time to react. She was grateful to be alive.

The girl trembled. Her lip was swollen.

"My God, did I do that?" Susan inquired.

The girl touched her face then shook it violently. No, Susan did not.

"Well, are you okay?" Susan persisted, suddenly curious why a girl with an enormous welt in a monstrous SUV should be distraught at *Susan's* tiny fender bender, albeit an expensive one. Susan reckoned the repair bill would run into the thousands. But California was a no-fault state. Wasn't it? The girl wouldn't have to pay a dime.

Several cars slowed to look. A young man in a Ford Escape pulled over between the two vehicles, stepped out of the vehicle and offered his assistance. He seemed young, nineteen or twenty. Cute face, thought Susan.

"Nice wheels, Ma'am," he said to Susan. "I hope you're insured."

"Ma'am?" thought Susan, somewhat deflated. She felt like the fender.

The teenager began sobbing uncontrollably. "Steady, miss. You okay?" She had not answered Susan's question, but managed to nod to the boy. "Your vehicle okay?" She gulped back a sob and nodded again. "Well, let's take a look anyway." He tried to sound gentle. A younger form of Jack, Susan thought, as he took her arm and guided her to the vehicle. Gallant, thought Susan, somewhat sarcastically. Like Jack.

"Hardly a scratch. Just some paint. Your father will understand."

"It's, it's not his car," she stammered.

A patrol vehicle pulled up before she could explain, a compact white suburban with a decorative green swoosh under the windows and the words "Pacer County SHERIFF" emblazoned on the side. An officer stepped out.

"Your car?" she asked Susan.

"Yes, officer. I couldn't see much when I made the turn; the sun was so bright."

"Gets that way this time of day. I see she gave you a kiss," nodding to the Pathfinder. "Not much damage, but I bet that'll cost you your allowance."

Susan started. "How did she know that?" She did not, Susan scolded herself; it was a joke. Besides, American Express would cover this. The platinum card covered everything.

"Okay, both of you, I need to see your driver's license and registration." To Susan, who stood by her car and hesitated, "It's your rental contract."

The officer inspected the documents.

"Ms. McDonald, I'm sorry to dampen your day further, but I am going to have to cite you for running the stop sign. There's no question the sun is bright, but not if you stop and look both ways like you're supposed to." Susan just nodded. She was lucky to be alive, lucky she paid with the platinum card, lucky the other driver and vehicle were unhurt. And besides, what did it matter if she acquired points on her license? Higher insurance rates? She didn't own a car.

"Yes officer, I should have come to a complete stop."

The officer turned to the teenager. "Miss Watkins, this is a learner's permit. You are supposed to be accompanied by a licensed driver, preferably your mother or father. And you are supposed to drive in Nevada. Who is George Underhill?"

Miss Watkins could barely stand. The boy from the Ford Escape was now supporting her. "He's, he's a friend, no not a friend, he's…" and she began weeping hysterically. She tried to resume. "I have, I have an appointment at the Forest Hospital, in twenty minutes." She tried to choke back the tears. "He said he couldn't drive me. He said he never wanted to see me again."

"Who, Miss Watkins? George Underhill?"

The girl mouthed "Mm-hmm" between gulps.

"Yet you have his vehicle."

"He said it wasn't his, it couldn't be. But it was. It was. I told him if he didn't help me, I'd make a scene." Susan and the boy cast their eyes downward and fidgeted, bound by a shared sense of embarrassment. The girl sobbed.

"So, he lent you his car. Where is he now?"

"He's, he's the foreman on a construction project in Brockway, on … on Dip Street." The girl paused in visible torment before volunteering the last bit of information. The officer nodded. She knew the site. Brockway sat twenty paces from the Nevada border and a mile and a half from where they stood. It was still in Pacer County, still within her jurisdiction.

A car slowed to observe the girl bawling on the side of the road. "I'd cry, too," the driver shouted, "if I dinged a car like that." It drove on.

The officer continued, "And he hit you?"

"He threw the money at me, called me a whore, told me to return the tank full. Or else." The boy tried to console her. The officer paused then walked the two of them out of earshot. She returned several minutes later. She handed Susan a slip of paper.

"I assume you have a cell phone?"

Susan nodded.

"Call Volker. I've written down his number. He'll bend the fender back or cut it off. Either way, you'll be able to drive. You can call the Pacer County sheriff's office for the accident report. Oh, here's your stuff. Remember, full stop at every corner."

Susan was stunned. The "stuff" was her driver's license and rental contract; it was not a ticket. She immediately dialed the number on the slip of paper.

The officer returned to the boy, who led the girl to the passenger seat of his vehicle, then got into the driver's seat. He spoke with the officer for several minutes before edging onto 28, presumably toward the hospital in Truckee. The officer strode back to Susan's car, keys to the Pathfinder in hand. "You call the old man?" she asked but did not hear Susan's reply. The officer turned to greet a "toot-toot" from the other direction.

A tow truck slowed to a stop and a grizzled old man in overalls stepped out. "I vuz 'round der corner at de Gar Vhoodz," the man grinned, "chatting up der talent." He winked at the officer.

"Well, Papa. Here's some more talent, Ms. Susan McDonald from New York City, only something tells me she has more expensive taste than you. See if you can get her on the road again, will you?"

"Sure ding, boss. Vot about de Podfinder?"

"I'm about to visit the owner to straighten a few things out." The officer nodded curtly to Susan, kissed the man warmly on the cheek, then opened the door to her suburban.

Volker Dierich watched his daughter roar off in the direction of the state border. "Kinder," he said, shaking his head, "sie haben es immer eilig."

"I'm sorry, Mister … Mist … Sir, I'm in sort of a hurry. I promised to meet a girlfriend from New York."

"Genau was ich meinte," replied the mechanic. "Dis girl from Noy York. Vos zee called?"

"Hannah," responded Susan, biting back the impulse to reply, "What difference does it make?"

"What if I answered Peggy or Frieda or Gertrude?" she thought, "What difference would it make to *you*?"

"Genau was ich dachte!" exclaimed the mechanic excitedly. "You find her at de bar in den Gar Vhoodz, five minutes dat'a way," he said, pointing in her car's direction. "Only you better get a ticket. I already in line."

Susan stood speechless. Hannah was … the "talent"? For geezers like Folker, Fucker, or whatever he was called?

Volker read her mind.

"Iz OK. There young people, too. Children, same age as you. But real men? Men mit rich experience? They hard to find."

Susan laughed. Well, at least Hannah was scouting the terrain. She overpaid Volker for his work but made him promise to buy her a drink.

"Mit pleasure, Kindchen, mit pleasure," were his parting words.

The Miata crawled into Tahoe Vista shortly after dusk. It was a good thing it crawled. If Susan had driven any faster, she would have missed it. She turned the car around when she reached the sign for Carnelian Bay and tried again. No sign of the Chamois Chalet. Hannah swore she stayed there ten years ago. This time she looked for the address. A "For Sale" sign stood on the lawn next to a somewhat larger vacancy sign for the Vistaview Grande. A mangy reddish-brown dog resembling a small husky sat on its haunches in the driveway. Enormous bat-like ears protruded from its head and its eyes gleamed yellow in the headlights. Its muzzle was narrow and angular. Susan slowed to a stop. The dog gave a high-pitched yip and skulked off, tail drooped low between its legs. Later it would gather with its friends and howl at the moon. Hannah told her later they were jackals. "You Americans call them coyotes."

"Good thing we're not roadrunners," quipped Susan.

Hannah smiled. "Oh, they hunt anything that moves – mice, birds, pet cats, even deer. They'll attack people if they think they're injured."

"I'll keep that in mind," thought Susan, "and my door locked."

"Hannah wasn't kidding," thought Susan as she drove up the small incline between the buildings. The parking lot was deserted. A row of white bungalows lay to each side in evident disrepair. The motel's office lay ahead, completing a horseshoe. A roadside copse of pines shielded motorists from the eyesore but blocked the bungalows' view of the water. Susan parked below the office, climbed the stairs to a rickety terraced landing, and untaped the envelope from the door. "S. Roberts," read the envelope. Inside Susan found a map of the grounds and the key to 3A.

The light was on, just as Hannah promised. Hannah was not there, of course, but her clothing was strewn over the king-sized bed, recliner, table and two chairs. Her equipment lay sprawled on the floor. A Dixie cup on the table served as a makeshift ash tray. It contained several butts, each bearing traces of lipstick. Old smoke hung in the air. Susan thought of her sublet in Hell's Kitchen. Hannah would have fit in fine.

Susan read the note for her on the table, threw her bags in a corner, and returned to the car. She could pee at Gar Woods. It was bound to be more comfortable.

Chapter 5

"Honest, the little man wore a hat and suit in Berlin. And he was pudgy. They say he was modeled after Erich Honecker. Only perkier. Naturally, the West Germans and French had to be different, so their guys were anorexic and naked."

"Au naturel."

"I guess that's why ours are, too. You know, allies and all."

The woman considered the stick figure that recently replaced "Walk" and guided her husband across the crosswalk. No, she decided. Too tangential.

Monday afternoon, October 15, 2012

The cursor blinked, a sans-serif "I" wedged between the paragraph mark on the right and the light gray margin indicator on the left. The cursor blinked uninterrupted for nearly an hour.

present
day

An old woman glanced up from the screen and gazed into the small sitting area to her left. Beyond it lay a still smaller area that doubled as foyer and dining room. The wall behind her divided the sitting area from the kitchenette. The wall in front set the sitting area off from the bedroom and a narrow passage connected the dining area to the bathroom and bedroom. A Maltese terrier sat on the small chaise lounge marking the end of the sitting area. Its dark, unblinking eyes met her gaze, ears perked in anticipation. The woman acknowledged the terrier with a faintly perceptible nod and turned back to her computer.

Bold canvases lined the walls, a violent black, brown and white neo-expressionist piece by Anselm Kiefer, a cubist portrait of two kissing figures in harsh tempera-like tones by Rainer Fetting, and a collection of early sketches by Joan Miró. The large canvases were unframed but the sketches were protected behind glass by simple black metal frames. None of the sketches were matted.

The apartment's wall coverings were of damask silk, gilded taupe in the living room, gilded claret in the bathroom, gilded rose in the bedroom. The kitchenette was tiled in black granite and fitted with brushed steel appliances and a mirrored backsplash. The furniture in the living room, dining area and bedroom was Queen Anne period, nearly every piece authentic, and the drapes that framed the wall-sized casement windows to her right were of brown and gold Milano Lucia silk. Above the drapes hung a scalloped pinch-pleated valance of the same material. Identical drapes hung in the bedroom.

Silk sheers blurred her view of the apartments across the well and softened the daylight that angled in at noon from overhead. It was 7 pm and the panes were dark. Hand-painted Cantonese ginger-jar lamps illuminated the sitting area. Above the foyer hung a cluster of Strass crystalline grapes within an 8-inch tall, 23-inch wide parchment-colored silken drum with polished nickel rims. Three recessed bulbs bathed the dining table in a warm, fire-like glow. The table was set for two.

A small walnut desk supported the woman's elbows. An open collar and pearl choker supported her head. And a red-cushioned walnut side chair supported her petite figure. She wore a Castleberry tweed A-line skirt with matching Chanel jacket. Metallic gold buttons dotted the jacket's black crocheted trim.

A hand-knotted 9-by-12-foot red Heriz Persian carpet peeked out from underneath the furniture. Six artisans labored six months to complete it. Her son said so. 7,776,000 knots, 500 per inch, she was sure her son inspected every one. "You can't be too careful with the Iranians," he remarked upon returning from one of his extended vanishing acts, this time presumably in the Middle East.

Her son could not have returned too soon. The rug covered at least eighty percent of the living room's usable floor space, precisely what the house rules of the cooperative required.

In truth, Mildred Whiting had no idea whether the rug covered eighty, seventy or ninety percent of her usable floor space. But she knew the penalty if one of her neighbors complained persuasively about a house rules violation: a $250 surcharge to the monthly maintenance for the first failed inspection, $500 for the next, $1,000 for each month's violation thereafter.

Mildred's renovation had been painstaking, flawless. It was just what she envisioned ... except the floor. She replaced the dark oak parquet with Venetian marble. A black, brown and yellow compass rose marked the center of the room. The rose was ringed with wide disks of white and grayish-white marble and the room was bordered by a rectangular black marble frame with lustrous pearl-white veins. Mildred thought the floor divine, worthy of mention in *Architectural Digest*, but the incessant click of Mildred's sling-back pumps against polished stone displeased her downstairs neighbor. Mildred received a citation from the board then a fine. And then another. A luxurious oriental carpet now cushioned her footfall but concealed her inlaid masterpiece.

Mildred learned about house rules the way most resident-owners did, in a six-page attachment to the cooperative offering statement and bylaws. She scanned the rules, many of them common sense, some of them bizarre, nearly twenty-five years ago then filed the papers away. "Away" meant, as it did for most residents, in a commercial off-site storage facility. Space was precious in Manhattan. Mildred paid $180 a month to store old files, photo albums, and her spring and winter wardrobes in an 8x10-footlocker in Long Island City. This was considerably cheaper than buying a second bedroom, and the brief forays into the "outer borough" were grist for the aging writer's imagination. "Let's face it," she admitted to herself, "you don't get out much anymore. Who knows what you might discover 'over there'?"

Mildred regarded herself as an adventurer. Most of her neighbors rented storage space in Chelsea or Yorkville. Venturing beyond the East River into the shadowy wilderness of Queens or

Brooklyn was considered bold, if not foolhardy. Venturing beyond the Harlem River into the Bronx was out of the question. But Mildred was not born and raised in Manhattan. Her neighbors indulged her quirky South Chicago ways. She enjoyed the gypsy cab jaunts down Thompson Avenue and Queens Boulevard – the honking and jostling for position onto the bridge into Manhattan, the swarms of students dispersing at all hours from the 7 platform into Bard, LaGuardia and DeVry colleges plus half a dozen public high schools and middle schools. She loved the crazy-quilt juxtaposition of single-story diners, noodle shops, gyros stands, pizzerias, kick-boxing studios, furniture stores, men's clubs and tire shops. And she adored the quaint planned communities that stood a couple blocks from the main thoroughfare.

At times she idled away the hours charging up and down the tree-lined streets of Sunnyside Gardens, admiring the 1920s English-style red brick row houses with their immaculate front and rear gardens and landscaped central courts. Mildred prided herself on having visited the second of only two privately owned and maintained parks in New York City, the first being Gramercy Park, just off 20th Street on the East Side. Sometimes, when her blank screen mocked her, she would Google the listings in Sunnyside Gardens. There weren't many. There were only sixty-six units in the entire community. Still, a two-and-a-half story row house in a national historic district might be just the thing to rekindle her writer's imagination. And if she bought one, she could admire her interior renovations in peace.

The history of Sunnyside Gardens fired Mildred's imagination. The landscape architect was a woman, Marjorie Sewell Cautley, orphaned at twelve, graduate of Cornell University at 25, successful landscape architect in a man's world at 34, and thereafter a highly-sought lecturer at Columbia, MIT and University of Pennsylvania on the subject of urban blight and renewal.

It was the sketchy personal details of Cautley's life that intrigued Mildred. Cautley suffered nearly 25 years from a mysterious, debilitating disease that left her hospitalized for months at a
time. She died without obituary in 1954 yet left behind a legacy
that includes Sunnyside Gardens, Roosevelt Common in Tenafly,
New Jersey and the wondrous gated parks of Fair Lawn, New
Jersey. Her exclusive use of native species and orientation of
structures and gardens to face a shared arboretum were revolutionary in her time and widely copied thereafter. Most intriguing
of all, her father was a decorated naval commander who, as governor of Guam, initiated major economic, judicial, penal and cultural reforms, including the restoration of the right to wear traditional clothing, cohabitate with Caucasians, and consume alcohol. Alas, he also raised property taxes to the point where many
natives defaulted and lost their land. The increases were re-
scinded once he saw their unintended consequence, but the insult
could not be disowned. He contracted a mysterious intestinal ail-
ment and died in California seeking treatment. "How perfectly
marvelous," Mildred exclaimed when she chanced upon his biography. Mildred borrowed liberally from the life of William El-
bridge Sewell and his daughter, Marjorie Sewell Cautley, when
framing one of her novels, and she returned periodically to
Sunnyside Gardens for inspiration.

"I'm afraid I am not going to buy a house there, Ruby. Houses
are high maintenance." Mildred glanced over at the terrier as she
spoke. Its shiny black eyes continued to meet her gaze. "There's
no man to help out," she sighed, "and I'm not as strong as I used
to be." Still, Mildred regretted not seeing her marble flooring.

"House rules, Ruby. I suppose they serve a purpose." Ruby
did not reply.

Mildred paid attention to only one set of house rules when
she moved into her apartment on Central Park South, those governing pets. She checked them off carefully. No four-legged pets
other than dogs and cats. Check. No loud barking. Check. No use

of the balconies as a substitute for the outside curb. Mildred's apartment faced the well. Check. No unleashed or un-carried dogs in the common areas. Check. Short leashes only. Check.

The house rules grew with the years. They were a collective thirty-year record of the special peeves and preferences of individual cooperative board members. The rules governed whether you could grow plants on your terrace (only with the prior written approval of the co-op and only in approved planters), smoke on your terrace (no), place blue, white, red, pink, orange, yellow or purple furniture on your terrace (no, only brown, green and black), use planters larger than 18x18 inches (no), leave shoes or umbrellas outside your door (no), bring indoor furniture onto the balcony for a cocktail party (no, only "outdoor-designated" tables and chairs with rubber protective cushioning), wheel bicycles or scooters through the lobby or onto a passenger elevator (no), illuminate a window at Christmastime (only with written permission of the co-op, which was invariably withheld), play in the halls or stairwells (adults only; "children shall not play in …"). The list went on and on.

Amendments to the house rules were neither published nor debated before board ratification. They appeared in her mail cubby before the annual meeting of the tenant shareholders. In fact, the last house rule stated that "these House Rules may be added to, amended or repealed at any time by resolution of the Directors." Mildred could not remember whether that was rule 32 or 33. Its identifying number rose each year.

A tenant's recourse against a board member's dictatorial impulse was to raise a ruckus at the annual meeting and hope a large number of attending residents agreed. Or the tenant could rally support behind a board candidate who promised to examine the issue more closely. Mildred engaged both tactics when the board dropped the bomb on house rule 3, the rule governing ownership of pets.

For whatever reason, a majority of board members decided to crack down on pet ownership. Overnight, ownership of pets became the exclusive privilege of grandfathered residents. Existing resident shareholders could continue to shelter their pets on the premises and replace deceased ones with breeds of similar *or smaller* size, but new tenants could not. Neither could longstanding tenants who had not previously owned pets. Small dogs were to be carried at all times in the lobby and elevator. Owners of larger dogs were asked to bypass the lobby by entering from the service entrance or garage. And tenants without pets were entitled to enter elevators first and could, if a pet made them squeamish, insist on riding the elevator alone.

Fortunately for Mildred, others shared her fury. The board relented and only the elevator amendment survived. But the incident made Mildred wonder. She wondered whether the board entertained a similar set of rules for children. "They must have," she decided. Nearly every board member was older than Mildred, and Mildred was pushing eighty. "They probably detest kids, or anyone under fifty for that matter." She already knew the board would euthanize puppies if allowed. Mildred resolved to consult the latest copy of the house rules the next time she visited Long Island City. She probably missed the announcement, as focused as she was on the rules for pets. "Sheesh. They might even have phased out Republicans."

Mildred chuckled. She could imagine the apoplexy of her late husband, learning that "his kind" had been phased out of the building. "It's okay, dear," she imagined saying, trying to allay his anger, "you've been grandfathered. But your son, well he's just going to have to register like me or live elsewhere."

As it turned out, Geoffrey registered as a Republican like his father, unlike his mother, who was a Democrat. She hailed from the south side of Chicago, Daley country. How could she be anything but?

In fairness to her late husband, the Republican Party had changed. Gerald would not have recognized its leaders. Gerald voted for Mayor Lindsay, for Governor Rockefeller, for Senator Javits. Mildred knew none of them would have joined the Republican Party in its present form. They would have been tarred as traitors, as "liberals." Both Mildred and her late husband hailed from Illinois, the Land of Lincoln. Gerald never considered it odd that he surrendered his firearms when he left the Navy. He did not have a private telephone listing. He participated actively in and contributed willingly to his union. He paid his taxes. He was glad to see Nixon go. In short, he was a proud and caring Republican.

Mildred's son Geoffrey joined the ROTC at Northwestern, just as his father did and served four years in the Navy. Geoffrey's father served on a battleship and a cruiser, Geoffrey on a nuclear submarine. Beyond that their paths diverged. Geoffrey's father became an engineer with the Metropolitan Transit Authority and, thanks to his wife's thriving career as a writer, the only municipal employee ever to reside in the building. Geoffrey became a spy. He did not reside in the building, not even under an alias.

Geoffrey worked for the Central Intelligence Agency, initially in field operations but more recently in administration at the George Bush Center for Intelligence, an oxymoron if Mildred ever heard one, until her son explained the agency's Langley, Virginia headquarters were dedicated to its former director, George Herbert Walker Bush, not his son, the forty-third President. "Well, if you ever *do* dedicate it to Dubya," quipped Mildred, "would you please name it the George Bush Center for Deciders?"

"Sure, Ma. Any other requests?"

"Yes. Send me some interior shots of mosques and mansions in and around Baghdad … and a map of the U.S. compound. I want to try my hand at international intrigue."

"Sorry, mom, I'm not going to Baghdad. Anyway, the last item is classified, and you'll find better photos of mansions and cultural shrines online. Besides, why do you want to complicate your formula?"

"What formula?" she demanded, somewhat indignantly.

"I'm sorry. I didn't mean it that way. I meant only the majority of your readers are teenage girls who clamor for your next historical romance – whether it takes place in the antebellum south, bootleg Chicago, or pirate-infested waters. The point is, you don't write about present-day crises with present-day actors who will likely scrutinize and take offense at every contrived detail. Why put yourself under that kind of microscope? Why reinvent yourself? You've had so much success writing young adult romances."

Mildred winced at the phrase "young adult romance" but knew it aptly described what she wrote. Fifty-four volumes and counting. It was the only thing she could count. The protagonists and settings were a blur, a phantasmal runway of period costumes, swashbuckling Adonises, spurned Aphrodites, and exaggerated sexual innuendo. The deeds themselves were reserved for "adult" novels.

Geoffrey was correct. Her teen romance formula paid for everything. Mildred resolved more than once to break the mold. But romances were easy to churn out and, until recently, remarkably easy to sell. It was a lot easier than chasing down stories for the paper.

The Maltese terrier sat erect on the chaise lounge, ears cocked in anticipation. "I don't suppose you remember those days, do you, Ruby?" The terrier did not reply.

"Well, I do," continued Mildred Whiting. "I survived on SpaghettiOs and Fruit Loops. I can't believe I ate that stuff."

The author thought a moment. "I can't believe my characters *never* ate that stuff." Surely among all the peasants' daughters, milkmaids and young charwomen was a girl who fortified herself against life's adversities with stale bread, rainwater and … Cheerios. But there wasn't. And for the last few weeks, there were no new peasants' daughters, milkmaids or charwomen. There were no fabled locales and no finely chiseled Adonises. Mildred Whiting's ink well had run dry.

Mildred's agent of fifteen years called that morning. Again. The publisher was impatient to see the fruits of her advance. They rejected the previously submitted synopsis with a polite but stern lecture about cannibalizing previous work, and the exhortation to explore characters and plot devices that would resonate better with today's audience. So Mildred spent several weeks surveying the most popular television shows, online portals and works of fiction for her target demographic and came to the conclusion that she was hopelessly ill-prepared to expound on paranormal phenomena, vampirism, lycanthropy, advanced sorcery and intergalactic warfare. She somehow missed the edict conferring superhuman strength and weaponry on all protagonists, did not realize that romantic entanglement required saving the planet, or, in the case of true love, saving the galaxy, nor that the course of history, and thus romance, was shaped exclusively by physical blows.

Mildred scratched her head. When did she lose sight of reality, of what made drama truly compelling? She wondered whether the clock had run out on "timeless" classics, whether they were hopelessly out of step.

Poor Emily Brontë, she thought. How cathartic Heathcliff's vengeance upon Hindley would have been if he just unleashed his inner werewolf and dispatched him there on the moor! But no, Brontë tortured readers with a long-winded account of the sworn enemies' reversal of fortune, of Hindley's engineered demise at the hands of grief, debt and alcohol. So depressing! So implausible! The Lintons would have put Hindley in detox. Then what would Heathcliff have done? "Summon his inner werewolf," answered Mildred.

Mildred reflected on Catherine, Heathcliff's spiritual soul mate. How gratifying the story would have been if, before Catherine died, Heathcliff quaffed unsparingly on her blood so they could be forever united as vampires! Then he would not have fallen stupidly to his death chasing her spirit. And they might have rid the world of feckless aristocrats. On that theme, how much less exasperating would Catherine's effeminate husband, Edgar Linton have been if the author just came forward and "outed" him? Gay, gay, gay! Why all the subterfuge?

Mildred's head spun. She realized she knew nothing about modern romance, about the real world of teenage literature, yet her livelihood depended on it. Mildred gazed over at Ruby and felt depressed. She made a mental note to speak with Joan, the Jamaican woman who stopped by once a week to clean.

"Joan needs to shake Ruby out," she thought. Lint clung to Ruby's fur like a dust mop. He had not been properly brushed in weeks.

Mildred regarded the muse on her sofa. "It was a bit morbid, wasn't it? Having you stuffed, I mean."

"But then you were such a dear, my precious little prince. I couldn't part with you, not then." Mildred shuddered at the memory. She remembered lying on the pavement, cradling Ruby in her arms, trying to coax his limp form back to life, then wailing for an eternity in grief, anger, bitterness, and finally loneliness until a kind man led her back into the building. She sat vigil over Ruby's body for two days then struck a decision. She retrieved Ruby from the taxidermist two weeks later.

At first, Ruby stood sentry near her bed. But the weeks of sleepless nights abated, the agitation subsided, and Ruby assumed his present post in the living room. Mildred could peer into the dark glass eyes of her muse, mine the stories secreted beneath, and commend those thoughts quickly to paper. But the sparkle in Ruby's eyes had dimmed. They no longer conjured up fantastical tales of bloody deed and derring do. Neither did they conjure torrid romances that could enthrall the next generation of Mildred Whiting readers. Perhaps it was time to retire old Ruby, lay him to rest. At the very least it was time to give him a good brushing. Yes, she would certainly speak with Joan.

∂∾∾

Joan cleaned several apartments in the building. Working for Mrs. Whiting was the most pleasant. That was because Mrs. Whiting let her manage the laundry. So Joan whiled away the hours in the basement, gossiping with the other maids, bemoaning the clients who denied her this privilege, waiting patiently for washers and dryers to free up. She folded and ironed the wash leisurely. Most days she could kill three hours without raising so much as an eyebrow on Mrs. Whiting's fastidiously painted face. She could burn another twenty minutes bringing Mrs. Whiting's garments to the cleaners. A flourish of the mop in the bathroom, a quick rumble of the vacuum, and a perfunctory feather-dusting of the furniture sent Joan off to lunch and her next client.

Mrs. Whiting was definitely her favorite client, even if she had peculiar taste in trophies. It was okay, though. Ruby was less intimidating than the stuffed bear Mr. Gossman kept in the library, the rhinoceros foot that served as his umbrella stand, and the stretched elephant dick he used as a cane. Joan did wish, however, that Mrs. Whiting would stop offering her signed copies of her books. Joan felt obliged to read them, or at least skim their first and last chapters, but they were boring. And there were so many! "Why can't she write about wizards? Or the undead?" She sighed then thanked Mrs. Whiting for the eighty dollars and excused herself for lunch. Yes, she nodded, next week she would remember to beat the drapes.

∂∾∾

Mildred did not plan to be an author. She planned to be a journalist. That is how she met her future husband, Gerald, back in 1954. Mildred Whiting was a student at the Medill School of

Journalism at Northwestern University. She lived at Chapin Hall, one of several dormitories for female students who chose not to join a sorority. The women's quarters, the library, the College of Arts and Science, and the college administration were all housed on the south end of campus within a three or four block radius. Chicago and its many attractions lay a short El-ride to the south. Mildred had only one reason to venture north, to attend a football game at Ryan Field, and that she rarely did.

Gerald lived in the netherworld between Ryan Field and the campus hub to the south. He was an engineering student at the Northwestern University Technological Institute, which was housed in a massive limestone structure several hundred yards north of the library, and an even farther distance north from Mildred's dorm. The giant Work Projects Administration-style complex was framed on the north by men's housing, west by Sheridan Road, east by Lake Michigan, and south by an observatory, mathematics department and a dozen acres of empty field.

Mildred had never knowingly met a student from "Tech" until she was assigned to write an article for *The Daily Northwestern* about two men's dormitories being constructed near the institute. Tech students kept to the labs. Very few were athletes. They couldn't be. The institute was legendary for its demanding curriculum and parsimonious assignment of passing grades. It was rumored that students slept under their desks, that it was more efficient than fighting the frigid wind off Lake Michigan at three in the morning, only to face it again at seven. No sane liberal arts student took an engineering course. That was grade point suicide. So Mildred did not know any "techies." Mildred overheard another phrase and it resonated: "nerd."

Mildred was assigned to interview male students who would not or could not join a fraternity but who nevertheless needed campus housing. Her best bet, the editor assured her, was to visit the Technological Institute. She was thus assigned to interview techies and her new favorite subject, nerds.

Mildred stared up at the stone and limestone colossus, its 730,000 square feet stretched above, around and as she would later learn, underneath the stepped plaza on which she stood, the plaza that led to three widely-spaced and imposing double doors. The structure reminded Mildred in scale of the museums that lined the National Mall in Washington, DC but in architecture of the enormous New Deal-era post office in New York City.

She paused on the plaza, inhaling the arctic lake air, trying to imagine the building in the sunlight. It was only 3:30 pm, but the sun hung low behind her, shielded from her primly dressed figure by an unbroken sheet of gray. Nature tucked Evanston into bed in late October and lifted the gray sheets in early April. Mildred could count the sunny days on one hand.

Mildred Whiting had no idea how to proceed. She stood before three large doorways, frozen by indecision. She watched as students scampered into and out of the building, bracing their bodies as they exited, anticipating the arctic blow. She noticed all the students were men. She watched more students enter and exit, just to confirm her suspicion. The editor was right. Her best bet for interviewing male students not pledged to a fraternity was at Tech.

A young man stumbled on the step beside her, awkwardly righted himself then lost control of several books and a notebook. The notebook flew open and a page ripped free. Mildred lunged for the paper and managed to spear it with her heel. The man collected his books and thoughts and thanked Mildred for saving his assignment.

"Impaling it, you mean," laughed Mildred.

"Yes, ma'am. I mean thank you for skewering my homework. It is but a prelude to what Professor Harris will do when he grades it, and, if I may say so, much more pleasant."

Mildred was astonished by the reply. It was so spontaneous, so natural, yet so polite and witty. Mildred was even more astonished by his appearance. The boy was handsome. He stood erect, not slouched, sported a neatly trimmed beard, and wore a uniform. "Marching band," she thought. "I bet he plays the trumpet." Mildred found her first quarry.

Gerald Błaszczyk was not in the marching band. He was in the Reserve Officers' Training Corps, a college-based program for training commissioned officers of the United States armed forces. In Gerald's case, he was training to be an officer in the United States Navy. ROTC was the only way his family could afford to send him to Northwestern. Gerald glanced at his watch then graciously consented to an interview but insisted on conducting it inside. He could see the girl's lips were blue. At the conclusion of the interview, Gerald asked Mildred directly whether he could call on her. If there was timidity in the request, he disguised it well. Mildred was secretly delighted he asked. She had hinted at a follow-up interview three times, omitting the inconvenient fact that the article would already be published.

Mildred did not conduct further interviews for the article. She surveyed the boys who entered and exited the building then peered into the main lecture hall and several classrooms. She imagined where each student came from, what they played as children, what music and movies they liked, and whether they had wives or girlfriends here or back home. She did the same for the professors. Then she wrote her article. It was so much easier than interrupting the students' thoughts as they bustled from one classroom to the next, and so much more lucid. The editor was sure to enjoy it.

Mildred Błaszczyk's first paying job was cub reporter for a small, independent daily in Des Plaines, Illinois, a sleepy Chicago suburb ten miles west of where she graduated. She covered births, deaths, marriages and divorces, embellishing and inventing sources when it was convenient, which was frequently the case. She eventually aroused the suspicion of her superiors. The managing editor called her "an affront to journalistic integrity, to everything Mr. Bushkevitz stood for." Mildred presumed Mr. Bushkevitz was the founder; she had not stumbled into him in the hallway.

Mildred was given twenty minutes to clear her desk and strongly encouraged to consider another profession. Mildred agreed she should seek a new line of work but resented the attack on her journalistic integrity.

"I have never submitted an article," she fumed inwardly, "that a reader would consider boring, which is more than I can say for you!" She was referring to the managing editor, not the mysterious Mr. Bushkevitz. She was sure she could charm him if given the chance.

Still, Mildred regretted writing about the newlyweds being hoisted and whirled about in chairs. The story was just as entertaining without it. But "Wasserman" did not sound Catholic, did it? "The editor should have told me the gerbil was his niece, told me *before* he assigned me the story."

The future Mr. and Mrs. Wasserman submitted photos of themselves to the paper, together with details about their lives and wedding, several weeks before the planned ceremony. This was customary in the suburbs, where reporters seldom rose from their desks to chase stories. The stories chased them.

Per custom, most of Mildred's piece was written before the bells chimed on Saturday morning. Saturday should have been the tip-off, the Jewish Sabbath, but Mildred paid little attention when she switched off her desk lamp on Friday evening. She assumed the affair was Sunday and that she would turn the story in on Monday. She did not plan to attend the event; few reporters did. But some choice tidbits about the reception would please the readers – all but one reader, it seemed; the one who instructed her to consider another line of work.

Mildred thought about her skills – her innate penchant for contrivance and prevarication – and decided on the obvious. She would raise a child. The father was at sea and six months' growth pressed against her diminutive figure.

Mildred resumed writing when Geoffrey entered kindergarten. Gerald rejoined the civilian workforce two years previous, first in Philadelphia, then in New York. The three Błaszczyks lived together in a flat in Brooklyn. To distance herself from the reporter summarily dismissed for fabricating sources, Mildred wrote under her maiden name, "Whiting." A case of forsaken identity was how she described it. She tapped into Gerald's rich account of Korean and Philippine waters to compose her first novel, an uncensurably erotic 90,000-word adaptation of Jane Austen's novel, *Persuasion*, to the French plantations of Cambodia.

Rejections poured in from the major publishers denouncing the plot as predictable, the research as slipshod, the vocabulary as slight, and the protagonists as caricatures of *Pride and Prejudice*. "Hah!" thought Mildred. "They don't even know their Jane Austen." But that did not help Mildred sell her novel. After two months of rejections, she was inclined to throw in the towel.

The letter arrived on a Friday. Mildred remembered counting the hours until 10 am Monday morning (sixty-six!), when she could place a collect call to Winnipeg, Manitoba. Harlequin Books, a small Canadian re-publisher of out-of-print books, had begun printing original works in 1953 and started assembling a stable of promising authors. Harlequin became a publishing industry fixture in 1957 when it secured exclusive North American publication rights to the works of Mills and Boon, a British publisher known for its short, erotic works of romance for unmarried, working-age women. Harlequin sold these slim paperbacks to readers via direct mail subscription and for twenty-five cents at newsstands, five-and-dimes, and general stores. The company developed such a voracious following that it resolved to corner the market on romance literature. The agent wrote Mildred because he thought her book could be trimmed and repackaged for

Harlequin's target audience. Mildred had not previously considered the publisher but was familiar with its business. In fact, she secretly read many of its novels. She signed a contract the following Friday.

Mildred churned out novellas like clockwork, earning workman's pay, but it was the publication of Kathleen Woodiwiss' *The Flame and the Flower* by Avon Press in 1974 that legitimized her genre, made it worthy of literary review. Publishers began competing for her talent. Her works appeared in genuine bookstores. And by 1978 several became bestsellers. Mr. and Mrs. Błaszczyk were suddenly blessed with the wherewithal to visit places Mildred Whiting wrote about. They bought a *pied a terre* in London, another beside Lake Zurich and finally one on Central Park South in Manhattan. For the first time in her life, Mildred and her husband conducted field research.

"Oh, Ruby, weren't those days fine?" Mildred's question was rhetorical, wistful. She did not expect a reply. The house phone rang in the kitchenette. It rang again.

"Just one minute," she shouted, perhaps thinking the caller could hear her. "I'm coming."

Mildred slipped on her pumps, rose from her chair, and stepped toward the kitchen. The house phone rang a fifth time. Mildred cursed the apparatus mildly. All Mildred's curses were mild, much like the ones she saved for her novels. "Loathsome annoyance! Why can't I connect it to my answering machine?" Mildred's answering machine sat on the table near her bed. Her telephone sat beside it. A second phone sat on her desk. But the phone in the kitchen was an older and plainer model, a chocolate brown wall-mounted Trimline with touchtone handset that, despite its nine illuminated buttons, routed directly to the lobby.

"Yes, John, what can I do for you?" Mildred tried not to sound impatient, but her computer screen waited. Ruby waited. Her agent waited. And she expected guests within the hour.

"It's me, Truman, Mrs. Błaszczyk." Truman was the superintendent. "The woman in 12N has a leak in the bathroom. We need to enter your apartment to see if it's coming from there."

"That woman!" thought Mildred Whiting. "If it's not the flooring, it's the plumbing."

"You mean now, of course, don't you?" Mildred inquired, thinking about her planned clandestine meeting with another agent. "Very well, I'm not planning to go out. I'll be here all evening."

Mildred returned the handset to the cradle and clicked down the short hallway to her bathroom. "Eighty percent of the livable floor space. Not one inch more," she resolved.

"Oh Lord!" Mildred gasped. "Oh Lord!" she repeated. "Oh Lord," she rasped, only this time the words were a prayer. "Tell me I'm dreaming," she pleaded as she surveyed the sagging wall, the soaked damask wall covering, the gaping hole in the ceiling, and the pool of debris on the floor.

Somehow the damage made her think of Gerald. He would know how to comfort her. "All hands on deck! I think the building is listing," she heard him console.

"No dear, it's we who must do the listing. Let's sell this place and move to Morocco."

"Abandon ship? Not while I'm the captain. We'll swab the decks and consider our options. Meanwhile, let's assemble the crew."

Mildred rushed to answer the door. The crew had arrived.

Mildred stepped out of the narrow hallway to give them passage. She seated herself next to Ruby and stroked his fur. "You're a good muse, Ruby," she reflected, "but Gerald was better." She stroked him again and a dust bunny settled to the floor.

Chapter 6

The reporter fidgeted impatiently at the curb, waiting for the walk signal to reappear, forced like everyone to endure the insolent salute of the bird. Some wag had inked out three of the signal's fingers.

Jack jerked himself away from the conversation. His wife's voice silenced the room. "You've got nerve, standing here in judgment. You and your entire profession. You're fucking hypocrites."

A woman recoiled in indignation. She strained to compose herself before responding. "Careful," she thought, "You crashed this woman's party, she is surrounded by friends you don't know who can identify you, and you purposely brought up the Roger Clemens trial because he is controversial. What did you expect?"

Meryl Scott Rupert of Fox 5 News New York had a weakness for free libations and a nose for stories. She sniffed about incessantly for both. Right now, she was passing time until she received a call from the camera crew on Sixth Avenue. She was sipping this woman's Roederer Cristal and feasting on her hors d'oeuvres. She surmised the name was Susan and the stiff on the other side of the room was her husband. She passed the gathering *en route* to the ladies' room and espied several distant acquaintances. One was the retired president of Planned Parenthood. Maybe she could provoke a rise out of her. Another was a Morgan Stanley banker whom she interviewed following the collapse of Lehman Brothers in September 2008. She recognized the weatherman from NBC News, although she did not recall ever meeting him. These were surely sufficient credentials to join the party. The television crew was idling down the street if she needed them. She and the crew were waiting for a story to develop. The gist of the story was still uncertain.

Mahmoud Ahmadinejad, the sixth president of the Islamic Republic of Iran, holed up the previous September at the Warwick Hotel on 54th Street and Sixth Avenue before addressing the United Nations General Assembly. He called on the body to launch an investigation of the United States government's role in perpetrating the 9/11 attacks because, he asserted, there was no evidence Al-Qaida even existed. More plausible, he insisted, was a United States government conspiracy to incite war against the Arab world by murdering its own citizens. When his speculation provoked a diplomatic walkout, Ahmadinejad explained himself. He was just trying to allay the Arab world's natural suspicion of the US government. An "independent and impartial committee of investigation" could do that. But "any opposition to this legal and human demand [could only mean] that 9/11 was premeditated in order to achieve the goals of occupation and of confrontation with the nations." To paraphrase the venerable president, "We have no factual basis for investigating the United States, just a suspicion rooted in paranoia, but if you deny us a full-blown investigation, you will confirm our suspicion beyond reasonable doubt. Moreover, if you challenge any aspect of our suspicion, you will legitimize debate about it, thereby legitimizing the suspicion itself."

The president of Iran plied Meryl Scott Rupert's favorite form of innuendo, the well-placed "I'm just saying" to justify without a scintilla of evidence the most preposterous accusation he could concoct. That was how six percent of Americans came to believe the Apollo 11 moon landing was faked, how seventeen percent of the voting public concluded President Obama was a Muslim, and why sixty-four percent of Republicans doubted he was a natural born American. A hack commentator's naked insinuation, "I'm just saying," could sway more public opinion than a freight load of countervailing evidence, the more implausible the insinuation the better. Meryl could not fault Ahmadinejad for learning from Fox News and her associates. The only awkwardness was that he aimed his insinuations at the United States of America, not the Democratic Party.

"Time will cure that," thought Meryl. "The Administration is Democratic. In time, Obama will own 9/11."

Predictably, the Iranian president's address also described the Shoah as a myth contrived by Zionist sympathizers, foresaw the destruction of the State of Israel, and defended Iran's everpeaceful right to enrich uranium. The address drew global derision plus hours of colorful Fox commentary. Meryl hoped the 2012 address would be even more incendiary. The morning bartender at the Warwick tipped her off that Ahmadinejad's security team just checked in and that a New York City police detail had been assigned to the building. Meryl considered this curious. The next General Assembly meeting was not until September. A lower-ranking diplomat might have scheduled meetings at the United Nations, but the Iranian government maintained a permanent mission on Third Avenue and 40th Street. Surely it was not fully occupied. Granted, the Iranian president had a penchant for advance planning, but six months? Meryl sensed something was brewing and, if not, felt she had enough information to sow, broadcast and cover a protest.

Meryl interviewed police officers stationed at the hotel, cajoling them to question aloud their duty to serve and protect foreign tyrants. They accommodated splendidly but could not or would not identify the Iranian VIP inside. She recorded sound bites from voluble passers-by, sidewalk pundits whose salty, off-thecuffs remarks, like those of self-appointed experts in the studio, filled the inconvenient synapse between paid advertisements more cheaply than genuine programming. What she most desired was to foment a protest. Her editor counseled her to conduct more surveillance instead. Even Fox News needed something tangible. So a skeletal crew sat in a van across the street, awaiting signs of activity, and Meryl sipped complimentary Roederer Cristal at this woman's party, trying to conjure a story.

Meryl could have chosen a bar closer to the Warwick. But Rockefeller Center and thus NBC were in the vicinity, CBS was a block-and-a-half away at 53rd Street, and the former headquarters of ABC were even closer. China Grill, Milos, Circo, Connolly's – the nearby watering holes were likely crawling with reporters, writers, anchors and producers from the "Big Three" commercial networks, self-described guardians of the Fourth Estate. "Fourth Estate, my ass," she thought. Their only shared convictions were a mutual disdain for Fox News and contempt for those who worked there. Meryl did not need to be a pariah. There were plenty of acceptable places along Seventh Avenue.

"They have a lot of nerve," she fumed, as she marched westward along 55th Street past the brass doors, round marble columns and multicolored tiles of the New York City Center, a domed, neo-Moorish structure constructed in 1923 as the meeting place, or "Mecca Temple", of the Ancient Arabic Order of the Nobles of the Mystic Shrine, *aka* the Shriners. It was a performing arts center now, gloriously refurbished, and where Meryl went if she wanted to see a Gilbert & Sullivan operetta or a performance by the Martha Graham Dance Company. She breathed conservative fire into her news reports. But the Fox connection did not make her a boor. She saw the Spanish production, *Flamenco Hoy*, at the City Center just three weeks earlier and a revival of *Bells Are Ringing* in November. She supported the arts. What difference did it make that her employer railed against public funding?

"Who are *they* to stand in judgment?" she bristled, glancing at the poster for *Where's Charlie?* What did anyone at ABC, NBC or CBS know about the viewing public? They couldn't even hold their audiences. She and her colleagues gloated over the weekly Nielsen ratings. The commercial news networks played to 29 million fewer viewers than they did in 1980 and controlled less than a third of the total viewing audience. Rupert Murdoch's cable television upstart, founded in 1986, boasted two million viewers, nine percent annual revenue growth, and viewer loyalty that was second to none. Better still, their news operations were profitable. They captured a superior demographic – younger, whiter and more affluent. The half billion in annual news-service profit was the envy of the industry. Let CBS pander to the poor and the elderly. Meryl Scott Rupert did not worry about keeping her job.

"They're fucking hypocrites," she concluded. She saw terror in their eyes, the desperation of rats aboard a sinking ship. They would abandon it in a second to enjoy job security but would not risk the stigma of being branded editorially nonobjective. It was a pox on her entire profession.

"I beg your pardon," Meryl responded to her interrogator, "the evidence shows Roger Clemens perjured himself before Congress, even if the grand jury didn't see it that way. I'm just saying he's as guilty of using steroids as Mark McGwire, only his case is worse. He refused to come clean. I think it's shameful anyone is defending him."

"Oh God," thought Jack, "it's that reporter from Channel Five. How did she get in here?" Jack already committed one faux pas. How had he possibly committed a second?

Susan didn't need to articulate the first mistake. He felt the dagger lodge in his chest the moment she glimpsed her mother, and then twist as she turned and glared at him.

Susan's mother sat in a wheelchair in the corner, huddled in a yellow floral gown that hung in loose folds about her shriveled body. The high collar and ruffled hemline reminded Jack of a Hawaiian mu'umu'u, the kind tourists bought at Hilo Hattie's and never wore. Jack knew his mother-in-law sewed it when she was size ten and not size two. She wore a simple white crocheted shawl. What hair she had was pulled back in an awkward whitish-gray mop. A nurse sat beside her, placing a soda straw in a champagne flute of Ensure. Susan's mother shook her head, nonverbally reproaching the nurse for implying her approval of alcoholic beverages or even a celebration. Drinking dinner from the can was satisfactory for children of the Lord. Jack pitied the nurse. She wanted nothing more than to sample the champagne. He asked the maitre d' to slip a bottle into her handbag.

Susan did not see her mother often. Their relationship was strained even before she and Jack began dating. It was utterly unbearable thereafter. And now her mother suffered from Parkinson's Syndrome, muscle atrophy and dementia. They placed her in a nursing home outside Atlanta four years ago. She needed full-time care and they could no longer rely on Susan's younger brother. He was in prison, this time for an extended stay. Jack did not pry much. The Reverend moonlighted on occasion by trafficking narcotics – generally marijuana and seldom for profit, but the court took exception to the minister's attempt to shine a godly light on substance abuse. Susan and Jack had no choice. Besides, Susan's mother no longer held a position in the ministry choir. Forgiveness was divine in principle but awkward in practice. There was nothing more to bind her to Decatur.

Susan's voice brought Jack back to the conflagration. "You don't get it, do you? You're a hypocrite for thinking yourself worthy of judging him. You all are," she shouted, directing her gaze at the stunned assembly of neighbors, parents and friends. "Let me finish," she demanded, brushing away Jack's arm. "You think you're defending the higher moral ground, stripping athletes of everything they have because, in your words, 'They cheated and set a poor example for your children.' Well what the fuck about you, Miss Rupert? There isn't a person in this room who doesn't remember the nose you began with or can't detect the scar line where your jowls were tucked. They know because they've all had surgery themselves. They've all had their breasts lifted. They've all tried Botox. Hell, your friend the weatherman lost two hundred pounds, didn't you? Can anyone spell 'lapband?' What kind of a signal do you think you're sending my daughter? What kind of a signal do you think you're sending the poor reporters who stand on the sidelines, competing for your job only you just won't age? Your plastic surgeon makes sure of that. And I am positive, just positive, it's all medically prudent, isn't it?"

Meryl began to protest but was cut off. "I don't give a rat's ass whether Roger Clemens used steroids. You stand here skewering him, yet you secretly risked nerve damage, disfigurement, even death just so you could stay on the air. You're pathetic. You've transformed an otherwise glamorous profession into a cosmetic-surgery arms race. Don't lecture me about steroids, not until you and every newscaster out there who's had an eye lift, nose job, liposuction or other form of cosmetic surgery forfeits their job to reporters who didn't cheat their appearance by doing something insanely risky. My God, have you seen Jocelyn Wildenstein?"

"If honest people want to throw the book at Clemens, let them. But I don't think you'll find a quorum. You've already made that impossible. A whole generation of girls has grown up thinking the only way they can get ahead is with a Barbie doll figure and a nose job; medical risks be damned!" She expanded her indictment, "That goes for all you guys who pop Tylenol and Advil like candy, just so you can prove you're still durable. 17,000 of you are going to die this year and more than 100,000 will wind up in the hospital, just so you can survive your next 10K. Only you'll die of liver cirrhosis and gastrointestinal bleeding first – a bigger toll than homicide. Great role model, Dad!"

She thrust aside Jack's arm in disgust. Her guests backed awkwardly toward the coat check room and exit. The kitchen staff abandoned its post and stood transfixed at the entrance to the private dining area. "What really makes me puke is that you take your holier-than-thou piety out on kids from the slums, kids who struggled with school, didn't have a family business they could fall back on, who gave everything they had for one chance out of the sty. But you feel so self-righteous with your surgically enhanced boobs that you just kick them back into the dumpster as if you're doing this country a favor. Get this through your thick plastic skin, you're making the country more elitist and unfair than it ever was, because *it was never* a few fringe cheaters. It was just like your profession – nearly everyone for a generation. Only athletes aren't in higher office. And they don't control the air waves. So they don't get to say, 'Oh, we're different,' like you do."

"You're worse than the Gestapo. At least they shot one of their own. Instead, you firebombed a path out of the hood to divert attention away from where it belongs – at the top of the food chain, where you have the power and authority to be fucking hypocrites."

She was almost through. "It was in today's paper. I don't suppose you read the *New York Times*. There were two million cosmetic surgeries last year in the US. The majority were medically unnecessary and uninsured. Add several hundred thousand medically unnecessary weight loss surgeries. By my reckoning, that's two, perhaps two-and-a-half million fucking hypocrites who cheated their looks last year to keep more deserving unenhanced people from taking their jobs. God knows what the cumulative statistic is, probably tens of millions. You want to penalize someone for trying to stay on top of the heap. Fine! Begin at home."

Susan brushed past the enormous white marble breasts and buttocks and exited the restaurant, leaving Jack in a nearly empty room with his mother-in-law, her nurse, his daughter and the reporter from Fox 5 television. Susan's mother glanced up from her straw in seeming confusion.

What to say? The marble ear on the wall pricked up in anticipation. Jack turned to the woman from Fox 5. "Ms. Rupert, I don't believe we've been introduced. In fact, I am quite sure you were not on our guest list. You no doubt mistook this for a complimentary wine tasting. Just as you no doubt mistook the revival of *Bells Are Ringing* at the City Center for an opportunity to show off your hat to those seated behind you. The wine tasting, as you can see, is over. Feel free to take an open bottle back to your colleagues. There is no sense letting it go to waste, nor perhaps this advice: It is considered inappropriate in polite company to pummel the guest of honor with matters he or she considers disagreeable, just as it is considered rude at a Rupert Murdoch soiree to pontificate about phone-tapping and journalistic integrity. This is a private party, not a press conference, and we are not celebrities. My daughter will show you and your reshaped nose to the door. Good luck on your story at the Warwick." He recalled passing her *en route* from his office. She tried to interview him about United States relations with Iran, but he declined. Had she removed her hat at the theater, he might have lingered.

Melissa yanked insistently on the reporter's arm. The interview was over. She stormed out the door. Jack paid the woman's bar tab then Melissa sobbed in his arms. "Mommy cheated, didn't she?" The medals at home seemed a lot smaller.

The voice behind them was scarcely audible. "John, chapter 8, verse 7: 'He that is without sin among you, let him cast the first stone.'" A long, scraping slurp followed the grandmother's declaration. She returned her attention to the straw.

Chapter 7

"There weren't any traffic signals in Beijing. Or streetlights. Remember the mule carts trying to cross the freeway? Cars were wheel-deep in cabbage for a week."

"That's 'real deep,' Ezra. You shouldn't make fun of their accents."

"I'm sorry, Allie. You're correct as usual."

WEDNESDAY MORNING, APRIL 4, 2012

"They found her at the base of Rock Garden, just beyond where Home Run forks off from Mountain Run – two kids from Truckee making their first run. We got there in five minutes, seven tops."

"And you say she was alone?"

"Crazy, right? She wasn't carrying much, just identification, a couple credit cards, keys to a rental car. Parking says it's a Japanese roadster, fender smashed, but they couldn't find anything inside, just a pair of Oakleys. Oh yeah, she had a Samsung Galaxy, but it's locked."

"Who flew?"

"CALSTAR. They were pulling some yahoo off Jake's Peak and managed to get here in ten minutes. She lost a lot of blood, though."

"Renown?"

"Yeah. Forest begged off. Her condition was too serious."

Susan N. McDonald, sex female, eyes brown, hair brown, date of birth March 29, 1972, New York driver's license ID 638 708 213, lay in the trauma unit of Renown Regional Medical Center in Reno, Nevada. Her right femur was broken midway up her thigh and breached the skin, she had severe swelling and contusions in the abdomen, her left anterior and medial cruciate ligaments were snapped, and her pelvis was shattered in two places. An eye was swollen shut and bleeding.

Surgeons worked feverishly to stitch the ruptured spleen and lacerations to one of her kidneys. They lay partially submerged in urine. Another team raced to stanch the blood loss from her thigh. They used local anesthesia, but she didn't notice. She was deep in a coma.

Administrators tried to reach the patient's family, but the address on the driver's license was invalid. Developers bulldozed the block of walk-ups six years earlier to make room for a skyscraper. An officer tried the number on the rental car contract, but a recorded voice said call back Monday after 8 am. The Internet directories listed several Susan McDonalds in New York, but many of them answered the phone or voicemails in person. Other entries had the wrong middle initial. An orderly lent the officer his cell phone charger. The patient's Galaxy would ring eventually. It had to. In the meantime, the officer dialed American Express. Surely, they knew where to send the bill for her platinum card.

Chapter 8

The pain was persistent, dull, only distantly connected to his sense of being. A muffled throb pried at his thoughts, but they eluded capture. They diffused into the milky white fog that coddled him, yet pinned him to this indistinct, supernatant cornice, prodding and poking him atop an unseen mountain, disrupting his sense of equilibrium. A premonition unsettled him. The fog would release its grip. His head would tumble off the precipice into a long glacial slide and be deposited beyond eternity in a deep, hazy pit, disembodied yet connected in torment to the aching torso on the peak. Shadows flashed in and about the fog. A beacon flashed white in the distance, beseeching him to cross over.

TUESDAY, OCTOBER 15, 2012

"So you see, Allison, Mr. Roberts here has arranged everything … everything …." Sheldon tried to adjust his glasses but could not. He must have left them at his bedside in the Bronx or at the nursing home in Brooklyn among his father's tools. Mrs. Pfouts was a vague, shadowy blur. Her attorney was the darker shadow in the corner. Thank goodness John Roberts was there beside him. Sheldon felt otherwise hopelessly ill-prepared.

"Mr. Roberts has restored your account with … with interest." Sheldon knew the "with interest" part was untrue but allowed that his thoughts came slowly. The words clung deep in his throat and emerged only reluctantly from his lips. They felt stretched, elongated, and the effort made careful word selection impossibly tedious.

"John here will explain what I mean. Isn't that right, Mr. Roberts?"

Sheldon reached again for his glasses but could not lift his arm. It felt disconnected from his body.

"I'm sorry to have caused you so … much … trouble, Mrs. … Mrs. … misses? Yes, Marian misses Helen terribly. It's our worst nightmare, burying our only child. Marian tosses and turns every night, hoping it was all a dream. I miss her too."

"Marian?" He felt a hand grip his arm and knew it was hers.

"Yes, Marian. I remembered to sign Helen's permission slip." The hand released its grip.

Sheldon shivered. He wondered whether he had forgotten his blazer. His eyes flitted about futilely for a mirror. It was too foggy. "That's right," he reassured himself, "Marian inspected me." It was all right then. Marian always knew what to wear.

The shadows loomed overhead. They were still indistinct. Sheldon tried to squint but his facial muscles failed him. He imagined his face, so placid as he and Mr. Roberts hammered out the details of their settlement with Mrs. Pfouts. Mr. Roberts would approve his countenance. It would be their secret; Sheldon's expression was anchored in place by the dense fog. He could not have displayed emotion if he tried. Sheldon tried to smile beneath his mask but even there the tissue was indistinct, un-pliable.

He heard reassuring voices but struggled to discern their words. The shadows drifted from view. Moments passed, or an hour. It was difficult to tell.

The deal was concluded; he was sure. Jack Roberts had taken care of everything. Sheldon cast a disconnected eye to his left. He willed his vision through the stubborn lids. "He's a fine lawyer, Marian," he murmured. "John Roberts will handle everything." A badge flickered momentarily into view. He could not make out the text, but was sure of the words that greeted him, "Marian Willis, Nursing Assistant." He pined to ask her out, if only he could summon the courage. Torpor swept over him and he slept.

∽✿∾

"I'm sorry, Dr. Martinez, Mr. Vogel's next-of-kin are dead. He never updated the emergency contact form." The resident manager was installed just two months ago but had encountered this situation before. No one expects to outlive their children. And at seventy, eighty, or whatever age Sheldon Vogel was, he did not bother to update the contact form, no matter how many copies were slipped under his door. The Department of Social Services intervened in the other tenant's case. It would probably do so again.

"Well, you have access to his apartment. Your own staff found him unconscious in his tub. Would you please check whether he has an address book or Rolodex?"

"That's not something we're permitted to do. Would you like the number for the police or Social Services?" The management company rehearsed its building staff well. Besides, the resident manager was not especially eager to help the patient. So much water had spilled from the tub that the wet walls in at least four apartments beneath had to be opened. There was a chance they would have to open every wall to the basement. Thirteen floors. Thirteen remodeled baths. One of those baths was his. He secretly wished Mr. Vogel would die.

Thirteen floors. "My lucky number," he thought. Crumbling ceilings were another headache, three and counting, but not yet his.

The doctor tried again. "No, I'm sure we have the number for Social Services on file. It's just that he keeps mumbling the name of his lawyer, Mr. John Roberts. I thought we might learn whether the patient signed a living will or health care proxy."

The manager bolted upright and responded, "Mr. Roberts lives in our building. I'll have the front desk connect you to his apartment."

The resident manager was delighted to volunteer the information. Now there was someone the cooperative could bill for repairs. And he could get Mrs. Błaszczyk and that annoying woman in 12N off his case. He hung up in satisfaction after passing the caller to John at the front desk.

ॐॐ

The resident manager picked at his lunch, a tuna melt with coleslaw delivered by the Greek diner at the corner. The diner billed itself as "Parisienne" but was as French as Paris, Texas. The melt was edible but cold. The manager moved into the building just seven weeks ago but was used to that. The melt lay on his desk for an hour.

The manager dialed his occasional partner, Andrew. They had not hooked up for several weeks. Randall knew he touched a nerve during their previous tryst. He should not have carried on about the other partners.

"Stupid gamble," he thought. "You can't bind a bonobo." Bonobos were frugivorous. So was Andrew. Or vegan, he was not sure which. Bonobos were also notoriously promiscuous, the most promiscuous species on the planet. "Topped only by Andrew," sighed Randall.

The resident manager was stressed and needed to unload. "There is no shortage of overbearing tenants in the N-line," he thought, "in any line, for that matter."

Randall despised the building. It teemed with dowagers and self-important old men – imperious, overweening dinosaurs who slunk about the lobby, lying in wait, hoping for the slightest provocation, any excuse whatsoever to sink their impossibly white dentures into the building staff, the menials, because they were the only ones left whom they could chew. These dinosaurs were fossils outside the building's walls, faint shadows of no interest to anyone except their eventual undertaker. But here they were prima donnas to whom each of the building's thirty-two employees, especially the resident manager, had to kowtow.

Contempt for staff was universal, perceptible even among the youngest tenants. That was to be expected, he supposed. Building management was a service business, and most of this building's tenants were wealthy, or at least pretended to be. But the pungency of their contempt grew when they retired. There were so many retirees, sixty or seventy percent, maybe more. They became positively nauseating when they were elected to the board. Because then their powers were absolute. Outside the fortress they were long forgotten, mere shadows, but inside they were crazed tyrants, responsible to no one. Demotions, reassignments, firings were just a few of their arbitrary powers. And what good are powers if you do not exercise them?

Randall pored over the previous years' binders. He saw how tenants scratched and clawed to become directors and how they schemed to retain their positions. The exchanges were caustic, more vitriolic than anything he observed in this year's Presidential election PAC ads. Losers frequently left the building. It was easier than muddling through without services. "Oh, Mrs. Lowry, I am so sorry. The handymen are all at work on another emergency. You'll have to call a plumber if you need help." The board knew how to discipline tenants who tried to muscle in.

Outwardly, board positions were honorary, unpaid. But inwardly, they were the difference between a life forgotten long ago and one of ugly, undying relevance to several hundred households and thirty-two employees.

For forty-eight hours, the board and a dozen angry tenants directed their holier-than-thou wrath at him, the resident manager, the one employee who could not leave work behind. It followed him home because this *was* home. He determined to unload on Andrew.

෧๛෨

The young man cradled the handset against his ear, leaned back in his chair, and listened as he played Angry Birds on his iPhone. The sun reflected off the building across the street into his twelfth-floor window. He could not imagine surviving the drudgery of his job without phone apps. Steve Jobs made modern employment tolerable. He answered a text from Norbert.

"job blows   hungry 4U2   CU L8r? 7ish"

"The guys said she didn't rise from the sofa to let them out. She just sat there, stroking this grotesque dead dog, staring into space, muttering about the caterer."

Andrew shifted his position. "Dead dog?" He wondered whether the building's insurance would cover that. He could not imagine how debris falling from the ceiling could have killed it. "Stupid mutt," he thought. He read Norbert's reply. Seven o'clock was fine. Norbert was fine. Norbert was definitely fine, well, for tonight at least.

"John said she didn't answer when the caterer arrived or later for her guest. It was really awkward. Truman let himself in, just to check on her, but she signaled she was okay, even though she was not okay. I mean her bathroom was impassable. We had to close it off. John said the guest took her to the Essex House. I'm guessing she spent the night there."

Andrew congratulated himself. "Nice score." He savored the latter word then jotted down the superintendent's name. "True Man," he thought. "Randall simply must introduce me." He began giggling.

"Andrew?"

"I'm here." Andrew coughed, suppressing a chortle. The superintendent caught her in the act – *corpus delicti*. The thought of hiring a caterer to prepare dog for the family feast somehow tickled him. *Corpus delectable.* The woman must be from Thailand, he thought, or the Philippines. "Oh Randall," he mused, "What kind of stink hole did they assign you to? Remind me to keep my cat clear of your building." Andrew turned his thoughts to the coming evening and contemplated what to wear … over the thong, that is.

"The guy in 8B denied being his lawyer but dashed over to Roosevelt Hospital anyway. I guess they were pretty close."

Andrew lost his train of thought again. "8B? Close? How close? Like raincoat close?" He restarted the game. No matter. This conversation was boring. Randall Dykeman was boring. He wasn't even randy. He was more of the cloying sort. But the surname fit. Andrew could not deny that. Norbert was another story. He was definitely randy, almost too randy. There were never enough raincoats for Norbert, even if he never used them. What good would they do anyway? The missionary stuff was just foreplay.

Andrew giggled inwardly at his puns then apologized to Randall for having to take another call. He tapped the red icon and returned to his birds.

The birds were angry, but Andrew was just bored. Mother was away and he had no clients of his own. The only time he was busy was when mother shared one. He hoped the next one would want some icing on his services, so to speak, but he would not.

"Let's get together to exchange briefs, shall we?"

'May I conduct a deeper probe?'

'Let me depose you at my place."

They never caught his gist, never. They were stiff old farts, every one of them, tintypes of his mother, only with dicks. He forgot; she had those too. She kept them as souvenirs in her desk.

Andrew played on his phone and fantasized about his dream client.

❦

"Well yes, Doctor, I do happen to be a lawyer, just not *his* lawyer. He's a neighbor. We met for the first time on Sunday."

The doctor frowned. He would have to make the decision himself if the patient did not wake soon. He detested being put in this position.

"I'd like to visit him," the voice continued. "It's possible we might have been the reason for his injuries."

"We?" The doctor shot back. The word returned him from his dilemma. This fellow was a lawyer. What was he trying to insinuate? That the patient's dire condition was somehow *his* doing? How audacious!

"I meant my wife and I."

"You know what happened?" interrogated the doctor. "Well?" he insisted three seconds later.

"It's just a feeling," was the reply. "Mr. Vogel pushed my wife's wheelchair away from a bus the other day, the day before you say he was admitted to the hospital. He was in the crosswalk next to her. I was in a crowd and couldn't see much. Still, I'm pretty sure he saved my wife's life."

The doctor waited impatiently.

"I heard a thud. I thought the bus hit my wife. I honestly did. But there they were after the bus passed – one pushing the other, both looking stunned but fine. Mr. Vogel even kidded with my daughter. But that thud… Do you think the bus might have swiped him?"

The doctor's tried to moderate his imperiousness. "Perhaps you could describe what happened again." Being solicitous did not come easily. It was not something they emphasized in medical school.

Roberts' account made sense. But why didn't the patient seek help immediately? That made no sense. He must have been in agony, even with God knows how many tablets of Percocet.

৵৹

Roberts appeared an hour later. It was evidently his turn to interrogate.

"The nurses mentioned a ruptured bladder. Is it serious?"

Martinez hesitated. What could he tell him? This man wasn't family or a legal representative. He was just a character in a patient's dream, no more relevant than the name of the patient's deceased wife. He would have a word with the nursing staff about patient privacy.

"It could be worse," the doctor offered. "Urine is sterile. It's just liquid sloshing around the abdomen. There's not much."

He hastened to add, "And we've inserted a catheter – standard procedure for unconscious patients. We don't want them relieving themselves in bed. The catheter should reduce pressure on the bladder and allow it to heal."

The visitor nodded. "Broken bones?"

"None detected. The bus could not have hit him directly, a glancing blow perhaps. We'll learn more about the joints and connective tissue when he regains consciousness." This was superficial information. There was no sense making Mr. Roberts interrogate the nurses. At least this way the doctor could control the dialog.

"Have you been able to speak with him?"

"Not yet. He's been heavily sedated, and he entered the hospital unconscious. But I'm hopeful." He could say that with impunity, couldn't he? Even a surgeon could express hope. Right now, he yearned to be hopeful. He hated making surgical decisions without consent.

The doctor excused himself but encouraged the visitor to stay. "A familiar face will lift his spirits when he comes around."

"Soon," he hoped secretly. The doctor retired to the break room and shut the door.

Dr. Martinez cursed himself for not detecting the thrombosis earlier. If Mr. Roberts' account was accurate, Sheldon Vogel lay immobilized in his tub for fourteen or fifteen hours. He was at the hospital for another thirty. The emergency room personnel checked his ankles, as they should have. There was no abnormal swelling. But they did not measure blood pressure in his thigh. Neither did he. They focused on the area of impact, the left side and torso, where the body was a dark bluish mass.

Sheldon Vogel suffered deep vein thrombosis. The press called it "economy-class syndrome" – a blood clot that forms deep within the body after sitting or lying still for long periods of time, allowing blood to slow down and thicken. Vice Presidents Dan Quayle and Dick Cheney suffered DVT as a result of their trans-global jet-setting, but most cases of DVT arose in hospitals, where lying in a single position is commonplace. Untreated, the clot can migrate to the lungs, choking off blood flow, sometimes killing the patient.

The Department of Health and Human Services estimated the number of deaths from pulmonary embolisms at 200,000 per year, more than AIDS, breast cancer, and motor vehicle accidents combined. It was the focus of a major care-improvement initiative at the hospital, in part because so many cases were preventable, but also because insurance companies mandated it. Medicare now refused reimbursement for *any* DVT or pulmonary embolism following knee and hip surgery and scrutinized other cases carefully. Given the amount of time the patient lay unconscious in his tub, Dr. Martinez knew his phlebitis risk was high.

ICU detected the first embolism when the patient's pulse oximeter reading plunged below seventy. They injected him with the anticoagulant heparin, which kept the reading from plunging further, and put rhythmically inflated stockings on his legs to promote blood flow. The clot buster tPA was postponed because the risk of internal hemorrhage was too great; he was too extensively bruised.

The readings stabilized but did not improve. A clot lingered somewhere, continuing to deprive tissue of sufficient blood flow.

Dr. Martinez pondered his options. He already "upgraded" the patient from the standard formulation of heparin to a more expensive designer formulation, but the patient's risk of pulmonary embolism was still, in his opinion, too high.

The doctor's second option was to insert a temporary filter in the vena cava, the large vein that carries blood from the lower body to the heart, to block further clots from reaching the patient's lungs. He could thread the filter into the vein at the patient's bedside with a long, thin wire and an ultrasound device for guidance. It was the same procedure he used to thread central lines for chemotherapy. He could remove the filter once stronger anticoagulant medications were advisable, that is, after the bladder and other bruised tissue began to heal.

But the IVF procedure was risky. The only generally accepted justification for use was "the presence of a recent proximal DVT plus an *absolute* contraindication to therapeutic anticoagulation." He was mired in semantic hell. "Absolute contraindication? What in Hades does that mean?" Dr. Martinez yearned to discuss the options with the patient, but he lay unconscious.

The doctor's internship and first three years of residency were in Nevada. He was uncertain about New York law, but knew informed consent came from the patient or, if the patient was incapable of providing consent, a chain of vicarious representatives, beginning with signed health care proxies, then next-of-kin and state-appointed surrogates. The attending physician could challenge this chain of command in a life-threatening emergency, but not always with legal impunity. The fact that the patient's vital signs were not deteriorating gave him pause. The fact that Dr. Martinez was in the break room and not presently resuscitating the patient gave him further pause.

The doctor waffled. His training said life's hour glass was bleeding sand. His scarred fingers said there were still too many grains. The decision would be so much easier if the patient stopped muttering to himself and opened his eyes.

"Open your eyes!" shouted Martinez, slamming his fist against the table. He rose from the chair and reopened the door.

Sheldon sensed movement. A cool breeze chilled his face. He sensed the flutter of garments, presumably his. His form rocked gently left then right. A faint rustle disturbed the heavy silence and the sensation of movement ceased. A chime intruded on his thoughts. He felt his body lurch forward then halt. The chime rang once, twice, thrice. A slight breeze greeted his face and he sensed movement. Sheldon was going for a ride. He could not turn his head but knew Marian was driving.

The orderly wheeled the gurney out of the basement elevator and into radiology.

☙❧

"Back again?" The doctor seemed surprised to see him.

"I'm looking out for him," Jack replied. "He looked out for us." The doctor regarded the lawyer's answer as uncomfortably vague. Jack continued, "My family understands."

Dr. Martinez did not understand. The patient and this man were practically strangers.

"I see you're giving him enoxaparin. That's the high-potency heparin, isn't it? Was there an embolism?"

The question staggered Dr. Martinez. Who was this man? How could he know about this stuff?

The lawyer continued. "My wife had a pulmonary embolism in ER following an accident. Her legs were a mess, lots of blood loss. A clot lodged in her lungs. She almost died."

The doctor exhaled. He was relieved to hear this. The man was speaking from family experience, not as an ambulance chaser. Dr. Martinez transformed his expression from one of profound relief to sorrow. He did not want to injure the lawyer's feelings. "I'm so sorry to hear that. I hope she's better now. Yes, the patient suffered a small venous thromboembolism event. We're monitoring the situation."

"You didn't have to insert an IVC filter, did you?"

The question dismayed the doctor. Where was this leading? Was he psychic? "Not yet," he responded. "We're monitoring the situation."

"Thank heaven for Dr. Seldinger," the lawyer added. "He made the operation a lot safer. Still, a lot can go wrong."

Dr. Sven-Ivar Seldinger was the Swedish radiologist who in 1953 introduced the procedure for inserting, threading and guiding a small medical device through the body via a blood vessel, rather than more direct, open surgery at the ultimate site of implant. Only a doctor would know that speck of history, or a malpractice attorney. The doctor held his breath.

"My wife's surgeon misread the ultrasound. Too much bowel gas. The first filter wound up in her iliac vein instead of the vena cava. It's still there. She couldn't dislodge it. My wife takes aspirin every day to reduce the risk of blood clots from the filter, but her doctors are considering Coumadin. That's pretty drastic for a forty-year-old. The second filter tilted. When the surgeon finally removed it, part of it was missing. It's still floating around somewhere. It just made a bad situation worse."

The doctor did not know how to respond. This was the very procedure he planned to perform that afternoon. He affected a more detached tone and changed the subject. "Where was your wife treated?"

"A small hospital in Reno – not in the same class of this one," conceded Jack. "Renown Medical Center. It's where they airlift patients from Squaw Valley."

The room began to swirl. Dr. Martinez braced himself against the bed to regain his composure. He tried to suppress the next question, but his mouth disobeyed him. "I'm so sorry to hear that. When was this?"

"Early April," responded the lawyer, "this year." His eyes were fixed on the patient.

"Would you excuse me, Mr. Roberts?" White knuckles clasped the bed stand to prevent the doctor from falling. "I need to check another patient."

Dr. Martinez locked himself within a bathroom and vomited into the toilet. He dictated into his cell phone: "The risks of the procedure outweigh its potential benefits at this time. The patient will remain on enoxaparin."

John Roberts made the decision for him. His wife was the trauma center patient of Dr. Lester Martinez's mentor and ex-fiancée, Dr. Abigail Weinstein. Les Martinez assisted her with the procedure.

Chapter 9

"Does he have a name?"

"What, the walk signal? It's just a pictogram."

"He greets you every day."

"Christ, I don't even know the name of the doorman, and that's pinned in brass to his chest!"

"So by your elitist standard he's 'the walkman,' just as Robert Faulk is 'the doorman.'"

Jack checked his anger. Why on earth had she left him alone with Hanife?

WEDNESDAY EVENING, APRIL 4, 2012

"Hello, Wally?"

"Speaking."

"It's me. Jack Roberts."

"Oh. Evening, Captain."

"Uh, Ev'nen, Guv'ner."

The honorifics were habit, exchanged whenever they crossed paths. It was a private joke, the commiseration of ungrateful namesakes.

Wally's full name was George Wallace, as in the late George Corley Wallace Jr., the four-time presidential candidate and governor of Alabama best remembered for his unbending, vitriolic support of segregation. It was not easy bearing the name of that snarling little man, a man whose 1963 gubernatorial inauguration speech contained the vow: "In the name of the greatest people that have ever trod this earth, I draw the line in the dust and toss the gauntlet before the feet of tyranny, and I say segregation now, segregation tomorrow, segregation forever." It consoled Wally that others bore names as awkward as his own.

Jack's full name was John B. Roberts, as in Captain John "Bartholomew" Roberts, the feared Welsh buccaneer "Black Bart" who captured 470 vessels during four rapacious years of piracy, and whose exploits became the inspiration for Walt Disney Studios' popular pre-Depp theme ride, "Pirates of the Caribbean."

John Bartholomew Roberts was not to be confused with John Glover Roberts, Jr., the Chief Justice of the United States Supreme Court, except perhaps in their mutual respect for *stare decisis* and rule of law. For Bartholomew Roberts, this meant sworn allegiance by his crew to the pirate's code, which governed decision-making (one man, one vote), personal conduct (no women or gambling on board, curfew at eight), resolution of personal disputes (duels by pistol and sword on shore), division of spoils (equal shares except for the captain, quartermaster, master gunner, boatswain, and officers, but in no instance more than two shares apiece), fraud (marooning), dereliction of duty (marooning or death), dissolution (no discussion until each mate accrued 1,000 pieces of eight or 800 if crippled, which never happened) and musicians' rights (rest on Sunday evenings).

Roberts was in all other respects ruthless, known for torturing and butchering entire crews when they engaged in armed resistance, or merely because it amused him. He raided indiscriminately in the West Indies, the North Atlantic and along the west coast of Africa. No nation's flag offered sanctuary. His own flag was black, adorned in white by his likeness, cutlass uplifted, standing astride two skulls. Another flag depicted him holding an hourglass jointly with the skeleton of death. He dressed for battle in finest raiment, eschewed alcohol, and seldom let his fleet shrink from armed conflict. Black Bart's reputation preceded him. Most opponents surrendered without a fight.

Alas, Black Bart's spree of terror preceded Governor Wallace's by 244 years. It was a mere speck in the contemporary conscious, but it was nevertheless relevant to Wally's. It consoled his fragile psyche that Jack's parents wittingly named him after a depraved but resourceful miscreant. He wished his parents, like Jack's, had chosen a forgotten one.

The exchange of pleasantries masked the urgency in Jack's voice.

"Susan has been in an accident. I need to get hold of Hannah."

Wallace hesitated. He wanted to reply, "Get in line. She only communicates through her lawyer," but said nothing. After all, Jack was a lawyer and Wallace did not wish to be disrespectful … or get on his bad side. He got on the bad side of counsel at NYL and look how that turned out.

"They were supposed to meet in Tahoe for spring skiing, but no one knows how to reach her."

Wallace stifled the retort, "Serves Susan right for relying on her," and remembered he introduced them.

"I thought you might have her cell phone number."

Wallace paused then finally relented. "She won't pick up. She screens everything, but you can try." Wallace recited the number.

"Thank you, Wally. You're a lifesaver!"

"Sure thing, any time." The answer was reflex, just like his greeting. He closed with, "Good luck trying to reach her," unsure whether Jack would detect the bitterness.

The realization struck after hanging up that Susan's injuries might be life-threatening. "Imbecile!" he screamed at himself. "The call was not about you or Hanni. It was about Susan. Why must you be such a jerk?"

Wallace pondered how he would broach the subject the next time he saw them. "If I see them," Wallace corrected himself. The correction had nothing to do with Susan's condition. It had to do with Wally's. Most days he stayed inside. He was loath to enter the lobby. The sidelong glances tortured him. He was sure he detected whispers.

"It's him, I'm sure of it, the man who locked himself out during the blackout."

"Manny said he was arrested for defecating in the bushes, that he was discovered sleeping in his vomit."

"Manny told me that too."

"No one claimed him, not even his wife. He had to call his former employer to post bail."

"I bet that was awkward. Wouldn't bank on a job reference."

"Can you imagine the expression on the doorman's face when he showed up with the locksmith?"

"Manny said Robert nearly fainted. The stench was so bad."

"And he still lives here, right?"

"7H, although my wife says it's listed."

"I'd sell too if I did that. Hell, I'd move to Wyoming."

"What was his name, again?"

"Wallace. George Wallace, like the governor."

"But isn't he … isn't he … not white?"

"Neither is Clarence Thomas. But he's entitled to his opinion."

"You mean his parents' opinion."

Wallace muted the imaginary device. At least they did not see what the bank staff gave him: a pry bar and prepaid telephone card emblazoned with the logo of Empire Bail Bonds.

Wally's middle C did not stand for Corley. But what good would it do to explain? It made an inauspicious name outright laughable. His grandfather was christened Charlie Cornwallis after First Marquess Charles Cornwallis, the general who, in the face of exhausted food supplies and munitions, on October 19, 1781 surrendered six thousand British troops to French and American forces. The Battle of Yorktown closed six years of armed conflict, began formal recognition of colonial independence, and secured Cornwallis' place in history as loser of the American Revolutionary War. Wally's grandfather was ribbed mercilessly as a child. He changed his name when he was eighteen to Charles Corn Wallace. He also devolved that name on his only child.

Like Charles Senior, Charles Junior was a native son of Georgia. He was stationed during the Second World War in Birmingham, Alabama, servicing supply planes for the military. The Birmingham Municipal Airport was a staging area for deploying combat troops to Europe and is where the Air Force sent him for service after blowing out his ear drum during the first week of training camp. His duties were non-technical; in fact, they were janitorial, but he still wore his uniform.

Charles Junior remained in Birmingham after the war, finding work at the bottling plant that bordered the airport's main runway. He stood in front between shifts, staring up at the F-51 fighters as they roared past, wincing slightly as they broke the sound barrier. He retained partial hearing in the left ear. A sergeant's bark and the roar of a jet fighter still commanded his attention. He knew most of the ground crew after the war and brought them cases of employee-discounted Coca-Cola when the thermometer broke ninety. It was a ritual his son remembered well.

Charles Junior met his wife at a post office in the Ensley neighborhood of Birmingham, not far from his small house by the Oakland Cemetery. She worked in a garment factory nearby. A wooded ridge framed the southeast edge of the city and an enormous statue of Vulcan, the Roman god of fire, stood sentry. Their third son, George Corn Wallace, remembered lazy afternoons on their back stoop, Coke bottle in hand, musing about the forge in heaven.

He was born in 1957. George Corley Wallace Jr. was just a fiery circuit judge from the southeastern corner of the state. Fifteen months later, when the judge ran unsuccessfully for governor, Charles Jr. and his wife were still content with the name they had chosen. After all, Charles III and Edward were already taken. "Charlie Cube" was their eldest son and Edward was their second, named in honor of Lieutenant General Edward Cornwallis, founder of Halifax, Nova Scotia and uncle of General Charles Cornwallis, loser of the American Revolutionary War. They toyed with Frederick, another distinguished Cornwallis, but settled on George Corn Wallace. George Cornwallis-West was, like Charles and Edward Cornwallis, a famous British officer, albeit more because of his matrimonial conquests than anything else. His first wife was the mother of Winston Churchill, which rankled the future Prime Minister completely because he was Cornwallis' junior by a scant sixteen days. Cornwallis then married the beautiful actress Stella Campbell whom George Bernard Shaw cast as Eliza Doolittle in the first stage production of *Pygmalion*. "George Wallace" sounded propitious too. The NAACP endorsed George Wallace Jr. in the 1958 election. It was his rival, John Patterson, who bore the imprimatur of the Ku Klux Klan. George Corn Wallace's parents congratulated themselves on the auspicious turn of history. Their son had a name he could be proud of. By 1963 it was too late for regrets. Wally was already enrolled in grade school.

ॐॐ

Wallace's thoughts returned to the call. He struggled to remember how he met Jack Roberts. Of course, Wollman Rink: the skating fiasco!

Wallace received the call at work, back during his bank days, back when life seemed normal. He was overseeing installation of a backup system. He was furious his wife couldn't handle the matter herself. The director of skating demanded a conference with Alya's parents – both of them. No, Alya was fine. Yes, it was urgent.

Wallace gave instructions, excused himself, and cabbed to the park's entrance at Sixth Avenue and 59th Street. He glanced up at the statues of the liberators, Simon Bolivar, José Martí and José de San Martin. Martin's horse threatened to trample him but it was the statue of the Cuban patriot and poet, José Martí, which caught his attention. Wallace noticed for the first time that the likeness was severely wounded, fighting for life as it clung to its rearing steed. Wallace silently thanked the sculptor, Anna Huntington, for the anguish and intensity the other sculptures lacked. The quest for liberty wasn't easy. The artist knew it was written in tears and blood.

The gilded statue of General William Tecumseh Sherman at the southeast corner of Central Park irritated him. Led by Nike, Greek Goddess of Victory, the general's horse treads on a Georgia pine branch. Was that the best the artist could do for the 618,000 men who died from wounds and disease, the 375,000 men who survived the war but were physically maimed, and the countless women, children and grandparents who were uprooted, killed or torn from their loved ones? Did the artist honestly believe they were honored in death by a golden homage to more war?

The statue of Martí revealed the price of freedom, albeit romantically, in a way no Congressman nowadays dared. The President's exhortation after 9-11 was to go out and spend. The liberation of Iraq was a grand frolic, a media-scripted demonstration of shock and awe, a mission declared accomplished before substantive sacrifice began. He remembered when *Life Magazine* devoted page after page to the hundreds of soldiers who died each week in Vietnam – a plain one-inch photo for each fallen American, accompanied by several pages of harrowing wartime images. Naked children seared by Napalm, anguished soldiers cradling lifeless friends, bodies mutilated beyond recognition by modern weaponry, violent clashes on campus – the magazine reminded Americans of the price they paid daily by waging war, of the price his brothers paid.

Wallace's mother recounted how she scrimped during the Second World War, how everything was rationed, how she volunteered at the Vulcan factory, how every civilian pitched in, and how they sought out the paper each day, not to read the local news, but to learn who among their neighbors would be grieving. Today, the only thing restraining the country from firing on all sides was budget. Boys were cheap. They weren't Senators' sons or corporate scions. They were "volunteers" so it was all hunkydory – conscripted only by their race, poverty and level of education. The statues of Martin and Bolivar angered him. The great

American ambivalence began here, in the artists' contempt for those who gave their country everything. They exhorted modern media, the public, and the politicians who fed off them to do the same. Contempt for shared sacrifice – that was the prevailing incantation. People shed more tears for Dumbledore than they did for their flesh-and-blood cousins. And *Life Magazine*, like photo journalism in general, was dead – killed by the same general complacency that killed his country.

Wallace struggled to contain his anger. He struggled often. He wished he could desensitize himself, but the offense was raw, visceral. He wondered whether others were more composed than him or just emotionally stunted. He wondered whether they shared his reverence for rectitude or merely extolled lofty values so they could cheat, exploit and defraud those foolish enough to believe in them. Wallace unclenched his fist and drove it into his pocket, forcing it to count change, count keys, anything except life's manifold inequities and insults.

Wallace hurried along the park drive then found the path leading to the rink. From above, the rink was a pearl-white guitar pick, a distended and rounded triangle with a surface area approaching two professional hockey rinks.

The afternoon figure skating academy was in session. A soft, black removable barrier bisected the rink into eastern and western surfaces, and orange cones near the entrance demarcated a zone for toddlers. Group lessons were conducted on the eastern surface. Children skated by themselves or with private coaches on the western surface. Wallace scanned the ice for his daughter but labored to descry her. There were more than a hundred children. All but three were girls, more than half wore identical lilac fleeces, and many of the others wore identical black ones. With three exceptions (the boys), their skates were white and pants black. A languid neon swirl down the left leg distinguished Tania Bass' line of sportswear from the stripes and swooshes of noviтiate rivals.

The reigning world pairs champions, Pang and Tong, skated to victory in her designs. So did the world ladies champion, Miki Ando. As did Olympic champion Sarah Hughes. Each of the older girls, the ones who could do axels, owned a pair of spandex-polyester skating pants from Tania, and each of the younger girls marked them on their Hanukkah or Christmas wish list. Alya did not have to wait for Christmas, or Eid al-Adha for that matter. Hanni learned that the designer's factory was on the upper floor of a crumbling structure in the garment district, three subway stops south of her apartment. She marched there unannounced, climbed the stairs, and refused to depart until Tania sold her one of her samples. Wallace spotted it now, a black pant with Tania Bass' signature leg swirl, this one in neon cadmium red.

Alya and another girl stood at the rail. They scooped snow from the mounds that ringed the rink and sculpted a miniature snowman. They accoutered it with twigs and leaves from the willow that stooped over the rink's southwest corner. The tree would not finish shedding leaves until February. Alya and her friend leaned forward to admire their creation. Wallace chuckled. The $7,600 he budgeted for ice time and lessons were paying dividends. Wallace called down to them but his voice was muffled by the program music, instructors' shouts, and children's laughter. The two lost interest in the snowman and darted into a sea of black and lilac. He spotted them near the dividing barrier practicing spins. It was Alya's turn. She arched her back slightly as she spun, tilted her chin skyward, then embraced an imaginary beach ball. Wallace thought she was attempting a layback. She had a long way to go before resembling Sonja Henie. "No, Dad," Alya explained later. "That was an attitude spin. It's supposed to look that way. Who's Sonny Henson?"

"Attitude spin – appropriate name," thought Wallace. "I bet Hanni dreamt that one up." If her girl couldn't spin like a champion, she could at least stick her chin out and let everyone know what she thought of them. Wallace didn't realize until the local competition that other girls spun that way as well, and that Hanni had nothing to do with it.

Wallace strode past the iron gate, parked Zamboni and closed ticket windows, and entered the building adjoining the rink. It housed the administrative offices, pro shop, rental desk and cafeteria. It was carved into the earth underlying a popular dog patch. Tourists gathered on the lawn and patio above the building to snap photos of the skaters and Manhattan's skyline. Artists gathered to sketch portraits and paint landscapes.

Wallace worked his way past the shoes, coats, backpacks and Zucca bags that lay strewn about the floor, benches and tables and wondered whether this was where Hanni learned about neatness. No, thought Wallace. Hanni hadn't stepped foot in the Wollman facility until three years ago. These were habits of the young, the newly born. Hanni just hadn't outgrown them. He discovered Hanni with an issue of *Cosmopolitan* at a table opposite the cafeteria's first cash register.

"Hello Darling, I'm so glad you hurried. The director will be finished with lessons on the hour and will see us then. Oh, I know, you don't have to tell me. The timing is wretched, isn't it, right in the middle of your workday? But you know how it is. She insisted on speaking with both of us." Wallace knew it was pointless to interrupt. His wife was habitually long-winded. He leaned down and kissed her lightly on the lips. That was the best way to cue a pause. He shoved aside assorted garments and sat himself beside her.

"What did we do wrong this time?" he inquired. They were summoned to the principal's office the previous week.

"There you go again, rushing to judgment. Who said we did anything wrong? I just said it was urgent that she see us."

"Okay," conceded Wallace, "But you really don't know what this is about?" Wallace was apprehensive; Hanni thrived on being evasive.

"Well of course I know what this is about, silly! Why do you think I called you?"

Wallace tried hard to control his temper. He confined himself to two words, "Please tell."

Hanni deliberated for a moment, then blurted out, "Oh darling, I was just trying to spare us more agitation. If the director is there, you won't blow up, will you? I mean, you will, but the trees will still be standing, right? Honey, I think I pissed off the coaches; in fact, I'm sure of it. I'm pretty sure they want me expelled." Wallace stared dumbly. He did not know whether to begin with the offense or the punishment. Either topic would unleash a torrent of countercharges and rationalizations. What he most wanted to do was burst out laughing. Instead, he realized this was the closest Hanni would come to genuine contrition. He leaned over and hugged her tightly.

"It's okay, sweetie. You just felt strongly about something. You can't help it if everyone else is sensitive. Promise me this: help me keep my cool with the director and I'll help you. Everything will be fine. Alya loves it here, and she's getting exercise after school. In fact, I saw a magnificent layback from the top of the hill. How many parents can say that?"

Hanni thrust her arms around Wallace and kissed him fervidly. Her cheeks were wet. Wallace was sure they created a scene, better than the ones they typically provoked, but a scene nonetheless. Hanni released her grip, wiped her face with her sleeve, and affected a dignified pose. She rustled the magazine to indicate the therapy session was adjourned. Wallace smiled gently then walked outside to watch his daughter. That night, Hanni and Wallace clutched each other as impassioned lovers. Their marriage survived on drama.

Hanni surmised correctly. The skating school adored Alya but was not as enamored with the mother. They stopped short of expulsion. She was suspended for thirty days. Thereafter she could return on probation, meaning no interference whatsoever with the coach-student relationship of *any* child. According to the director, Hanni was jealous of the extra attention conferred on another parent's student, the one Alya incidentally befriended. Unlike other parents, Hanni broadcast her jealousy widely. That and several other incidents, including an incorrigible predilection to smoking in the girl's room, persuaded the coaching staff that Alya's mother needed a "time out." The staff dealt with children all day long. Dealing with an older one did not alter the remedy.

During the thirty-day suspension, Hanni could sign Alya in and return to sign her out, but she was not permitted to advance beyond the front desk or wait inside the doorway. Wallace shielded her from the disgrace of banishment to a winter bench by enrolling her in afternoon classes at the Art Students League, two blocks south of their apartment. All she had to do was drop Alya off. She spent the rest of the day sketching nude men and women, an ever-fertile topic for evening discussion and a great boon, she averred, to her event planning ideas, if not business. Wallace circled by the rink between five and six to pick up Alya. Most evenings, they rendezvoused on the street with Hanni and dined out. It was the best thirty days of their married life. He secretly wished the skating school would revoke her probation and slap her with another suspension. But they never did, even if Hanni occasionally gave them cause. The couple returned to their largely separate lives.

"Is that your daughter?" the man inquired, pointing in Alya's general direction.

"Uh-huh. She yours?" Wallace replied, indicating the girl beside her.

"Yes, that's Melissa. Your girl's Alya, right? I think we're neighbors. My wife says she passes Alya in the lobby before school." He extended his gloved hand. "I'm Jack Roberts in 8B and my wife is Susan. I'm usually here on Saturday and Sunday mornings. Susan brings Melissa during the week. She seems to be fast friends with your daughter."

Wallace removed his glove and shook Jack's hand. "The name is Wallace, George Wallace, but please call me Wally, not George. It avoids a lot of tiresome explanation."

Jack grinned. "I can imagine. My name has baggage too. Search 'John Bartholomew Roberts' online when you get home. You'll find me, of course, but you'll also find the other Bartholomew. He'll give you a chuckle."

"What was he, a mass murderer?" Wallace thought of John Wayne Gacy.

"In a matter of speaking, not like Jeffrey Dahmer nor so recent, but you will still get a chuckle." Jack would not explain himself further. Wally's online research that day hatched their habitual exchange of honorifics, Captain and Governor, and a neighborly friendship that, if not deep, was nevertheless pleasant. They stood at the rail of the rink most Saturday mornings, trading snippets of information about their respective lives, cheering on each daughter's progress. Susan and Hanni began hosting play dates for the girls. Occasionally, they organized field trips to the movies or zoo. The play dates wrapped up when the fathers left work and joined for a cocktail. For the first time he could recall, Wallace's apartment bordered on neat. And for the first time in years, Hanni and Wallace felt the marriage was solid, meaningful, validated by a building and city that so often seemed hostile and uncaring.

Hanni was sensitive in that regard. Her citizenship was fresh and her memory of 9/11 even fresher. She felt under suspicion, especially in Manhattan, despite her birthplace in a NATO ally and member of the European Union. When she travelled on business, she dressed as professionally as possible but was regularly pulled aside for pat-downs and luggage inspections. She eschewed covering her head with headgear, even in winter. The closest concession she made to cold and implied religious conviction was an earmuff. In truth, Hanife was a nominally Catholic atheist, persuaded, as Wallace was, that organized religion was the root of more hatred, suffering and evil than all other forces in world history, and that each denomination was equally blameworthy. Still, she could not escape the name on her driver's license. So her friends and colleagues knew her as Hannah Kaplan or Hannah Wallace. Neither name was outwardly suspicious.

Wallace was in a similar predicament but knew thirteen percent of Americans could cite experiences as wearisome as his own. And no one mistook him for an enemy combatant. Nor, thank goodness, for a gang member. He was too old, overweight and balding. No, his biggest peeve was that he was mistaken occasionally for succeeding to his late father's occupation, janitor, rather than becoming Chief Technology Officer of a large hospital network. When the mistake was committed by a fellow employee, he got even. System crashes could be a colossal nuisance. But when it occurred on the street or in his building, he was defenseless. He had to swallow his anger or create a scene, something that nearly always precipitated regret.

Wallace recalled the time he returned home from a workout, lugging six large bags of groceries from the market. One of the porters, Rafael, stood at the elevator bank, filling in temporarily for the attendant. Rafael regarded him condescendingly then motioned silently down the hall to the concierge, implying without words that delivery boys should know better than to head directly to an apartment.

How many years had Rafael's name been on the staff's holiday card? How many years had he handed him a thick envelope on December 24th? Wallace reckoned it was eleven. He stared fiercely into Rafael's eyes but said nothing. He turned and trudged the long wide corridor back to the front desk. He walked slowly, erect, shoulders rolled back the way his mother taught him, fingers sore from the six bags of groceries. Fine! The staff regarded him as a delivery boy or imposter. Who cared that he made five times any one of them? Without his jacket and tie he was nobody. John saw him return to the front and smiled inquis-itively.

"I need to be announced. Rafael says so. Perhaps you should ask Mrs. Wallace to come down and fetch me." Wallace tried to sound as pleasant as possible. Inwardly he screamed.

John reacted in horror. Robert, the doorman, signaled down the hall to Rafael and shouted frantically, "It's okay. He's Mr. Wallace in 7H." Three or four tenants passed through the lobby. They inspected Mr. Wallace in turn, deciding for themselves whether he was indeed "okay."

Hanni pleaded with him afterward to treat Rafael kindly. He had helped her so many times. He was one of the most reliable and friendly porters in the building. He was just doing his job. Besides, it happened to Hanni all the time. That is why she frittered away their savings on designer outfits and expensive perfumes. Otherwise, some woman, inevitably some woman, would inquire whether the store carried a larger size or whether there was a table near the window or whether she could direct her to the ladies' room. It was the first lesson she learned upon arrival at JFK. Never dress or behave in an understated manner. Always dress and behave like royalty, even if you could not afford it. And if women still regarded you as staff, reply in French or German until they gave up, not in English and never in Turkish or Spanish. Hanni spoke all five and claimed she could still decline Latin. Wallace resented the double standard but knew Hanni was right. People treated him respectfully when he stood beside her. It was immaterial that she was drowning in credit card debt to Saks Fifth Avenue and Bergdorf Goodman when they married. Wallace promised he would turn the other cheek and Hanni made ardent love to him. Wallace treated Rafael as if nothing had happened.

Wallace missed the old Hanni intensely. They argued about everything but beneath each seismic argument was an ardor that bound their tectonic plates closer together and steeled them against the world's ambivalence and derision. Fighting with each other was their nature, yet they would have defended each other to the death. Such was their devotion, but Alya robbed them of that satisfaction, robbed them of … everything. He felt his body tremble and struggled to shake free of the looming despondency. He progressed so far since the previous summer, but the bog still menaced him. It bulged and oozed and changed form relentlessly, towing at the brink of his consciousness, straining to engulf him.

Wallace gazed at the building across the street. He sensed coldness where Alya previously stood beside him. They stood on the balcony giggling at the remodeled aquatic center. Only in New York, they laughed, would an institution like the New York Athletic Club replace frosted glass with five enormous casements of fully transparent un-tinted windows. Only in New York would they broadcast to their neighbors a brightly illuminated aerial view of the hot tub, sauna and 30-by-75-foot swimming pool until 9 pm each evening. And only in New York would they replace the shutters on the men's and women's locker rooms with windows that could be thrust wide open for ventilation. Alya begged her father for a telescope, preferably a Meade ETX 60AT with Maksutov-Cassegrain optics. There were three of them for a buck a peep at the boat pond in Central Park. Each was trained on a point below the gable of a townhouse that poked above the foliage concealing Fifth Avenue. The scopes were there to spy on Pale Male, the red-tailed hawk who nested there in 1991, and who returned each successive spring with a mate to breed.

Alya also wanted to spy on a pale male. Chubby white men without towels were a choice source of merriment. The women were amusing too, but there were so few. Women were not admitted until 1989, and then only because the New York City Human Rights Commission decreed it. Twenty-three years later, women comprised a mere ninth of the club's members.

Alya would have enjoyed the melee Thursday evening. It spilled from the second floor Tap Room onto the streets. Wallace

counted six or seven squad cars. The papers reported three ar-
rests and two hospitalizations. Club policy forbade discussion of
the brawl, but the *New York Times* and *Daily News* quoted liberally
from an anonymous blog titled WallStreetJackass: "The best fight
I've ever seen … a non-discriminatory ragematch … two broken
noses right off the bat … three wolfpacks … no one could leave
unless you wanted to go through the lion's pit … 10 cops were
arresting all of them." Alya would have found the account hys-
terical and trained her telescopic lens each evening on the building. She would have texted Melissa in her apartment, beseeching
her to do the same, and then shared photos and videos with their
friends at the rink. Had she opened a Facebook account, which
he strictly forbade, her photojournalism would quickly have gone
viral.

Wallace concurred; the club's giant windows offered better
programming than reality television. Perhaps that is how the
overwhelmingly white, overwhelmingly male private club preserved its 501(c)(7) tax-exempt status – free public entertainment.
Wallace suspected his personal property and income taxes were
higher than those of the club's, a club whose 8,600 members paid
$8,500 initially plus $3,000 annually for the exemption-subsidized
privilege of remaining ethnically, racially and sexually exclusive.
Maybe a telescope wasn't such a bad idea.

Wallace stepped foot in the club once. The cooperative rented
a ballroom there to host its annual resident-shareholder meeting.
Wallace was grateful for the dress code. It was the only way to
distinguish him from the janitors and porters. He was conscious
of the dozen eyes that followed him as he and Hanni entered the
lobby, and of the doorman who followed them at a discreet distance to make sure they did not veer from the path to the elevator.
He recalled how they were escorted to the exit at the meeting's
conclusion, while other shareholders were allowed to linger. He
wondered what the protocol was for decontaminating the premises. How would they know which glass he used, which urinal he

pissed in? They could throw out all the glassware from the meeting, but the urinals? The answer came quickly enough. The club began renovating that floor the following month. Wallace voted by proxy thereafter.

Wallace stared at the athletic club and sighed. He promised Alya the telescope and Facebook account when she reached twelve. She never made it.

Part II:

The Lives

Chapter 10

The city wagered on decades of harmonious cooperation, but smog and grit frayed the LEDs. The bent figure and raised hand flared in unison – one flashing, one loping – both straining for attention. The city limped on despite them. Their dysfunctional feuds were commonplace and, like posted speed limits, largely ignored.

"No. You can't have him. He's not part of the bargain."

"You think we planned this? We've already planted our own people … and gotten nowhere. They don't have the skills … the cred. They wither in some administrative backwater – processing patient records. That's not what we're after, Miss Kaplan. This new position … it couldn't have been better timed. Your husband has the perfect cover – C-Suite credentials, the inside track."

"Why, because I know the chairman?"

"You're more than just acquaintances. Or must we explain that to your husband? You can plant the seed, in both of them, then nurture it, make it grow."

Hanni turned in disgust. "Even if I get him in, why on earth would he help you? What makes you think he's a boy scout?"

"Not everyone needs to be coerced, Miss Kaplan. We know a lot more about your husband than you think, just as we know a lot more about you than the INS."

There it was, the reminder. She wanted to stab him, drag the blade upward and watch the eyes bulge in surprise. But the knife was on the kitchen counter and the cut of his blazer betrayed a revolver. Plus, she wanted desperately to preserve the fairy tale of her last ten years, to mix cocktails for her husband and their neighbors, reheat TV dinners, watch *Aladdin* for the thousandth time, and cuddle with the only remaining innocent people on earth. She was in no hurry to become a fugitive.

The man continued, this time softly. "It's not as ominous as it sounds. We're not asking him to be a spy. If you play this right, he won't even know we exist. It's just a job – a really prestigious one. Curiosity will do the rest. I'll wager it takes less than a month before he smells something fishy."

Hanni suppressed a guffaw. "I don't know who drugged your coffee, but Wally's the most introverted, gullible guy you'll ever meet. He's no rocket scientist and he sure-as-hell isn't a detective. He's a G-as-in-gosh-golly, gee-willikers, god-I-love-my-cheese-grater Geek. And he's my husband. Find someone who might actually help you."

"He doesn't talk much about the old days, does he?"

Quizzical stare.

"Well, that's good; I'm glad he's taking his business and family responsibilities seriously."

Hanni fidgeted. Wally said he was contract programming in Birmingham so he could look after his aging parents. She never inquired further. Job descriptions bored her. Guys who droned on about their jobs bored her even more, guys like Jack Roberts in 8B or Gürhan Erdoğan at NYL Health Systems, her biggest client and subject of intense interest by her erstwhile employer.

She'd assumed Wally couldn't find a job in the city after college and returned home. He was black. It was the 1970s. His break came when a local bank expanded into the Northeast and offered him a position on Park Avenue.

Błaszczyk's insinuation irritated her. What did he take her for? Her husband wasn't evasive, and he certainly had nothing to hide; he was shy, the shyest and most forthright man she ever met. So what if she never ferreted around his past. Thank God he didn't ferret around hers! She changed the subject.

"What about the Bureau? Does Julianne Moore's understudy want in on this too?"

"*Julianne Moore? Understudy?* Ha-ha, that's rich. You mean 'stand-in.' No, this is just between us. Give it a chance, will you? The promotion and esteem will do him good. The bank's dead; Congress destroyed it. I bet without any covert assistance your husband discovers something sinister and calls the appropriate authorities, and then we can tear the place apart. That should be worth millions in whistle-blowing fees. Neither of you will have to work again. Your husband *is* a boy scout, Miss Kaplan. That's what we're banking on. Aren't you?"

He cut off her reply. "If it works, life will be easier for both of us. Fewer problems with admissible evidence, fewer indelicate encounters on your part."

Hanni struggled to control her rage. "You dismiss them as if they're amateurs. You haven't caught any of them in six years. My husband will be at the bottom of the river before anyone dials 9-1-1."

"Not likely. We've watched you like a hawk – every step, every shrug. You can't even pee without us seeing. Makes you feel safe, doesn't it, knowing we watch that?"

Hanni didn't feel safe, just denuded. Directly or indirectly, she always felt denuded. She shuddered. The man was abhorrent.

"So we watch him too. We don't even need extra cameras, although we'll just see his backside … when he's peeing, that is. No matter; economies of scale. Even the US government needs to economize. But don't worry, we'll add eyes when you're apart. Otherwise … otherwise it's Plan B, Miss Kaplan. Plan B One Step. You'll need it, I assure you. You'll need it often."

The man's chuckle made her nauseous. His puns were worse than Erdoğan's. She wanted to thrust him out the door and cry.

Chapter 11

Orange, white, a spasmodic flicker of appendages and groping hands. They flared voraciously, frantically, thrusting and compressing into a singular incandescent discharge. And then darkened. It took three weeks before the city replaced the walk signal with a new one.

WEDNESDAY MORNING, APRIL 4, 2012

Susan woke before dawn, pried herself from the woman lying beside her, and crawled out from under the blanket. She could feel her breath condense as frost against her face but did not switch on the heat.

6 months ago

present day

The aging unit had two working settings: fiery hot and off. The first setting roared like a blast furnace, searing anything within its proximity. The bed sat within that proximity. Had they left the heater on, the blankets would have caught fire. Hannah already melted the tops of her Dalbello boots by tipping them against the unit to dry the liners. The two spent an hour reheating the deformed plastic against the heater then gingerly bending the cuff of the ski boots back in place with gloved hands. The heater had evidently roasted the thermostat years earlier; it was as functional as the "close door" button on the elevator in Susan's apartment building. So she and Hannah switched the unit off, eventually generating their own heat.

Susan crept into the bathroom and shut the door quietly but firmly. The fluorescent light flickered then bathed her in a pale greenish hue. The figure that shivered in the mirror was ghoulish, an apparition. It bared its teeth, checking to see if it had grown fangs. The inside of the jaw was black – lips, tongue, gums – all but a set of bluish-white teeth. Her hair lay in a wild black tousle about the shoulders.

The visage in the mirror inspected the nape of its neck, where Hannah bit playfully the night before, here, there, then again before venturing to the breasts, the navel, the thighs. The reflection shuddered.

The dim lighting disguised any redness. Susan remembered finger painting when Melissa was a toddler. Melissa swirled the colors of her set together, attempting to create a rainbow. Instead she produced a dark brownish-gray smear. Melissa daubed more paint on the smear, trying to restore the colors to their original vibrancy. But she could not. Her creation grew darker, grungier. Susan's skin was that dark grungy smear. Even after she bathed, even after she scrubbed, the filth would reappear, as soon as she reentered this cell. Susan yearned to flee, to howl at the coyotes. Instead, she double-checked the security of her door.

Susan reached down to lift the toilet lid but there wasn't one. Rusted bolts were evidence of where it had been ripped free and commandeered as a makeshift sleigh. Susan seated herself on the rim, not bothering to inspect for grime, then examined her surroundings. The toilet area stank faintly of urine and fecal overflow. Mold was visible on the wall where the water valves fed the toilet and the basin. Paint peeled from the ceiling. The floor of the plastic shower stall was stained, and mildew clouded the transparent plastic shower curtain. Tape covered the spot on the door where a clothes hook had been ripped from its mooring, and the linoleum flooring was worn and warped. The room was as shabby as the one she slept in. It reminded her of the apartment she shared in Hell's Kitchen sixteen years earlier, of the rooms she shared when she lived off campus in Tallahassee, of all the places she lived after cutting ties with her family. She was on the verge of cutting ties again.

She didn't bathe. So what if others detected the sheen of dried saliva on her skin and the pungency of days-old cigarette ash in her pores? So what if her hair was a raven's nest of snarled matted knots? Or if yesterday's mascara ran smears across her cheeks? She didn't care. Susan thought about the woman on the bed. She thought about the men who bedded and discarded her when she was single. She cupped her hands under the spigot, swirled water between her teeth and spat.

The light flickered out and Susan reentered the bedroom. A shadow lay under the blanket near the window. What did she know about it, really?

She dressed quickly, selected a couple items from her purse, then locked the purse in the small safe on the closet floor. She hoisted her boot bag, contemplated leaving a note for Hannah, then closed the door behind her.

"Dumb ass," the ghoul in the mirror followed her from the bathroom and smirked. "You left the motel key on the table." Susan paused for a second, thought twice of waking her roommate, then threw the boot bag in the car.

"I'll text her from the slopes."

Susan needed to be alone. She strove to rationalize the evening as Hannah's machination but could not; as the interaction of alcohol and high altitude but could not; as a desperate cry for liberation and could. But the events only left her more asphyxiated and confused. She inhaled deeply but her hair and coat reeked – of a dozen chain-lit cigarettes and rancid day-old musk. Susan did not smoke and most certainly did not wear musk. The pungent odor quashed any reticence about leaving and she barged to the driver's side of the vehicle.

She regarded the MX-5 in the morning light. The exterior was caked in rime. The hood and windscreen were filthy, splattered grayish white by the parade of trucks, SUVs and cars that barreled up Route 267 the preceding afternoon and despoiled it. The skis were lashed to the car, covered in the same whitish-gray grime. The bicycle rack and duct tape, which seemed so clever the day before, looked ridiculously out of place. The taped misshapen fender completed the picture. Tears welled in Susan's eyes. She kicked a tire in frustration and opened the door. A tailed creature scurried into the underbrush. Susan slumped down in the driver's seat and clenched the wheel. Her hand shook as she turned the key in the ignition and reached to shift into reverse. She could see her breath rise but knew her jittery grip was not from cold.

Susan pulled into the near-vacant lot at Squaw Valley. It was still two hours before the lifts opened. She selected a spot deep in the lot's interior. SUVs trickled into the resort. Most of the early arrivals were resort personnel and ski patrollers. Several came with dogs.

Steam rose from her coffee. It traced curls between the cup and the visor. Invisible currents spun the curls about, feathered them into wisps then swallowed them as they dispersed. The landscape in front of her was alien. Monstrous four and five-story condominiums crowded the base area. Gabled roofs lent it a Tyrolean feel, but the oversized windows and ubiquitous concrete slabs robbed the visage of charm. Susan remembered none of these structures from her previous trip. The signature structure in 1997 was a large white concrete and tinted glass bunker that housed the aerial tram. The other buildings were rustic wooden structures, each associated with some aspect of resort operation. The closest lodging was along the access road or off to the left at Squaw Creek. Tickets were dispensed from simple wooden kiosks resembling those at Disneyland, and she could see the base of most lifts from the parking lot.

The tram and its bunker were still visible, but little else was familiar. The scale of development bewildered her. Her memories of the place, so vivid as she drove along the lake and up the access road, were muddied by what she saw now. Her emotions rebelled. "What right have they to destroy this? It's Forest Service land!" She did not want Melissa to see this. Ever.

"So what if the resort gets to host the Olympics someday? Do you think the athletes care? Do you think they want *this*?" Susan sympathized this moment with her husband. How many dreams, how many memories, how many lives had been bull-dozed over just to make room for this vision of tomorrow or the tomorrow that rose back home on Wall Street? Jack's world had been kidney-punched so many times his outer demeanor reflected it – a crumpled and beaten man, serving out his time. He seemed so strong when Susan met him, so deft at sidestepping misfortune. But now he was lost. It infuriated Susan that his strengths were an illusion. She was angry at the world for dragging him down, but angrier at Jack for succumbing placidly. He was not who he feigned to be when she fell for him. And this was not the rugged resort it purported to be. It was Vail II, III or VII. Who could keep count? Who would want to?

Susan debated whether to drive to Alpine Meadows, the neighboring resort, but suspected it would anger her more. She read Squaw annexed it the previous year as part of its bid to host its second Winter Olympics. Concrete foundations for a base "village" were probably already poured. Alpine Meadows was liable to be an eyesore. At least this Vailplex was reasonably complete.

Susan gazed past the riot of gables to the craggy peaks that marked the summit. Several of the lifts creaked to life. She could see ski patrollers with their packs. They would begin detonating charges within the hour. She recalled how they exchanged greetings with the avalanche control team from Alpine Meadows the last time she was here. The team used the KT-22 chairlift to reach the backcountry ridge running above the sister resort's access road.

Susan strained to see if they were there this morning. There had not been much snow during the night, mostly rain, but the water trickled into the snowpack, boring rivulets into the lower layers, compromising the snowpack's integrity. The lower layers were a crystalline sponge. At any moment they could crumble and send a dozen feet of densely packed snow, heavier than concrete, hurtling down the mountain, crushing anything in its path.

Jack's brother had been a parking attendant the day a wall of snow demolished two chairlifts and the operations center at Alpine Meadows, then buried the parking lot in twenty feet of snow. Jack's brother survived, but seven of his co-workers died. Even within the tightly controlled confines of a ski resort, avalanches happened. Secretly, Susan wished one would happen to the Vailplex at Squaw.

Susan sipped her coffee. The name inscribed on the cup was "Syd's Bagelry & Espresso." It belonged to a café in Tahoe City. The café stood on the northwest edge of the lake, about five hundred yards from the Route 89 turnoff north into the mountains and five miles from the access road to Squaw Valley. Susan had been there sixteen winters earlier, the second time she went skiing with Jack. She corrected herself, the second time she went skiing. It was Café O'Lake then. Jack pointed out the owner, Tamara McKinney, "the most decorated skier in American history. My brother and I idolized her."

She wasn't much older than Susan. Or was she? Susan couldn't tell. She knew she should be impressed but was struggling. Or jealous.

"Does she race against Picabo Street? Glenn Plake?" Susan chanced upon their names in an issue of *Skiing Magazine* at the lounge in the San Francisco airport. There was an article about Street, a rising star on the downhill circuit, and half a dozen ads featuring Plake. She remembered Street because of her unusual given name and Plake because of his unusual hairdo. Eight-inch Mohawks were uncommon.

"Same team as Picabo," Jack volunteered, "but a little earlier." Susan could not comprehend this woman skiing "earlier." She looked like a child. Jack seemed to read her mind.

"You'll look fabulous in ten years too. You're an athlete and have exceptional bone structure. You'll age well."

"Will you recognize me in ten years?" she inquired, half kidding.

"Intimately," he replied, "and hopefully twenty years after that." It was the first time he alluded to the future. Susan had alluded to it for months.

It seemed comical in retrospect that her husband taught her to ski. The man she knew as her husband was impossibly at odds with the image of a boy raised in a cabin in the Adirondacks. But he was not so at odds with the image when she married him.

Jack greeted Susan at Salt Lake City International Airport in late January after a week of meetings in San Francisco. A private van service drove them to Little Cottonwood Canyon, initially along the interstate, then up the narrow, winding, left face of a gorge whose steep cliffs towered over both sides above them. Nestled in the gorge were groves of short, shrub-like trees, each topped with a hundred small tufts of snow. "Cottonwood," Jack explained. Clinging to the mountains were dense stands of pine and spruce.

The van strained against the incline, coming eventually to rest at the turnoff for Snowbird Ski and Summer Resort. Jack instructed the driver to use the second turnoff instead, just before the Iron Blossom Lodge. The van drove to the end of the turnoff, dropping them beside the Cliff Lodge and Spa, a ten-story glass and concrete complex with sweeping views of the resort and canyon. The top two floors were a full-service fitness center and spa, complete with an enclosed Olympic-size rooftop pool and outdoor skating rink. Jack reserved a room with king-sized bed, wet bar, and separate sofa and desk areas. It was twice the size of Susan's sublet in Hell's Kitchen and had an unobstructed view of the slopes. A 120-person aerial tram emerged from somewhere beneath them and climbed up the steep face of the resort, disappearing after clearing a ridgeline. She learned later that the ridge was called the Cirque, but it was not to be confused with the outrageously stuffy and expensive restaurant Jack took her to the previous weekend.

"French is full of homonyms, just like English," Jack explained. "Words that sound or are spelled the same but have different meanings, like *bare* naked and the little brown *bear*." Susan said nothing but was grateful for the explanation. Jack was considerate that way. He somehow knew she had forgotten about homonyms from English class and proffered the definition, as if he would say the same thing to anyone, even an English professor.

"Well, the restaurant we went to was Le Cirque, the Circus, and I promise, I will find something less stuffy next time. But this cirque is different. It means a rock cauldron, in this case, a really steep one. Nothing stuffy about it."

"And we're going to ski that?" Susan inquired, her interest suddenly piqued.

"Quite possibly," Jack said, "it depends on the conditions." Jack declined to volunteer the conditions, namely, that she first learn to ski.

Jack didn't pack much. His boots were his only equipment, a pair of well-worn Salomon Force 9s. He said if Susan had to wear rental skis, so would he. Doing otherwise would be unfair. "We'll wear matchies," he said. Susan liked that.

It was still early but Susan asked to dine in. She threw him on the bed as the SnoCat began its long winding descent down Chip's Run. "Now let me teach you something about the barenaked brown bear," she teased, straddling him and yanking off her top.

They giggled when the doorbell rang with room service. Susan ran naked into the bath and Jack somehow managed to appear dignified. Susan wondered whether the porter noticed the bulge protruding from Jack's towel. No, she decided. His eyes were fixed on Andrew Jackson.

Dinner was cold when they woke. They could not remember who ordered what. So they left all but the wine and bread and resumed what they had been doing before dozing off. They went through the same ritual at breakfast. "I suppose this is one way to diet," said Jack.

"Speak for yourself," replied Susan. "I've eaten twice." Jack blushed red, almost purple. And Susan dined again.

Jack signed Susan up for a morning of private instruction then escorted her to the ski shop to rent equipment. He returned to the room to make calls after depositing her back at the ski school. Susan spent an hour on the bunny slope behind the lodge, insisting to her instructor that she could step into and out of her bindings, safely mount and dismount the Chickadee lift, fall down and get up on her own, snowplow the gentle Chickadee Chutes (chutes they were not), and even manage a hockey stop. The instructor was impressed, or rather, endeavored to seem impressed. His tip depended on it. He spent the rest of the morning accompanying her down the well-groomed beginner runs that crisscrossed the fall line below the Gad I chair lift. The last run took them from the top of the Wilbere chair down Bass Highway to the doorstep of her lodge. She found Jack waiting with his equipment and her poles.

"Let's ride the gondola," she exclaimed. "I want to ski down from the top."

He glanced at the instructor. The instructor shrugged as if to say, "She's your responsibility now." But he did not say, "I don't think she's ready," or choke on whatever he sipped from his bota bag, so Jack replied exuberantly, "My thoughts, exactly." He placed forty dollars in the instructor's hand and thanked him warmly.

Jack guided Susan down Chip's Access and Chip's Run, a narrow catwalk that wound back and forth into the bowl formed by Mount Baldy on their right and Hidden Peak and the Cirque Traverse on their left. Steep chutes drained on either side of them into the bowl. Skiers swooped down off the cirque, whooping with laughter, flew briefly along the catwalk, then veered off into the trees.

The catwalk joined the fall line at certain points and Susan accelerated, losing control and landing in an awkward jumble. Giggles followed. Susan's giggles. She placed her skis sideways below her as instructed and rose from the fall. It was much easier on an incline, she observed. Jack spun around after the third incident, leaned forward and grabbed the tips of her skis. He held them in a V position and skied backward as she slid down the next embankment. He did not say much, just asked her to pressure her knees and feet to hold that position, to dig deep with her edges.

When the run resumed crisscrossing the mountain, Jack stood up and skied behind her. He told her to keep her knees bent and let the skis run parallel, encouraging her to shift her weight from ski to ski, to get used to the feel of weighting and unweighting, and of guiding the skis into a snowplow and back to parallel.

They rode the tram again but veered off Chip's Run onto Rothman's Way, a catwalk that traversed left under the tram to the lifts she rode in the morning. Susan's feelings sank as they approached the familiar beginner-level terrain. She wanted desperately to impress Jack, to prove they belonged together. He sensed her thoughts. "I'd like to show you a couple gems, Bassackwards and Bananas. They're hidden at the top of Gad Valley. We need to take two lifts."

Jack was right. The trails were gems, wide open groomers that followed the fall line, but not nearly as steep as those under the aerial tram. And it was quiet. There were almost no other skiers. Jack pointed out the glades that bordered Black Forest and Organ Grinder, somewhat steeper trails that curled down from Bassackwards. "I like to lose myself in there when the powder's deep. It muffles all the sound. You're twenty feet from a marked trail, but it feels like a hundred miles. It's so peaceful."

"Show me," demanded Susan.

Jack hesitated. "After a couple more lessons. It'll be your graduation present."

Susan fought back the urge to argue. "Well, at least let me see *you* ski it."

She had not thought about how she herself would ski down without a companion. "Bassackwards," should have been his reply, but Jack said, "Okay, I'll race you. Once you've seen enough, follow the blue squares to the base of Little Cloud lift and wait for me. It's just a few hundred yards from here. I'll take the Gad lift up and meet you there." Susan agreed.

Jack tipped his skis off an embankment and vanished. A moment later his head bobbed into view. Left, right, Susan watched Jack weave between the pines and disappear, legs bounding up, down and sideways like a hyperactive yoyo, upper body uncannily still. White plumes marked his trail. Jack was right. It was silent, like watching a movie with the sound off. But it was also beautiful. Susan was hooked. She pushed hard on her poles and made for the rendezvous.

For the next two-and-a-half years, Susan skied as often as she could, arriving at the resort before Jack, leaving after. She took lessons here and there, but relied mostly on swift reflexes and athleticism, a stack of issues of *Powder Magazine*, and a couple choice videos from Warren Miller. The next time they were in Gad Valley, Susan chased Jack into a densely forested section, found a particularly secluded powdery embankment, and made love to Jack with her skis on. She was glad she was not wearing a one-piece, glad he was not any taller, and glad she was bearing his child. She was proud of the engagement ring on her finger. That was many winters ago.

∽∼

Susan peeled the tape off her skis and poles, crumpled it into a wad and threw it on the driver's seat. The grime left whitish-gray streaks on her gloves, jacket and black stretch pants. She shouldered her skis, hoisted her boot bag, and trudged toward the village gate. The resort was ugly. She was ugly. What did it matter?

Once inside, she felt disoriented, uncertain whether she steered the Miata to the wrong resort. The walls crowded her. She considered returning to the car and continuing along the lake to Homewood but did not. The village was remarkably quiet. Its tenants still slept or, more likely, it was vacant. That aspect of Lake Tahoe remained unchanged. Tourist season was over. The dabblers moved on to golf, fishing or whatever else dabblers fancy once April arrives. Susan despised the dabblers for financing this monstrosity but was heartened they had flocked to their next artificial playground.

She gazed up at the mountain. She craved the crisp silence, the solitude that greeted her when she veered off the marked trails into the narrow chutes and secluded glades. Jack craved the stillness too, even if he could no longer enjoy it. The few times they pulled Melissa from school to go skiing, Jack proved he could still pick his way through the trees, smoothly, swiftly, upper body still, as if the feat were effortless. But the feat was not effortless. She glimpsed him at the base of a forested trail she and Melissa circumnavigated. His poles supported his shoulders. His chest heaved to catch its breath. He looked old, spent. He stood upright and smiled sheepishly the moment he saw her. "Counting snowflakes," he confessed when they caught up with him. "I lost track at three hundred."

Jack then swapped roles with Susan and watched as she bounded into the next stand of trees, lurching forward and backward over the uneven terrain, forcing her turns, thrusting her poles side to side, surviving on catlike agility alone. "She makes it look so hard," Melissa remarked, which indeed it was.

"The trick, you know," Jack replied, "is to make it look easy." Melissa knew. She was a figure skater. Susan, on the other hand, was a runner. She needed it to feel exciting.

"C'mon," said Jack, "I'll race you. Show me really clean edges." Melissa carved long fluid turns down the groomed terrain, upper body still, not whipping her tails around until she came to a hockey stop at the bottom. Her father grinned and followed. She was a natural. Susan arrived a minute later, winded but radiant. She knew she did not ski like her husband. He scarcely touched the mountain; Susan needed to tame it, make it quiver. Right now, peering up at Squaw Valley's ridgeline, Susan was determined to make it quiver.

☙❧

Susan found Hannah the previous evening seated at the bar. Behind her were a large stone fireplace and dining area. Light flooded out of the glassed-in restaurant onto a wooden deck and pier. The pier stretched into the darkness. Mountains lined the opposite shore, forming a thin black silhouette against a dark burgundy expanse. The expanse ripened into indigo and inky blackness as she tilted her gaze skyward. Slate and obsidian ripples lapped against the pier. A couple dined in the rear corner against the window and a family of five rose to leave. Hannah sat alone at the bar. The rustle at the door caught her attention.

"Quiet night," commented Hannah, without rising. "You just arrive?"

Susan strode over and embraced her. "Where are all the men? A mechanic with an accent said I'd find you here. Polish or Czech, I think." Susan did not mention reading Hannah's note.

"He's bayerisch, darling, Bavarian, and he's mine. He gave me his card, see? That makes us engaged."

Susan recited the name on the card, V. Dierich, enunciating each syllable. "vee-dye-rich."

"That's a capital idea, darling. But first, I'm going to marry the dear old lederhoser and a few of his friends, my little old men harem, then retire in comfort when each of them dies or I poison them. I just have to perfect my concoction. So how is *dear old* Jack? Still minting money?"

Susan flinched. Hannah was so direct. "He's working hard. He says the firm is falling apart."

"Dewey Ballantine? Inconceivable, darling. They wrote the book on survival. They'll muddle through; so will Jack."

Susan wasn't as sure. There were so many defections. She changed the subject. "What are you drinking?"

"Peach smoothie, all sorts of rum. Scotty, dear," she inveigled, "a Wet Woody for my friend." Scott's head popped up from beneath the bar. "I should have worn a skirt," she teased. "I didn't know we had a peeper."

The bartender blushed. "I was arranging the beer." Susan thought he looked fifteen, not much older than Melissa. He acknowledged her nervously then busied himself with the rum smoothie.

"You missed happy hour. Five-dollar Woody's until six-thirty. I think this is my third."

"Fourth, Miss Kaplan," corrected the bartender. "The last one was on me."

Hannah smiled. "You're absolutely right, darling, and such a sweetie for remembering. As I was saying, the place was hopping. But now the action is in Reno – subsidized food and beverages, courtesy of the Sands and Circus Circus. I don't suppose anyone here shells out for anything unless there's a promotion. Isn't that right, dear?" Scott pretended not to hear.

"I didn't peek into their cars but I bet they're brimming with coupons, all organized into bare essentials: booze, chow and gas. I tried to hand out my own coupon but there weren't any takers, at least not yet. Buffet special first." Susan began to speak but was cut off.

"Actually, some of the guys – boys, really – were tourists. They only made it to Incline. Someone said they reopened the Cal Neva Lodge, Frank Sinatra's place. Either way, Reno or Incline, they won't save money. They'll lose everything at slots or blackjack or blow it at the Mustang Ranch – that's a brothel, honey; a genuine licensed, tax-paying enterprise with a different kind of slots – then start over with nothing in the morning. No future there, I'm afraid. As I said, I'm not settling down until I find someone with a foot in the grave and a lot of unfrittered assets." She paused for breath. "Two or three of them would be better – old misers, that is, not assets. So, Jack is minding Melissa?"

Susan ignored the juxtaposition. "She's a big girl, now. She takes care of *him*."

Hannah didn't listen. The question was evidently rhetorical. "This place will fill again shortly. The dinner crowd, only they have dates. So, it's just you and me tonight or the casino, but you'll have to drive. There's enough alcohol in me to preserve a cat."

Hannah did look well-preserved, thought Susan, and on the prowl. "How about appetizers and bed instead? I've been running since four this morning, New York time." She stopped herself from saying "running away." Hannah probably knew. They shared an order of sliders and Ahi poki. The poki was not what she remembered from the Royal Hawaiian, but she volunteered nothing. Hannah did not have someone "with a foot in the grave and a lot of unfrittered assets" to take her there. Sierra-style poki would have to do until her benefactor materialized.

Susan corrected herself. The best poki wasn't at the Royal Hawaiian. It was at Fort Ruger Market in Kaimuki and Young's Fish Market in Kalihi, tiny plantation-era general stores that even the locals had begun to forget. How Jack found these places she never knew. They visited Hawaii nearly every summer. They spent their first evening of the trip in Waikiki in a swank hotel like every other tourist but instead of catching the morning flight to Maui, hailed a cab to the top of one of several gated communities beyond Diamond Head. From there, they climbed a ridge trail through low-lying brush, dense jungle, ferns and thick stands of long-needle pine to a windswept summit with breathtaking views of Oahu and the ocean on three sides, encountering only a dog and two hikers. They marked off the ridge trails over the years: Mariner's, Kuli'ou'ou, Hawaii Loa, Wiliwilinui, Lanipo, Wa'ahila, and plotted where they would begin their next ascent.

Afterward, they stumbled out of the mountains and took public transit south to Koko Marina. They ordered Portuguese bean soup at Zippy's, worked their way down the pier for a Longboard at the Kona Brewing Company, then caught the bus back to Waikiki. Other days, they emerged closer to Kaimuki. They bought malasadas at Leonard's, trekked to John's or Waiola Market for shave ice, then caught an open-air concert at the zoo. If it was July, they spent their weekend evenings at a bon dance. Other evenings they dined on lau lau, kahlua pig and lomi lomi salmon, or inquired where they could see Jake Shimabukuro or Amy Hanaiali'i. Compared to Oahu, the outer islands were a cultural wasteland. The newbies could golf all day, burn themselves to a crisp on the Ka'anapali, dine at their hotels, and never encounter anything more genuine than a New Zealander serving Mai Tais. Susan knew Hannah would have ordered three of them, flirted with the bartender for her fourth, and considered the vacation grand. Susan chewed the raw marinated tuna and washed it down with her smoothie.

Their conversation drifted. She could not remember much. The Wet Woody's were strong, and Hannah seemed averse to substance. She blathered for twenty minutes about Wally's mule-headed stupidity, not a word about Alya.

The poki steered Susan's thoughts back to Honolulu. Jack could have been kama'aina, a local. He blended in here too, wherever he went. He must have been a stranger here once, she reasoned. But everywhere they went – Hawaii, Tahoe, London, Munich, the Swiss Alps – Jack knew his way around; everything seemed familiar. She thought of all the places they reserved for the future and realized she would never see them. Jack did not know them and that made him uneasy. He would never admit it but something always postponed the journey.

Susan hated the word, but Jack was predictable. And old. She was relieved she had not mentioned the hikes above Oahu. They came to resemble his evening rituals with the Levitra. Only it was

Advil before the hikes, three or more, then a deep snooze afterward in the hot tub. Susan and Melissa knew the long pauses along the trail were just pretext. He was not drinking in the view, he was summoning the strength to continue. Jack could no longer keep pace with his family.

❧

"You look exhausted," observed Hannah, after they returned to the motel. Susan was surprised. These were the first words of genuine empathy either of them had expressed.

"My back aches," admitted Susan. "Too much sitting and driving. And yeah, I have a lot on my mind. How about you?"

"Just trying to keep it together. It's been hard. I'm really glad you could tear yourself loose. I am really grateful."

Susan leaned forward and embraced her. "I'm really grateful you invited me. I can't tell you how much I needed to get away." She sighed with relief. The other Hannah was tiresome.

But it returned. It sprang from the couch, a mischievous grin stretched across its face. "Let's check out the hot tub!"

"What?" Susan replied, bewildered.

"Come on, it will relax your muscles, and it's bound to be more comfortable than this sofa." She had a point. The spring where Susan sat was broken. Still, Susan protested, "I didn't bring a swimsuit."

"Neither did I," Hannah answered, defying the bikini on the bed to contradict her. "Did you see any other cars in the lot? Not a one. It's just you and me, babe. The Chamois Grande is our oyster. Or is it the Vistaview Chalet? I can't remember. Either way, we can say we were the joint's last patrons, the last pioneers to brave its deep fetid waters before it was condemned and converted to a cesspool."

"You make it sound so alluring," resisted Susan.

"Humor me. Wally and I enjoyed it back when this was a real joint. Grant me one good memory, because, believe me, these rooms are not doing the trick."

Susan relented. She detected a glimmer of the real Hannah. They tiptoed out to the tub in small threadbare towels. Water overflowed the whirlpool and dripped over the sides. Susan toed some leaves to the edge of the tub and stepped in. She giggled as she picked out sunken pinecones and fallen branches and threw them at Hannah's feet. Hannah reached down and placed an uncorked bottle of Southern Comfort on the edge of the tub. "Preventative medicine," she said, undoing her bun and shaking out her long, desert-brown hair. The towel slid to her feet, but she did not react. Instead she stood astride the rim of the whirlpool, legs spread slightly, and lit a cigarette from the pack she carried from the room. She inhaled deeply and stared up at the crescent moon. A coyote yipped in the distance as she exhaled.

Susan had difficulty reconstructing the evening. They splashed each other mercilessly, traded barbs about their sex lives, massaged each other's sore muscles, drank more than either of them could handle, and groped about helplessly as they stumbled over one another trying to reach the bottle. They retreated giggling to their room when the howling of coyotes became a chorus. Hannah made the first overture; Susan was sure of that. But Susan did not protest. She let the tongue probe the roof of her mouth and brush against the back of her molars. Hannah squeezed her closer and Susan rolled on top. She kissed Hannah passionately. A dam breached within her and a lifetime of emotion burst forth. The reaction shocked her but she reveled in its intensity. She yielded to where the swirling torrents took her. Hannah seemed determined to do the same. Later Susan imagined Jack lying fitfully on an enormous bed, tossing about, unable to sleep without his round of Levitra and obligatory lovemaking. But then she remembered Don Julio. No, she smiled, Jack slept with the Don tonight, both aged, but only the latter to perfection. And Susan slept with Hannah. 2,730 miles apart, there was symmetry in their lives.

∂∾∽

Susan sat on a bench and pried open her boots. The aging plastic cut into her fingers. She pointed her toes into the boot then pushed excruciatingly hard on her heel so that the top of her foot could clear the enclosure. There was no need to clasp the yellow buckles. The boot held the foot snugly without them. She threaded the Velcro power strap across the cuff of the boot and fastened it loosely. She gazed about for a coin locker. A small line of skiers gathered for the next tram.

Susan exited the building and climbed a small incline to the base of the KT-22 lift. She remembered it as a fixed-grip double chair without protective railing, a place where you lost yourself in thought as the jagged outcroppings and uneven moguls crept silently down-mountain beneath you. She remembered how the base of her feet would ache as they hung there, how her shins would scream in rebellion, and how relieved they felt when she stepped off at the top. The pain ebbed during the day, but it was always sharp, life-defining during her third and fourth ride up the mountain.

A couple stood beside her. The detachable quad circled glacially behind them and the couple sank heavily into their seats. Susan let the chair push her along for a moment and then sat. The couple already reached up to lower the safety bar and it crashed into the back of Susan's helmet. "Inconsiderate shits," thought Susan, as she reached up, grabbed the safety bar, and slipped in. The chair clamped hard on the overhead cable and the three skiers were swept forward up the mountain.

There was nothing peaceful about the journey. The swift-moving lift clanked and whirred, and the woman prattled shrilly about the meager amenities at her hotel. At Deer Valley they would have carried her skis. They would have waxed them overnight. They would have greeted her by name and assigned her an instructor she could understand, someone who spoke English. Susan glared at the woman, but she yammered on. The husband leaned forward to shield her from Susan's glare or to muffle the harangue. He said little, straining when he did to remain inaudible. They stepped off the lift and swerved to the right, directly in front of Susan. She cursed as she lurched to a stop then continued ahead for a view of the ridge leading down to Alpine Meadows. She thought of the brother-in-law she never met, the Roberts family's Jeremiah Johnson, the one who parked cars during the winter and died of AIDS before she and Jack met. Bozeman it was, in Montana. But the hospital was in San Francisco. That's where they held the service. Jack seldom mentioned Steven, but she knew they were close.

A snowboarder guided his board forward and reached down to clamp his boot. He wore studio-white Beats headphones but could just as well have toted a boom box. She recognized the song instantly. It was one of Jack's favorites, the Hendrix version. "All along the watchtower, princes kept the view, while all the women came and went, barefoot servants, too." The rider slid left over the lip of the G.S. Bowl, into the rudely carved traverse to the East Face and Olympic Lady. Or was it Ladyland? Susan could not remember. She considered following the rider but decided to begin easy. She hummed the next strain, "Outside in the cold distance, a wildcat did growl," but could not remember the rest. That irritated her. Forgetting lyrics was an affliction of age, she decided, and right now she did not want to be reminded of age, Jack's perhaps, but not hers.

She buckled her boots and pole-pushed her way right onto the Saddle, a groomed ridgeline that wound above and around the steep western face of KT-22 to the gentler lower basin of Squaw Peak. Another noisy couple stepped off the chair and brushed past her, then an even noisier foursome, each excoriating Barry Bonds for his use of performance enhancing drugs. She paused to wipe her goggles, fighting back her contempt. On impulse, she silenced the chatter by diving off the trail through a copse of pines then veered left to the top of Rock Garden.

A jack rabbit espied the approaching figure and scurried behind an outcropping. The skis cleared the icy mounds three at a time. The first two turns were labored, overwrought scraping affairs that thrust their owner back on its tails then forward as the skis accelerated. The figure tried to remember what it had been taught about moguls. Keep the tips down, stay in the troughs. Try to zipper the line, one mound to the next. Keep shoulders facing the fall line, hips over toes, arms extended in front, always reaching forward.

The figure reached forward with a pole and a ski tip lodged into a mogul, launching its body forward. The rider gasped from pain as her bindings held and the ligaments in her knee did not. The ski snapped off above the boot and flipped the skier over. The other ski freed itself from its boot and catapulted past her. She hurtled headfirst into and over the bumps. Jagged ice scraped at her face and clothing, but not hard enough to reverse the acceleration. Susan thrust her poles forward. The poles clawed a mogul; but the handle of the first jabbed hard into her midsection. The second slammed into her goggles, ripping them free from her face. The impact of the first pole knocked the wind from her. Her body spun around the second pole, feet forward into the steepest section of the pitch. She tried desperately to dig her one responsive heel into the ice, but the maneuver spun her sideways against and over a small outcropping. She groaned as her thigh slammed against the rock, and went limp as she slid another twenty feet then flew off a small drop-off onto a flat section ten feet below. She was dimly conscious of shattering her pelvis.

A coyote edged close, sniffed its prey and growled. Somewhere in the cold distance, Susan sensed two riders approaching, and the wind within her howled. She lost consciousness in the tumult of tortured chords from a vaguely familiar rock anthem.

Chapter 12

"'Ample man?' Why he's just a stick figure. What do they call someone who is actually fat?"

"They call him 'Herr,' darling, but with an 'e' – no Let-the-Sun-Shine-Aquarius bullshit for the Germans."

Wallace took the elevator from IT to the trading floor. He picked his way through a warren of cubicles, pausing when he found the name plate for "Stuart Chu."

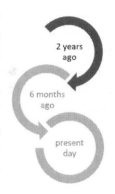

The desk surface was framed by empty cans of Monster Energy drink. A carton of 16-ouncers poked at Wallace's feet. Wallace noticed the can's ghoulish "M" was fluorescent blue against black, not the familiar glow-in-the-dark green.

"Stuart, are you trying to lose weight?" Wallace was surprised. The equity analyst could have doubled as a straw.

Stuart peered up through thick, Coke-bottle glasses. "Fending off diabetes. It runs in the family. I don't need fifty grams of sugar. I need fucking caffeine."

"Not sure caffeine's the answer," Wally volunteered. "I read it disrupts glucose metabolism." Wallace knew he was lecturing the master. Stuart Chu covered big pharma. But he couldn't resist. Diabetes ran in his family, too.

Stuart pulled issue #1 of the *Journal of Caffeine Research* from his desk and flipped it open to page 23. "This article came out yesterday: 'Caffeine, Glucose Metabolism, and Type 2 Diabetes.' Everything you need to know about insulin resistance and caffeine – fucking scary. I give myself three-to-five years." The ebb in jocularity was barely perceptible. "But the stuff's addictive. I can't fucking function without it."

"At least it's legal," he added, dropping to a whisper. "I'm not like our friend, Jilted Love in CB, sneaking OxyContin every couple hours just because his wife's a fucking whore. I'm sorry. He should quit moping and be elated we found out before he had kids. We spared him a fucking lifetime of paternity suits."

"We" meant Stuart and two colleagues – colleagues who entered a conference room they thought was unoccupied. His wife found employment elsewhere but the boss, well, the man in Commercial Banking just scowled. "The stuff's addictive," Stuart conceded. "He can't fucking function without it."

Stuart put down the can of Lo Carb Energy drink and straightened his posture. "What brings you to my hovel?"

Drained energy drink cans stood sentry to a jumble of computer printouts, SEC filings, analyst reports, magazines, data CDs, memo pads, Lucite cubes, Post-it notes and trade-show knick-knacks. The desk's contents spilt onto the floor. Wallace wondered whether Stuart and Hanni once roomed together.

"Tell me you're retiring this piece-of-shit Blackberry," Stuart implored, "that I'm getting a real phone." It was the most common refrain in the office.

"Sorry, no such luck."

"I met the chairman of NYL Health Systems last night," Wallace continued. "It turns out my wife and he attended the same high school ... in Istanbul. His name's Erdoğan – no relation to the prime minister. The *Journal* ran an article about him in the society pages. Well, he started peppering me with questions about credit lines and revolvers. Finally, I said, 'I'm just an IT guy,' but I got the impression he was trolling for capital."

Stuart shrugged. "Most of the big nonprofits are burning through cash or chewing through their endowments. Costs keep rising but Medicare and the insurers won't fucking play dead like they used to. They say, 'Run your business more efficiently.' But shit, that's the rub, isn't it? They're not a business; never were. They have no fucking concept of opportunity cost, what it takes to get investors to part with their money. My sources say several are for sale; they're tapped out. Shit, the majority won't make it past the credit committee."

He paused, appraised Wallace, then suddenly commended Erdoğan for running one of the tighter ships in the industry, whatever that meant. He added, "Maybe you *should* speak with the guys in lending."

He leaned closer. "But that's not why you're here, is it?"

Wallace jerked upright.

Stuart whispered conspiratorially. "They've been advertising a CTO position for weeks. I'm surprised Hanifa – that's her name, right? – didn't set you up earlier. I see them together at the trade conferences. She arranges all NYL's appearances, doesn't she? That must be a fucking big contract."

Wallace fidgeted uncomfortably.

"Serves us right for passing you over. Instead we have some shitty-assed greenhorn from Accenture feeding us doses of PowerPoint. Such lovely bubble charts! He'd be fucking lost without you – doesn't know shit about programming and wouldn't know a denial of service attack if it bit off his cock. Hell, yeah. Anything beats hanging around here, waiting for the next shoe to drop. TARP has us by the fucking balls, and all the bank can do is hire more consultants."

"But NYL? Shit, it's not going anywhere. It just has to cover its operating expenses every two or three years and the trustees think Guri's a fucking hero. Billions in property and equipment that will never see a fucking return and Guri's a fucking guru, just because NYL isn't bleeding cash."

"But us, Dolus Fucking Merc? I'm sending out résumés daily. We all are. My bet is RBS acquires us or we fold. We don't have the capital to survive and we're not 'too big' to fail. Sixty-to-ninety days and I say we're toast."

Wallace was stunned. He was vice president and director of network systems at a regional bank with commercial operations in Manhattan. He survived the first and second wave of TARP-related layoffs and his pay was respectable. It covered household expenses, Hanni's lavish wardrobe, and the mortgage on a converted one-bedroom on Central Park South, even if he could only see the park obliquely from the corner of his balcony. But everything Stuart surmised rang true. And he was right; Wallace deserved the promotion. The new guy knew nothing about managing and securing data. Stuart didn't have to finish the thought.

"Take me with you if you hear of an opening in business development – you know, acquisitions, joint ventures, research. I'd be great; I know everyone. Shit, I'd even work IT. I'm serious. This rust bucket heap-of-manure you call a trading floor would seize up and die without super geek Stu Chu. It's a fucking nightmare … and a conspiracy. Ever noticed how the system only shuts down when your too-fucking-smart-to-work boss calls a meeting? While you guys are over there gushing about his brilliant-as-shit PowerPoint presentation, I'm dragging his piece-of-shit trading system onto life support."

Wallace cleared his throat but spoke nervously. He was horrible at pretending. "Thank you, Stuart. I'm glad I could make the referral. Let's set up that meeting with lending."

Wallace gave three weeks' notice and alerted his future boss, Dr. Gürhan Erdoğan, to expect a call from Rory Jitlov, SVP Commercial Banking, office cuckold and closet OxyContin drug addict. It was the least he could do for his former employer.

He said nothing about the offer to his wife. It would be her anniversary gift, a surprise. Still, he couldn't hide his excitement. Alya ascribed it to "that time of month" and Hanni laughed at his new pair of pajamas.

❧

"I thought you'd be elated. Better benefits. Better pay. Better security. Listen to this. It's *The Wall Street Journal*, per Rory Jitlov

– yeah, Rory. He stood scowling at everyone during the Christmas party, remember? 'NYL Health Systems is the most viable healthcare facility owner and administrator in the United States.'"

"Did you hear that? Not *one of* the most viable, *the* most viable. He continues, 'Year after year, its hospitals beat nearly everyone in nationwide rankings among physicians, hospital staff and patients.'"

"And then there's Stuart Chu in *Fortune*. You remember him from the trade conferences. He writes this: 'Dr. Gürhan Erdoğan runs one of the tightest…' Honey? Are you listening? You're crying! What's wrong?"

Wallace glanced nervously at the wait staff. They had never been to *Jean Georges*. It was a block away but he could never justify the expense. Now he could. They could dine here twice a week if they wanted to.

He began rolling the edge of his napkin. What if Hanni made a scene? The announcement was supposed to be dessert.

"I'm happy for us, darling, I am. I'm … I'm just tired. Let's go home. I don't want to impose any longer on Susan and Jack. The kids have school tomorrow." Wallace sighed, partially in confusion, partially in relief, then beckoned for the check.

੶৽৵

IT management? Wallace groaned. None of the equipment matched. The hospitals had Gigabyte Ethernet but 10Base-T cables and 100Base-T routers. Almost none of the databases were shared. They were also hierarchical and poorly suited to data mining. There wasn't an OLAP server to be found. Backups were irregular and haphazard. Tapes were stored on premises. Servers were stuffed into unventilated closets and plugged directly into wall outlets. Firewalls and other basic forms of Internet security were porous. Accounts and passwords were shared. Employees of third-party contractors accessed hospital systems and patient records without background checks. There were no policies governing flash drives and other forms of removable media. Doctors and staff plugged their personal computers and smart phones into hospital servers, both at the hospital and from home. Policies against excessive personal use of the Internet, data streaming and hospital systems were spotty. There were no restrictions on social media. Enterprise resource programs were unheard of. Asset management was handled via spreadsheet. There was no records retention or litigation hold policy. IT training was nonexistent. And the only drinkable coffee was outside at the corner.

Stuart Chu nailed the problem two months ago. NYL wasn't a company – not in the conventional sense of trading on an established exchange and being responsible to shareholders. It was responsible to no one. And its management culture reflected that.

Security training. He could see Erdoğan color at the phrase. "Look, I'm sure we can keep it simple – perhaps just a daily 'security pointer' that pops up when a user logs onto his computer. You've got really bright people here, brighter certainly than me. They don't need to sit through classes. They'll pick up the security tips easily enough." Erdoğan nodded reluctantly.

Wallace broached a related topic, this time with as much sensitivity as he could muster: data centralization. The Chief Technology Officer position was new, the brainchild of one of NYL's trustees – not Wallace surmised a popular one. He was assigned fourteen previously autonomous hives of technical support. Each openly resented his supervision and fought consolidation. With reason. Wallace spotted inefficiency and redundancy immediately. But the organization was feudal. Getting the fiefdoms to recognize a titular leader was like orchestrating the Crusades. He needed someone to champion his mission. A king. He needed Erdoğan.

Erdoğan glanced at his watch. "Better hurry," Wallace urged himself.

"I'm sorry, Wally. I'm late for a meeting with Chuck Schumer. Let's discuss – what was it, centralized data? – next week. You're making fabulous headway, just what the board wants." Erdoğan left as Wallace fumbled for a reply.

He cursed himself. "Five minutes' face time and I couldn't get to the point." His vision for the first hundred days was a joke, dilated into a five-year plan that, like its Soviet counterparts, was only distantly attainable.

He was losing control of time. Skirmishes between the office of the CTO and its multiple support hives preoccupied most of his day. Brush fires consumed the rest. Once the board announced NYL's first-ever IT "owner," physicians and administrators knew whom to swarm for assistance. They were tenaciously impatient. Wallace began closing his door to box out the noise, the noise outside his head. The noise inside was practically inaudible but it unnerved him. He couldn't fight a war on two fronts, not this time.

He pored over the org chart and armies of staff who feared him. Or had they already divined the obvious, that he was toothless? And what of his direct reports, those who could rally their units if they just tried? They were too busy flinging manure at each other to think about long-term milestones, much less putting out brushfires. Wallace felt he was crisscrossing Gaza.

He repented the previous Crusades analogy. The Franks captured Jerusalem just once, and then only fleetingly. The Gaza analogy was even grimmer. And the Soviet Union? No, there was a better analogy, the goat sent into the wilderness on the Day of Atonement. Yes, that was him. He made a mental note to call Stuart Chu ... and to request more milk with his coffee. It was making him queasy.

❧

"Listen, you know I was against it, so stop complaining."

"Against it? You introduced me."

"At Erdoğan's insistence! What else was I supposed to do? Tell NYL to fuck themselves? Their fees cover the cost of Alya's tuition, her skating and lots more. If I play my cards right, they'll pay for college. But *you*? *You* could have stayed put. Or found a job anywhere, anywhere but there." She put down the hair dryer and reached into the medicine cabinet.

Wallace struggled to maintain composure. His wife was a work-from-home event planner. Her main clients were trade organizations – organizations that hosted seminars, small-scale trade shows, fundraisers and other publicity events. Before meeting Erdoğan, she was a bottom-rung subcontractor; she had fewer contracts than a first-year realtor.

But Erdoğan changed that. Dr. Gürhan Erdoğan was a celebrated oncologist, head of two of the premier research hospitals in Manhattan, and, more important, an alumnus of St. George's Austrian High School in Istanbul. Hanni graduated thirteen years after him but leveraged their shared background and experience into an enviable, ever-growing book of business. Wallace rinsed his thin corona of hair and stepped out of the shower.

Whatever friendship Hanni and Guri projected was evidently an illusion. She just needed NYL's business. Couldn't she have divulged that earlier?

Wallace resumed his monolog, the one Hanni interrupted. "I hate saying this, but I don't think NYL's any better managed than the bank. At Dolus we had meaningful performance metrics. We knew we were playing with other people's money. But here? They think they're rock stars just because they can beg and borrow enough to pay the bills. Oh sure, the reports show an operating profit. But enough to cover financing costs? Not while I've been there. And the balance sheet? It's a joke, beneath anyone's dignity even to acknowledge."

Hanni interrupted again, this time more forcefully, "Listen, darling. You're not in Kansas anymore. Respect, prestige, pay, endowments: everything at NYL is linked to the size and growth of the department, to the number of physicians and researchers employed, to the number of patients treated, to the number of facilities owned. Size matters; nothing else. There's *Grande*, *Venti* and *Trenta*. Get used to it."

Wallace slumped. He felt like one of the four middle-aged men in *Hot Tub Time Machine* but transported back in years to a clueless hedonistic 1980s corporation instead of a clueless hedonistic ski resort. Well, at least he had recruited Stuart. He could commiserate with Stu. Hanni tugged at his towel, pushed him into the bedroom, and shut the door to the corridor. Alya could hear her mother chortling, "Let's see, are you a *Grande*, *Venti* or a *Trenta*?" The T-shirt Alya bought him for Christmas was XXL. *"Trenta!"* she volunteered from the corridor. Hanni looked up at Wallace in shocked amusement.

Wallace had no illusion Erdoğan would teleport the hot tub, sailboat, dingy or whatever he was in forward. The executives played golf when they could and with other people's money when they could not. The only time they'd do anything was if wolves were baying at the door, threatening to dissever fat from the meatier morsels. But what wolf could menace a privately held foundation, one that somehow miraculously paid its bills?

Wallace recalled the warning sign going in – the flaming orange hand at the building's corner. It kept pulsing, pulsing. Cowering behind it was a thin white figure, waiting for the wrecking crew. Wallace crossed anyway. He had only himself to blame.

ཚོ◈ལྦ

Wallace was just four years into the workforce when civic leaders and unions vilified T. Boone Pickens for going after Mesa Petroleum. Their indignation rang hollow then. It was nigh laughable today. How many years was that? Yet here he was with just such a dinosaur – the top predator in its industry, a veritable Tyrannosaurus Rex, but just one blistering asteroid from oblivion.

He reminisced about Mesa at the rink with Cap'n Roberts. Instructor Todd romped with their daughters near the railing. He swept Alya up, launched into a scratch spin then held his arms outstretched as he flung himself into a layback. The funnel cloud cleared a swath in the front of the rink. Patches of hot pink spat from the blue-and-black vortex. The dust devil emitted a joyous shriek as it accelerated, decelerated then released its grip. Seventy eyes blinked in envy. Melissa bounded up and down, pleading for the next ride on the academy's "E ticket."

"I used to work there. Drexel, I mean. I spent a lot of long hours on that deal," Jack ventured.

"For which I presume you were well-paid."

"*Jerk!*" he chided himself. "What I meant was…"

Alya crumpled suddenly then regained her footing. "Dizzy," thought Wallace. "I'd be dizzy too." Alya breathed hard for several seconds then bounded off. Wallace realized Jack was speaking.

"It was a pact with the devil. You wouldn't have enjoyed how it ended."

"Probably not," conceded Wallace, and he changed the topic.

&ca&

"Best in class, Mr. Wallace. Our organization will not rest until we stand toe-to-toe with the top corporations in America in terms of data technology and governance." Gürhan Erdoğan was evidently impressed by Wally's vision for information technology. "I expect the Board of Trustees will agree. It is not just quality of care anymore. We're judged on the whole package – quality of care, economic efficiency, civic leadership, professional management, innovation. We thoroughly intend, Mr. Wallace, to be the vanguard of computer technology and innovation. I look forward to having you on our team."

That was six months ago. Wallace reflected suddenly on how "the whole package" excluded pay practices – performance measurement criteria and incentives. Without those, he and his "team" were shepherding cats. "Try barking orders to a cat."

"Meow," purred Hanni, rolling from bed and slinking into the kitchen to see about dinner. "Seeing about dinner" meant selecting the appropriate take-out menu. There were so many to choose from. She ordered the evening's kibble from a pan-Asian restaurant across from Carnegie Hall – salt and pepper shrimp with tom yum soup; sashimi for dessert. Like most felines, she preferred her tuna raw.

Alya was asleep in bed with a fever. He could put it in the toaster for her later. Poor girl. Flu season arrived early.

Chapter 13

Erdoğan commended Wallace on his work again as they stood on line at the catering truck in front of the hospital. The line stretched to the corner but the man with the apron was efficient. Nearly everyone's order was ready before they stepped forward in line. He never forgot a customer, nor apparently their order. An orange hand flashed insistently from the corner, but Erdoğan ushered Wallace inside.

THURSDAY, DECEMBER 2, 2010

"Damn it, is that acute *lymphoblastic* leukemia or acute *lymphocytic* leukemia?" He could not believe the diagnosis. Hanni said it was an asthma attack, just a precautionary trip to the hospital.

"They've ruled everything else out. Her leukocyte counts are sky-high, and they're deformed. They don't function properly."

"But the gasping, the wheezing, wouldn't that relate to oxygen intake, to her lungs, to her red blood count? And what about the nosebleeds?" Wallace grasped at straws. Any explanation sounded better than cancer.

"I'm not a doctor, damn it. Do you think I want to hear this? Do you think Alya wants this? Stop interrogating me and get over here. We need you." "Here" was NYL North in East Harlem.

Wallace braced himself against the wall before answering. "I'm sorry, sweetie. I am really sorry. I'll be right over." He righted himself and reentered the conference room.

What were they discussing? Social media? Yes, that was it, and data streaming. Aside from productivity concerns – Who's working when everyone is on Facebook and YouTube? – usage was crushing their networks and exposing the foundation to an array of potential liabilities. This was important. Wallace was adamant about it. The issue had to be addressed.

"I'm sorry. I have to excuse myself. There's a crisis at the other hospital." He paused for a second, "a family crisis. You can fill me in later." He gathered his papers. One face registered concern. The others were indifferent. He addressed them when he reached the door. "I almost forgot. I need a computer-by-computer breakdown of the heaviest data streamers. I want to approach them discreetly about scaling back. They need to know we're monitoring them. Andrea, could you make sure someone takes charge of this?" Andrea nodded politely. He thanked her and excused himself once more.

"Yes, sire," grumbled Andrea after the door was safely shut. "Just how are we supposed to assemble that information? Self-reporting?"

Stuart didn't answer. Neither did anyone else. It was the easiest task in the world. Summarize the network and ISP logs. But why should he volunteer that information? He could rescue the mission when Andrea failed. The techies from North Campus were twits. Shit, they all were. "I hope everything's okay, Wally. I'd owe you if this wasn't so damn BORING. But fuck, I can still trade. The equipment is better than what we had at Dolus, I'm closer to the research, and … fuck yeah … no one's watching."

⁂

An inner voice mimicked the hematologist. "Apply chemo, resect spleen, irradiate body, reboot corpus with stem-cell transplant … pray." Wallace jotted notes to camouflage his trembling. Déjà vu. His father contracted Non-Hodgkin's lymphoma in 1997. The doctor's intonation was identical. He scribbled faster. Vincristin, Cytoxan, Ara-C, methotrexate, prednisone. *Was that his father's protocol? CHOP? No, Hyper-CVAD plus alternating cycles of methotrexate and Ara-C.* He couldn't believe he remembered. Wallace asked Dr. Kher to spell asparaginase and daunorubicin.

The doctor paused. Wallace pressed him about monoclonal antibodies, the closest science came to silver bullets.

"You mean Rituxan? It depends on the diagnosis. Your daughter could have T-cell leukemia, in which case it would be useless. If the histology is right, we'll include it in her frontline therapy. That's why she's here, so we can immuno-phenotype the disease more precisely." The doctor looked forty, perhaps forty-five. Hanni was subdued. Her eyelids were swollen, the mascara somehow intact.

"I'd like to keep your daughter here to complete the tests and begin the first cycle of chemotherapy Saturday or Sunday. We'll watch her for a couple days after that, but if she responds well, we'll send her home until the next cycle. She'll have to come in for blood tests and a couple subcutaneous injections, but they're just pin pricks, not painful at all."

Wallace knew the rest. Twenty-one days. Then she'd sit in a chair for hours, receiving infusions through a porta catheter – a receptor sewn into her chest for channeling chemicals directly to her heart. Or they'd use a Hickman, a hose-like contraption with leads dangling from her chest. It didn't matter. Either method was barbaric.

Hanni looked pale. He rested his hand on her shoulder. The shoulder quivered; so did his hand. He tried to disguise his unease.

"We'll manage … together," he mustered.

The rebuke was telepathic: "Don't start with your father. I don't give a damn whether he 'tolerated' the treatment, or even achieved remission. He died."

"He died because mom drove into an oncoming livestock trailer, not from some incurable disease."

"No, Wallace – the truth! She drove because your dad was too loopy from all the Kytril they gave him to prevent nausea. It was the disease. One way or another it got him."

The accident killed his parents instantly and set off an eleven-car pileup. Only the cattle emerged unhurt, but they were herded onto another truck and butchered five days later – Dad's gift to everyone for trying to defeat cancer.

Hanni stared silently at the floor. This time Wally's thoughts ventured from his mouth.

"Honey, I know it's hard, but our baby is NYL family, and NYL's the best cancer research hospital in the East, some say the country. The administrators know her by name. I'm sure even Dr. Erdoğan will check in on her." He wasn't convincing, even to himself. Hanni's depression was infectious. Or was it the coffee? His stomach had been knotting up for weeks, it was increasingly difficult to concentrate, and he was having trouble silencing the voices.

"Damn it, son." It was his father. "You're a Cornwallis – descended from British military aristocracy. A leader's blood courses through your veins. We named you George Corn Wallace for a reason."

"With all respect, Dad, the black Cornwallises never commanded anyone, just inherited the surnames of their masters."

Wallace felt his mother's hand gripping his shoulder. He remembered the sealed caskets of his brothers, so disemboweled there was nothing left to display. But *Life Magazine* memorialized Edward's moment – the instant a 130-millimeter Soviet shell shredded him into a thousand unidentifiable ribbons. The next week he was whole again, one of 253 black-and-white head shots festooning the magazine's weekly gallery of casualties. Edward visited Wallace in his sleep – sometimes in a thousand unidentifiable ribbons, sometimes in jeans. He brought his friends, grotesque, limbless GIs, and invited him to come out and play. "Cowboys and Indians, Wally, Cowboys and Indians!" Those were the good dreams. At least he recognized the voices.

"You're older now," his mother pleaded, "a big man. Don't let them menace you during the day." But he wasn't big. He was eleven. He swallowed the tablets and cowered in his room until the cacophony dimmed to a hum. Twice or thrice daily for twelve years, and then gradually silence. Peace. Today he was 54. A voice whispered, *"Happy birthday, Wally!"* but it was his own.

There was a protracted pause; the hematologist awaited a response. Wallace jolted himself into the present. "That's really encouraging: eighty percent cure rates. Thank you, doctor!" *Moron. You get better odds playing Russian roulette.* "And the pediatric staff seems so upbeat!" *A mask. They lose as many patients each week as they did 15 years ago.*

$90 billion: forty years' spending on cancer research and treatment by the National Cancer Institute. $2.2 billion: the collective annual budget of 260 nonprofit cancer research organizations – more than the US spent each year on AIDS, Alzheimer's disease, strokes and heart disease combined. Yet the hospital was still fighting cancer the way it did in 1995, in 1970. Wallace wanted to scream, to run as fast and far as his legs could carry him.

"Thank you, doctor. Our daughter is in great hands."

Chapter 14

"In good hands? Saçmalık. Horseshit!" Hanni remembered the crossing signals. They were flashing incoherently when she entered.

Hanni remained silent. She huddled on a stool, crumpled under the weight of the diagnosis. Wallace's reassurances mollified no one, not even himself. She felt the desperation of an animal trapped in a forest fire. Their words were harsh wind and dry timber. They fanned the flames that lapped at her hide and would soon devour her. Hanni tightened the grip on her stool, unable to blink, scarcely able to breathe. Dr. Kher and Wally droned on about  "Alya's protocol" but the words remained incoherent. Even their bodies were indistinct. It was her mother's words that rang with clarion sobriety. "This is how God repays sinners."

❧

Hanife Kaplan's mother was a tyrant – an illiterate, hijab-shrouded despot whose bearing vacillated between intense brooding anger, icy bitterness and righteous self-pity. The self-pity and bitterness were directed at her daughters, Hanni and Beril, only secondarily the domestic servants and outside world. The imam promised she would bear sons. But the birth of Hanni left her barren. Hanni somehow desecrated God in her mother's womb. The imam said so. Her mother could not forgive that.

Hanni's father called his wife the Shah of Batman, a thinly veiled reference to Mohammad Reza Shah, the second monarch of the House of Pahlavi, the last Shah of Iran – not incidentally a reference to Adam West or *DC Comics.*

Batman, site of the Batı Raman oil field, was a treeless city on the hot, dusty steppes of southeastern Turkey. It grew with the discovery of oil in the late 1940s from a village of 3,000 inhabitants into a boomtown of several hundred thousand laborers. Batı Raman was the epicenter of Turkish oil production – Asia Minor's answer to the Permian Basin. Its topography was hostile and barren, as hostile and barren as the actual Permian Basin in western Texas, or as Hanni's mother for that matter, but it bore Hanni's father great wealth. He eventually sold his foul, despoiled acreage and precious subterranean mineral rights and moved the family to Istanbul.

Like his namesake in Batı Raman, the Shah of Iran was also a tyrant, an especially ruthless one. He was overthrown during the Iranian Revolution in February 1979 by Shiite Islamists and the Ayatollah Khomeini, a still harsher and more implacable despot. Hanni was only five but remembered the events well. Batman was not far from the Iranian border. In fact, many of the oilfield engineers and workers were Iranian expatriates. Refugees flooded in by the thousands. The border was long and, in many places, unmarked. Mohammad Reza Shah Pahlavi spent the last seventeen months of his life in exile, a guest of President Anwar Sadat and the State of Egypt. He died July 27, 1980 of leukemia. Hanni's mother died three years later of … acute non-lymphocytic leukemia. President Sadat also died during that interval, assassinated by fundamentalist Muslims during a military review. Fundamentalists – yet another form of cancer.

Wallace and the hematologist were pathetic. They chatted with such seeming clear-headedness, but she knew better. It was nonsense. They knew nothing of terror, the terror that drove her small family to Istanbul. The air in Batman was acrid with the dark smoke of wellhead flares. The water stank and tasted of benzene. A lit match could ignite the kitchen tap. She and her friends scooped ochre-black clay from the caves and marshes along the Tigris and made imaginary castles. They gazed at the hills of Hasankeyf and saw only thick smog. Petroleum oozed from her father's pores. Leukemia was more common there than tuberculosis, and inexorably fatal. Medical studies in the United States confirmed what she already knew, what everyone in that God-forsaken wasteland knew for forty years: leukemia was environmental. It was God's vengeance against the wicked men and women who despoiled his planet.

Hanni dreaded this day since the day her mother died, since several of her friends died, except the next victim was supposed to be her, or Beril, not Alya. She remembered the article in *Cosmopolitan*. Children in the United States with leukemia were 5.4 times more likely than children without leukemia to have consumed water from wells in areas with a history of petrochemical contamination. They were six times more likely to develop leukemia if their fathers worked with benzene, alcohol, petrochemicals or other hydrocarbons prior to their conception. They were eleven times more likely if their pregnant mothers were exposed to pesticide sprays or foggers. And that was in places like Dover Township, New Jersey, where exposures were measured in parts per million. What were the statistics when toxins reached parts per thousand? Hanni's hometown of Batman swilled in pesticides and hydrocarbons. It was part of the town's DNA. And now it was part of her baby's. Wallace and Dr. Kher were salaklar, trottel, blithering idiots.

❦

Wallace reviewed Stuart's report. He wished Stuart had collaborated with Andrea. The gamesmanship was childish. He tried to concentrate on the report but worried about Alya.

"Dad," she asked, "will you and Mom stay together if I die?" Wallace stared at her in disbelief. "That would be a good legacy, wouldn't it? I mean my life would mean something."

Legacy! How had the word entered her vocabulary? Wallace pulled her close and cried secretly. "You are not going to die, honey. I promise. I won't let Mommy drive." Alya knew she was supposed to laugh but could feel her father choking back tears. Her father was frightened. She would have to comfort him, just as she comforted her mother. How would they survive without her?

"I know, Daddy, I know," she reassured him. "I mean just in case…"

❧

The IP address of the worst offender was vaguely familiar. His or her Internet utilization was immense, several gigabytes per day. The next few entries were also huge, but the rest of the list was unremarkable. These were employees who most likely watched reality shows or soap operas but seldom more than five hours per week. He could send gentle reminders to everyone on the list without even identifying who they were. He just needed to assign pop-up reminders to their IP address. If abuse persisted, he could increase the frequency of the pop-ups or, if necessary, identify recalcitrant users by name. He entered a purchase order for web filters. They would allow him to block instant messages and filter content by category, URL and file type. They were also effective firewalls.

❧

Hanni hovered over her child. A cold glare banished Wallace to the corner chair. The first course of chemotherapy was decidedly un-mundane. Wallace and the simpleton hematologist knew nothing. Alya's reaction to the Rituxan was severe. She was still in the green faux-leather recliner when it began. Rituximab was still pouring into her veins. She felt her lungs and bronchial airways constrict. Her breathing became irregular. The spasms became pronounced. She began gasping for air. Hanni and Wallace stood helplessly at her side as her face contorted and turned blue. The attending nurse clamped the tube dripping Rituxan and raised the drip rate for the anti-inflammatory corticosteroid. Another nurse rushed over with a bronchodilator and instructed Alya to inhale deeply. Disheveled old men and women fidgeted in their recliners, glancing about in alarm, each tethered to their

special blend of intravenous poison, each clutching a can of Ensure.

An unfamiliar doctor swept into the room, followed by an
equally unfamiliar team of interns. *Does anyone here even know the
patient?* He attached a bag of epinephrine to the IV pole and instructed a nurse to dose "the child" with 3 ML then repeat the
procedure ten minutes later if the situation did not improve. Epinephrine was just adrenaline, he explained, the hormone secreted to help prehistoric man fight or flee when threatened. It
would widen "the girl's" blood vessels and bronchial passages,
easing her ability to breathe. An intern could monitor her.

The doctor did not have time to excuse himself. "The girl"
clutched at her heart and stared up in terror. The doctor grabbed
Alya's wrist then placed a stethoscope against her chest. "Ventric-
ular fibrillation" was all Hanni could make out. An intern plucked
a defibrillator off the wall. Alya's irises rolled upward and disappeared into her skull. Her body jolted and then collapsed as 125
joules of electricity coursed into the upper right and lower left
quadrant of her chest. The doctor listened intently through his
stethoscope. The child was unconscious but breathed easier. He
called for a gurney to take her to intensive care.

⚝

"He's nosing around, monitoring our data."

"Let him. He'll never figure it out."

"But what if he yanks the cord? He's got this bug up his ass
about bandwidth; doctors can't get enough of *General Hospital*.
The best transfer scheme in the world won't matter if he yanks
the cord to free up bandwidth."

"Your kids ever play Wack-A-Mole?"

"And what makes you think he isn't one? It'd be just like the
Feds to plant one."

"Wally? Pretty sorry choice for a spy if you ask me. Besides,
he'll never figure it out. It's too innocuous, too good. If he blocks

the transmission, we'll just transmit from another server. There are thousands."

"But that's the problem. He's centralizing everything. He'll impose system-wide traffic controls if he has to. And then we're back to square one. Why'd you have to get someone from banking? We just needed a hotshot idea guy, someone to get the trustees off our back, not someone who can actually do stuff."

Silence.

"Accenture, KPMG, McKinsey, you had your pick. Instead, you listened with your dick."

"Enough! We control her, we control him. It's that simple. And now that his daughter's sick, we really control him. You do your job and I'll keep the data flowing. And if not, we'll play a different kind of Wack-A-Mole."

⌘

Dr. Kher described the reaction to Rituxan as "unfortunate." Asparaginase was no longer an option; the risks were too similar. Wallace wrote furiously in his notepad, trying to keep pace. The doctor mentioned daunorubicin – better tolerated but less effective. And the infusions could be elongated, with more premedication. Wallace's hand cramped. Why didn't Kher mention the other "mores" – more time in the chair, more apprehension, more dread of complications?

The complications arose next evening, thirty-six hours after the partially aborted infusion. It happened to lots of first-time Rituxan patients – blood poisoning. Alya's circulatory system began choking on the toxic detritus of dead and dying cancer cells. The kidneys couldn't keep pace with the buildup of uric acid. Dr. Kher called it lysis.

⌘

"I told the parents in advance she was high risk. Her leukocyte count was astronomical. Most of those cells were dysfunctional, and we both know Rituxan targets dysfunctional cells like a machete. It dispatched them so quickly and in such quantities that her blood literally oozed with their sour remains. Yes, Dr. Erdoğan, I understand. Yes, I know but I've got to get back. I'll update you later."

Dr. Kher pre-medicated Alya to inhibit uric acid production, but she evidently required a stronger dose or a different enzyme that degraded uric acid into more soluble substances that her kidneys could more easily excrete. Whatever. What mattered now was that the patient's creatinine levels were too high, and her kidneys were failing. A simple loop diuretic wasn't going to solve anything.

What to say? The mother was crumbling. He observed the frantic clenching and unclenching of her fingers, the pupil dilation, the labored breathing. *God, she's beautiful.*

The father nodded at his explanations. "Of course he did," the doctor reminded himself. "He works here. Anal geek; pop-up warnings and tutorials every time I turn on the computer. What on earth did she see in him?"

๛๏๛

Wallace mumbled words of encouragement. Lysis meant the chemotherapy was effective. Alya might get by with as few as three or four cycles, in contrast to his father's seven. The toll on her body, her heart muscle especially, would be lightened. Alya might even be cured by summer. He watched in dread as the staff connected her to a dialysis unit. Hanni just wept.

๛๏๛

Wallace compared Stuart's report to the network logs he downloaded from the server. The pop-ups seemed to be working. The casual offenders eased their usage. A victory, a small one, but one he needed. If only there was a way to measure its effect on productivity.

"That's bullshit, Wally."

Stuart could be blunt. "Patient volume rises and falls hour-to-hour, day-to-day, week-to-week. And it's not 100-fucking-percent predictable. Your daughter's hemodialysis is proof. They can't just say, 'Make an appointment and come back tomorrow.' So, they're intentionally overstaffed."

"Your point?" Wallace bristled at the mention of his daughter.

"All you've done is move standby staff from fucking around on YouTube to fucking around at solitaire or email or the water cooler. The only benefit to the hospital is reduced traffic on an overburdened network. How that translates into cost savings, productivity or patient care is anyone's guess, but shit, go ahead and boast about it in your report. It's not like this place has shareholders. And what am I anyway? Just a repurposed equity analyst with fifteen fucking years' experience."

Wallace sighed. "We're not done."

There were still several major bandwidth users. Two had migrated to other workstations: same bad behavior, different ISP location. He consulted a table of internal addresses. The new workstations were on the same local area network as the old ones. So he directed the network's web filter to intercept incoming streaming media. He or Stuart could lift the block if an administrator or physician protested; he was more concerned about sending the appropriate message.

The third user was problematic. The volume of data transfer was undiminished, greater in fact than in Stuart's report. He wondered whether the workstation was streaming video at all. If it were, a pop-up would have alerted the user he was monitored. That surely would have impeded abuse, or, as was the case with the other heavy users, motivated migration to less-protected PCs.

Wallace consulted the PC's backup log. The last successful backup was three weeks earlier. He constructed a "to do" list for when he returned from NYL North:

- Restore/inspect previous backup
- Mandatory backup on reboot (delay 2 weeks; need time to investigate)
- Monitor large file transfers from target workstation
- Inspect backups of 4 other workstations

His first guess was the hospital had become a file-sharing hub and repository for pirated videos. His second guess was a data breach. He'd fill Stuart in when he had more data.

❧❧

Hanni kneeled in the second row of pews, gazing up at the serene robed figure of Jesus of Nazareth, his white marble arm extended in welcome, his left hand pointed at his exposed heart. She fumbled with the string of beads. It lay untouched in the back of her wardrobe for thirteen years. She could not recall why she kept it. Wallace kidded her about it but secretly scoffed. She struggled to remember the appropriate words, words she swore long ago to forget.

She did not wish to be seen entering St. Patrick's Cathedral. Instead, she climbed the dark red steps of the Church of the Sacred Heart of Jesus on a quiet residential street in Hell's Kitchen. There were no pedestrians in view. Hanni counted five parishioners as she crept down the aisle. Two huddled in the back. The others slept among the pews, seemingly homeless. The red brick and terra cotta structure was one of the largest churches in Manhattan. It had high vaulted ceilings, tall white arches, large white copings, and wide white bands between the floors. Nothing florid, a staid example of late nineteenth century Romanesque architecture. It was designed to reassure parishioners of the sturdiness and permanence of the Catholic Church during the tumultuous closing years of the Victorian era. A gargantuan child might have erected it from Lego.

If the church's architecture signified permanence, its neighborhood signified change. The studied dignity of Clinton gave way during the early twentieth century to the harsh disharmony of Hell's Kitchen, a roiling stewpot of first-generation immigrant laborers – counted on by the diocese as an inexhaustible font of new parishioners. But the neighborhood had other plans. Investors scooped up properties during the 1980s and real estate values soared. Immigrant families were squeezed west and into the boroughs. Gentrification brought residents, but the young professionals who renovated and inhabited the walkups expressed little appetite for spiritual nourishment, or they sought it online and in the bars. Archbishop Dolan singled out the parish school for closing. It was the plight of so many churches in the region. Too many Christians abandoned their faith. Wallace and Hanni openly denounced it. And yet she was back, not for salvation, but for divine intervention on behalf of her child.

Hanni's mother was right. This was how God repaid sinners. But which God? Her family revered so many. Her ancient Kurdish ancestors were Yazidi. Their cultural heartland was Tur Abdin, the hilly southeastern corner of Asia Minor, a dusty, abandoned outpost on the Silk Road. Their religion was indigenous. Some still worshipped its deity, the one who created the world and entrusted it to the Seven Mysteries, a confederation of holy deputies, among them the Peacock Angel. But Arabs conquered the region in the seventh century, just as Alexander the Great conquered it a millennium earlier. The teachings of the "Black Book", *Mishefa Reş*, were outmanned by the teachers of the *Qur'an* and the Prophet Muhammad. Most of the Yazidi converted to Islam, as did her mother's ancestors, specifically to Alevism, a Kurdish-Islamic sect with mixed Shi'a, Sufi and Zoroastrian teachings. Her father's ancestors sampled everything else: Judaism, Sunni Islam, Orthodox Christianity, Catholicism, Zoroastrianism. The Silk Road connected the world to Tur Abdin and Tur Abdin to the world. There were so many religions to choose from. Hanni's father secretly declared himself agnostic. Who wouldn't be, he implored, given all the conflicting messages? Like many Kurds, he assumed a somewhat eclectic, moderate stance when conversation tilted toward religion.

There were only 30,000 Yazidi left in Turkey when her father moved the family to Instanbul. The trade routes beckoned for centuries. Some Yazidi sought fortune in those distant lands.

Others sought the amenities of modern society. But the majority sought refuge from ethnic violence. Like most Kurds, his grandfather renounced his Kurdish name and adopted a more palatable Turkish one, Kaplan. The grandson did the same by naming his daughter Hanife. He preferred Hêlîn but Hanife was less ambiguous. Turkey adopted a Surname Law in 1934 to improve the polyglot nation's sense of Turkishness. In so doing, it extinguished many tribal names, especially Kurdish ones. The tension between nationalism and ethnic identity festered as Hanni's father aged. Syria, Armenia, Russia, and Germany each now quartered larger Yazidi populations than his ancestral home in Asia Minor. The Diaspora covered the globe, dispersing as far as New York, in the form of Hanife *nee Hêlîn* Kaplan Wallace. There were fewer than five hundred Yazidi in Turkey when Alya fell ill. By then, nearly all the Yazidi had emigrated to greener or safer pastures, but their hydrocarbonated genes emigrated with them. It was God's retribution on their offspring.

Hanni braced herself for confession. She prayed that the Catholic god would be just and merciful. She did not believe her mother's "all-forgiving" Al-Ghaffur would get past the justice part. Hanni abandoned Salah, the practice of Islamic formal worship, when her mother died. It was much easier to practice agnosticism with her father and then Catholicism when it offered a path to higher education. Al-Ghaffur would demand justice for defecting, for worshipping another god. Justice would be her firstborn, her only borne. Afterward he might forgive her, but how would that help her daughter? If there was a god, Hanni wagered on the Christian one. She had not discarded him for a different god, just lost faith, as had so many of his followers. Surely he would see these were sins of the mother, not the daughter.

Hanni did not know where to begin. She struggled to recall the Seven Deadly Sins but confused them with the Ten Commandments. Surely there was a catechism for that. There were so many. She remembered her second tutor, the one hired after settling in Istanbul. She trembled. The first tutor, her governess, came with them from Batman. Formalized female education was still primitive in the eastern provinces, so a tutor was the only way Hanni and Beril could compensate. Hanni knew the governess slept with her father, but they were discreet. Her father hired the second tutor to foist his children off as Catholics, never mind the intended school was secular. "It's named *Saint* George. No arguments! Susmak! Silence!"

The second tutor believed in inculcating life skills, believed passionately. And Hanife was an invigorating case study. No good came from repulsing his advances. He outweighed her by eighty pounds and would accuse her openly of prostitution if she complained. Her shamed father would have to emigrate or kill her to reclaim his honor. Neither prospect appealed to her. No, the tutor's lessons were loathsome but no worse than those in the Bible. She carried the lessons with her to St. George's, but there her tutor was a priest from the nearby church, a step up the ecumenical ladder. Her father complimented her on her quick assimilation and academic success, which she openly attributed to cramming. He never inquired by whom.

The Catholic training was many years ago and secondary to the life training she carried into adulthood. She scarcely remembered the Lord's Prayer. She tried to enumerate crucial elements of her confession. She disbelieved God but would atone if he gave her a positive sign. Her christening documents were fabricated, as were the recommendations that gained her admittance to St. George's Austrian High School. She slept during religious instruction at church because the lecturer tested her earthly knowledge at night. She cheated on her husband because her bosses were insistent and well-connected – both of them. Their voices were more credible than hers. One held a sword over Hanni and Wallace's career; the other held a sword over their lives. Hell, they both did.

"So, that's it, God. My family destroyed the ancient heartland. They ripped out the pistachio groves that shaded the banks of the Tigris for three centuries and left behind an ugly moonscape of craters, interconnected pipelines and pumpjacks." She remembered the hulking stick horses that never slept. They bobbed their heads up and down week after week, year after year, sucking oil into a rusted labyrinth of metal straws that spewed into refineries and tankers along the Caspian Sea. Her family despoiled the river Tigris, the wellspring of the cradle of civilization. It was runoff from her land and others' that buried the basin in toxic sediment and raised salinity to oceanic levels. The profit financed her escape from tribal Turkey and seeded her well-accoutered life in America. She fingered the issue of *Cosmopolitan* in her handbag. Perhaps she should have left it at home.

Her thoughts returned to the confessional. Hanni defiled tradition and her family. She married outside the caste. She did not even marry a Kurd. To her father's consternation, she married a black man, someone who wasn't even human. Her father never met him, never dignified the marriage with his assent. She was forbidden to return home and communication was routed through her sister. Her daughter was a crime against nature.

A roommate flew from New York to Birmingham, Alabama to give Hanife away at the wedding. It was a quiet ceremony before a local pastor. If Mr. and Mrs. Charles Wallace were troubled by the family's absence, they didn't show it. Air fares were exorbitant. The truth was, they thought Hanni was the loveliest and worldliest person they ever met. Especially later, when her father-in-law was sick, Evelyn called and asked Hanni to recount stories about Istanbul and Hamburg and Paris, and about her short career as an interpreter. They asked her to speak to them in French, German and then Turkish, although they scarcely understood a word. They begged Hanni to show their "little boy" – the one who lived at home until thirty-seven except during college, and who dared not date a girl until she practically tackled him – that big, marvelous world. They did not mention the cold sweats, the recurring nightmares or mortal fear that he would lose his mother and father if he did not spend every waking moment with them. Instead, they transferred responsibility to Hanni and hung on her every word. Hanni embodied the airplane that Charles Junior never got to fly. She was Wally's savior after they were gone. He was so fragile. No, not fragile, special!

Evelyn looked up Hanni's surname, Kaplan, when she and Wally began dating. Genealogy was her pastime. That was how she endured hours on her feet at the public library, and why she initially volunteered. She shushed obstreperous children, helped them locate video cassettes of popular movies (books were passé), and researched tidbits about her extended family tree. The tree brought her places she and her husband couldn't otherwise visit. Its canopy spanned five continents and twelve countries. Each leaf was a relative, distant yet connected – an embryonic pen pal and future MySpace acquaintance. The tree swept Evelyn beyond Birmingham into the rich foliage of the world. At the base of a new family branch was a chaplain or priest. That's what Kaplan meant in German, Swedish, Yiddish, Czech, Polish, Hungarian and Norwegian. So declared *The Dictionary of Surnames*, a weighty, black tome that stood alongside *Encyclopedia Britannica* in the reference section. Evelyn lobbied for its purchase in 1989 and never regretted her decision. It was the most-handled reference in the library. Kaplan was a propitious match for her son … as propitious as being named after a gallant British commander.

Evelyn became the mother Hanni lost but never possessed. The Wallaces were proud their son married her, the son she presently betrayed. They esteemed her as God's gift from heaven. She did not tell them their son married a government-trained call girl or that Kaplan meant tiger in Turkish. Neither did she tell the son. Now she wept. She needed Wally's parents more than ever.

Hanni gathered her belongings and left the church. There was clarity in her mother's pronouncement, "This is how God repays sinners."

"No, mother." Hanni's body shook with anger. "God forsook us the day we were born, just as he forsook your granddaughter. He forced sin upon us and then goaded us into thinking it was the other way around. He is capricious and unjust and indulges rapists. He is the biggest con of them all. I will not prostrate myself before a fraud!" Hanni's rosary lay on the pew. So did her issue of *Cosmopolitan*. The homeless woman in the eighth pew slid forward to see if there was anything of value.

Chapter 15

Rain penetrated the yellow casing, sputtering as it burrowed deeper. The figure flickered, then plead, then shrieked, but all anyone heard was meaningless crackle. The hand returned briefly to wipe the tears.

WEDNESDAY, MARCH 22, 2011

"I'm frightened, too, sweetie. But Alya's a fighter. And her blood work is encouraging. There is a chance the next chemo cycle will be her last."

Hanni said nothing. Her baby was in the hospital after another harrowing emergency and the completion of chemotherapy just meant the beginning of another terrifying procedure.

"We should be pleased. She didn't need a splenectomy." Hanni said nothing.

"Look," said Wallace in exasperation, "How were you supposed to know she would self-infect?"

Hanni glared at Wallace. Her thoughts were murderous. "How dare you suggest I caused this! I was the model mother, the model host."

⁂

"I can't talk to him. I can't talk to anyone. They're beyin ölümü, brain dead."

She approached Susan. After all, she owed her an explanation, a better one than sending Melissa home in frightened mystery.

She recounted the events in her mind. Alya was mid-way through her third chemotherapy cycle. There was her old friend Rituxan – this time with extra premedication – plus an arsenal of other, less-discriminating weapons, each aimed at blasting cancerous cells into oblivion. Rituxan was the designated sharpshooter. The others were cluster bombs and artillery. Collateral damage was inevitable. Dr. Kher said so.

"The doctors said chemo would make her weary, maybe nauseous … and her hair would fall out," Hanni steamed. "They didn't say anything about this!" Susan remained motionless so she continued.

Alya's chemotherapy progressed in cycles. By the end of the first week, her blood counts were always low. The frontline agents purged millions of blood cells, bad and good, leaving her body defenseless. White counts dropped to zero, red counts became anemic and platelet counts were those of hemophilia. Because she received anti-nausea medication and steroids, she felt tolerable but was nevertheless highly vulnerable to infection. The "nadir" lasted three-to-five days. It was temporary because the body fought back after excreting the therapeutic toxins. Her bone marrow generated fresh blood stem cells, which in turn ripened in the bloodstream into red cells, white cells and platelets. Dr. Kher accelerated this recovery by injecting hormones subcutaneously: Neupogen to spur granulocytes; Epoetin alfa (EPO) for red blood cells; and thrombopoietic growth factor for platelets. Wally had written it down. He showed her the notes – so many times she tore up the notebook and threw it at him.

"I get it, you imbecile. You want to recharge Alya's circulatory system before injecting her with more poison. Satisfied?"

"Well, we rushed Alya from school to the hospital during the first cycle's nadir. She spent four days there with pneumonia. I should have told her, 'You need to spend a few more days at home, just to be safe.' But she missed her friends and she was afraid of falling behind. What followed was that damned hospital's fault, not mine. They should have known better."

"Alya began scratching her scalp and chest and arms. Hives cropped up everywhere – a thousand misshapen insect bites. Her breathing became uneven, forced. She was scratching furiously; said the itching was unendurable."

"'Allergic reaction to the antibiotic,' is all they said. They pumped her up with Benadryl and some steroid I can't remember. Turns out she's allergic to sulfa drugs, same as Wally. Duh, they have Wally's medical records! Couldn't they put two and two together? *'Stay away from Bactrim!'* Well, they found a substitute but Alya had burning in her palms and grittiness under her eyelids for weeks, longer than she had the pneumonia."

Susan reached forward and clasped Hanni's hands. Hanni continued.

"We kept her home during the second nadir, and she fared better, except she got excruciating bone pain from the Neupogen. The pain was as bad as giving birth but she's only nine, just nine! Dr. Kher said the hormone was more effective than intended. No shit! The marrow in her pelvis and femur churned out so many blood cells her bones felt like they were going to explode. They hospitalized her and had to sedate her with morphine."

"Alya. My baby. She swore then and there she would never have a baby, not even if she married a prince."

Hanni swore then and there she would kill herself when it was her turn for leukemia, but she kept that vow to herself. It was just a matter of time. God was a sick bastard but otherwise predictable. As predictable as Boss One and Boss Two. Kill the ones she loved. Make them suffer. Make her watch. Then kill her. Why give that unholy shit the pleasure? Alya's medicine cabinet was a fountain of poisonous elixirs. Hanni could snuff her own life in an hour. Let God practice sadism on someone else. Hanni turned back to Susan.

The latest episode arose during the play date.

"Melissa was so sweet. She showed up Sunday evening with a gift-wrapped DVD of the fourth *Twilight* movie, *Eclipse*. But you already know this. It was for a viewing party over the holidays, but Alya got sick and it kept getting postponed. I can't believe Melissa worked up the courage to knock on our door. She wanted the play date to be Alya's birthday."

Susan remembered.

Melissa included a skating medal with the DVD – a small gilt-bronze maple leaf that dangled from an inexpensive blue fabric ribbon. It bore the inscription "The Wollman Open" on the front and "Skating Club of New York" on the back. She won it earlier that day, but said Alya's program was better, that she deserved it. Alya could land an axel. Melissa's was two-footed. Susan remembered it vividly.

Hanni struggled to continue.

Most of the girls in the skating academy signed the giant birthday card – a composite of skating-related *Peanuts* strips that Melissa photographed when she visited the Charles M. Schulz Museum in Santa Rosa. Melissa described how Schulz built an adjacent rink for his children, Snoopy's Home Ice Arena, that she visited while Jack and Susan toured vineyards in Sonoma Valley.

Hanni knew Melissa invested months of training in the gilt-bronze trinket, a trinket every non-medaling skater deeply envied. In addition, Melissa spent hours laying out the card and collecting signatures. Bewilderment registered in Alya's eyes. Tears welled in Hanni's. Had she ever had such a friend, even in childhood? No. She had oversexed Catholic tutors. She excused herself from the girls, rushed to the kitchen, fumbled with a cigarette and sobbed.

She returned to Alya's bedroom forty minutes later. The girls sat side-by-side on the floor, staring up at Kristen Stewart and Robert Pattinson. Melissa wore Alya's wig. Alya wore the fiery red Ariel wig she bought at the Disney Store in Times Square when she was seven. They both wore clothes from Hanni's expensive wardrobe. They were perfectly normal preteens enrapt by an interspecies love story glorifying a teenage girl's suicidal obsession with a vampire. Life's truths could wait until later. Hanni sighed then asked them what they would like to eat. "Popcorn, please!" came the simultaneous reply. Hanni watched Kristen Stewart jump from a cliff, plunging to certain death in the churning waters below, or to yet another rendezvous with her undead heartthrob, Robert Pattinson. Hanni was unsure which. The plot was complicated. She could watch it later. Alya would explain.

Hanni returned fifteen minutes later with a large bowl of Orville Redenbacher. Strawberry smoothies followed. The movie ended and Melissa went home in her own clothes and hair. Thanks to Mrs. Wallace's lipstick and eye liner, Melissa resembled Boy George. Alya resembled RuPaul. Alya hugged her mother and said it was the best "after-birthday" party ever.

Cold shivers and violent shaking began around five-thirty. Alya's temperature rocketed to 104. Ninety minutes earlier, a partially popped kernel scratched her intestinal wall. She spent three days in the hospital with sepsis, a life-threatening bacterial infection of the bloodstream. She improved by the end of the second day, courtesy of high-dose vancomycin, but Dr. Kher said it was the closest Alya came to actually dying. Hanni was apoplectic. She nearly killed her baby.

Hanni rebuffed Melissa coldly when she asked the following day to see Alya. "I'm sorry, Susan. I'm afraid I took my frustration out on your daughter. Let's plan a play date, shall we? Without popcorn."

≈≈

The first two workstations were encrypted BitTorrent implementations. They acted as seed and peer sites for a vast electronic database of copyrighted music and film. Usage spanned multiple departments – doctors, nurses, administrators, paramedics, orderlies – and was accessible to users around the globe, provided they installed the workstations' distinctive BitTorrent implementation. Wallace reckoned there were tens of thousands of connected remote users. The peer-to-peer file-sharing network was nearly seven years old and had become many employees' *de facto* entertainment library. Wallace flew into a rage when he broached the topic with Andrea. The network was nominally within her charge.

"BitTorrent is not data streaming," Andrea protested. "It has nothing to do with progressive downloading. It exchanges data in encrypted non-contiguous pieces with dozens of peers, assembling what it receives *after* the transfer. Your policy talks only about *streaming* audio and *streaming* video."

"Do not lecture me about file sharing," Wallace thundered. "Distributing copyrighted material you do not own is illegal, and it is especially illegal over the Internet. My God, do you live in a cave? Do two hundred thousand lawsuits under the Digital Millennium Copyright Act mean anything to you? Or is that why you use the hospital's servers, so each of you can point to someone else and say, 'It wasn't me'?"

"I never *up*loaded a thing."

Wallace noted the omission but ploughed forth, "You ignored the problem, let it fester, and seem to know the underlying technology really well. The foundation has hundreds of millions of dollars of potential damages on its hands, possibly even criminal liability, and you're trying to downplay it, as if it's a harmless diversion."

"It *is* harmless. Most of the files are backups of movies and CDs the employees already own. They can produce the original copies."

"I'm sorry, Andrea. I am not drinking your Kool-Aid. The 'first sale' doctrine says you can resell CDs you own. It does not say you can lease, rent, license or distribute them. Your network is not a public library, nor is it a small restaurant or venue that can play music without paying ASCAP. The users are engaged in illegal file sharing, there is no way around that, and not just among themselves. This isn't a Darknet. It's a friggin' free-for-all. God knows how many viruses have been transferred into our servers from anonymous, outside peers."

Wallace wasn't through. "$750 to $30,000 per work per infringement: that's what ASCAP and United Artists are entitled to. They don't have to show lost sales. They don't have to show illegal intent. They just have to prove infringement. Judging from the network logs, there were somewhere around 2,000 infringements yesterday alone, presumably that many each day for the last three years, before which thank goodness we are protected by the statute of limitations. So that's 2,000 infringements times, what, 1100 days, or 2.2 million incidences – each entitled to a minimum $750 in statutory damages. The total is $1.6 billion, Andrea. If we use $30,000 fines instead, the total is $66 billion. Do you honestly believe the hospital can afford that?"

Andrea began to speak but Wallace interrupted. "Andrea, the less you say, the better. Delete all the files today. Track down each of the users in the hospital. Do it in person and do not use email. Stand beside them until they delete every mp3 and video on their workstation, even the ones they say are backups of purchased copies. Then make sure BitTorrent is uninstalled and defragment their hard drives. Merely clicking the Delete key is reversible. It is something they should do anyway; their machines will run faster. If they refuse, take down their names. They will be the first ones we turn over if we are sued. Stuart will work with you on redacting the backups."

Wallace paused before concluding. "This is important, Andrea. Do not delegate this, do not try to do this via email, and do not drop the ball. Delegate your other responsibilities. As long as no one has lodged a complaint, we can fix the problem. But the moment some lawyer says 'Boo,' there will be a litigation hold and we will have to preserve everything."

"I have an appointment at two-thirty with general counsel. He'll probably retain outside experts to conduct an investigation. That's standard practice in the financial services industry. Let's show him we've been proactive. Shall we?"

Andrea nodded and turned to leave. "Fucking blowhard," she muttered as she rounded the corner. "It's not like we're the only ones doing this. Megaupload has, what, fifty million downloads a day. We're not even rounding error." Andrea would do what the jerk insisted, but she sure as Hell would not play grand inquisitor, taking down names of the uncooperative. "Let the outside investigator earn his pay," she thought. She marched to the office of the first big user.

ॐॐ

"'No space in the transplant ward,' what does that mean?" Dr. Steiner's announcement confounded him.

"It just means there's a backlog, Mr. Wallace. Bed space will clear up in fourteen to sixteen days." Dr. Steiner tried to be courteous. Wallace approved nearly all her requisitions, even though he terminated her access to free movies. Steiner's husband was furious.

"Who ever heard of such a thing? The movie reeked. Why should we waste money on garbage? Hasn't he heard of sampling – sniffing before buying? Face it, Becky, you're being steamrolled by a bureaucrat. Who does he think he is, telling you what's right or wrong? Has he ever tried returning a DVD he didn't like? He's not even a doctor. I bet he's not even a lawyer."

Dr. Steiner fought back the impulse to reply, "Neither are you, dear," but knew Stanley was vicariously entitled to assert her brilliance as his own, contrary evidence notwithstanding. Dr. Steiner secretly adored the movie *Precious* and would gladly have bought the DVD, were it not for Stanley's derisive commentary about the "porker" on the cover. And yes, they did have money to waste on garbage. She earned $486,000 in 2009 – less than what her male colleagues made, but enough to support Stanley's on-and-off career as a squash pro and insurance agent. She wondered how much money the actress Gabourey Sidibe made as receptionist at the Fresh Air Fund before she debuted in *Precious* and earned her invitation to the Oscars. Sidibe was born in Bedford-Stuyvesant and grew up in Harlem. Her father was a Senegalese cab driver. Dr. Steiner wondered how many actresses answered phones and bused tables or starved while her husband fretted about stretching *their* $508,000. Stanley was easier to look at than her first husband and a lot younger but was undeniably dim. Why was that always the case with second husbands?

"That's a long time without chemotherapy," Wallace demurred. "What if the cancer comes back? We've worked so hard to bring it into remission." He tried to hide his consternation.

"We haven't performed PCR, but her blood enzymes are clean. Dr. Kher and I will play it by ear. If we detect cancerous cell development, we'll give your daughter another course of Rituxan. That should tide her over and not interfere with the stem cell transplant. Your daughter will be fine, really she will. Okay?" Wallace nodded reluctantly then led his wife to the door.

"It will be all right, sweetie. Think of it as a vacation for our baby — nothing to worry about for two weeks." Hanni nodded silently and stepped into the taxi.

∂∞∂

"George, don't you think you're over-reacting? We're a hospital, not a bank. Disney is not going to sue us for damages. It would not be in their best interest. Can you imagine the headlines? 'Disney bleeds life from nation's largest not-for-profit research hospital.' 'Disney tells displaced patients to wish upon a star.'" The joke made Hotchkiss chuckle. "Copyright cases are matters of public record, George. The press would be all over them. They would paint them as greedy, patient-hating bastards. If the studios are irate, they'll send us a take-down notice, not a process server."

The general counsel had a point. Still, Wallace was disconcerted. He was not sure whether it was because Hotchkiss thought so little of the problem or thought so little of him. "Why is he still calling me George? He knows I can't stand it."

Hotchkiss tried a different angle. "Look, George, you did the right thing. You nipped the problem in the bud. We'll sleep better knowing we run a tight ship, but that doesn't call for an outside investigation. We're a private foundation. We don't have Congress or public stockholders or the SEC up our ass. At some point, you need to think outside that box you came from. Your paranoia is driving everyone crazy."

Hotchkiss regretted the comment about paranoia. Those were Andrea Lyden's words, not his. Andrea barged into his office whenever she received marching orders from her new boss. Hotchkiss did not know what to do about her. She could be so pliant and nice but then so touchy. "She's worse than my wife," he conceded, "but a lot younger and light years more … more inventive." Why were the frisky ones so complicated?

Outside the box. Wallace nodded assent. He would be more permissive and accommodating than he already was. The organization was fortified on the outside by a thin porous membrane and on the inside by warring egos. It was as defenseless as his daughter's immunosuppressed body, but that was their general counsel's decision. He recorded it on his Dictaphone just to be sure. Wallace admitted to himself this was neurotic. Three hundred thousand malware assaults daily did that to you. Wallace rose to leave. "Thank you, Sanford." Wallace knew Hotchkiss preferred Sandy. "I should have taken my lithium this morning, but it gives me gas." Wallace smiled politely then pulled the door shut behind him, making a note to quarantine his medical record in case Hotchkiss became curious. He made another note to research whether lithium tablets stimulated gas. The joke made Wallace chuckle, but only slightly. He hadn't intended to be sarcastic. And why had he screamed at Andrea Lyden? That wasn't his nature. His mother glared at him sternly.

"I'm sorry. We can't admit her. We can reschedule her transplant when she's clean."

"But she only has a mild fever – 99½, 100 tops. She says she feels fine."

"I'm sorry, Mr. Wallace. Your daughter has a vanco-resistant staph infection. She cannot remain in the transplant ward. The patients here have no natural immune system. And there's no point keeping her isolated in a regular hospital room. She is well enough to recuperate at home and will be a lot more comfortable."

Wallace knew it was silly to argue with Dr. Steiner. She was right. But he was discouraged. The family took months to psych itself up for the procedure, for the three-to-four weeks they would be parted. Alya was drained. Hanni was terrified. They wanted the treatment to be over.

"It's not uncommon for a mediport to become infected because of prolonged non-use," Dr. Steiner explained. "It's just uncommon for the infection to be so highly drug resistant. Dr. Kher has your daughter on three powerful antibiotics. She should feel better in a couple days, but she must finish the full two-week course before she can return. It's crucial we prevent the staph infection from mutating further. We don't have any other antibiotics we can give her."

Wallace thanked Dr. Steiner for taking the time to explain everything and apologized for coming across as "prickly." These were emotionally trying times. He reached into his coat pocket and handed Dr. Steiner a shrink-wrapped DVD. "Your husband took me down a couple notches in an email. I guess my address wasn't hard to find. In any case, I'm really sorry. I've pissed off everyone. It's taken way too long for me to figure out this isn't a bank. Accept this as a peace offering. Please. I hope it wins Best Picture."

Rebecca Steiner accepted the DVD in consternation. "What in God's name did Stanley do?" She fumbled with the DVD to see the front. The actress Gabourey Sidibe wore an open black jacket and gray sweat pants and strode defiantly toward the camera. The watermark of a crown and butterfly wings framed her. The title in lowercase was *precious*. Wallace guided Hanni and Alya toward the door before Dr. Steiner could react. She dropped into her chair and gripped the package with both hands. They trembled uncontrollably and she blinked furiously to flush back the tears. She would have given everything at that moment to trade places with Mrs. Hanife Kaplan Wallace.

❧

The first set of backup tapes was mystifying. There were some Word documents, spreadsheets, mp3s, a couple videos, not much else – three gigabytes on a five-terabyte hard drive. But the drive registered full. He visited the actual computer after hours and inspected the unformatted partition, the supposedly unused portion of the disk. Erased data? There were thousands of scientific papers, progress reports and data – not encoded, just on an "unformatted" partition and therefore invisible to backup. And to Windows Explorer. Curious.

But it was nothing. The reports weren't so much patient information as scanned copies of scientific research, most of it dated. Plus some out-of-place videos. Most of them looked amateurish and erotic – grainy. They shouldn't have been on hospital workstations, but they weren't kiddie porn either. Nothing of interest to film studios or the authorities. But the bandwidth usage flummoxed him, kept him focused, quieted the voices.

❧

"It's his job, Sandy. Play along. He'll eventually reformat the drive and move on. By then we'll be done."

Hotchkiss wasn't mollified but said nothing. The new CTO made him uneasy. It was so much easier when IT reported to him. Fourteen departments – so balkanized he could run an online casino and no one would have noticed. But Guri had to ass-kiss the trustees, demonstrate NYL was as state-of-the-art as NYU, as if NYU had any fucking idea what it was doing. And then hire a real engineer instead of an ideas guy, a management consultant? What the fuck was Guri thinking?

"Yeah, Guri, it's his job. It's our necks."

Chapter 16

The rain abated but the figure still wavered. A hand reached forward midst the remnant crackle and brushed it aside, but the walkman's hesitation was infectious. The hand didn't flash; it dimmed — slowly, inexorably — it just dimmed.

THURSDAY, MAY 5, 2011

Alya tried to swallow the membrane and nearly gagged. Her gums burned and she could not chew. She slurped the membrane back again and felt it slither down her throat to her stomach. Another membrane sloughed free. One by one, her mucous membranes molted, delaminated from her oral cavity then sloshed about in her saliva. It was painful to swallow and hard not to gag. Layers clung to the interstices between her teeth and she fum-

bled with her tongue to dislodge them. Skin sloughed off her tongue as well. The more she worked it free, the more other layers followed, the closer she came to gagging. The consistency reminded Alya of steamed okra. She told her mother not to serve it but who could she talk to about her dissolving gums. She pulled a membrane from her mouth and kept pulling. She choked as the last bits cleared her throat and slipped past her teeth. There wasn't room in the cup. It spilled over the side and the loose end slipped to the floor, drawing with it what she regurgitated into the cup. It lay in a puddle of clear, pinkish goo beside her bed. She did not realize until then that she sloughed more than her mouth and gum lining. The lining of her esophagus molted as well. She swallowed the saliva accumulating in the back of her mouth and realized it was just another layer of membrane. She felt it slide partway back her throat and get stuck, lodged like a warm slippery noodle above her larynx. "There must be thousands," she moaned as she pulled it forward. She regretted making jokes about the ray gun.

Total body irradiation. Alya remembered donning a small protective vest then standing at attention in front of a metal box for twenty minutes. It was cold in the room and she had to pee. She thought the box was a giant washer/dryer. It didn't look high-tech at all. The radiologist said it was a ray gun. Alya thought he was lying. It did not even look like a radio. What did a hospital have to do with radiology anyway? Didn't that department belong in a broadcasting booth? She asked the technician whether he was a talk radiologist or a jazz radiologist like the one her father listened to. The man seemed puzzled and stepped inside the other room. He spoke to her through a microphone but did not answer her question. "So, you *do* have a broadcast booth!" she shouted. She lowered her pitch to a baritone and intoned, "Testing, testing, one two three. Can you hear me? Are we live?" The voice from the booth reminded her to keep still.

Her parents were so worried. She told them afterward it was nothing, boring, and that the hospital had a long way to go if it wanted to be in show biz. The radiation was no worse than the super-duper chemotherapy they started with. The bags weren't any bigger, and they didn't run any longer than the previous chemotherapy sessions. They just did four days in a row instead of spacing them out in three-week intervals. Alya was not as chipper after the second day of irradiation. She was morose.

Wallace and Hanni sat at Alya's side, gazing with concern at the large puddle of clear goo at their feet. A pint of blood hung on the IV. They banked twelve pints before she entered the hospital. Two came from Wallace and Hanni, two from their neighbors in 8B, the rest from Wallace's friends at his previous employer. Only one came from anyone at the hospital. The donor was Dr. Gürhan Erdoğan, their champion and benefactor. Just two of the bags matched Alya's blood type, B-positive, but the bags were exchanged with the bags for other transplant patients. That was standard practice. The six days of intensified chemotherapy and radiation had two objectives: (1) exterminate any vestige of the disease; and (2) obliterate Alya's circulatory system – its marrow, its blood cells, its platelets so it could be rebooted with a fresh, uninfected copy. For the next two weeks, she would rely exclusively on donated blood to fulfill her immune and circulatory system needs. A nurse entered the room and hung a half-liter bottle of chalky white sludge on the IV pole.

"That's dinner. Same as breakfast, I'm afraid. How's our little princess doing?"

The little princess answered for her parents. "Tell the talk radiologist I'm using the radio booth next time. He can stand outside at attention."

The nurse furrowed her brow inquisitively. "I need to check her blood pressure and then I'll leave you three alone."

Wallace marveled there was blood pressure at all, then realized there remained plasma, irrespective of blood cells, and that Dr. Erdoğan's blood coursed through her veins. If that did not cause pressure, he couldn't imagine what would. Their little princess spoke again. "I know it's not milk. But do you think you could add some food coloring. Like chocolate milk or strawberry? Or would that make me pink?"

Hanni wiped her eyes then thrust her arms around her baby. She could not embrace her. The fluids were infused through the portocatheter in her chest. The bed was an ugly tangle of tubes. Wallace seemed to puzzle through the answer to Alya's question. The nurse smiled broadly. Their little princess would be just fine.

Hanni ripped off the surgeon's mask and hair net then struggled out of her gown. "Can't you see she's in agony?" she demanded.

"Yes, sweetie, but…"

"But what?" snapped Hanni. "No one said we had to approve the stem cell transplant. It was optional, remember?"

Wallace glanced about uncomfortably. He lowered his voice to a conspiratorial whisper. "Dr. Kher said it was advisable. So did Dr. Erdoğan."

"Dr. Kher, Dr. Kher. Don't even get me started with your precious Dr. Erdoğan." She began quietly but gave up the charade. "Dr. Kher wasn't around to resuscitate Alya from the Rituxan or to rescue her from sepsis. He has no idea who he's talking about. Alya's just a statistic. He doesn't even put on his glasses when he reads her chart. Why the fuck does he dangle a pair of glasses from his neck if he doesn't use them? Don't you think that's a wee bit peculiar?"

A nurse nudged past. She glanced down awkwardly then scurried along the corridor.

Wallace admitted it was peculiar but maintained the transplant was the best course of therapy. "Six weeks of remission is nothing, Hanni. The disease could come roaring back. That's why they do the transplants. The chemo isn't necessarily enough. This is so Alya never has to look back, so she can live the rest of her life with confidence. Eight out of ten, honey, that's the cure rate for her regimen. She's made it this far, so she's probably doubled her odds."

Wallace moved her from the doorway. She was blocking a man and his walker. He was frail, decrepit actually. His eyes were sunken deep in large brow-less sockets. He wore a New York Giants ski cap low over his ears. The gown draped loosely from his shoulders, exposing his bony clavicle and flaccid folds in his pale splotchy skin. His cheeks were hollow, a post-apocalyptic study by Edvard Munch. A relative, his daughter perhaps, followed somberly with the IV pole. Plastic tubing scraped along the floor, entangling itself in the processional. The woman placed her hands to her cheeks and looked ready to scream, but then dropped them to her side and shuffled on.

"You're wrong. She's withering before our eyes. Just look at her. Why am I the only one who sees this?" Wallace tried to hug her but she thrust him away. "I don't need your kindness. I need my baby." Her sobs came in convulsive waves. A nurse kept her distance, waiting for the right moment to skitter by.

Wallace tried a different approach. "Look, this is the worst stage. There is practically zero risk of rejection once they re-inject the stem cells. It's autologous. They're her *own* cells."

The transplant for Wallace's father was homologous, not autologous. The donor was unrelated and lived in Baltimore. He registered with the National Marrow Donor Program six years earlier when his brother battled another form of lymphoma. Charles Wallace Jr. was lucky to find him. Charles had no siblings and his son's HLA protein markers ("human leukocyte antigens") were incompatible. So were his wife's. Remarkably, the donor matched on all six markers. Alya, like most patients, did not find a match. The pool of half black, half Kurdish donors was rather small, smaller than a droplet. Even if she found a prospective donor, he or she could have declined. Most donors sign up to help a relative, not a stranger, especially after learning the mechanics of the procedure. It was considerably more time-consuming and uncomfortable than donating a pint of blood.

Wallace's father thought he won the lottery when they found a willing donor. But it was a mixed blessing. There's no such thing as a perfect match, except among identical twins. The body still rejected implanted stem cells in the absence of compensating medication to block the immune system. This was called graft-versus-host disease and was often fatal, exactly what the oncologist counted on. He called it "immunosuppressant prophylaxis." Wallace found it profoundly ironic. The disease was a failure of the immune system, so the antidote was to annihilate it entirely, then hope another's immune system could take root and flourish in his father's body. The first bone marrow transplants took place fifty years prior but they still seemed like science fiction. Wallace's father fought rejection for months. He was on methotrexate and cyclosporine when his wife ploughed their Rambler into a cattle car, and probably would have required a glucocorticoid for life. Wallace was secretly glad Alya could not find a match. He wanted her to lead a normal life. The nurse saw her chance and bustled past.

"That's exactly why this torture is bullshit. It's not like they're cleaning her cells before injecting them. I distinctly recall your precious Dr. Kher saying, 'No, Mr. Wallace, this institution does not believe in purging. It weeds out too many healthy cells and is not foolproof in weeding out bad ones.' So he put her on a gurney for four hours and pumped her blood through a centrifuge. I don't see how the bag of cells they harvested is any cleaner than the ones they just killed. All they've proven is that little girls can't hold their urine for four hours. She peed all over the table and was an emotional wreck."

Wallace stared at his feet, fidgeting. His imbecility was exasperating. They should have ceased treatment after the chemotherapy. The six-week delay was God's sign – first the wait list for bed space then the staph infection. Hanni realized she'd been wrong. God was benevolent after all. His message could not have been more obvious. "You've suffered enough to appreciate my power. Now appreciate my benevolence and go home." Why couldn't Wallace and those imbecilic doctors see it?

Hanni knew the answer. The doctors were corrupt, greedy. The esteemed Gürhan Erdoğan was a bastard. He didn't suffer at all. Only the women he claimed as playthings suffered. The doctors were snakes, all of them, wrapping their coils around anyone they could ensnare. Hanni wished Wallace had remained at the bank. Then Alya would be at Memorial Sloan-Kettering instead of here, anywhere but here.

Wallace gave up. "Look, Hanni. It's water under the bridge. Her circulatory system is at this very moment in a syringe in a hospital refrigerator. Dr. Kher is going to re-inject it on Saturday. We have to continue treatment, or she dies. Okay?"

Hanni glared at him. "Water under the bridge!" she thought. "My baby is *not* water under the bridge."

☞◌☜

Dr. Rajit Kher admired Hanife Kaplan Wallace. He fantasized about her intensely. Beauty-wise, she was on a pedestal with Sophia Loren and Salma Hayek. Personality-wise, Kher wasn't yet sure. Sarah Palin?

Gury Erdoğan and she were having an affair. Kher smelt it. Erdoğan had a knack with attractive women – so charming, so rich. His cronies hung around for the crumbs. And Kher hung around the cooler.

The Chief Administrative Officer was the worst. Hotchkiss gloated for weeks about Andrea Lyden (she was no Salma Hayek!), confiding between sips that she was "high maintenance – a real pain in the wazoo when she wanted something but wazoo plenty when she did not."

"Thank you for sharing," thought Kher. "I'm so glad I became your confidante."

Kher found Hotchkiss crude, the opposite of Erdoğan's suave but somehow equally repulsive mien. He disliked all Erdoğan's cronies. There was something about them that was not quite right, not just cheating on their wives. "Are all 'happily married men' like this?"

Kher was unmarried. He never had time for dating, for cultivating relationships. He worked. When had he truly slept? Most nights were a succession of impromptu naps, interrupted by late-night rounds and emergencies. Even when there were no emergencies, he slept fitfully. Emergencies crowded his dreams. He shuddered at the previous one. Hanife rode astride a camel, or was it an elephant? Her face was draped by a veil. Her body undulated with the motion of her transport. The sun seared his eyes, a blinding white fireball that blotted out everything except the rider. Soft dunes shimmered and shifted beneath her. The sand leapt up and swallowed the camel. Its rider tumbled free and rolled to his feet. But he wasn't standing. He was on a gurney in a loose-fitting gown tethered to an IV pole by plastic tubes. The goddess smiled down at him as she wheeled him into the operating room. She pulled her veil tighter as the nurses and assistants adjusted their masks. She bent down, lifted the veil, then kissed him longingly before shoving a scalpel deep into his chest. Kher woke in a violent sweat.

No, the hematologist had no illusions about bedding Hanife Wallace. She was indisputably gorgeous, but her husband Wally was his colleague and the only corporate officer he did not detest. He thought about saving their daughter night and day. It was his sworn duty, if not to his profession, to his wife – Wally's wife. Dr. Kher could recite the daughter's charts by heart. He memorized them so he wouldn't have to wear glasses; he did not want Mrs. Wallace to regard him as "Owl Eyes." Kher admitted he was vain, hopelessly lonesome and vain.

Wallace steadied himself, sipped his coffee. When had he truly slept? His evenings had become a succession of impromptu naps, interrupted by late-night harangues about Alya's treatment and genuine treatment-related emergencies. Even without interruption, he slept fitfully. His brothers were back, their unnamed platoon-mates were back, his father was back. And so were the voices. Even during the day. Even during this meeting.

"It makes no sense, Stuart. Why would so many scientific documents be flowing in and out of the same IP address? And from the executive offices? When was the last time any of them picked up a scalpel?" Stuart was the only capable troubleshooter on his team. Where did Hotchkiss dig up the others? Accenture? Wallace felt the coffee in his stomach churn.

"It's an enormous library. Look, this file is from *Lancet*. This one is from the *New England Journal of Medicine*. Then there's the

Journal of Clinical Oncology and the *Clinical Journal of Oncology Nursing*." Stuart could also have said, "Look, this file is inner-genital-fetish pornography, and this one is a recording of heavy breathing," but those files comprised a distinct minority. He and Wallace stumbled upon the world's largest trove of medical articles and data without any obvious unifying theme. "Shit, maybe you should just ask around the executive offices. It could be the communal compost heap for articles and reports that doctors send them."

"Agreed, but..." Wallace felt nausea, dizziness. He suppressed the urge to vomit. The bouts had become routine, just as they had during childhood. "Concentrate," the voices entreated him. For once he agreed.

The network usage perplexed him. "If this is just a communal inbox, why is there so much traffic, and why is it so tightly secured? This has to be indexed somehow. There are articles flying in and out every second. Someone somewhere is reading them and refreshing them, even if it's just a Google bot."

Wallace opened a random document on his screen: "Congenital Bronchial Atresia Associated With Spontaneous Pneumothorax," by Kotaro Kameyama, Norihito Okumura, Yujiro Kokado, Kentaro Miyoshi, Tomoaki Matsuoka, and Tatsuo Nakagawa, *Journal of Thoracic Surgery*, 2006; 82:1497-1499. Figure one was a chest x-ray of a spontaneous pneumothorax. The article described a 36-year-old woman and her treatment. The three pages of text and exhibits were precisely what the title described. He opened another file: different journal, same conclusion.

"Curious," thought Wallace. "Curious," echoed the choir. He googled *Journal of Thoracic Surgery* and was guided to the homepage of *The Annals of Thoracic Surgery*. It was a comprehensive electronic archive of articles dating back to 1965 for the Society of Thoracic Surgeons. All the articles were free. He verified the article by Dr. Kameyama, *et al* was listed. "Why would someone go to the trouble of scanning and saving pages from a journal when they could search and access an electronic version for free?" Stuart did not have an answer. "Why?" repeated the choir.

Wallace reexamined the scanned version of the article, enlarging it 20 times. The answer was scattered in barely visible dots across each page. He checked another file, filtering it through a blue channel, then a yellow one. They were there too. "They're bar-coded!" he exclaimed. Stuart leaned over to see for himself. "Free rounds for everyone," exclaimed Charlie Cube. "It's not that kind of bar, son," responded his father.

"That's horseshit, Wally, they're just tracking dots."

"Tracking bots," the assembly murmured.

Tracking dots were microscopic water marks that laser and inkjet printers included on printouts to assure federal authorities they could not be used anonymously for forgery or counterfeiting currency. The water marks included each printer's encoded serial number and a time stamp. "The articles could have been scanned from computer printouts rather than directly from a journal."

Wallace persisted. "All the printers I've run across use yellow dots on white backgrounds. These are multi-colored. What printer manufacturer does that?"

No answer.

"Let's open the really big files. I'm looking for email archives."

Stuart looked at him incredulously.

"This is a litigation database. It arose from a motion for discovery."

"What the fuck, Wally? I need whole notes. Whole notes."

Wallace spoke slowly. "Banks get sued all the time by stockholders, debtors, counterparties, you name it. Hospitals do, too – for example, by disgruntled former employees – only you don't see the files because HR networks aren't your department. Once a complaint is filed, each party subpoenas the other for documents. They search for smoking guns – *'Guns?' inquired the troops* – incriminating evidence that will prove their case or discredit the other side. The bar codes are how legal teams keep track of the millions of documents that arise in electronic discovery. We once used Bates stamps. Remember those?" Stuart shook his head. The soldiers shrugged. "Self-inking numerical stamps that increment by one each time you press down on a sheet of paper. They're great as long as you have only thirty thousand pages of documents and an army of paralegals to index them – *'Army,' they intoned* – but with e-discovery we're talking about millions and millions of pages. Bar codes are the only way to keep track."

Stuart interrupted. "So you think this is some fucking database Hotchkiss arranged for his legal team and outside counsel. And the data is flying back and forth because they're busy running it through electronic algorithms to sniff out nefarious words and phrases, or to make duplicate copies for co-counsel and the other side."

"Precisely." Stuart was quick.

"You're an idiot, Wally. If it was a high-tech law firm – and that's a fucking oxymoron, you know that, right? – they'd use conventional bar-code technology on the bottom corner of each page. They wouldn't try to conceal it."

"But what if there's super-sensitive information – information the lawyers don't want subject to discovery, yet need to analyze?"

"A smoking gun?" *"Guns again!"* "You think someone's email database, a PST outlook file, is somehow encoded among these files?"

"Several of them. Look, email databases contain really private and personal information. We're not the only ones who can access this server. I sure as hell wouldn't want someone opening my Outlook folders. That's why we use really secure passwords." Stuart nodded but said nothing. His password was qwerty456, the second row of keys when he pressed NUM lock. Besides, both he and Wallace knew there was a back door to Outlook. Wallace taught him how to open it.

"Sure thing, Wally. But I'm the big-pharma research analyst, remember? I don't think this has anything to do with lawyers. I'm betting on simpler shit – trade secrets. Someone's selling this hospital's research ... or buying it. Wally, are you listening?"

The voices pummeled Wally on all sides. But they were suddenly lawyers. Dozens of them, all in perfectly accoutered pirate suits. When did this lawsuit arise? Did he violate a litigation hold when he ordered the destruction of all those audio and video files? Was he guilty of spoliation – tampering with evidence? The voices were unanimous, *"Hotchkiss!"*

"Huh? Oh, I'm sorry, Stuart. I need to talk to legal. We probably shouldn't be leafing through attorney work product."

"Uh, sure Wally, but let's keep this secret, just in case I'm right. Okay?" Wally fumbled his way out without responding. Stuart shook his head and returned his attention to the screen. He'd be messed up too if his daughter was in NYL's care.

∂∼∾

The injection of harvested stem cells was uneventful. The initial indication was they migrated toward the larger bones and were engrafting themselves deep in their interior. In time, they would reproduce the patient's depleted circulatory and immune system.

Dr. Steiner cast a sidelong glance at Mrs. Wallace's shoes. The smock covered her dress, but the shoes shone plainly. They were beautiful shoes – beige crocodile sling pumps with dark tortoise points, straps and three-inch heels. Dr. Steiner bought nice shoes too. But they made her feel ungainly. She resigned herself to nondescript flats. Mrs. Wallace looked like a desert queen. Dr. Steiner felt like the desert itself. She wished she knew Mrs. Wallace after her divorce. She could have learned so much. Then she could have found a man like George Wallace instead of her Ken-doll husband, a husband who was permanently expelled from the New York Athletic Club for brawling. Becky sighed. It was too late now. The Midtown North Precinct released him into her custody. She paid his legal fees but was unprepared to pay alimony. The NYAC was his most consistent source of income. "For better or for worse," she sighed.

Hanni acknowledged Dr. Steiner's presence with a thin smile then looked downward. Both she and Alya were subdued. Several days had passed since the trauma of exuviation. Alya's gums, mouth and throat were swollen and tender, but the incessant molting was over. She glanced up at the half-liter bottle of nutritious, intravenous white gruel. No, they could not infuse her with chocolate or strawberry. But soon she could use a straw. Then they could feed her milkshakes. The nurse displayed a can of Ensure, and said it came in five delicious flavors: homemade vanilla; butter pecan; creamy milk chocolate; coffee latte; and strawberries and cream. She said she would drink one with her except that she wanted to lose weight. Alya nodded, unconvinced about the flavor, not about the nurse's weight. The old men and women drank Ensure during chemotherapy. They drank it constantly, smiling wanly at her as she sank into her own green recliner to concentrate on her Nintendo DS. They never wiped their lips heartily with their sleeves after finishing a can of Ensure, not the way her dad did after a stein at P.J. Carney's. The milkshakes weren't even cold.

"Oh, excuse me," apologized Dr. Steiner. She backed into Dr. Kher as she was exiting. "Miss Wallace's tests are good, and she looks terrific. She'll be back on the ice in no time." Miss Wallace didn't feel terrific, and knew ice in June was expensive, but she understood Dr. Steiner's confusion. Dr. Steiner spent the entire exam gazing at her mother. What she really meant to say was, "*Mrs.* Wallace looks terrific."

Dr. Kher stared at her mother too, except he was furtive. He did it when no one else was watching, no one but Alya, that is. Alya was always watching. Her eyes were the only sensation she still possessed. She could not eat. She could not smell. Her hearing was damp and muted. The only things she felt were dull and achy. But images still blazed with clarity. She knew Dr. Steiner would be embarrassed if she caught her watching, but Dr. Kher would be mortified. Her throat hurt too much to giggle. Dr. Kher tried to look dignified and in control but was hopelessly stilted. Even his casual poses were contrived. She imagined her skating coach barking out instructions. "Roll your shoulders back. Tuck your butt in. Keep your head in alignment with your spine. You're strutting around like Groucho Marx. I did not choreograph a Keystone Cops comedy!" A tear rolled down Alya's cheek. She missed being yelled at by her coach. She missed the bitter wind against her face and the dizzy sensation after coming out of a spin. She missed her friends at the rink. She missed her friends at school. She even missed her teachers. Most of all, she missed her room on Central Park South, the only home she knew. She dreamt once of distant adventures, but they were banal, superficial yearnings, like Dr. Kher's fixation on her mother. Alya wanted desperately to go home, where she could play with her dolls and heal the gaping wound between her parents.

☙❧

"Uh, why yes … of course it's litigation-related." Wallace caught Hotchkiss off guard. He discovered the directory too soon. It was hidden and password protected. The operatives were touted as experts, the best in their field. Wallace wasn't supposed to stumble across the hidden partition for months, and then only if Plan A failed. Hotchkiss improvised Plan C.

"Price discrimination, George: it is the cornerstone of our industry, just as it is for hospitality and education."

"Quick thinking, old boy!" Hotchkiss imagined Gury's reaction. Hotchkiss resumed character. He adjusted his suspenders and addressed the tribunal. "Prices for airline tickets are all over the map for the same seat, depending on when you buy, what membership level you've attained, who's bidding against you;

same thing for hotel rooms and college tuition. No surprise: hospitals do the same. Medicare and private insurers press us hard. They negotiate rates that in some instances are a fraction of what hospitals charge the uninsured. But it's a mirage, George, because the uninsured are lousy debtors. They default on their bills. Or their assets vanish from their estates when they die. The average amount eventually collected, as opposed to billed, is less than what Medicare would reimburse us."

Hotchkiss paused for drama. "It is a price discrimination suit, George, a fishing expedition by eight state attorneys general to discover whether hospitals are pocketing more than their fair share. And I do not mean just NYL. I mean every hospital in the country. Can you imagine the enormity of this paper chase? We are spending millions and millions to comply with their so-called omnibus discovery motion. They want the combined works of mankind and by God we shall deliver them! Meanwhile, Congress harangues us for raising prices and hospitals are squeezed out of business. It is madness, but it gets worse. The motion for discovery is amended. Now they want the combined *unabridged* works of mankind. It's become a never-ending story – a black hole sucking up everything in its proximity, including, it seems, your perspicacious eyes." He gazed sternly at the witness. The witness fidgeted uncomfortably in his chair.

Hotchkiss cut to the chase. "The investigation is secret, George. There have been no hearings, no grand jury indictments, just the biggest unpublicized investigation of all time. Surprise, surprise, the preening, strutting investigators do not want publicity unless it comes from them. They say it would compromise the integrity of their investigation. If traced to us, they might construe it as obstruction of justice. You don't need much these days. I'm sure you've heard about the *Pension Committee* case."

Wallace nodded. He began thinking about it the moment Hotchkiss mentioned an investigation. "Damn it," he thought, "why wasn't I informed of a litigation hold?" "Why indeed?"

came the pirates' refrain. Per the ruling, negligence could be presumed whenever the subject of an investigation destroyed *any* electronically stored information (ESI). Failing to issue a litigation hold or take it seriously ratcheted the offense up to gross negligence, for which judges could issue punitive, outcome-determinative sanctions, notwithstanding the strength or weakness of the underlying case or actual relevance and prejudicial impact of the "spoliated" evidence. Wallace did not enjoy where this was heading. The chorus within abandoned him. He sat there naked, afraid.

"I am not sure what to tell outside counsel. If they learn you pored through various documents, we might lose attorney-client privilege for the entire database. I mean, who is to say what you as non-counsel were privy to?" Hotchkiss interrupted his performance. He just had to appease his curiosity. "That was clever connecting the … the dots to a discovery motion. Tell me, how did you even know about the partition? It was supposed to be hidden."

Wallace thought hard before answering. The Dictaphone was on. The pirates made him check before entering Hotchkiss' office. "The amount of data in the visible file partitions and directories is inconsistent with the amount of traffic flowing in and out of the workstation. Only four percent of the drive shows up as formatted − a few gigabytes out of five thousand. The rest was child's play." Child's play when Hotchkiss used passwords like "confidential."

"I know what you're thinking, George. You're sitting there shitting bricks because you destroyed those files during a litigation hold. Don't be a moron. They don't care about piracy."

"Pirates?"

"And they don't care about anything recent. The investigation has been going on for three years. We've turned over everything and then some. So, we could delete every file older than, say, six months, and the lawyers would still have multiple copies of everything. You're always fretting about this and that and not focusing on your job – securing patient records, reducing cost, improving speed." Hotchkiss softened. "I'm sorry, I misspoke. You *have* worked diligently to reduce cost … and improve speed. That's why you went after streaming video. Except it wasn't streaming, was it? So, the payoff is a lot of pissed coworkers and only modest improvement in bandwidth."

"I'll tell you what. This conversation did not happen. You found a hard drive with a partition error and were able to recover terabytes of otherwise lost information. I'd say that was a good day's work. Someone has been searching for those files for months. You've made his year. Why don't you go home to that beautiful wife of yours and celebrate?" Hotchkiss winced at his blunder. "I mean, why don't you spend time with your daughter, Myra? I bet she could use some comfort about now." Hotchkiss never met his daughter. He avoided the patient floors and detested riding the elevator with the sick and dying. Hollow compassion was Gury's department.

છૈઝ

It was like the shock she received once from an empty socket. Only this wasn't momentary. Every fiber in her body constricted. The once gentle tingle was now 120 ferocious volts, maybe 240. She couldn't count, couldn't see. Her lids were so tightly compressed they squeezed her eyeballs. She felt any moment they would pop. She willed her finger desperately from the socket. But the current flowed directly to her chest. She felt her brain sizzle. A drill bored into and tore at the tissue, first the frontal cortex, then deep into the occipital and temporal lobes. She tried to grab at the tubing, but her arm was pinned by hot irons to the bed, every sinew a broiling, tightly wound coil.

Her teeth clenched so hard the molars cracked. She could smell the fume of sizzling flesh, of spattering brain tissue, the first thing she really smelt in weeks. Mommy warned her not to place the radio near the bathtub. That was how they executed murderers. The talk radiologist plugged the radio into the IV bag. That must be it! She struggled to reach the orange panic button but could not. She tried to yell but her jaw locked shut. She used her tongue to pry it open, but her teeth clamped down upon it. She knew they chomped through but felt nothing – nothing but 240 volts seething through her muscles and brain. Except it was now 500 volts, maybe 1,000.

The nurse warned her it would be uncomfortable. It was supposed to kill fungus in her bloodstream. She thought about all the little mushrooms among the blood cells. She wondered whether it killed the leprechauns too. She knew it was killing her, thirty minutes after her mother and father hugged her good-bye. It jolted them apart, not just Alya from the living, but the living from each other. The nurse said, "Die, Flooken!" a word Mommy said meant "sacrilege." She learned it in high school. It was her coded expression of disapproval when a group of boys swore obnoxiously on the subway or offensive rap lyrics grated from someone's ear buds. "Dieses Fluchen," she muttered, rolling her eyes, and Alya understood her exasperation and displeasure. They shared a lot of code words; Daddy too.

"Die, Flooken!" The medicine was answering the nurse's command. It was exorcising the unholy being that drove her mother from her people. Oh yes, Alya knew about the shame. The nurse thought she was tricky, but Alya knew a lot of exotic terms. Auntie Beril made her swear to keep the secret – why Grandpa never spoke to Mommy, why Grandpa never met Daddy, why Grandpa never acknowledged his grandchild. She couldn't even tell her father. The infusion would restore her mother's family to dignity by reducing Alya's legacy to smoldering ash. Only what value was dignity if they couldn't survive? Mommy and Daddy were lost without her. Where was the dignity in that? She wished Daddy could seize her from the bonfire, unplug the current, then conceal her on a remote frozen island beyond the reach of medicine and Grandpa's hateful morality.

But it was too late. The panic button was out-of-reach, Mommy and Daddy were gone, and her own heart powered down. She was a charred rat, like the one they found behind the wall of the Alabama house when the fuse kept blowing out. Daddy picked it up gingerly and tossed it into the trash. 2,000 volts, 3,000; the nurse was a master of understatement. The talk radiologist was a sadist. The doctors were obsessed with her mother. And God was a bigot like her grandfather. She wondered how long she was supposed to be "uncomfortable" but the current shredded her thoughts into fragments. Vacant eyes saw the room erupt in flames. The flames incinerated Alya's cerebellum then her brain stem.

"Tonight's dinner, princess! Your last meal from a …" The bottle of parentarel shattered on the floor. Creamy-white gruel splattered then oozed across the broad terrazzo tiles. A slender arm hung lifeless from the bedside, its brown hand speckled white by the intravenous goo. The other hand lay clenched and frozen on the bed, mere inches from an orange-red call button. A bag marked Diflucan hung limply from the IV pole. A nurse in blue scrubs howled feverishly for assistance, searched vainly for a pulse, then crumpled in anguish to the floor. Shards of glass cut into her skin and the white goo that was intended for a precocious little girl seeped into her wounds and nourished a much larger one. The milkshake date was cancelled.

Part III:

The Co-operative

Chapter 17

The honking persisted, two brays per second, despite regular remonstrance by the hand. Its partner beckoned through the fog for the man to cross, but the man doddered, disarmed by the Audi's shrill alarm. Mist transformed the walk signal into the outline of a policeman. It placed a citation on the bleating car's windscreen then floated past and dissolved.

What was his name, the trust and estates professor who was thrown in jail because he found the honking so insufferable he smashed the car's window, shut the alarm, and left a signed note rebuking its owner for incivility? Too long ago. Jack couldn't remember. Upstairs his daughter shut the window.

THURSDAY AFTERNOON, APRIL 5, 2012

Jack stared. The hair was black and gelled, stretched taut over the cranium. It grew from a dense patch along the back of the scalp and ridgeline above the ears. The hair was thick, thick enough for the comb-over to be deceptive. Jack glanced up when he stowed his roller. He stood six foot two, perhaps six-three. The bald spot was undetectable until he reclined. So was the dandruff. White specks and gelled black hair met Jack's gaze minutes before the crew's interphone chimed at 10,000 feet. The seat reclined when the plane first lurched upward. Jack knew it was senseless to object. Besides, it was only a matter of minutes. For two hours the man could recline as he pleased. Still, Jack would have welcomed five minutes' reprieve.

6 months ago

present day

Jack's knees pressed against the seat. He was sure the man could feel them. It was not intentional, just unavoidable. Jack shifted his body, so the knees reached forward at an angle. He could shift the opposite way when his left side numbed. He resolved to be considerate. In all honesty, he just wanted to avoid gazing at the dandruff. The gel and aftershave did not help either.

Thankfully, the man did not smell of old cigarettes and body odor.

April 23, 1988. Jack remembered. He booked a flight to Boston for the experience – for the sheer joy of travelling smoke-free on a short domestic flight. No more second-hand smoke. It scarcely mattered that co-workers smoked cigars in their offices, that restaurants feted smokers as their best customers, that smoke-free hotel linen was a novelty, and that dry cleaners tended his suits weekly. Eighty minutes' respite was cause for jubilation, for a cup of the airline's finest cranberry juice, except the cup was half full. The man next to him smelt like an ashtray. And the woman he planned to meet in Boston wasn't home or chose not to answer the doorbell.

Three years since the divorce. He wasn't reeling anymore. He was numb. The separation stung, the divorce stung, the alimony stung. He resolved to move on, but his spontaneous weekend getaway fizzled. The woman stood him up.

He met her two weeks earlier at the Waldorf. He'd moderated a panel discussion on securities law compliance as part of a continuing education program for in-house counsel. The woman wasn't a participant, just a hotel guest who found herself seated adjacent him at breakfast and asked to read his paper. They exchanged pleasantries about the headlines, the hotel and their respective professions.

She was an assistant home-furnishings buyer for the Jordan Marsh chain of department stores in Boston. Jack thought she was cute. She had a rich, sumptuous smile and silky, cordovan-brown hair. She and Jack exchanged pleasantries then cards then invitations for lunch and dinner. Jack was ready to exchange vows. She seemed so much nicer than Marcia, the Marcia of late. Instead, he asked if he could call her when he visited Boston on business, which he said he did often. He lied. Jack hadn't been to Boston in years. She said "yes", then "yes" again when he called on Thursday afternoon, but apparently "no" when he arrived late Saturday morning.

Jack cancelled the 6 pm reservation at Michela's. They had a young chef who'd received rave reviews. "Next time," he thought, except he learned there'd be no next time. Todd English left that year to open his own restaurant and Jack's subsequent romances were kindled elsewhere.

Jack visited the Opera House and asked the box office attendant to resell his tickets to *The Threepenny Opera*. The founder of the company was Sarah Caldwell – a revered opera impresario and the first woman to conduct at the New York City Metropolitan Opera. Her image graced the covers of *People* and *Time*, but Jack knew it only from television – a Dick Cavett-hosted broadcast of *The Barber of Seville* twelve years earlier. Jack considered the visit timely. Caldwell had just presented "Making Music Together," a three-week, eighty-event festival featuring 250 performing artists from the Soviet Union. Jack read about it when Governor Dukakis, the presumptive Presidential challenger, and Secretary of State Schultz intervened to salvage the underfunded glasnost extravaganza. Three years later, no one would have noticed if it failed. But in 1988, the world was still embroiled in the Cold War. "Next time," Jack thought, except he soon learned there'd be no next time. The Opera Company dissolved in 1990.

Jack walked three blocks to the Boston Commons, found a bench at the Parkman Bandstand, and handed a bouquet of mango-tinged calla lilies to an old woman seated with her poodle. He then scribbled and mailed a postcard to the young woman with the rich, sumptuous smile and silky, cordovan-brown hair before hailing a taxi back to Logan Airport, just in case she forgot or had an emergency. The front bore a photo of Fenway Park, home to her beloved Red Sox.

He was astonished to receive a letter of explanation. She reconciled the previous evening with her boyfriend. It took the imminent threat of an affluent suitor to bring the young musician to his senses. She confessed she was wracked by guilt but realized receiving Jack would perpetuate a lie. She was glad he had business in Boston. It would have killed her if he made the trip just for her.

Jack thanked her for the candor, wished her utmost happiness, and reminded her she possessed his card in the event her relationship soured. "Jack and Jill," he thought, "the stuff of nursery rhymes … and Shakespeare." He closed his letter with a line from *Love's Labour's Lost*, "Our wooing doth not end like an old play; Jack hath not Jill," then scratched it out. It was liable to be interpreted as sarcasm. No one knew the play. Instead, he scrawled, "I will write you in twelve months and a day to see how you are faring. Warmest regards, Jack Roberts." Then 'twill end, he thought. And it did. The anniversary letter was returned as undeliverable. She probably moved in with her boyfriend.

༺๑༻

Jack's cup was half empty. His surprise date fizzled, and the man seated next to him smelt like an ashtray. He was still exhaling smoke when he took his seat. Jack marveled at the feat. He must have held his breath for two or three minutes. Jack noticed similar feats of endurance as he sat in the passenger lounge. Smokers gassed up before boarding. Entire packs were consumed in thirty minutes. Fumes were so dense in the cramped smoking enclosure near the boarding area that the faces of the passengers were indistinguishable. They looked miserable, like prisoners awaiting execution. Smoke seeped from their clothes as row numbers were called and they trudged down the jet way. They embraced their last draught as long as possible, coughing helplessly when eventually they slumped into their seats. Anxiety carved grayish-yellow furrows in their brows. The expectation of two hours' deprivation tortured them. It did not matter their blood was supersaturated with nicotine and carbon monoxide; the mere anticipation of denial was agonizing. On board just five minutes, they suffered the deep mental pangs of withdrawal. Jack drained the cup of juice, gnawed on an ice chip, and pondered why it was so difficult to meet people.

అంత

Congress stretched the in-flight smoking ban to long flights in February 1990, but Jack scarcely noticed. His employer of eight years was bankrupt. Drexel Burnham Lambert defaulted on $100 million in borrowing and fired its five thousand remaining workers, including Jack Roberts. He could not remember which came first, the universal in-flight smoking ban or Drexel's closure. They may have happened simultaneously.

Neither development surprised Jack. The smoking ban on short flights proved hugely popular with the American public, as did the crusade by then-US Attorney Rudolph Giuliani against Wall Street racketeers, especially insider traders. Prominent among them were Dennis Levine, Martin Siegel and Michael Milken – high-level Drexel employees. Levine and Siegel made headlines in 1986 and 1987 for their confessed roles in smuggling information about pending Drexel- and Kidder Peabody-advised deals to the arbitrageur, Ivan Boesky. The firms disavowed Levine and then Siegel, but their reputations were irrevocably tarnished. The circus of journalists and photographers Giuliani invited to each arrest made clients and business partners leery. They shopped elsewhere, anywhere but Drexel and Kidder Peabody, the two firms with employees under indictment.

Jack remembered the early days of the investigation, when Drexel was still fiercely defiant, convinced it could bulldoze through any ensuing scandal. Some wag posted a photograph of the US Attorney next to the coffee machine. The prosecutor's comb-over was conspicuous, as conspicuous as Michael Milken's toupee, yet horribly unattractive. The wag added a mustache, a short, Charlie Chaplin-style hyphen. The resemblance to another obsessed publicity seeker was unmistakable – an omen, Jack mused, of how the ambitious US Attorney dealt with those who defied him.

Old-line Wall Street firms gloated over the adverse publicity. They regarded Drexel as a one-trick pony, a hired assassin with ephemeral fidelity to its clients, a raffish upstart in the otherwise staid and intensely loyal world of investment banking. Drexel got a leg up on the competition by issuing "highly confident" letters to under-capitalized would-be financiers – Carl Icahn, Ted Turner, T. Boone Pickens, Ronald Perelman, Victor Posner, Kohlberg Kravis Roberts – assuring their senior lenders of adequate auxiliary firepower before laying siege to another company. The firepower came from selling high-yield sub-investment grade bonds, or "junk," to the public and, where necessary, buying those bonds on the firm's own account. Under Michael Milken's aegis, Drexel Burnham Lambert became the *de facto* global marketplace for complex high-yield securities. No other firm had the financial wherewithal and appetite to maintain a liquid market in what were essentially bespoke derivative securities.

Jack drafted several "highly-confident" letters while at Drexel. He also worked on dozens of bond underwritings.

Before joining Drexel, Jack was an associate at Brown & Wood, a premier law firm in securities underwriting. But it was boring work, not what he expected when he left law school. In law school, intellectual stimulation came from analyzing precedents – hierarchies of previously-decided cases that bore relevance to the disputes at hand. The lawyer's job was to dissect those precedents – to identify subtle differences in fact or circumstance that a judge could employ to rule in his client's favor without flatly contradicting previous holdings or legal reasoning.

Precedents were an intellectual vacuum in the securities world. They were previously-filed prospectuses – dense volumes of disclosure that had been accepted by the Securities and Exchange Commission when other companies sold securities to the public. Each document contained discussions of the security offered, the business to be financed, and risks intrinsic to the business and the security buyer. Prospectuses ran more than a hundred pages and were, for lay investors, generally unreadable. Most investors skimmed the cover page then flipped to the historical and projected financial statements. The vast tract of boilerplate in the middle was the work of lawyers. Their stated mission was to deliver the minimally sufficient amount of information necessary to mollify SEC staff and withstand future litigation. Their unstated mission was to do so in the most verbose and unintelligible manner possible. Jack's tool chest overflowed with such precedents, time-tested filings that had been fine-tuned in the art of opacity. Jack spent most of his time cutting, pasting, editing and adapting those documents, watching them grow in unwieldiness with each successive underwriting. If there were pearls of legal reasoning secreted within these documents that would inspire future generations to embrace his profession, Jack never found them. They were concealed beneath the neatly gelled comb-over of his client's actual risks and often balding prospects.

☞◈☜

Jack's leg began to cramp. He reached into the seat pocket and removed the airline magazine and in-flight catalog, hoping to create room. They were sticky and damp. He spread them gingerly on the floor then glanced at the safety information card. It was as he surmised. The rumble behind his seat, 27E, was unmistakable. The aircraft had rear twin engines – noisy, inefficient Pratt & Whitney JT8D low-bypass turbofans. Their design dated from 1963, forty-nine years before Jack's flight. The plane was an MD-80, a domestic airline favorite, a single-aisle workhorse that McDonnell Douglas designed in the late 1970s and stopped manufacturing in 1999. Jack remembered the plane as a stretch DC-9, a reinvention of McDonnell Douglas' bestselling aircraft from the 1960s.

The company changed the moniker from DC-9 to MD-80 in 1983 because, well, the association seemed dated. DC-9s had been in service for eighteen years. Jack chuckled, "Just eighteen years." The company stood by its MD-80 appellation for thirty years (still counting) and the Pratt & Whitney turbofan for fifty. For most business travelers, the aerospace industry was barely treading water. It put a man on the moon in nine years, called it quits after four and threw in the towel on domestic aviation. All the aerospace engineers worked on wide bodies and jumbo jets – twin-aisle 747s, DC-10s, L-1011s, A330s, 767s, 777s and, just recently, A380s and 787s. They improved intercontinental air travel but did nothing for typical business commuters.

Instead, they boarded an MD-80, an airframe designed in the 1960s, or a 737, which entered service in 1967, the year Jack entered high school. Jack's connecting flight from O'Hare to Reno was on a 737. The seats would be new, of course, more tightly configured than before, but new. And the overhead compartments would be larger, just as they were on the MD-80. There might even be electronic gadgetry in the armrest, but the aircraft itself would be an aging tube with all the noise, lack of comfort and fuel efficiency of a late-60s muscle car.

Was Jack an MD-80? He had been leased out over 34 years to four employers. And except for Brown & Wood, they each filed for bankruptcy: Drexel Burnham, Brobeck Phleger, Dewey & LeBoeuf. He might just as well have said Pan Am, Eastern and TWA. The Dewey bankruptcy was still of course just a rumor, but the firm was hemorrhaging at the seams. The only question was when.

Jack's engine groaned. His frame ached. He was pressured always to economize yet produce more, to improve top-line fees when all he was really good at was legal work itself. Schmoozing and marketing, marketing and schmoozing. He detested the role of partner. Maybe Dewey's collapse was best. He could hang a shingle in the Adirondacks, ski a couple mornings a week, yet save enough in living expenses to conduct most of his work pro bono.

A pipe dream, he conceded. Susan would object. Melissa could not possibly attend Johnsburg Central High School. Nor would Susan forfeit civilization, as she put it. She needed proximity to her friends.

The last thought stung. Susan dropped most of her friends when she met him. She and Jack were inseparable. *He* was her friend. Then Brobeck collapsed and Jack thrashed about until he could establish himself at Dewey. That meant starting over, working as many hours as a young associate, competing against colleagues twenty years his junior, whilst trying to buy an apartment on Central Park South and support an expanding, high-maintenance family. Then there was Marcia, drawing support at a level commensurate with his income during the heady days of Drexel. Drexel collapsed but his support obligation did not.

Jack regarded the small warped mirror in the lavatory. He hunched over to peer at it squarely. The debonair young man was a vaporous shadow, the after-burn on a vintage monochrome computer monitor. The actual image was shorter, stouter, feebler. Jack sought vainly for indications of zest, but the sign beneath the sink screamed "IMPOTENT." Jack recoiled in shame then realized he had not seen the "R" and misread the "A." Passengers were reminded as a courtesy to others to wipe the basin before returning to their seats. Jack complied meekly then shut the door behind him. He straightened his back, but his insides remained hunched – servile and beaten, awaiting the hands of time to sweep them aside. He berated himself for his lack of enterprise, for entrusting his career to the care and whim of titanic failures.

Jack handed the flight attendant his plastic cup and pretzel wrapper. When had he become so drained and discarded? Before he even met her? Jack reproached himself. His wife clung to life, yet he wallowed here in the disappointments of his charmed one. "How many thrice-unemployed baby boomers live on Central Park South?" he demanded, unsure how to answer the question. The financial crisis threw so many families into disarray. Still, Jack knew he had plenty to be grateful for. There must be a way to patch relations.

Jack longed to rise and stretch, to shake out his frustration, but he had returned to his seat just moments earlier. The passenger on the aisle slept. Jack shifted his legs and beseeched the Holy Trinity to watch over his injured wife, but the prayer only wearied him. He dozed as passengers queued to use the lavatory. The Father, Son and Holy Ghost dissolved into the fallen angels, Drexel, Brobeck and Dewey. And his dreams reverted to self-commiseration.

❧

"Jack" Roberts joined Drexel Burnham Lambert in 1982 during a hiring binge. The firm issued its first highly confident letter in 1983 to help Carl Icahn finance a raid on Phillips Petroleum.

"Hey Carl," paraphrased Marcia when she snatched the letter from Jack's briefcase. "Here's a 411 for those squirmy D&Os at Phillips Petroleum. We think you are sooo cool! What you did at Marshall Fields and American Can is, well, pure jazz, and just begging for a recital down old Route 66. We would absolutely love to harmonize with you on that gig. That's because we at Drexel Burnham Lambert are confident, indeed *highly* confident, we can scrape together enough coin to make old PP wet itself. We'll find you investors who are willing to forego common stock yet stand in line on an unsecured basis behind everyone else to get paid, just like real musicians. Or was that 'laid'? Hell, we're even confident they'll forego quarterly interest. That's how jacked everyone is about shaking PP down. Oh Carl, one last thing: don't hold us accountable for this – in court, we mean. We're so stoked about jamming together we can't contain ourselves. What judge wouldn't understand that?" Icahn's actual letter was longer, but Marcia's summation was accurate. She wrote a lengthy article about it for her school's law review.

The letter's impact was immediate. Phillips paid Icahn $25 million to sell his shares. Together with capital gain, his combined pre-tax income was $65 million. Senior lenders sang Drexel's praise. The firm was now officially feared. "Highly confident letters" became synonymous with cash.

Jack shook himself awake. Marcia! He could not dream about Drexel or Brown & Wood or the Holy Trinity without summoning the ghost of Marcia Wasserman Roberts. Bipolar, sharp-as-a-razor Marcia. Bipolar, raving-mad Marcia. How many times did he have to explain to his colleagues why they wed in a church, why Marcia worked on Saturdays, why there was no rabbi in her life? She was sensitive about that, extremely sensitive. "Why the fuck can't they understand my parents were Catholic, that my grandparents were Catholic, that I have to earn a living on Saturdays, same as them?" Except she did not have to earn a living, not really. Jack paid her living expenses. He still did. What she made as a Second Circuit judicial clerk after graduating from law school was pocket change. It didn't help that she taunted his boss. "Go on, tug on my hair if you want to. I know you think it's a wig … and that you want one, just like those English barristers!" His boss laughed nervously. He was unsure Marcia was joking. Jack wasn't sure either.

"It was so much easier on the North Shore. Everyone knew my family," except her family was in actuality obscure – a minor name in Chicago-area publishing. She received the same surprised reaction when they first dated, but the questions didn't seem to bother her. Married six years, everything seemed to bother her.

Jack saw the cracks widen daily. By the time she lampooned the letter to Carl Icahn, Jack knew their marriage was over – just not with such draconian gusto. Two years later, the First Judicial District of New York issued a highly confident letter of its own. It ruled Jack could support Marcia's $84,000 per year lifestyle until she remarried. She also kept $230,000 in joint savings. Her earning potential as a highly coveted Second Circuit judicial clerk never entered the equation.

Judge Dinardo considered the decree restrained. He was confident Drexel's unorthodox tactics would redouble Jack's annual income. Jack wasn't as sure. He saw the fault lines at Drexel but was sworn as a staff attorney to silence. The tsunami struck hard. Drexel tethered its fate during the Ivan Boesky scandal to Michael Milken, the most successful Wall Street dealmaker in history. Milken's four-year pay surpassed $1 billion. His compensation in 1987 alone was $550 million. Yet it was a fraction of what he delivered to the firm. Michael Milken, alias the "Junk Bond King," was Drexel Burnham Lambert's alter ego. He was too big to disavow, alas not too big to fail.

Milken was the government's bull's-eye from the beginning. The felons Boesky, Levine and Siegel turned state's evidence, implicating Milken and his employer, Drexel Burnham Lambert, in a wide range of questionable legal practices. The SEC mounted a formal investigation of the firm in November 1986. The US Attorney followed suit immediately thereafter.

Chairman Fred Joseph stood behind his man. He had to. The allegations of Dennis Levine were, the firm maintained, the invention of a desperate confessed felon. Privately, Drexel's managers were uncertain. The legal team, Jack included, sent out résumés daily. Most found it disconcerting that their leading public figure, Michael Milken, steadfastly refused to cooperate with the firm's own internal investigation. The US Attorney brought criminal charges against the firm in September 1988 for stock manipulation, insider trading, defrauding its clients and stock parking. Jack no longer took weekend excursions in quest of romance. He no longer sought out productions by Sarah Caldwell. A forest fire raged at 60 Broad Street. Jack's exclusive concern, shared by each of his colleagues, was individual survival.

The threat of imminent RICO indictment brought the firm to its knees. It expelled Milken, pled no contest to three counts each of stock parking and stock manipulation, closed its retail brokerage operations, fired 5,000 employees, agreed to stricter oversight procedures, and paid a fine of $650 million. Michael Milken pled guilty to six counts of securities and tax law violations and was sentenced to ten years in prison, later commuted to two.

To service debt and pay expenses, Drexel needed to unwind its billion-dollar portfolio of junk bonds. But a pox descended on the instruments themselves. It mattered little that they were legitimate claims on the income of genuine bricks-and-mortar companies. One by one, state regulators ordered insurance companies to divest their holdings. Congress followed suit in the savings and loan industry. Pension funds and endowments were peer-pressured to do the same. Sub-investment grade bonds were written off or sold *en masse* at staggering losses – often to long-term overseas investors, the only parties sensible enough to buy and hold them. Drexel shuttered its operations, whole sectors of American industry wrestled with insolvency, and the economy wallowed in recession.

ॐ

Jack wallowed in San Francisco, watching his brother waste into a gaunt, hollow shell. The apparition at baggage claim shocked him. He thought Steven was parking cars at Alpine Meadows, making long, fluid tracks in the Sun Bowl, living from a camper near the lake, processing biofuels before anyone realized a diesel generator could run on discarded grease from a fryer.

Steven was an outdoorsman, a loner – a self-sufficient hunter, fisherman, lumberjack, mechanic, conscientious objector, and occasional freelance journalist and photographer. He survived for weeks at a time in the wilderness, foraging on roots and fish he speared through the ice – the stars and long daytime shadows his only beacons. He diarized his wanderings, devoting more ink to the mental journey than the physical one. Even his photographs, breathtaking as they were, were introspective. The snippets of reflection that appeared in *Snow Country*, *Field & Stream* and *Powder* were disarming – plaintive cries from a distant, long-forgotten way of life.

Steven had no patience for Vail or Breckenridge or any other planned recreation facility. He was a John Ford western. He was Ansel Adams' depiction of Half Dome. He tolerated the slow double chairs at Alpine Meadows because they brought in enough dough to pay the lease on Forest Service lands. But he explored the leased property on skins – touring skis with *randonnée* bindings that allowed him to venture far from the lift-serviced areas.

Jack's brother was intensely rugged and, like most of his gay contemporaries, dead or dying. A gaunt, bony hand stretched forward to take his luggage.

"Hello Jack, you look tired. Let me grab that."

Jack stared in embarrassed dismay at the twin orbs protruding from deep sunken sockets and the thin, broad fleshless smile. Reddish stubble carved a deep hollow on both sides of his lips and joined underneath as a still-prominent chin. His nose was narrower, more pronounced than Jack remembered. He wore a nondescript navy cap low over his scalp.

"And you look like a bird of prey," Jack answered, wrestling his luggage from the outstretched hand then embracing his brother closely. Jack loosened his grip. One arm alone could encircle his shrunken frame. Together they would crush it. "I am so sorry," he continued, "I had no idea."

"It's my cross to bear," the brother replied matter-of-factly. He freed himself from the embrace then continued, "I'm in a tow-away zone. We can talk on the road." Jack marveled that the skeleton could walk, much less drive. But he walked erect, proud – seemingly oblivious of the many averted stares and hushed whispers at baggage claim.

Jack later told Susan he nursed Steven. That wasn't true. He only nursed Steven during the final month, and then only because his brother had no choice. Until then, Steven nursed Jack. Steven cooked, did the shopping, ran errands. Jack accompanied him to medical appointments and treatments, but it was Steven who furnished the life counseling and insisted on driving. He showed Jack where to buy things in San Francisco, where to dine, how to navigate the vineyards of Napa and Sonoma, where to find the best lines at Kirkwood, Alpine Meadows and Squaw Valley. More important, he introduced Jack to a wide circle of friends in the Bay Area. The self-avowed trapper and frontiersman from upstate New York somehow amassed a Rolodex of close business, financial and art-world contacts that would make any prospective banker salivate with envy. Jack just wanted a job, the right one of course, but a job. Somewhere among the listings for North Beach, Mission District, Nob Hill and Pacific Heights was a friend who could plug Jack into the right investment bank or law firm.

That friend lived in Haight Ashbury, a rough-and-tumble neighborhood not far from Steven's own apartment. The friend owned a painted-lady Victorian on the edge of the Golden Gate Park panhandle. The head shop and tattoo artist on the corner sat in stark contrast to the mansion's stately, renovated interior. Steven introduced Jack to a senior partner at Brobeck Phleger & Harrison, legal specialists in high-technology and start-up finance. Jack took his time deciding. He stayed with Steven until the end. But the fit was good. He could even work in New York.

"New York's got the ways and means," his brother offered, "but just won't let you be."

"Chicago, New York, Detroit and it's all on the same street," replied Jack, continuing the refrain. "Takes time, you pick a place to go, and just keep truckin' on. I'm a goin' home, Steven. I have to get back home."

"Me too, I suppose, me too," Steven answered slowly. He shook his near-lifeless skull, "What a long, strange trip it's been." Jack rested his head on Steven's hand and wept. Eleanor leaned against the bed stand and clutched her elder brother's foot. The Roberts family spent their last evening together in ICU.

Jack organized a funeral service at the Red Victorian Theater, not far from where Janis Joplin, the Grateful Dead, Mamas and Papas, and Jefferson Airplane proclaimed the Summer of Love. The theater was nearly empty. A line of gaunt, hollowed figures ascended to the stage and delivered eulogies. "Together, more or less in line," he thought. "They just keep truckin' on." So much loss, an entire generation. Jack closed his eulogy with a line from the same Grateful Dead song, "Sometimes your cards ain't worth a dime if you don't lay 'em down." Jack lay down the weary bones of his brother, the do-dah man, then helped Eleanor bring Steven's few belongings back to New York. He signed with Brobeck Phleger the day he left.

Chapter 18

The stick figure flashed urgently, momentarily distracting the man seated below. "Why do they still install no-smoking lights above each seat? And shouldn't they always be illuminated, not just on take-off and landing?" Jack shrugged. There was no accounting for old habits and equipment. The fasten-seatbelt light winked on.

THURSDAY EVENING, APRIL 5, 2012

Jack glanced at his watch, then once more at the passenger safety card. MD-80. He shook his head; same craft Susan flew. TWA bought 111 of them. American Airlines still used 78, perhaps even the one he was sitting in. They seemed newer in 1995 … and so much quieter. Back then he sat in 3B, the bulkhead – twenty-nine rows ahead of the noisy twin-engine turbofans. His seat was spacious, sectioned off from rows seven and beyond by a curtain. He boarded the plane first then engrossed himself in a stack of financial statements and offering documents. His client was a global mining conglomerate with zinc operations in St. Louis. His goal was to discuss a partial spinoff and public offering. He had additional business with a publicly traded food processor and a hospital network, and hoped to squeeze in dinner with a classmate who worked at Emerson Electric. He did not recall requesting a beverage, but he shot upright in his seat when the orange juice arrived in his lap.

"Oh, my heavens, I am sooo sorry. Here, use these," said the flight attendant, thrusting half a dozen cocktail napkins into his lap. "I'll fetch a towel from the galley." She began to dab his shirt frantically. He grabbed the towel from her hands, wiped dry his documents then tried to soak the wetness out of his crotch. He stood in the aisle glancing down at the puddle of yellow liquid on and around seat 3B. Seat 3A was thankfully unoccupied.

"I wet my pants once … in high school," he remarked to no one. "It was the most embarrassing day of my life. How will I explain this to my clients?" Jack did not demand an answer. He was thinking. He could probably procure a shirt and tie at the airport, perhaps even socks, but trousers? At least they were gray. A rinse at the Crown Room then a gentle drying with the hand dryer? Was there a Crown Room? Any club room? He most certainly would not strip down to his wet, yellowed underwear in a public bathroom. He realized he was mumbling his thoughts audibly – a good reason for not becoming a litigator.

A stifled giggle jerked Jack's attention upward, but the source vanished. It reappeared seconds later with another towel, some club soda, and an outward display of utmost repentant sincerity. The flight attendant began dabbing methodically at his crotch. He stepped backward and burst into laughter. Chortles emanated from rows four through six.

"The airline will give you a voucher for dry cleaning. I am really, really sorry." The voice was earnest, plaintive. Jack looked at the woman in sympathy. He caught himself staring then glanced down. She was no more than twenty-five, a child, and yet her face …. Jack wiped dry the scattered drops of orange juice on seat 3A and seated himself there. His thoughts raced back to his own childhood, to a stove-heated three-room cabin in the Adirondacks. He shook his head then glanced furtively at the flight attendant. She met his gaze full-on, frowned slightly in curiosity then gathered the remaining cups for takeoff. The flight attendant's face was … her face was beautiful.

Jack miscalculated. There were no shops open when he landed, neither at the airport nor in town. He survived the day's meetings by buttoning his suit jacket, including the lower button that no one else bothered with. The day was hot, well into the nineties, and Jack perspired copiously. Air conditioners strained to keep office buildings in the upper seventies. He was encouraged by each client in succession to doff his jacket, even take off his tie, but thank goodness no one insisted. They accepted him as they would any New Yorker – aloof and socially inept. Jack resolved to make a less formal impression next time. He begged out of the dinner engagement with the former classmate and caught a 7 pm flight to New York. His seat was 3B in the same aircraft he arrived in that morning. The seat was clean but the carpet noticeably darker than the surrounding area. The flight attendant asked whether she could take his jacket and then gasped. Jack laughed.

"Yes, please, but no orange juice. If I'm thirsty, I'll gnaw on my trousers." The woman blushed. "I'm kidding. Everything worked out fine. I told clients I met the woman of my dreams. She's a mermaid. Well, you can't meet a mermaid without getting wet, can you?"

The flight attendant stared blankly then turned her attention to other passengers. The man in 3B was crazy.

Jack listened attentively to the boarding announcement. The cabin personnel were Lionel, Claire and Susan. The woman's name was Susan! Jack's thoughts whirled. He was an obstreperous child, unbowed by years of labor and loss, clambering over an ancient, glacier-sculpted outcropping, dangling from a narrow limb that jutted out over the headwaters of the Hudson. He plunged into the frigid waters, shivered deeply, and let the still-powerful June current sweep him to a shallower section twenty yards downstream. He climbed to his feet then heaved his heavy legs against the current and back to shore. He scrambled up the muddy embankment and along the craggy outcropping back to the unofficial launch point. His friends shrieked with delight and fought for turns. A sensation of intense joy and sorrow suffused him. Jack simply had to know this woman.

The flight attendant served a light snack and retreated to the galley. The captain dimmed the lights. Jack rose to use the toilet, paused for a moment then turned instead to the galley.

"I'm afraid we got off to an awkward start this morning. My name is Jack. Jack Roberts."

"I know. It's on the manifest, except it says 'John B. Roberts,' not 'Jack.' I don't suppose you are the same Mr. Roberts."

Playful response, thought Jack. That's promising. "I'd like to think so, only John is still glued to his seat, on account of his citrusy fresh trousers. We don't let him out much."

The flight attendant arched her eyebrows. "And why is that?"

"Vitamin deficiency – 'C,' I think. He spent his entire adult life dreaming about a special woman, a very special woman, a flight attendant actually, but when at last he found her, he was completely inept, a clod. He stammered something about drying his drenched yellow underwear in a public bathroom and that, well, that just killed the moment. You don't suppose there's hope for him, do you?" Jack searched her eyes beseechingly.

Susan regarded the man in the custom-tailored Paul Stewart gray worsted trousers. She read the label on his jacket in the morning. She had never ruined a suit before, especially not an expensive one. Lionel nearly choked when he saw the label. "Oh honey," he told Susan as they confided near the jet way, "ain't no way TWA is going to replace that one. They'll send it to the cleaners fifty times before they shell out $2,400 to Paul Stewart." She rifled surreptitiously through his wallet. The passenger was so rattled he forgot to remove it. Nice cards: platinum Amex, platinum Visa, New York driver's license, Upper East Side address, two hundred eighty dollars, twelve neatly embossed white velum business cards with his name and a law firm in New York, and no photos. Make that eleven cards, she corrected herself. She slipped one into her pocket.

"Tell me," she responded, "this friend of yours, is he married?"

"He was," Jack replied, "but not for … for some time." He stopped himself from saying eight years. "I think he started too young, before finding the right person, at least that's what I tell him. But I'm certain he's found the right person this time. Look at him, sitting there writhing in angst. He's afraid to ask her to dinner. He's wringing himself into knots. There's orange juice dripping on the floor. He doesn't know where to start." The skepticism in the woman's face was unmistakable. "Look, accept his card, would you? And tell me your name so I can at least cheer him up. He's had such a long, forlorn journey."

The woman burst into laughter as he dug into his back pocket, then his other one, then glanced about nervously for his wallet. She brought it forward from behind her back. "Your friend left it in his jacket this morning too," she explained, nodding toward the coat closet. "I put a dry-cleaning voucher in the billfold with the woman's number on it. I'm pretty sure she has Thursday off. She might even accept his call. Now if you'll excuse me, I have to attend to the other lovesick passengers aboard this aircraft." Except she did not. She parted the curtain between first class and coach, walked straight to the rear galley, and began an animated discussion with Claire and Lionel. Jack made reservations at the Rainbow Room and Windows on the World the moment he stepped off the plane then called her three mornings later, just as she prescribed. He felt the exuberant childhood thrill of plunging into the frigid headwaters of the Hudson River and swore he would get it right this time. Vitamin C. "Acerbic acid." That's how she mispronounced it in grade school.

❧

The tall man with the gelled black comb-over stepped off the jet way. A woman in a navy-blue skirt suit and white cotton shirt swept forward to greet him, blocking the remaining passengers from deplaning. Jack rolled his eyes. Was this necessary, here at the exit?

"Doctor Erdoğan? I'm Jill Kroll. I was sent by Doctor Michaels to greet you. I'm so glad you could make it to our conference. This is Mr. Błaszczyk, Geoffrey Błaszczyk. He will be helping with arrangements." A man stepped forward from the seating area.

"Pleasure," frowned Dr. Erdoğan as he shook Mr. Błaszczyk's outstretched hand. Erdoğan arched his back and rolled his shoulders. He regarded disconsolately the rumples in his otherwise impeccably tailored gray herringbone suit. He straightened the light blue, heavy-twill tie and stretched his calves by rolling forward onto the toes of his dark tan crocodile loafers. He emitted an audible sigh. Jack aped the exercise. If Erdoğan had yawned, he would have yawned too. He recognized the tie as Hermes. "It was a bit cramped in back." The man's tone was sharp, in evident admonishment. A chestnut brown leather two-wheeler cowered at his side.

"Nice," thought Jack, "not the remark, the luggage. Swaine Adeney? It must weigh a ton." Jack compared his black nylon Tumi favorably – light and indestructible. "He won't like the scratch on the side, and, yes, I'm not used to coach class either." Jack refused to call it "economy." It was a desecration of his undergraduate major. He agreed with the man with the comb-over, the disgruntled impediment to his egress. "It was indeed cramped back there."

Błaszczyk cracked a thin smile at the doctor's rebuke. He wore a dark, inexpensive suit, a plain, soot-burgundy tie and sensible shoes. Ms. Kroll relieved Dr. Erdoğan of his luggage and motioned for them to exit. He budged slowly.

"That's curious," thought Jack as he and the eleven other remaining passengers squeezed past the ill-situated trio. "How did they get through security? Gate-area receptions ended on 9/11." Jack consulted the large display monitor then made his way down Concourse K to Concourse H.

Ms. Kroll's heart skipped a beat but she gave no indication of recognizing the gentleman with the Tumi two-wheeler. She lost her opportunity eons ago. She was too concerned about blowing her cover. She followed him then just to learn more. He never suspected he was tailed. "Well-trained, I suppose … and lonely."

She grabbed Erdoğan's elbow – too roughly judging from his reaction – and strode toward the exit. She kicked herself for steaming open the man's follow-up letter, then returning it as undeliverable. She remembered the scratched-out words on the postcard, the one she saved at home in a volume of Shakespeare. "Come challenge me, challenge me by these deserts, and by this virgin palm now kissing thine, I will be thine," she yearned to respond. She should have flown directly to New York and into his arms. No one ever gave her mango calla lilies and she never dined at Michela's. She flung open the passenger door of the waiting sedan. Dr. Erdoğan glanced over in nervous alarm. Mr. Błaszczyk relieved her of their guest's luggage. "Jack hath not Jill," she reminded herself, then motioned Erdoğan stiffly into the backseat of the sedan.

સ્જ

A mechanical ventilator pumped fresh air via plastic tubing into the patient's lungs. The patient slept in a medically induced coma. But the mind was alert, flitting from one indistinct shadow to the next. Walls of light pressed in and then retreated. Flickers of luminescence occasioned pain in distant corners of the room. Aches flared as muted, ill-defined glows. A tangle of emotions struggled to find expression. Embers of clarity smoldered but were as quickly extinguished. "There must be some kind of way out of here," cried an inner voice. "Said the joker to the thief," came the modulated reply. "There's too much confusion," she suddenly gasped, eyes flitting about the indistinct confines of a bridal limousine. Walk and Don't Walk signs blinked simultaneously. "I can't get no relief."

Jack shook himself awake. He caught himself humming as he dozed. A Hendrix riff wailed from the gate H15 intercom.

Chapter 19

A traffic signal swung furiously on its cable, jerked loose then crashed into the pavement – its shards swept down the road aside tumbling trash cans, newspaper vending machines and fallen branches. The walkman watched dispassionately, brightening when its timer said to cross. But the riot of debris continued. The hurricane heeded no one.

WEDNESDAY, APRIL 4, 2012

Hanni's eyelids gripped each other, the entangled limbs of doomed lovers. They squeezed her eyes desperately, gaining weight with each labored breath. She pried them open but then relented. Orange sunlight bore through the olive sheers and drew menacing patterns on the opposite wall. The patterns  seared her retina. Purple and black after-images danced against the mustard-green curtain of her eyelids. She groaned and rolled onto her belly. The vise gripping her head winched tighter. "Ungh," she commanded, and the ripe melon within her cranium sloshed and thudded against its cage. Her mind reeled in momentary dizziness then regained focus in a gelatinous fog. Her throat was parched, her tongue a distended slab of smokehouse bacon. The smokehouse used cheap tobacco instead of choice hickory and mesquite. Foul ash insinuated itself into every membrane, every pore of her dry, aching body. She clutched at the blanket and coiled the dull pain into a shivering ball. The harshly lit room was freezing. Why didn't she remember to pull the drapes? She knew the answer. It was more sensual, more seductive, knowing others could peer in. She pulled a pillow beneath the blankets and squeezed it between her thighs. An eternity passed. The melon in her head grew larger, pressing against its shrunken confines.

Hanni reached for the packet of cigarettes but it was empty. Her arm retreated to sanctuary beneath the blanket. She was dimly aware of the figure that rose before dawn and jangled its boots, but Hanni's brain was still swirling, her stomach too nauseous to risk moving. It was remarkable she hadn't retched on the bed. If she did not drink something soon she would become a desiccated husk. Buzzards circled the toxic figure and moved on. Their flapping wings cast dark fluttering shadows against the ochrous interior lining of her eyelids. Her saliva, what little she could produce sucking as she rolled her tongue against her palate, was clammy and foul, as nauseating as giving head to that bastard Gürhan Erdoğan after he returned from a workout.

Fucking creep! What gave him the right? She could feel his hands clutch every follicle in her scalp, each thrust of his malodorous groin tightening the vise further, flinging her brain forward against the temple wall. It throbbed from pain then nausea, but dutifully it rallied her cheeks and tongue to suck harder as their quarry thrust and quivered ever more violently, quaked with the force of La Prieta, then shriveled in a series of meek, shivering aftershocks. Only then would the vise release its grip, but the foul, clammy taste of the workout remained, lubricated by the salty, viscous phlegm of a million doomed baby Erdoğans. That thought alone impelled Hanni to suck more furiously, to extirpate every last fugitive spermatozoon. But there would be more baby Erdoğans in the morning before breakfast and then again before evening cocktails, perhaps even before the luncheon. And somehow, he would still manage to probe her repeatedly after dinner, after sending their conference hosts off in inebriated joviality. She wondered if he would procreate if she did not take precautions. Or were there billions of baby Erdoğans secreted within his being, each clamoring to conquer some corner of the world and deliver misery? The owner of the uncompromising cranial vise lay back in his chair, inhaling deeply the musk that bathed his powerful hands and fused with his trenchant aftershave. He shuddered slightly, then tucked the flaccid, moist appendage back into his Savile Row trousers. Hanni would have vomited all over his privates were she not so practiced. But gagging never came into question. Her childhood tutors were determined educators. She scarcely disturbed her lipstick, and she never soiled his trousers.

Hanni hauled her cell phone beneath the blankets and pressed the Sleep/Wake button. The screen remained dark. She groaned and pressed again, this time harder and longer. A partially eaten apple illuminated the screen. Hanni was certain the apple winked at her before dissolving into a moons-eye photograph of planet earth. Was that a snake or Eve, she wondered? What did it matter? The earth flickered suddenly and faded out. "Shit. I should have plugged in the charger."

Hanni needed to urinate and considered peeing into the pillow. Someone had done that on a flight to Chicago. They left it in the seat pocket in front of her. Even the clean-up crew decided to overlook that one. She handed it gingerly to the flight attendant as she passed through the aisles to close the luggage bins. The look of appalled disgust was unforgettable. No, Hanni would not do that to the cleaning lady. Hanni gathered the blanket loosely around her and stumbled into the bathroom.

What time was it? Her iPhone flashed momentarily but she forgot. Was it 10:48? What time was housekeeping? Hanni willed herself from the seat-less toilet to the sink and to the shower. A glint of life bathed her battered chassis. She arched her head back and drank copiously. She stood there, mouth open for an eternity. She willed the fluid into her bloodstream, into her tissues, into her bosom, taking short light breaths because inhaling deeply risked exploding the melon that throbbed within her head. Vapor condensed and dripped from the ceiling as she patted herself dry with the small threadbare towel she used the previous evening at the hot tub. At least it was not one of the towels Erdoğan spread beneath her splayed limbs when he poked and probed her double-orifice. She became practiced at drying her entire body with a face cloth – the only towel she could secrete from his voracious gaze, the only clean towel he did not reserve for himself. "Selfish bastard!" He enjoyed seeing women helpless. He would have a hard-on if she used the towels from the bed. It would have primed him instantly for the next round of "love-making." But she was never helpless, not like his other "sweet things." She had resourceful, industrious tutors, the most impassioned educators money could buy. The next round came quickly enough anyway. He was so pumped with Cialis and Dexedrine he could poke and probe all night. He sometimes did. The evenings at the hospital were the worst. Hanni told Wally they were business dinners. Then the good doctor had his 'tools'. "Jesus fucking Christ, he's a surgeon! How much deeper and closer does he need to get?"

Hanni despised Gürhan Erdoğan, just as she despised her early educators. He would have his day. She made sure of that. His little toolkit would betray him. She had the best instructors in the business. They did not miss a trick, and neither would she.

Hanni rummaged through the toiletry kit for her deodorant. She pulled out a bottle of assorted narcotics, Vicodin and Percocet mostly. Bless Alya! They were her bequest to help stave off the pain. Except they did not. They only emboldened Hanni to drink more, to smoke more, to shred every last connection to her pathetic past. My God, she bollixed their lives! And for what? She did not need the money. Wally made ends meet. Extravagance on her part was met with frugality on his. He'd wear patches on his Brooks Brothers trousers if it meant paying off the bills at Saks Fifth Avenue. Hell, he'd still wear JC Penney's if she had not burned them.

Hanni laughed mirthfully, then ruefully and then trembled. She planned a picnic on the Great Lawn of Central Park north among the pines. She even reserved a table and grill pit. Such enterprise on her part was unfamiliar. The Hanni he knew would have called a caterer. He watched with bulging eyes as she emptied a full bottle of Gunk Liquid Fire Starting Fluid on the charcoal briquettes, stepped back, flung a lit match into the kettle, and

watched the match explode into a fireball that singed the surrounding branches. Without waiting for the charcoal to smolder,
she unsealed the wheeled Igloo ice chest and tossed his polyester
and poly-blend suits on the fire. Wallace had no time to react.
They burst into flames, crackled and simmered like discarded
Christmas trees his father collected from the side of the road and
crammed into the family hearth. Wallace caught an impish sneer
through the dense, noxious smoke as he groped his way forward
to stop her. But the sneer dissolved into gay, riotous laughter as
his wardrobe howled then perished at the stake. She was an en-
chantress – mischievous, petulant and intoxicating, a sylph whose
innate powers were discord and crazed emotion. Wallace realized
as the black smoke cleared, he was under her spell. Against his
better judgment, he let a twenty-four-year-old freelance interpreter reorder his life.

The giddiness of the prank transported Hanni. A humble
man, a kindly man, but not a simpleton – she rather liked George
Wally Wallace. Hanni bought him a hot dog after the park rangers
expelled them from the park. She ate most of it and made him
buy her a second one, this time with sauerkraut and mustard. Had
she bought him cotton candy, he would be just as pleased – and
just as ready to surrender it. Wally tried to tease her, to requite his
incinerated wardrobe.

"You are a wight, if ever such wight were to suckle fools and
chronicle small beer." He confessed later that he memorized the
line from *Othello* during a college Shakespeare class. He had a
knack for warehousing seemingly random bits of information.
They spewed out at the oddest moments, as if proffered by an
inner librarian. Sometimes the inner librarian was another person,
someone with their own distinct voice and identity.

"Iago?" replied Hanni, "You?" She laughed uncontrollably.
The juxtaposition was preposterous. Guile was Hanni's trade-
mark, not his. "You'll excuse me if I am ever fair and always
proud, have tongue at will and am sometimes loud," she parried,

tossing the second wadded hot dog wrapper at him. It caromed off his T-shirt and landed on the pavement. Othello was the only Shakespearean play she knew.

"You are a green-eyed monster for mocking me," he responded, picking up the wrapper, looking about for a waste basket, then depositing it in his pocket, "I who'th raiment thou hath doth slain."

Hanni tittered at the riposte, jerking her head back to avert the spittle of a half dozen lisped syllables. "To mourn a mischief that is past and gone is the next way to draw new mischief on."

"Thou hath mith checkmateth," he mumbled. There was no telling what she would incinerate next – his size-34, white Fruit-of-the-Loom briefs and matching T-shirts? Wallace tipped his king and resigned. "I will wear my heart upon my sleeve for daws to peck at."

"You're not going to burn them too?" he added sheepishly.

"Not to worry, 'tis neither here nor there," she replied, "They will find a nice safe home at Goodwill." She lifted his right arm, cradled her left arm into it, and stretched up to kiss him on the cheek. The Moor promenaded her down Central Park West to his tiny studio apartment off 58th Street, pulling the now-empty picnic cooler at his side. Hanni resolved to find him a better castle in the morning … and a bigger cooler. He staggered at the price of the castle – a spacious one-bedroom apartment in a luxury building facing Central Park. His fiancée evidently dreamed large.

"Think of it as an investment, darling. It's safer than investing in a bunch of companies you don't control and know nothing about. Besides, the interest expense will lower your taxes."

"And my income!" he murmured. She held his hand as he signed the sales contract … and the marriage license.

"A suitable residence for our newest permanent resident," was his toast. Wally radiated happiness. Hanni radiated contentment. Alya was born seven months thereafter.

"The robbed that smiles steals something from the thief," sighed Hanni, as she studied the bottle of Vicodin and Percocet. "The overgrown boy stole my heart." No, Hanni did not throw Wallace over for money. He was kind and humble and in his shy, quirky way, adorable. His rumblings about neatness and spending and the conspiracy of world leaders to lobotomize themselves were the only stability Hanni ever knew. The vows she made she intended to keep. It was Beril's green card and his father's pension and the contemptuous INS agents twisting and distorting aspects of everyone's past. It was the overlooked flight incident when she applied for permanent residency and citizenship. All Błaszczyk had to do was release the file, flagellate his loathsome pickle and her citizenship would be revoked as fraudulent. "Hug your daughter," he advised. "She may be a pixilated image on Skype tomorrow." Kosher or not, Vlasic was as vile as Asskiss and Erdrutschen.

Hanni opened the bottle of Vicodin and Percocet. Her daughter lay moldering under a simple granite marker in Alabama, next to two uncles she never met and two grandparents who pre-deceased her. "My baby never knew her grandparents," she moaned. She cursed her father and fought back the impulse to sob. Her body convulsed, her lungs heaved, but Hanni refused to yield. That chapter of life was over. No more Alya, no more com-mitments, no more debauched perverts at NYL Hospital, and no more cretinous, Shakespeare-offending husband. He could not protect her. He could not even comprehend what she was up to.

She told Wally after the funeral she was not returning. She did not bother notifying Gürhan Erdoğan. She left the egomaniac to book his own flights, to suck his own hyper-distended dick. She even dropped the account with the Greater New York Hospital Association. They never cornered her with pricks but NYL was part of their association – two campuses allied by a team of in-satiable pulsating cocks, each waiting their chance to pork the company's prize sow. "Curds and whey," rasped Erdoğan, as his prostrate convulsed and ejaculated its last gametal contents into the suction-sealed cavity against his crotch. "Miss Muffin" he called his acolyte, probing her later with an experimental fiber optic hysteroscope that displayed images via iPhone – so infatuated was he with whether his gametes found their quarry. The mere possibility aroused his libido, whipped him into a frenzy of violent thrusting. Erdoğan dropped the pretense of gentleness when he discovered she was a Kurd. Thenceforth she was Miss Muffin, devouring her Kurds and his whey. He seemed determined to impregnate her then abort the fetus. It was not enough that his staff tortured her daughter daily, eventually killing her. He made doubly sure he could wound her. The bastard thought "Miss Muffin" and "Kurds and whey" were clever. What did he call Andrea Lyden? She wracked her imagination but gave up trying. Hanni lacked Erdoğan's knack for "inventiveness."

The terror on Wally's face was pathetic. At first he just shouted, refused to believe anything, thought she was provoking him. But then he shouted louder, begging her to stop, to spare him the harrowing details. But she could not. He cowered in the corner of his childhood bedroom, the one with the window facing the cemetery, cringing with each shameful confession. She lashed him until he was a quivering, beaten dog. She knew she had peeled back more than a century. Alya's death was devastating. But this topped everything. He was enslaved again. She could have urinated all over him and thrust him in front of a train. She could have flung him on the flames instead of his pathetic, polyester Pierre Cardins. He would have endured it. But she did not. She was not the prurient sadist, Gürhan Erdoğan. She was not Lie-down's sugar daddy Asskiss or the tutors she conciliated in high school. They nauseated her. Her husband's meek reverential terror nauseated her even more. "Get up, God damn it and hit me! I need you!" But he squatted there cowering, eyes popping out of his sockets, hoping the nightmare was just a cruel joke.

The boy who parried *Othello*, she scoffed. I could have suffocated him then and there with his Charlie Brown pillow.

No, she assured him. It was the only truthful thing she ever told him. Susan and Jack had to put him on the plane, help him with the connection in Atlanta, and escort him home from LaGuardia Airport. Hanni cleared out her belongings unannounced while he was at the office. He did not even know she was in New York. The act plunged him into denial. He waited four months to acknowledge the exodus via voicemail. What a helpless, spineless sack of shit! Where was the Moorish general when she needed him?

∂∞∫

Wallace hobbled about the hospital in dazed silence. Each step was a trial. He wavered, regained his footing, tread further. A file clerk said something about the men from the government, but he just nodded. He held the papers from Hanni's lawyer in one hand, a cup of coffee in the other. How did she prepare them so quickly? Had she begun before Alya died? Why was he so woozy? The papers slipped to the floor and a nurse bent down to help reassemble them. He dropped his coffee when he turned the corner. Caramel streaks radiated from his feet. He glanced about nervously then plodded on. Dr. Steiner stopped him in the next corridor "to say good-bye," whatever that meant. "Unh-huh," he replied. "You and Stanley have a wonderful vacation," he ventured. "Hanni and I just love … just love …." He lost the thread; it was back somewhere with his coffee. Becky Steiner looked at him quizzically. She decided not to correct him. She had accepted a position at Mount Sinai Medical Center. She needed a change of atmosphere. Andrea Lyden brushed by him, almost toppled him over. "Why don't you look where you're going? Fucking dumbass," she bellowed, "I'm surprised they let you in here, or are you here to download your mp3 files?" She flashed a derisive grin and marched past. Andrea's words echoed in his head and came out garbled. "I don't have any mp3 files. Do I? Let me in from where?" Stuart looked up startled as Wallace entered his office. He glanced around nervously at the cardboard boxes filled with files to be destroyed and with desktop items belonging to its former occupant.

"I was just settling in," he offered nervously, "I placed your personal items in this container. You can take them with you if you like. Hotchkiss told me to send the rest to legal." Wallace struggled to comprehend. What was it the papers said? Constructive abandonment? Cruel and inhuman treatment? Imprisonment? Irretrievable breakdown? Yes, of course, Hanni's lawyers would want everything. He would not contest. How could he? His employment was part of the estate. He had to turn that over as part of the divorce, just as he had to turn over custody of his daughter. She would probably want the suits too, to make the bonfire complete. Wallace nodded dumbly and turned to leave.

"You forgot your box," Stuart offered, but could see that Wallace wasn't listening. He secretly thanked him for installing him at NYL, even if he was a traitor. "Litigation database, my ass! I'm not a fucking moron?" No matter, the guy put on a good show. He was the only one in the organization who seemed to care about it – the organization, that is, as opposed to winning brownie points or screwing Andrea Lyden. No need, I guess. He had Hanife Kaplan. "Fuck, I suppose that's how they infiltrate our defenses – such a nice, unassuming family. And a pretty good boss."

Wallace trudged past the office of Dr. Gürhan Erdoğan to the office of Sanford Hotchkiss. He knew Sandy would relish the moment – the moment he had to turn over his wife, his office, and his entire estate to NYL Health Systems, joint claimants in her petition for divorce. He prepared to empty his pockets. They would want his unlimited-ride Metro card and Alya's membership to the Central Park Zoo. He wondered whether they needed his gym pass. He did not need it, not in his run-down ranch house in Alabama, the one abutting the cemetery, the one overlooking the graves of his remaining family. He searched his pockets frantically for the bathroom pass. Miss Terrell would be furious if he lost it. He could not produce the keys to the house. He would sit on the stoop until his mother came home. "Please, God, let Mama be first." He did not want to incur the wrath of his father or play cowboys and Indians with the mangled corpse of Charlie Cube or Edward. The formation of F-51s was deafening. His father hardly flinched. A refueling tanker flattened him to the ground as it leapt into the air and retracted its landing gear. He glanced around at the narrow walls and marveled at the agility of the aircraft. He saw an opening in the wall and crept through.

Hotchkiss stood up and beamed. He looked genuinely pleased to see him. Wallace smiled back. He looked like such a gentle man, not like the previous principal, not like Mr. Walters. Mr. Walters took him out back with a paddle, made him do horrible things before letting him re-zip his trousers – Mr. Walters' trousers. Two figures emerged from behind the door, grabbed Wallace's hands, and cuffed them. No, Mr. Walters did that too. Sanford Hotchkiss was not a nice man after all.

"George C. Wallace, you are under arrest for violations of the Espionage Act of 1917 and the Computer Fraud and Abuse Act of 1986. You have the right to remain silent. Anything you say can and will be used against you in a court of law. You have the right to speak to an attorney and to have an attorney present during any questioning. If you cannot afford a lawyer, one will be provided for you at government expense. Do you understand?"

Wallace gazed at the woman and then the man and then the cuffs in front of him and the still-beaming face of Sanford Hotchkiss. He realized he was not at school or in detention. That was yesterday or Friday or last month. He remembered Mr. Hotchkiss was a lawyer. Wallace saw him about the videos, the ones children were borrowing from the library without permission. The librarian was upset. Except he couldn't recall the librarian's name. Why was he so tired? A voice within him screamed.

Hanni, is that you? *"There is no librarian. You're a fucking adult, Wallace. You're a 54-year-old man arrested for crimes against your country. Say something in your defense!"* Wallace struggled to slough off the dream, to wake up, shower, shave, and get to the office.

A voice repeated, "Do you understand?"

Wallace woke from his trance. What did divorce or the death of his daughter or spoliation of video files have to do with espionage? He shrugged dumbly and let the two strangers guide him down the corridor to the elevator. A crowd of employees converged to witness the procession. The Cheshire smile of Sanford Hotchkiss burrowed a trench between Wallace's shoulders.

✌

Hanni read the report five times. She received it the previous Monday – six months after they released him. She did not even know they apprehended him. That explained why he did not protest her exodus or beg for her to return. Deceitful bastards! She screwed the lights out for them and still they did not trust her. She searched her bloodshot eyes. She resolved the previous afternoon to swallow thirty-seven tablets of Vicodin, one for each blighted year of her existence. That's why she bought the Southern Comfort – 750 milliliters of insurance.

She was so drunk after the hot tub she passed out. And now the thought just nauseated her. She emptied the pill bottle into the seat-less toilet, thought momentarily about scooping the pills out, then flushed them. God would claim her soon enough. She did not need to accelerate his satisfaction. "Stupid fool," she murmured. "I'm sorry I dragged you into this."

Hanni dressed impatiently. She needed caffeine and cigarettes. "Damn, I should have charged the phone while I was in the shower." She threw it into her purse. She saw the extra keys on the table and, without thinking, tucked them in with her cell phone. She shook the Moncler jacket several times forcefully then donned it over a wool sweater from Dale of Norway. She wore nothing underneath. She could search for her bra after fetching coffee. "My God, this place is a dump." She meant the motel, not what she had done to it. There were times when even Hanni could not find her possessions among the clutter. At least she found panties and a pair of socks. She borrowed them from Susan's roller. It was so neatly organized. Too bad she didn't wear the same size sport bra. She tried squeezing into it but it was cramped. She did not want to look like she was wearing a dirndl – wrong Alpine adventure.

Hanni rummaged through the passenger seat of the white Honda crossover SUV. There among the debris were two intact cigarettes. She lit the first one and inhaled deeply. She kept the windows sealed and the ignition off to reduce circulation. She needed to inhale the exhaled fumes before her grip on the wheel loosened enough for her to feather the gas and turn on the ignition. She lit the second cigarette and pulled out of the driveway. She closed in on Gar Woods but drove past. "Wet Woody's," she shuddered, bemoaning the crushing throb in her temple and still-aching torpor in her spine. She remembered the empty bottle near her bedside and re-ascribed her torment to "Southern Discomfort." She liked that. She did not have to walk a mile for a camel. They were humping in her passenger seat where she left them, and they unburdened their precious cargo in her lungs. Her bloodstream began to emerge from purgatory. She just needed coffee … and more cigarettes.

She buzzed through Carnelian Bay and found a place near the end of Tahoe City, not far from the turnoff to Squaw Valley. She wondered whether the guy behind the counter was really Syd, or whether people here used aliases too. "Everyone has something to hide," she thought, "everyone except Wally."

"I could have used some help back there," she screamed at him, "What the fuck did I see in a capon?" He was probably too frightened to look up the word, probably bracing himself against the worst. "Your balls went up in flames with your suits," she said, but she chided herself for being so harsh. Among all the unanswered voicemails, he did not once mention the arrest, later expunged, or the four months caged in isolation. That most certainly was not expunged.

She sipped her double latte then crossed the street to the Chevron station. She purchased a carton of unfiltered Camels and clutched them as she returned to her vehicle. They had camels in Batman too – big, smelly, disagreeable ones. They would just as soon spit at you as obey you. Her father laughed as they bullied her around the arid fields. Alya would have enjoyed that, she moaned. "Fuck it," she stammered, rubbing the dust from her eyes, "I should have switched to Marlboros."

The town siren blared for fifteen seconds. She glanced at her dashboard for confirmation. She had not eaten anything in eighteen hours. Susan would understand if she snuck in lunch. She could not imagine Susan skiing the entire day – not after last night, not with a three-hour time lag from New York, but Hanni could not hold out until three or four. She reentered Syd's and ordered water and a "Gobbler" sandwich to go. She ate the turkey, pesto and Swiss cheese concoction in the car. She was not ready to rejoin civilization.

She backtracked route 28, determined to find her clothes but missed the "For Sale" sign and continued into Incline Village and Nevada. "The hell with them," she declared, and drove on. She remembered touring the Ponderosa Ranch when she visited here with Wally, a well-preserved outdoor studio for the 1960s television western, *Bonanza*. Wally loved watching it as a child. Hanni took his word for it. She did not recall reruns of *Bonanza* in Turkey. Still, it was an interesting way to pass the hours. She drove all the way to South Lake Tahoe before realizing it was probably dismantled. Erased; Hanni wished she could erase the past too – or just a season, the way Pamela Barnes did on *Dallas*, a more modern and more *risqué* television western that did in fact make it to Turkey. Hanni was surprised her father let her watch it.

Hanni spent the afternoon on a small plot of sand between bleached, rounded boulders, a copse of fragrant cedars, a couple mating ducks, and a cold blue expanse. The sun numbed her spine and helped weaken the throbbing in her head. The lake appeared lifeless. She expected minnows and tadpoles or at least algae. She saw nothing – just cold, clear water, a small patch of sand, and a lakebed of bleached, rounded stones and partially-submerged boulders. The ducks paddled around amiably, hugging the shore, perhaps scouting for nesting sites. Hanni would have to do that soon herself. It was an adventure when she was engaged to Wally. Now it was just a chore. Clouds crept out from the mountains and occluded the late afternoon sunlight. The chill chased Hanni back to her car. She reclined the seat and dozed.

She woke after dusk, disoriented but no longer immersed in fog. She felt her way back to the path leading to the water and relieved herself between two boulders. She climbed back to her vehicle and returned to the California border, eyes keenly fixed on the passing road signs. A coyote in the driveway was her signpost.

Susan was not there. She must have given up waiting and went to dinner. Hanni remembered the extra set of keys. "Crap, she couldn't let herself in!"

Fifteen messages greeted her when she charged her phone – not completely, just enough to see who called. Several were from Wally, two were from her lawyer, and the rest were from a 646 number she did not recognize. Not one call from Susan – obviously pissed off for being missing-in-action or too busy carousing. No matter. She let her phone charge a few more minutes and lay on the bed. Torpor overcame her and she slept.

Chapter 20

"No flashing hands, no sirens, just an unwavering line. The sign for crossing over was different at the hospital."

Hanni dressed quietly. Her clothes were scattered about the luxurious seating area of the suite. Her brassiere lay draped over the muted 40-inch flat panel television. Kristen Stewart dove off the cliff into the right C-cup. Hanni was still confused by the movie's plot. Alya never had the chance to explain it.
She inspected her makeup in the bathroom mirror, fetched her coat from the couch and slipped into the corridor. She followed it to the elevator bank, rode the cab to the lobby and stepped out the main entrance onto 54th Street. The man in the hotel suite still snored. He would not miss the Gilchrist & Soames Spa Therapy bath amenities or the terry-towel bath slippers unless, of course, he planned another diversion – Miss Lyden, perhaps, or some novitiate member of the management team. The man took a keen interest in the talent of his new employees. "He'll have to contact housekeeping if he has any more visitors," sneered Hanni, "unless of course they bring their own body lotion."

The charade was over. She would not demean herself this way again. The report on Wally coerced her back into service, but just this once. There would be no more encores. Henceforth, Wally and country were on their own. She strode west on 56th Street to Seventh Avenue, nearly toppling the news reporter from Fox 5 television – the one who lurked outside the hotel all afternoon with her film crew. It was remarkable Hanni slipped in and out un-accosted. The reporter continued past her in a huff.

There were just two familiar faces when Hanni peeked into the back area of Trattoria Dell 'Arte. The birthday girl was not among them. Hanni cursed the lecherous bastard for detaining her and hailed a cab back to her apartment. No, Gürhan Erdoğan would not miss the Gilchrist & Soames Spa Therapy bath amenities or the terry-towel bath slippers, but he might be surprised by the gift she left for the cleanup crew. Hanni had just enough time to pack and catch the last evening flight to Chicago.

It was not the first time Gürhan Erdoğan stayed overnight because of work. The drive to Greenwich, Connecticut was taxing after an evening entertaining hospital directors and business associates. The sixty-seven suites at the Warwick Hotel were quiet, elegantly appointed, and spacious – a comfortable place to recuperate during a hectic week of conference appearances and meetings. His wife and teenage children did not object. They had not been here long enough to adopt Western ways or demands. He resolved to keep them cloistered a bit longer – until he determined whether it was safe to remain. He chuckled. He said that to himself eight years ago. He would probably say it again in ten. His family was in equilibrium. He afforded his wife and children supreme comfort, for which they acceded to mute obedience … and ignorance. He plied a similar managerial style in the boardroom.

The bank balance in Cyprus troubled him. He expected the sum to be larger. He discovered the transaction record in the hollow tube of a toilet paper dispenser, per his employer's penchant for quirky, cloak-and-dagger subterfuge. His employer was old world, ancient world, actually; so utterly predictable. He gave up insisting on safer distances – ones measured in miles rather than hotel floors. Management needed to see things for itself, to assure itself he was not feeding them garbage, although how a brief, overlapping hotel stay accomplished this perplexed him. No, Marja just wanted to plant the seed of fear, so he would not be tempted to betray them. And for that he would risk late-night cocktails in a public dining area, under the watchful eye of New

York's finest and an alphabet soup of federal agencies. But Marja was not part of the state delegation, the high-security entourage. That was a ruse; it was always a ruse. Marja traveled alone. He fobbed himself off as Pakistani. The previous encounter he was Egyptian. One time, he entered the country as David Newsome, an alias the deposed Shah of Iran used in 1979 when he underwent surgery at the New York-Weill Cornell Medical Center. Marja's code name was apt – "source of emulation" – the same as the great Sayyid Ruhollah Mostafavi Musavi Khomeini. He was a trained medical doctor, nominally at least, so he blended marvelously with the guests assembled at the conference Hanni arranged at the Hilton New York on Sixth Avenue.

It was good to have Hanife back. She was a *great* travel coordinator. He did not mind admitting that. He would never find a more competent or efficient one – not one botched flight or reservation ever; conversant in four or five languages. Gury missed the lush, lascivious Kurd. Her breed of filth aroused him – outwardly worldly, the epitome of sophistication, inwardly a seething, impure kettle of lust. Gury had no illusions. There were no dates or honey or virgins awaiting him in heaven. What use had he for sweets and inexperienced virgins? Besides, he had dissected too many cadavers and attended too many dying patients to believe anything remained for the hereafter. He did his best as a surgeon to prolong each person's banal existence on this planet. It was the only existence and planet they would ever know. Still, God and country! He believed at least partially in the latter. The man seated opposite him probably wondered.

The man known as Marja reminisced with heartfelt satisfaction about the summer Gury began his internship at NYU. "Thirty thousand miscreants, Gury. Can you imagine? They were hunted down like dogs and slaughtered." Marja pointed his lamb chop at Gury then picked clean its last sinew. "Those were the days, my friend."

"We thought they'd never end," reprised the classmates left behind, the ones he never saw again.

"The bastard is rejoicing. He probably pulled the trigger," seethed Gury. Did he know one of them was his brother, Veli? Would it matter? The brotherhood seemed to have eyes everywhere, to be awash in clandestine intelligence, but it still could not manufacture what a crazed, dirt-poor spit of land in the Yellow Sea detonated six years ago. It could not run an assembly line without centrifuges flying out of alignment and into pieces. And it could not safeguard its own defense systems against malware. Were there legitimate prize money, Caracas and Havana would succeed before them. But there was not. It was economically suicidal saber-rattling, yet in complete character with every religious dictatorship he'd worked for. He wondered if he would be happier in the service of Kim Jong Un.

"You did not expect us so soon – a full six months before the General Assembly. I cannot say I blame you. I came in person to make sure there were no hard feelings, no misunderstandings. You see, we appreciate your long record of service and strong sense of … of enterprise. But our authorities, our *scientists* say you have exhausted your … your budget. The recent research is either unhelpful, redundant or, how shall I put it, incomplete?" Gury held his tongue. It was better to let Marja meander.

"These *scientists* want to freshen the … *your* investigation, introduce a new protocol for reporting, and shed more light on a couple nagging treatment complications. As a man of science, you surely empathize."

Gury coughed to disguise his unease. The information they were trafficking was extraordinary. It far surpassed in detail and reliability what his counterparts were peddling from Pakistan and Russia. Why for heaven's sake were they upset? There must have been a leak. Hotchkiss? Lyden? They wouldn't risk it, would they? "Fucking Americans, they think they're invincible. Have they any idea who they're dealing with?" Or was there another screw-up with their pathetic former CTO, George Wally Wallace? He and his wife were supposed to be their cover, damn it, not a red flag. Why the hell did the girl have to sicken and die – then of all times? Fortunately, the man went totally insane. His mutterings were incoherent nonsense. Hotchkiss witnessed most of the interrogation personally. He told me. Wallace neither knew nor divulged anything. He's still incoherent. That Kurdish bitch destroyed him. Gury felt his dick harden. For no evident reason it sought to avenge the disgraced husband's honor.

Gury struggled to think. He resolved to scale back the Dexedrine. It kept dragging him back to his libido, distracting him from concentrating on the man in front of him. He dismissed the possibility of scaling back the Cialis. He sold and forsook his integrity, that much was true, but not his masculinity. He measured a man's worth by his harem. Erdoğan still had oviducts to conquer. Impotence was out of the question. Instead, Gury attempted to catalogue his precautions. He parked the proceeds of his latest enterprise in an account in Cyprus, except the balance was less than expected. He had holdings from previous enterprises in Zurich, the Cayman Islands and a half dozen other tax havens, or did when he last checked. Now he was less certain. He was also not sure money would help him. He took mental inventory of his passports. He waited for Marja to continue, willing his bulging penis to smaller proportions.

"We would like you to make a trip home to … to Istanbul, to discuss the next phase of your research. You will be away for a week, two weeks tops. I am sure the Board of Trustees will acquiesce. You have made the foundation very proud."

Erdoğan's penis shriveled abruptly. It did not want to return from his brief sojourn in a casket. Its custodian checked out of the hotel before midnight. Four police officers stood at the corner, ready to quell any unrest, but the news crew from Fox 5 television was no longer there. Police were investigating a murder suicide on the Upper West Side – a high-ranking hospital executive and his female employee. Meryl Scott Rupert and her team were on Central Park South at that moment, banging on the apartment door of the man's widow and three children, trying to force an interview. They entered from the garage and bribed an employee to switch on the service elevator. The concierge watched it unfold on security camera and called the police. They shoved Ms. Rupert and the film crew out of the building, but not before Mrs. Hotchkiss clicked on the 55-inch 4K Ultra HD flat-screen Sony television for confirmation. Her children were awakened by the commotion at the door and watched the grisly images unfold in awkward silence.

Erdoğan glanced about nervously then waited impatiently for the doorman to hail a taxi. The driver thought nothing of his request. The last train to New Haven departed at 11:22 pm. It was not unusual for businessmen to arrive at Grand Central Station moments after the last train left, seek lodging somewhere for the night, and discover the hotels fully booked. Grand Central shooed them onto the streets at 2 am. They had no choice but to pay $130 back to the suburbs. The man in back obviously thought he could secure a room at the Warwick Hotel. Fat chance! The woman from Fox 5 News New York said it was booked to capacity by Iranian delegates.

The driver would have firebombed the hotel in his youth. Now he just watched the news in stony silence. What good had protesting served? Most of his fellow students were dead. And now he fought New York City traffic twelve hours a night, seven nights a week – a man with a PhD in civil engineering! He shook his head and drove the man to his home in Greenwich, Connecticut. The police officers at the Warwick Hotel continued to patrol the sidewalk. They placed wagers on whether their comments to Meryl Scott Rupert would make the morning news. Gürhan Erdoğan kissed his wife on the cheek then hugged separately each of his sleeping children. He could not hug their pixilated images on Skype.

೧೮

Hanni woke at 10 pm, groaned, and clutched the pillow tighter. By 3 am she felt rested and famished. She reached over to snuggle closer to Susan but shot upright in alarm. She wasn't there. She flipped on her cell phone and checked for messages, the same fifteen messages as yesterday. She rummaged through Susan's luggage to see if she somehow snuck in and snuck out, missing key notwithstanding. Same panty selection as yesterday; no one had been there except the maid. She dialed up the first message then clicked replay, then clicked it again.

೧೮

Hanni stuffed some belongings into her empty boot bag and stumbled toward the car. She jarred her head against the door frame and swooned over the steering column in dazed shock. The key jammed twice before negotiating the narrow slit to ignition, and the engine howled in protest as she wrenched the key and pressed the accelerator into the floorboards. Hanni managed to extract a few confused words from Wally. Thank God it was already six in New York. She could not have called him earlier. She tried Jack Roberts' landline but could not reach him. The nausea she tamed the previous day keeled her over. She knelt for twenty minutes before the seat-less toilet, vomiting what might once have been a pesto Gobbler, praying Susan was better than described. Her lawyer spoke briefly with the hospital, "as a courtesy mind you," and related via voicemail what he knew. "Courtesy?" she fumed to herself, "Susan is my closest friend." The hospital could not tell her anything. They were still working to save her. The best answer they could provide was to come and see her.

She did not stop at Syd's for coffee, did not even buy a bagel. She stormed past the Chevron station and branched right on Route 59 to Truckee. She would fly down Interstate 80 into Reno. It was not the most direct route, but it was the one she knew. The needle on the dashboard flitted with ninety, bounced around a bit then settled at zero. She ran out of gas in the dark, desert outskirts of Reno. A billboard shone the bright red letters "BOOMTOWN" into her left side mirror. A green and black digital display declared, "We Still Give CASH," whatever that meant. Thankfully, there was a smaller billboard, tucked to the side, announcing a Chevron station. The exit was half a mile back.

Hanni cursed herself. Gas was Wally's department. She was not even sure how to pump it. She made a point of refueling their rental cars in New Jersey, even if they were touring Long Island because New Jersey still had full service. The price was forty cents per gallon cheaper than in New York, yet the state still managed full service. Hanni resented pumping her own gas. She resented anything that brought her in contact with that filthy substance, the substance that poisoned her mother's body and her unborn daughter's embryo. She resented having to stub out a perfectly good cigarette, ravaging poison notwithstanding, while waiting for the pump to finish. Hanni pounded the steering wheel and debated what to do. She called Wally.

Chapter 21

"Next, I suppose they'll replace 'STOP' with the image of a policeman and a whistle. I wonder what they'll use on street signs instead of 'Broadway' and 'Park Avenue.' Theater masks? A bench? Why the Hell do they tax us so much if kids can't read 'Walk' and 'Don't Walk?'"

"Easy, Allie, I think it's toddlers and tourists they're concerned about."

"Toddlers shouldn't run around unsupervised and tourists should be observant ... like Americans. We didn't need a game of Charades to realize cars drive on the left in Hong Kong. But it's all about the foreigners here, isn't it? Making them feel at home. How long before we're ordering meals by photo?"

Ezra was silent. He had just returned from McDonald's.

Allison pored over the brochure from Lindblad Expeditions and National Geographic. "As astonishing as the photos in *National Geographic* and an exhilarating life adventure," declared the brochure, "A Lindblad-National Geographic Vi-etnam and Cambodia Expedition." Allison returned four weeks earlier from a river cruise from Nuremburg to Budapest but already itched for more. It would be too cold to book a voyage along the Elbe or the Rhine, so the brochure from Lindblad was timely. Southeast Asia in early winter sounded wonderful. She could even stop in Hong Kong before flying home. It would be a travesty flying all the way to Vietnam without first paying respects to Stanley Market.

Allison loved Hong Kong. She could live there if it weren't so British, or so Chinese. She loved the geography and the climate. And she loved Stanley Market. It was the world's loveliest bazaar, tucked into the picturesque backside of the island, accessible by double-decker bus along a narrow, winding road that clung for life to the treacherously steep mountainside. The bus passed the golf club at Deep Water Bay, where space between the highway and enveloping mountain was so precious that the eighteen fairways crossed each other like spokes of a wheel. Even her late husband Ezra, fanatic as he was, would not risk golfing there. "Pity the man whose drive falls short," he said. "I don't regard dodge ball as a death sport." No, Ezra Pfouts did not play golf with the Chinese of Hong Kong ... nor with the English for that matter. He was not sure which inhabitants actually played there.

The bus followed Island Road to Repulse Bay then climbed and descended into the town of Stanley, a small peninsula jutting into the South China Sea. Allison had ridden there many times. It was the perfect place to shop for the holidays (silken scarves, hand-embroidered handkerchiefs, all manner of counterfeit ties), and she met so many fascinating people– people from everywhere – from Ohio, California, North Carolina, Florida, Texas. She even befriended three Canadians – *real* Canadians, not the ones with foreign-sounding accents. "Merci, my ass," she declared after stepping off the jet way at Montréal-Trudeau International Airport. "If I want to converse with an effete Frenchman, I'll book a flight to Paris." Ezra did not correct her. He hustled her over to porte huit for their connecting flight to Nova Scotia. He regretted not visiting the fortress city of Old Quebec. He first had to convince his wife it was Canada's answer to Epcot. Yes, Allison befriended many intriguing bargain hunters at the Stanley Market. She would definitely include a side trip to Hong Kong.

Allison Pfouts ventured nearly everywhere her 81-year-old frame could carry her, but she had not yet visited Vietnam, Laos or Cambodia. The pain was raw and she never felt safe venturing there as an American. Naturally, she had been to Germany and Japan and Korea, but Vietnam? We did not win there, not even partially. What would stop them from abducting her and trying her for war crimes? Hell, we set the precedent at Nuremburg (she learned that during her previous trip) and then the Hague. What would prevent Vietnam from establishing, say, a Ho Chi Minh tribunal for ensnaring every American tourist who unwittingly thought the war was over? Weren't the Cambodians doing something similar this very moment?

Allison shuddered. For the same reason she never visited India, although she could not exactly remember in which war India fought against us, but it surely did. Its constant state of agitation with Pakistan was testament. Pakistan was our ally against terrorism in Afghanistan. They were prickly but there was no mistaking their intentions. They ran political cover for our drones, allowed us to take out Osama Bin Laden, and sent us the doctors who cared for Ezra. There was surely something suspicious about India. No matter; she could sort out South Asian politics next year. The brochure she held described Vietnam.

July 8th marked the fortieth anniversary of her only child's death, Private First Class Sidney Pfouts, United States Army. He died during a skirmish outside Camp Horn in Da Nang. The attack lasted seconds, just a few random shots actually, but no one took anything for granted. The unit returned fire, inadvertently shooting one of its own. The officer who was dispatched to inform them described it as "friendly fire." Allison saw nothing friendly about it – ironic perhaps, but not friendly. There were so few American infantry deaths by that point in the war. Most of the grunts had been withdrawn or redeployed. The ground war was now fought overwhelmingly by ARVN rangers and Vietnamese infantry. Ezra and Allison Pfouts had every reason to expect their son home shortly. He was just three weeks shy of completing his in-country tour of duty.

Allison and Ezra could have celebrated Sidney's sixtieth birthday in November, only Ezra and Sidney were deceased – felled by forces that sounded mild or incidental on paper, but cruelly ironic in real life: friendly fire and *peripheral* T-cell lymphoma.

No, Allison had not yet visited the Mekong River delta, but the photos in the brochure enraptured her. A young Vietnamese woman in traditional silk *áo dài* and conical *nón lá* hat smiled invitingly from a doorway. Could Sidney have fathered her mother? Allison knew he fathered an infant girl. He wrote declaring his love and devotion to the mother, a villager, and how he planned to bring them back to New York. Allison turned the page. Lush limestone formations jutted out of Halong Bay at dusk and cast eerie shadows on a two-masted junk plying its tranquil waters. Did Sidney see only menace or also beauty? Two Buddhist monks in saffron robes shielded themselves from the fiery sun with a lime-green collapsible umbrella while gazing at the twelfth century ruins of Angkor Wat. The secret bombing raids began in March 1969, shortly before Sidney was inducted. His number came up in April. Would they have deployed him there if we invaded on foot? If he lived longer? Could they have defanged the Khmer Rouge before it butchered two million civilians? A woman's hands set down a large woven basket of red chile peppers between baskets of limes and calamondin. Sidney preferred military rations. He was on constant guard against dysentery. Had he ever savored a calamondin? A darling 24-cabin riverboat advertised its luxurious accommodations on two full pages of the brochure – just $13,450 for a solo accommodation plus $1,600 in estimated airfare. Sidney made $2 a day. How many tours of duty would he have required to afford just eight days on the *Jahan*?

Allison sighed. $15,050 was considerably more than the cost of navigating the Danube. The figure excluded the planned side trip to Stanley Market. Allison wished she had a companion. She could cut her overhead by $4,480, perhaps more. But who? Most of her contemporaries were dead, in assisted care facilities, or simply unfit to travel. Still, she knew the trip was worth it. Allison voyaged with this organization before, most memorably the fjords of Norway and the Galapagos Islands. That's why she received their mailings. She knew the expedition leader and naturalists from *National Geographic* would radiate expertise and help quell the demons that still pursued her. For the first time in many journeys, Allison wanted to meet the host inhabitants – not just glimpse them, but actually communicate with them. Who did her son fight for and alongside? Who were his foes? What if anything did the younger generations remember? Did the past haunt them as it did her? Was her granddaughter still alive?

The numbers were enormous – too large for Allison to comprehend. 58,209 American casualties were digestible, even if one was her own. They were a fraction of the 405,399 American soldiers killed during World War II. But the Vietnamese lost one or two *million* soldiers; no one knew exactly how many, perhaps thirteen percent of their entire population. By contrast, the staggering carnage of the American Civil War, 625,000 soldiers killed, represented only two percent of the country's population. The loss of an entire generation of men, an eighth of Vietnam's population, plus as many as a million women, children and civilians, was too immense for her to imagine. She yearned to understand this country better, a country that sacrificed everything. Somehow, she would finance this journey.

"Hi Shelly, it's me, Allison Pfouts. Call me when you get a chance. I'm planning my next trip but need to verify my account balances. I hear the market has been great."

Allison waited a day, but the suspense was unbearable. She called her attorney.

"Oh, she's not? Well, could you ask her to call me? Yes, that's right, Allison Pfouts."

Catherine Fallis returned Mrs. Pfouts' call at 5:30 pm. "Well, shouldn't you ask Sheldon Vogel? He's across the hall from you and has on-line access to your account."

"That's just it, Mrs. Fallis. I can't reach him. I've been trying for four days." Allison exaggerated. "I called you because you have access to the account in case anything happens to Shelly."

Mrs. Fallis paused before replying. "Look, I'm in Philadelphia on business until at least next Tuesday. I'll have someone in my office download a copy and send it to you by overnight courier.

Would that be okay?" Mrs. Fallis resisted the temptation to add, "Or you could go on-line yourself and save everyone the trouble." She knew her client was eighty-one. Still, her mother used a computer and was in her nineties. "It's just as well," she thought. "Andrew needs something to occupy his time." Networking and finding clients on his own was too much to ask … and probably beyond his faculties.

Catherine Fallis regretted encouraging Andrew to follow her into the law. He would have been so much happier and more productive as … as…. She gave up. Catherine had no idea what motivated him, except perhaps his stomach, but she was his mother and couldn't just starve him. So Andrew was in reality an overqualified, under-skilled office assistant in an office where the actual assistant was terrific and $120,000 per year cheaper. "Why, oh Lord, was I not blessed with a daughter?" Catherine's mother was a lawyer and a damn tough one too, a labor-law battle axe. You had to be tough to hang a shingle in a man's world. "Fallis *et fille*, Attorneys at Law" sounded so much better than "Fallis and Sponge" or "Attorney and Slouch."

Andrew could put down his iPhone long enough to look up Allison Pfouts' portfolio. Why didn't Shelly just call her back? That was so unlike him. Catherine softened. "No Lord, you did not curse me with a son. I would have been delighted with someone like Shelly – okay, he's my age, I know, but someone like him. You cursed me instead with *Andrew*." She did not complete the thought, but the accusation was plain enough. Andrew was not really a son … not in the Biblical sense. Of course, he was a man but then again…. Mrs. Fallis shook her head. The world had become so complicated.

Andrew shouted in indignation. "No, Mother. Ask Denise to do it. That's clerical work!" He could not believe his mother was so insensitive. He was a lawyer, God damn it, not some grunt paralegal.

"Andrew, listen to me. I am not going to ask you again. I do not want to entrust the login ID and password to our receptionist or even you, but I have to trust someone, so it might as well be you. I am sorry you have to postpone your after-work activities for fifteen minutes. If your friends are good people, they will understand. You will find Allison Pfouts' file in the leftmost credenza when you enter my office. You know where I keep the key. The URL, ID and password are in a sealed envelope stapled to the inside of the folder. Put the folder back when you are done. Do not leave it lying on the desk or by the copier."

Andrew rolled his eyes in exasperation. What did she think of him, that he was a moron? Of course, he would put back the file. He flipped off the game of Angry Birds. It was impossible to concentrate with his mother carrying on like that. "I get it, Mother, I get it. I will take care of everything immediately. Have a nice retreat in Philadelphia."

The idea of a dozen harridan fussbudgets coaching impressionable young women into being successful lawyers nauseated him. Andrew switched off the speakerphone. "I need another job. It's unbearable living in her shadow." He stretched back in his chair, picked up his iPhone, adjusted his crotch, and resumed his game of Angry Birds. It was no use. She was impossible. He threw the phone down, glanced about nervously, then retrieved it from the carpet. "Now see what you've done!" he screamed, carefully inspecting the iPhone. "You could have damaged it!" The target of his rebuke was in Philadelphia, encouraging young women to follow her example, just as she encouraged Andrew. He did not intend the rebuke for himself.

Andrew checked the time. If he hurried, he could still get home to change and hook up with Norbert as planned. Mother would have to pay for the car service, of course. He was not going to work late at the office and take the subway. He was a lawyer, after all. No self-respecting lawyer stayed late and took the subway. What would his friends say? They would laugh him out of the state bar.

The file was labeled and located as Mother described. She even typed the ID and password. My God she was anal … and so tight-fisted. Andrew chuckled at the metaphors. He and Norbert would take turns deciding whether these were good things. Andrew hastened back to his office. He wanted to share this *bon mot* with Norbert. Meanwhile, the *bon moteur* in his trousers pressed him to work faster. "Insistent fellow," he thought approvingly. "Teacher's pet," he added, although it was unclear whether he meant anything untoward. He was already nineteen, a legal adult, when he began exchanging views with his Aesthetics professor – posterior views mostly. Aesthetics was such a sensual topic, about which the professor was passionate. He expressed his passion in every sinew of Andrew's exterior, in every membrane of his reachable interior. The man's reach was remarkable, Andrew sighed, farther even than Norbert's.

Andrew spread the file on his desk, blew the dust off the keyboard and switched on the unit stowed beneath his desk. He glanced at the logo on the monitor. "Dell," he sneered, regarding it the way his contemporaries regarded "Blackberry." The brand was out of touch, as irredeemable as Kodak and Xerox. Andrew's derision brought forth a nursery rhyme. "The child takes the cow, the child takes the cow. Heigh-ho the derry-o, the child takes the cow." Andrew knew exactly what he would do to the cow if she were not in Philadelphia. He broke every other sexual mores. Why not incest? Norbert could pork her from the other side. "Heigh-ho, the fairy-o, the cow tastes the pig."

"$1,438,576.24, Norb. The woman had a fit because her statement is two weeks old and she needs an update – now! Can you believe it? A measly $1,438,576.24. I'm doing her broker's job just so the crone can sleep better. Yeah, I'm clicking the print button now. I'll be out of here in five minutes. I'll see you at seven prompt. Promise."

He terminated the call and put down the iPhone. The investment summary in the top corner of the screen caught his eye.

"That can't be right," he remarked, "Can it?" There were a few hundred dollars in dividends, a couple thousand dollars of unrealized capital gain, a thousand dollars of interest income, but more than ninety thousand dollars in recognized capital losses and fees. That was a substantial hit, even in today's volatile market. He clicked the tab labeled 'Transaction History."

Andrew switched off the monitor. He spent longer at his desk than anticipated. He would not have time to change his wardrobe … or fetch his thong. He and Norbert would have to improvise. He lost some of the urge. His ever insistent *bon moteur* wasn't pressing as hard. It hardly pressed at all. His mind raced through various scenarios. Andrew reached an executive decision. As acting attorney for the Pfouts Estate until Mother Fallis returned, he would bring action against its financial advisor for fraud, mismanagement and misappropriation of funds. At a minimum, he would instruct Mrs. Pfouts to terminate Sheldon Vogel's services and sue for restoration of misappropriated funds, commissions and fees. Depending on whether Sheldon Vogel had other clients, he might tip them off too – then represent them directly or collect something for acting as whistleblower. He did not need to tell Mother anything – not until he brought home the bacon. Andrew sang merrily, "The cat takes the mouse, the cat takes the mouse. Heigh-ho the derry-o, the cat takes the mouse." He was still singing as he closed the door to his office.

Denise emerged from the file room, jotted down the login information on Mr. Fallis' desk, and gathered her belongings. "The mouse takes the cheese, the mouse takes the cheese" she chirruped as she slipped out of the office. Denise made $28,000 a year and shared a filthy one-bedroom apartment with three flight attendants in Hell's Kitchen. $1.43 million was a lot of cheese.

Chapter 22

The dream dissolved and the patient regained consciousness. Tubing pressed uncomfortably against his nostrils. His arms and legs felt clamped to the bed. He jerked his head upward in panic, winced in agony then let it collapse against the pillow. A hand reached forward to adjust the half-moon-shaped tube running ear to ear under his nose. Two prongs aerated the nasal passages and made them itch. The white figure came into focus.

THURSDAY, OCTOBER 18, 2012

"Easy, Mr. Vogel. You've had an accident, that's all. You are at Roosevelt Hospital on the West Side." The voice waited for indication of acknowledgement. The patient's brow furrowed. The voice continued, "The building staff found you unconscious in your bathroom and called 911. They're really worried about you. A couple of them stopped by to see you."

Sheldon wondered whether this was another dream. He was lazing in the tub thinking about Marian. No, he was thinking about something else… The bus? He lurched upright to inspect his injuries but recoiled again in discomfort and reclined stock still against the bed. Pain stabbed him from every side.

"You're no match for the MTA, Mr. Vogel. Lay still for a bit. Your body took quite a beating. Dr. Martinez can tell you more than I can. I'm sure he will be delighted to have you back among the living."

The voice was familiar. Sheldon shifted his head slightly. The stiffness in his neck was excruciating. The last time it hurt this much was when he moved into his apartment forty-one years ago. The moving company could fit everything into the service elevator except the sideboard, a wide, all-purpose storage unit that graced his living room. It held the Wedgewood china, a dozen neatly-assembled photo albums, two cartons of unfiled photos, three Kodak instamatic cameras, a Nikon FG-20 35 mm single lens reflex camera, assorted photographic accessories, and a half dozen three-inch binders of bank statements and corporate records. Marian emptied it but the bulky, American walnut unit was still remarkably heavy. It took four men to maneuver it. The moving company sent just three.

They draped the unit in burlap blankets, making it bulkier and harder to grip than it already was. The first set of stairs descended from the sidewalk to the basement into a narrow warren of corridors leading to the service elevator. The moving company transported the sideboard that far without him but could not wedge it into the service elevator. They offered to climb the stairs for a supplemental fee, all fourteen flights, but needed Sheldon's help. To spare his back, they offered him a spot on the lower end.

The extra work was unexpected. Sheldon hoped he had enough cash left over for a gratuity. The men surely deserved one. Marian was upstairs rearranging furniture and boxes — some to the bedroom, others to the kitchen, still others to various corners of the living room. He wanted her to run to the bank for cash and stop at the corner for beer but was supporting the belly of her family's enormous sideboard. He couldn't whip out a cell phone. That was as fanciful as a Star Trek transporter, so the trip to the bank would have to wait.

Pain seized his neck beneath the tenth-floor landing. The spasm was sharp, raw, as if the sideboard reached down with its enormous walnut door, gripped Sheldon's head, then tried to wrench it free. It nearly succeeded. Sheldon crumpled to his knees and collapsed on the staircase after edging the unit onto the landing. The moving company reached the last four landings on its own. Sheldon took a twentieth century transporter to his apartment — the elevator.

Marian dipped into her purse and Sheldon emptied his wallet in gratitude to the movers. Marian rushed downstairs and returned with beer. The empties piled up near the door. After the men were paid, quenched and discharged, Sheldon lay on the wood parquet floor and moaned. He wore a neck brace for three weeks.

The man with the reassuring voice was John Roberts, his neighbor, the man who resolved that unpleasant matter with Allison Pfouts and her attorney, Catherine Fallis.

"Thank you," Sheldon managed to rasp, "for rescuing an old bungler from his missteps." A coughing fit prevented him from continuing. How had he caught cold? He felt healthy when he entered the park, healthy enough to challenge a moving bus, then climb back to his apartment. He imagined the color of his side, an inky, purulent slab.

Jack reached for the pitcher of water and Sheldon nodded. Jack poured a cup, raised the bed slightly and held the cup to Sheldon's lips.

"I'm sorry, I wasn't clear," Jack proffered. "I didn't rescue you. The co-op superintendent did. Truman discovered you unconscious in your bathtub and called 911. I imagine you'll see him later today. He stopped by twice already. Besides, Mr. Vogel, you're no bungler. You shielded my wife from a swerving city bus with your own body, didn't you? I thought for a second we lost her."

"Mr. Vogel." Sheldon liked that. John Roberts just saved his professional reputation yet still accorded him old-fashioned respect. "For heaven's sake, Jack, call me Sheldon. We're friends, and no, I did not intentionally inject my body as a shield. I just miscalculated." He uttered the last two sentences between coughs. His rib cage convulsed in pain. He choked a bit on his spittle and coughed again.

"Easy, Sheldon," Jack urged, "You have pneumonia." Sheldon's eyes widened. "The hospital has you on antibiotics. The one on the pole is Bactrim. It seems to be working. My understanding is that your lungs couldn't expand fully after the accident, not with all the bruising, so they were vulnerable to infection. And of course you were in ER with a lot of sick patients. No one seems surprised you contracted pneumonia; it evidently occurs quite often. The good news, knock on wood, is you are past the fever stage." Jack glanced about then rapped his knuckles against the bed stand. The plastic was dyed to resemble mahogany veneer. "I imagine it's still uncomfortable," he added. Sheldon nodded faintly.

Jack returned to the accident. "You can't imagine how grateful we are for what you did. It happened so fast, but I'm pretty sure you saved my wife's life. We are both so indebted to you but at the same time distraught by your injuries. I don't think you broke anything – shock, mostly, some really nasty bruises and a bladder injury, but Dr. Martinez can explain that."

For the second time, Sheldon's eyes registered alarm. He groped his crotch nervously with his hands. A Foley catheter extended from his penis and another tube projected from his abdomen. Sheldon trembled slightly. He frowned in resignation.

Sheldon detested Foley catheters but understood their function. Marian said they were routine. "No reason for patients to wet themselves, especially if they are bedridden." She inserted hundreds of Foley catheters during her years as a nursing assistant. The thought unsettled him. How many penises had she groped and threaded in Korea and then in Brooklyn? How many patients were conscious when she inserted or removed them? Was she gentler with some patients than others? Did she make mental notes and compare them to the phallus of the man she married? Was it ever erotic? Sheldon felt intensely ashamed and tried to shove the unflattering image from his mind. He fingered the other tube.

"It's a drain, isn't it?"

"Yes," Jack replied, "a turkey baster, only the nurse squeezes the bulb to suck urine out of your abdominal cavity, not inject it." Sheldon managed a weak smile.

"Is it bloody, the fluid from … the turkey baster?"

"Tequila sunrise, although weaker than yesterday's. Easier on the grenadine and, truth be told, on the OJ as well. I'm not a doctor but I would say you are mending."

"That's how Marian died," mumbled Sheldon matter-of-factly. "My wife – that's how she died."

"Urine is sterile," objected Jack mentally, but he remained silent. He leant forward expectantly. Sheldon was barely audible.

"The cancer would have killed her eventually, but she could have died peacefully, without all … without all this." He motioned feebly at the tubing in his lap, the IV apparatus and the monitors. Jack nodded, not comprehending where this was leading.

"They removed a large section of her colon back in 1990, but because she had lung cancer several years earlier, they gave her a lot of radiation, total body irradiation, not just chemotherapy. They did not know what else to do. The radiation fused tissue from the small intestine with itself and with tissue from other organs. Everything became entangled, especially the intestines … and fragile. There were all sorts of complications. Food rushed through her. The functional parts of her intestine were so small she lost forty pounds. There wasn't enough left to process nutrients. And simple foods like bread and milk caused intense gastric pain. She spent hours locked in the bathroom yet still had accidents. She spent the last twenty years of her life wearing Depends. But she was otherwise 'cured' of cancer – emaciated but cured. We managed just fine." Sheldon stared vacantly at the opposite wall. It was clear he and Marian did not manage "just fine," yet Jack understood. The couple survived.

"And the abdominal drain?"

Sheldon started suddenly and returned Jack's gaze. Jack detected scorn, but doubted it was directed at him. "No one dared operate when the cancer returned." Jack offered Sheldon a sip of water and he paused. "Her colonoscopies were clean for nineteen years – a small polyp here and there but nineteen 'unremarkable' colonoscopies in a row. Then suddenly she had dysplasia – a mass of precancerous growth near her rectum and another near the valve where the small intestine empties into the large one. There was nothing anyone could do. They could treat her with low-dose chemotherapy to slow the advance, but most everyone advised making her comfortable – taking a trip around the world or something. It was sad but sounded lovely. I think Marian would have enjoyed that." Sheldon paused. He was agonizing over what to say next. Jack reached forward and clasped his hand.

"I'm so sorry," he ventured, unsure whether Sheldon wished to complete Marian's story. He decided to spare him the anguish. "Sometimes cancer outwits everyone and changes the timetable." Sheldon's eyes flashed rebuke.

"No, doctors change the timetable; the disease doesn't, at least not in Marian's case. I pleaded for one last opinion, this time at NYL North – the top research hospital in the country, or so everyone told me. I did not want to let her go. You understand that?" Jack nodded.

"The surgeon was a young fellow – thirty-five, forty tops. Smooth as silk. Darrel L. Goldfein. He said the answer was simple: an ileostomy. He could remove what was left of her large intestine, sew the end of the small intestine to an incision in her abdominal wall, remove the rectum and anus, and, presto, she would never have to worry about colon cancer or wearing Depends again. She could move about freely, travel the world, perhaps even live past ninety. He never lost a patient, he assured us, not a single one, and eighty-five percent of them raved afterward about the choice they made. He showed us testimonials. Sure, the bag got messy, but patients became adept at emptying and reattaching it, about keeping it discreet. A trained nurse like Marian would have no problem. Dr. Goldfein could have Marian home and cancer-free in two weeks." Sheldon shook his head in disgust.

"It was a pact with the devil, Mr. Roberts. That's what it was. Darrel Goldfein could have offered me the Brooklyn Bridge and

I would have bought it. Even Marian was excited. Here we were, resigned to spending our last five or six months together, knowing the last two or three would be really rough, then this cherubic young surgeon from the reputed best hospital in the country pops up and says, 'You can have your cake and eat it too.' It wasn't just hope he was peddling; he peddled us salvation. Well, of course we lapped it up."

"He lied, Jack. He lied." Jack squeezed Sheldon's hand but said nothing. He held the cup forward and Sheldon took another sip.

"The surgery was impossible. The organs were a jumble. They had migrated to where the first section of the colon once was and fused themselves to her remaining guts. There was no way to remove one organ without slicing into another. Well, he excised the rest of her large intestine, just as he promised, but left a large gash in the bladder. Only Marian's bladder wasn't like mine. It was held together by rice paper. It wouldn't heal. He tried surgery but that only made it worse. Instead of one tear, the tissue shredded wherever he poked a needle. The bag didn't work either. She was so thin – just skin and bones – the bag wouldn't secure to her body. It leaked and fell off the moment food rushed through her small intestine. And believe me, it rushed through in crushing waves just minutes after ingesting anything."

"Removing the ileocecal valve was a really bad idea, her death sentence. It was the only thing retaining food in her small intestine long enough for nutrients to be absorbed. She was 98 pounds when she entered surgery. She weighed less than eighty four weeks later when she died. They pumped tPA into her veins to keep her nourished, but you can only use parenteral for so long. That's not living; that's life support. But it was the drain that killed her, Jack; it was that stupid drain." Sheldon paused for effect.

Jack gauged the man before him. His wife's ordeal haunted him, probably every day for, what would it be, two years? But describing it seemed to inspirit him. He could not see this man dying with an IV in his arm and a Foley catheter threaded into his bladder. This was not a man who needed IVC surgery or who would be felled by a few severe bruises. No, he would outlive his contemporaries and die peacefully on a park bench bearing his wife's name. Jack was sure of it. The doorman, Robert, pointed Marian's bench out the previous afternoon when Jack returned from his vigil.

"What's that mean, Mr. Roberts?" the doorman inquired, referring to the inscription. "'Without the hurt the heart is hollow.'"

"It means," answered Jack, "that love is measured in part by what it endures, although I daresay Mr. Vogel spent more of his time here reminiscing about the fire of September than the hurt of October."

"What fire?" the doorman asked, arching his eyebrows.

"The one that made them mellow," Jack injected, as if that clarified matters. The man in 8B was annoyingly cryptic, but Robert decided it was best not to protest. He could ask another tenant. Perhaps Mr. Vogel was a member of the New York Athletic Club. There were fire engines summoned there all the time.

"The Fantastick Mr. Vogel," Jack mused. "He'll outfox us all." Jack waited for Sheldon to continue.

"It was humiliating. She was cadaverous – too weak to rise from bed, but too nourished intravenously to die. She had three tubes jetting vile stuff from below her waist – bloody urine out of two and barely digested food out of the third. The food reeked and the raw stomach acids burned her skin. But if we salved the skin with cream, the damned bag peeled off. Oh, excuse me," Sheldon murmured, "the darned ileostomy bag. Hell, the seal leaked anyway, and she could not hide either urine receptacle. She just dragged them along the floor between her legs, her tequila sunset." Sheldon frowned in resignation.

"She was bitter. It was all so unnecessary. But Doctor 'I-Never-Lost-A-Patient' Goldfein needed to make his quota. She despised him. She despised me for being so gullible. Can you imagine that, the most loving woman in the world, hating everyone for robbing her of her dignity? I felt so ashamed." Jack wondered whether he erred when explaining the bench's inscription. Perhaps it was only the hurt that Sheldon remembered. The remaining lines of the song mattered little.

"She did not have to wait long. First one tube became infected, then the next. It was impossible to keep them sterile. It began with spiking fevers and uncontrollable chills. I rushed her to the hospital. They pumped her full of saline and antibiotics, then sent her home … until three days later, after the antibiotics were flushed from her system, and the tubes once again infected. Of course, Goldmine never witnessed any of this, just read the reports. He discharged her when they put her on parenteral and had the chutzpah to declare the surgery successful. He knew full well she would finish her days bedridden with four ridiculous sets of tubes jutting from her. She was one of Goldmine's ungrateful fifteen percent. Pompous ass! She refused treatment after the third episode and just died. It took seven hours of grimacing determination, but she just died. The death certificate listed the cause of death as cancer. It should have read medical arrogance and incompetence."

"Goldfein called me to express his condolences. Honest to God, his parting words were, 'If you or anyone you know needs a gastrointestinal surgeon, I hope you'll keep me in mind.' Can you believe that? I think he read from a script, just so he wouldn't falter. Marian would have known what to say. I just mumbled, 'Thank you,' and hung up. He lost no time sending me the bill for what wasn't covered by Medicare. He included a couple business cards too, just in case I wanted to make referrals. You probably came across them going through my things." The patient was obviously still disoriented. Jack tried once more to set things straight.

"No, Sheldon, I have not been through your things. The superintendent, Truman, found you and dialed 911. If you hadn't left the bath running, no one would have entered your apartment.

The water damage to the apartments below probably saved your life."

Sheldon winced. "Is it bad?" He no longer thought about Marian. He thought about the damage to Mrs. Błaszczyk's apartment. He brought her home after that horrible accident with the dog. The corner of Seventh Avenue and Central Park South was so dangerous. Just look at him!

Mrs. Błaszczyk's apartment was beautiful. Sheldon could not believe the unit was identical to his own. His was snug, modest and dark; hers was Buckingham Palace. The opulence of the apartment silenced him. He did not know who was in greater shock, the author who just lost her dog or the commoner who just crossed paths with the Queen. He fidgeted uncomfortably as she reclined on the divan, worried his shoes somehow wore the carpet. He did not know what condolences to offer. Mrs. Błaszczyk assured him she would be okay. He backed apologetically out of the apartment and closed the door. He regarded his apartment as shabby. He was ashamed he made his wife endure it.

"Not sure," answered Jack. "Truman can tell you the next time he drops by. The flowers over there are from his wife. Do you want me to fetch Dr. Martinez? I'm sure there are matters you and he would like to discuss."

"Actually, Jack, I'd like to rest a bit. Would that be all right?"

Jack felt suddenly embarrassed. "Oh, I'm so sorry. I was so gripped by your wife's story that, well, I forgot you were a patient in intensive care."

"It's okay, Jack, I needed to kvetch. I really did, but now I would like to rest." Sheldon closed his eyes. A thin voice trailed after Jack, "Thank you again for everything you've done, about setting matters straight, I mean."

Jack turned back uncertainly, then shrugged and continued down the corridor to the elevators. Sheldon was understandably disoriented. It was Truman and the building staff who saved him.

❧

Jack returned the following day with a box of cookies. Melissa and Susan baked them – Nestlé's Toll House chocolate chip cookies. They followed the recipe on the back of a package of milk chocolate morsels. Susan remembered following the same recipe with her mother in Decatur, Georgia – back before her mother discovered religion and drove away her father, back when Nestle was spelt without a diacritic e. The recipe and the packaging hadn't changed, but her family certainly had. She wished her family had exchanged places with the morsels. Let them grow humorless and spiteful. Let them drive each other apart. Let her family remain stable and sweet. Let it remain fun.

Susan's father was no angel. He drank, had boisterous friends, made passes at the supermarket cashiers, but adored his children. They adored him. Shortly after Susan turned twelve, Carrie Nation reached up from her grave in Leavenworth, Kansas and transformed her mother, a docile suburban housewife, into a God-fearing, Bible-thumping prohibitionist. Her mother found religion all right – the kind grand inquisitors invoked to reform pagans and slave owners employed to crush the human spirit. Her mother dispensed with the rack and the whip. She possessed a broom and a frying pan. Her demeanor careened between granite sobriety, as sympathetic of others as the driving winter rain, and volcanic Old Testament wrath. Her father abandoned them shortly thereafter.

Jack stepped off the elevator with the box of homemade Toll House cookies. Melissa tied a bow around the box and drew Sheldon a "get well" card. The cover of the card was a crudely-drawn Manga character – a Japanese schoolgirl on figure skates. Dr. Martinez stopped him in the corridor.

"Mr. Roberts, may I see you alone for a moment?"

"Of course," replied Jack, "Is something wrong?" Jack knew from the physician's countenance that something was.

"In here, where we can speak privately." Dr. Martinez gestured to a patient room. The bed lay fully made but empty. "It seems you have been dishonest with me."

Jack started at the charge but regained his composure. "How so?"

"I spent a good part of the morning with Mr. Vogel, *your client*." Jack began to interrupt but Martinez cut him short. "You deceived me into believing you were just his neighbor, a good Samaritan, so you could, what, entrap me?" Jack tried once again to interrupt but the doctor merely spoke louder.

"That bit about the woman in Reno. That was precious. What did you do, hire a private detective? Is that all he could dredge up? I wasn't even the attending physician. I was a third-year resident!" One shock supplanted another. Jack stared at Dr. Martinez in disbelief. Could he have treated Susan?

"It won't fly, Mr. Roberts. I've discussed your case with Legal. They have no patience with unscrupulous ambulance chasers. The hospital is filing a complaint against you with the ethics committee of the New York State Bar. I suggest you go back to your hole in the ground because you are not stepping foot in the patient ward without a court order. Those are doctor's orders – *my* orders. Until then, you can speak with your client by phone. I'll have Security escort you off the premises."

Jack stood in stunned silence. He did not know how to respond. He thought for a moment then met the doctor's gaze, "Thank you, Dr. Martinez, I can see myself out. My daughter baked these cookies for Mr. Vogel. She is neither a snake nor a lawyer, just a little girl. Would you be so kind as to make sure he receives them?" Jack did not allow time for a reply. He placed the box on the freshly made bed and strode out the door. He most certainly did not want an escort.

Jack stood at the corner of 59th Street and Tenth Avenue and stared up at the colossus. He recalled Sheldon's words the previous afternoon, "Thank you for setting matters straight," and wondered what story Sheldon unwittingly concocted during his coma. Whatever it was, it entailed retaining Jack as his lawyer.

༖

"Back so soon?" inquired Susan, evidently surprised by her husband's reappearance. Jack promised to return two hours later after swinging by the Brierley School on East 83rd Street to pick up their daughter.

"I have been banished from the hospital for, in Dr. Martinez's words, 'ambulance chasing.' It seems they want to revoke my law license." Jack shrugged but did not look especially indignant or distraught. Susan, by contrast, looked extremely indignant and distraught.

"You prepare securities filings. You don't know a thing about suing people!" Jack tried not to show offense. "You didn't encourage Mr. Vogel to sue the hospital, did you?" Susan considered that the height of hypocrisy. They hadn't sued Renown Medical Center. Why then would he encourage Mr. Vogel to sue Roosevelt Hospital?

Jack smiled and shook his head. "No, honey, you know I would never do that." Susan nodded. Jack hated confrontation. That is why he could never be a real lawyer – not like Perry Mason.

"What did you do, ask too many questions?" That must be it. Jack was so analytical. He asked dozens of questions but seldom gave answers of his own. He was like that Greek orator, Soccertease – all questions and esoteric, roundabout answers. So much of what he said was opaque – intended, she supposed, to be poignant but really just inscrutable. Susan was sure she hit the nail on the head. Her indignity and distress abated. She was just frustrated her husband asked too many questions. "You played Soccertease again, didn't you?" It was her patented rejoinder to Jack's inquisitiveness. She used it many times before. Jack wasn't sure whether she meant the philosopher, a video game, or Bruce Dern's little white rat. He responded obliquely.

"I suspect even one question is too many for Dr. Lester Martinez. Recognize the name?"

"No… Should I?" Susan was puzzled. She had not been to Roosevelt Hospital in years. "See what I mean?" she confirmed to herself, "He answers one question with another, and an off-the wall one at that. 'Earth to Jack, let's stay focused, shall we?'"

"He was half of the Abbott and Costello team that misplaced a metal filter in your ileac vein and strewed pieces of another one about your bloodstream. He's half of the team that has you taking aspirin and perhaps Coumadin for the rest of your life to prevent a premature stroke." Abbott and Costello? Jack seemed uncharacteristically sarcastic. Mr. Vogel must have been in a really foul mood.

"Vaguely. I only spoke with him once … at the beginning. I don't think I saw him after that." What did any of this have to do with Roosevelt Hospital?

"Exactly. He is Sheldon Vogel's physician. He transferred to New York by coincidence and is now tending Sheldon – at Roosevelt Hospital. He says Sheldon swears I have been his attorney since before the accident, and that everything I learned as a concerned neighbor was obtained under false pretenses. Were this true, it might be grounds for disciplinary action, but it's not." Jack threw up his hands in frustration and marched about the living room.

"Well you've just got to tell them Mr. Vogel is confused. He's been in a coma. He's probably confused about a lot of things."

Jack regained his composure. He leant down and hugged Susan close. She had a knack for stating the obvious. Jack feigned gratitude. "You're probably right, Susan, I have to set the record straight with the hospital. Thank you!"

Susan blushed. She enjoyed it when she was smarter than Jack. No, not smarter, wiser! Jack analyzed everything too much. Sometimes it was wiser to enunciate the obvious. She rolled the n's in her mind, "eñuñciate."

"Here, try this coffee," she offered. "I didn't think they sold it here. It's from New Orleans. It's got chicory."

Jack sipped from her mug and suppressed a grimace. "Lovely," he replied, "I could have sworn it was hemlock." Susan agreed the two herbs tasted similar. Actually, she did not recall tasting hemlock, but she did not want to admit that to her know-it-all husband.

The bitter-sweet concoction diverted Susan's attention from Dr. Lester Martinez. Jack was scarcely surprised. Susan spent her first three weeks at Renown in a coma. Jack slipped the rubber band off the bundle of mail he was handed in the lobby. Several of the envelopes were addressed to Sheldon Vogel. Jack sighed. He would set the building staff straight when he returned downstairs. He balanced Sheldon's letters on the armrest of his daughter's sofa then curled up for a nap before retrieving her from school. The top envelope slipped to the floor and slid beneath the wardrobe.

❧❦

"Damn it, Abby. Concentrate!" Dr. Abigail Weinstein had not slept in twenty-four hours. She allotted herself six before the operation but tossed, turned and spent most of the night abusing her pillow. "How could he do this to me?" She felt her world crumble – everything they planned and built together. Right now she wanted to remove the large trocar needle from the patient and stab it into the heart of her assistant … or her own, just to observe his expression. She imagined blood shooting out the hollow bore of the needle, the one used to thread wire from the patient's right femoral vein into the vena cava. The blood spritzed and made measles of his aghast expression. She extracted the needle from the patient and laid it on the tray.

He would still leave her, she decided. He would not even remain for her funeral. Duty called … only duty was in New York City, 2,741 miles from the gorgeous waterfront home she bought in Zephyr Cove. Most days, she could make the drive in an hour.

It would take Lester Martinez forty. At $5 million the property was a steal, at least $2 million less than the foreclosing institution's mortgage, only now the investment seemed foolish. She borrowed $3 million from her father, another $1.5 million from the bank, and for what? So she could enjoy the five bedrooms, sauna, Jacuzzi, patio and private beach alone? She and Les reckoned it would take four or five years to work the bank debt down to a manageable sum and then she could have babies – lots of them – perhaps field an entire ski team. They would single-handedly keep George Whittell High School from closure – no more declining enrollment, not with the Weinstein-Martinez family pumping out genius athletes. Their eldest children would watch the 2022 Winter Olympics unfold at Squaw Valley, right in their own backyard.

"Genius!" Abby harangued herself. How could she not foresee this? She thought it was just a phase, his moody detachment, the hours spent alone at the computer, the mad dash to retrieve mail from the post office. He planned to abandon her all along. He was waiting for the acceptance letter. New York City – it was another country, as foreign and unforgiving as his hometown of Los Angeles. Abby was just kidding herself. Les did not want a gorgeous waterfront home in a swank alpine retreat. He wanted the sensation of life in the gritty, urban maelstrom. He wanted the prestige of working in New York City and of living in a closet. He would never have settled in Lake Tahoe.

Abby threaded the stainless-steel water spider deep into the patient's vein. She concentrated on the fluoroscope but the man next to her made her angry. He should have tendered his resignation the moment he received word. Abby corrected herself. He did tender his resignation but gave the hospital three weeks' notice. What an asshole! She was stuck working beside him for twenty more days.

"Oh God!" she gasped, gazing at the monitor. It wasn't the vena cava. She opened the basket in the wrong vein. She glared at Dr. Martinez. Where were you? You could have said something.

Les glanced down in embarrassment. He felt terrible. He should have excused himself from OR. Abby would never have made that mistake on a good day. She was the most capable surgeon he knew. He chided himself. He would not have made that mistake either. He should have been concentrating on the monitor, not on whether he was a schmuck. "Damn it, Les, concentrate!"

Abby blinked furiously. The lack of sleep or the harsh lighting or Les' thick aftershave made her eyes water. She maneuvered the J-hook around the errant filter, but it was jammed. The iliac vein was narrower than the vena cava. She was surprised she fitted it there in the first place. Abby decided she was wasting time. She could remove the filter when the patient's condition improved. She removed the wire and fitted a sterile one with a second IVC filter. This time she paid closer attention. The filter lodged where it belonged, just below the renal veins. It would help protect the patient against pulmonary embolisms – blood clots migrating from her extremities to the lungs. Given the extensive damage to her lower body, not taking the precaution would be reckless. Abby retracted the apparatus, closed the wound then rushed out to prepare for the next operation. She was still trying to save the woman's leg.

❧❧

Jack did not ask Susan how to "set matters straight" with Roosevelt Hospital. It would not admit him to the building and probably would not answer his calls. He would have to address the finer points of setting matters straight on his own. The finest point, in Jack's devalued legal opinion as a securities lawyer, was that the hospital's hands were tied. Most juries would consider preemptive interference with the attorney-client relationship prima facie evidence that someone had something to hide. It was unlikely the hospital's legal team would file a complaint with the ethics committee, notwithstanding Martinez's wild accusations of misbehavior, unless corroborated by its own investigation. A smile crossed Jack's face. Susan could check up on Sheldon in his stead. That would unnerve the good Dr. Martinez. Jack decided to show Susan the tickets. He booked a cruise around Asia Minor and the Greek Islands during the Christmas holidays. He ordered the tickets before she emerged from the coma. It was an expensive gamble. He wagered two month's overhead on her recovery. Susan had to recover. She just had to. He could not face losing her again.

Jack had never been to Turkey, Susan perhaps, but not Jack. She flew everywhere before dating Jack, back when she was an impoverished but unencumbered flight attendant. That nettled her. He could tell. Jack hoped the experience would be new. It was certainly her first cruise – admittedly confining but so were a wheelchair and crutches. The latter were most likely unavoidable. At a minimum, the trip took Jack out of *his* comfort zone, demonstrated he could try someplace new. In the spring, they could hike the Andes. Somehow, he would finance it.

"I'll be back in a second, sweetie, there's something I want to show you." He rummaged through the three-inch file folder on his desk. New adventure or not, Jack believed in research. He withdrew the brochure for the cruise package and returned to the dining area.

Chapter 23

"They use the same guy in Tahoe but he moans like a distressed bird. 'Chirr...ip, chirr...ip.'"

The doppelganger back east moaned in silence. 12,000 whining harpies packed into 23 square miles of concrete was too unnerving for even New Yorkers. The thrum of traffic was tension enough.

THURSDAY MORNING, APRIL 5, 2012

Wally stared at his Blackberry. The display read 6:40 am. It was the second time Hanni woke him. He pulled the drapes and admitted the faint morning glow. He should have risen forty minutes earlier, after answering the first call. But he lay awake until 4 am listening to Dictaphone recordings he did not know he possessed and examining files he'd evidently chosen to archive  remotely. The files lay dormant for months – since before the funeral. Wallace answered the call before it diverted to voice mail.

"Hello?"

"Wally, it's me again. I'm stuck in the middle of nowhere and need you to do me a favor."

Wallace groaned. He fought the urge to reply, "I'm stuck in the middle of nowhere too – no job, no prospects, no life, no idea what I'm doing with four terabytes of files, and no idea what the government wanted from me." Actually, Wallace had a glimmer. It took months staring at the microdots before the patterns began to emerge, months more before he could dissociate them from his hallucinations. "Best coffee in the city!" Wallace spat the imaginary substance in disgust. "Why didn't they just ask me, as they had when he was in Birmingham? Far more efficient. Much less collateral damage." Wallace's eyelids began to constrict but still he did not cry. Not anymore. Some shred of dignity remained his.

"Why didn't they just ask me?" He posed himself the question a million times. His only answer: "Sadistic assholes!" They did it because they could.

The completed puzzle was still gibberish. There must be another way to rearrange the pieces. Wallace concentrated on the phone call.

"Sure, honey, let's go over Google Navigation one more time. It's not difficult. I'll have you at Susan's side in no time." Wallace sighed. He wished Hanni were at *his* side but he couldn't bring himself to say so.

"I'm not lost, darling. I have directions, and you can call me Hanni, not honey. We're divorced, remember?" Wallace fumbled for a rejoinder.

"Well then, Miss Kaplan, why did you wake me?"

"Wake you?" Hanni was suddenly indignant. "What business do you have sleeping this late? I'm halfway to Reno at 3:40 in the morning with no coffee, no sunlight and no gas in my tank, and you're still in your Spiderman pajamas? Get out of bed and help me!"

The pajamas were a gift from Alya. Wallace felt entitled to be indignant but chuckled. Old times. "Out of gas? I assume you are on Interstate 80?" No reply. "And that it's a big empty stretch of highway without much traffic?" He turned on his computer.

Bloody genius, thought Hanni, regaining her composure.

"Have you tried waving anyone down?" Wallace inquired.

Idiot, fumed Hanni. She declined to say, "You'd like that, wouldn't you, your ex-wife abducted, raped, murdered and discarded somewhere in a ditch? Then you'd be even." Hanni suppressed the urge to cry. She cleared her throat and responded, "No, darling. I would not consider that prudent. I have no way to defend myself against … against molestation."

Darling? Wallace entered his password.

"That makes sense," he conceded, "Stay inside with your doors locked … and put your blinkers on. I don't want you to get rear-ended."

Hanni fretted about the battery but did as Wallace instructed. Inwardly she shrieked indifference as to how she would be molested – molestation was molestation. What difference did it make which side they preferred?

Wallace continued. "I looked up Nevada Highway Patrol. There's no nine-digit hotline, just 911. I'm not sure whether it will work on your cell phone or if you'll be routed to emergency assistance here in New York. So, try two numbers when we hang up, 911 and the local telephone operator, 775-555-1212. I'll call them as well. Can you tell me where you are?"

"I'm on I-80." Wallace waited. Interstate 80 stretched from San Francisco to Teaneck, New Jersey. Hanni glanced at the left-rear mirror. "I just passed a casino, Boomtown. The exit is a few hundred meters back."

"And what kind of vehicle are you driving?

"A white one." Wallace waited several seconds. "An SUV, only smaller."

"Is there information on your key fob – a model or license plate?" There was. "That's great, Hanni. That's enough information for the state police. Just remember to say you need gas and possibly a jump start." Hanni interrupted him.

"Uh, darling?"

"Yes?"

"Wouldn't it be easier if I just called the Chevron station on the other side of the highway? I can see the billboard."

Wallace muted the speakerphone on his Blackberry, withdrew his hands from the keyboard of his computer, and massaged his face and scalp. He wanted to scream but was afraid he would wake the neighbors. So he tousled his hair and re-enabled the speakerphone. "The number is 775-345-8567. Check your inbox.

I just emailed it. Call me back if there's no answer." He hung up before she could reply.

"Thank you, pumpkin," she said wistfully, "for calling me honey. I like that, even if we're divorced."

The Chevron attendant told the woman on the phone to stop weeping. He would be there with his equipment in three minutes. "Yes, ma'am, I agree. The gas gauges on Hondas are notoriously unreliable." Stranded drivers always said that but this was the first one who didn't feign indignation to cover her stupidity. She just wept inconsolably.

A Nevada state trooper pulled in behind the white Honda crossover moments before the tow truck from Chevron. Wally thanked Highway Patrol, signed off Skype and returned to bed.

What was it about those files?

Wallace installed a fresh hard drive, keyboard and monitor after returning home from confinement. What else could he call it? He used the original system CDs and downloaded software from Internet hotspots in Central Park and the New York Public Library. The confinement fueled his curiosity … and his paranoia. It didn't lessen it, although his thoughts were decidedly clearer. He was seldom groggy and felt a lot less excitable. The inner conflicts still raged, but no longer animated themselves as tangible beings, as hallucinated mishmashes of childhood, marital and present-day anxieties. They presented themselves as they did previously – as devastatingly real, but distinct memories. He realized much of what he remembered after the funeral never happened or transpired differently from how he recalled it. What about before the funeral? For how long were his memories compromised? His entire life? Wallace struggled to establish his identity. He was reasonably certain, before the funeral, that he was the frustrated, hardworking chief technology officer of a healthcare giant, the caring father of an ailing child, and the temperamental husband of an exasperating wife, but *reasonably* certain was unsettling. The government released him but explained nothing, just that he should follow doctors' orders. Wallace's thoughts returned to the files.

He bought a cellular modem and handful of prepaid SIM cards from a stall in Spanish Harlem and inspected the system using tools he procured anonymously from the online digital security community. He installed a filter behind the cellular modem and two levels of traffic monitoring software. Only then did he check the encrypted access logs of his remote servers for tampering – the ones he cloaked as page hits at espn.go.com and news.turner.com and routed through a virtual private network and self-designed Tor browser, much better than what NYL cobbled together for its film audience.

The government report on Wallace was that he spent ungodly amounts of time reading the sports news. He was surprised no one questioned him about it. He would have been hard-pressed to name *any* New York Giant or Ranger. The remote servers seemed intact.

Wallace then programmed a backup computer to perform random daily tasks, some of it Microsoft Office-related, some of it browser-initiated, using his original hard drive, modem and Internet Service Provider. The FBI could monitor those activities, for all he cared, as could anyone else behind the mirror, including Sanford Hotchkiss. Only Hotchkiss and Lyden were dead. He never suspected they were lovers, or that she was so temperamental. He did not even know the NYL executive was his neighbor. He did now. The news crews were out front every day for a week, trying to scoop an interview with the wife. The apartment was listed; so was his. Except the Hotchkiss apartment was a three-bedroom E-line unit, facing the park – professionally renovated and decorated. The shares would sell in a week. His unit was another matter entirely.

Hotchkiss: Wallace tried but could not mourn his loss. The pompous jerk witnessed his interrogations. He boasted about them in his email briefings to Erdoğan. It took Wallace ten minutes to hack into the backup tapes of Hotchkiss' account. He did not consider "kissmyass" an especially secure password, although it was definitely superior to "confidential." He chided himself for taking ten minutes. He could have halved that ten years ago. Wallace did not bother penetrating NYL's active systems and servers. He had everything he needed on the backups. Besides, the active systems were now more closely monitored, although not much, he suspected. His five-year plan for IT security was a pipe dream.

"Pipe dream," he repeated, imagining the hookah-smoking caterpillar from *Alice in Wonderland*. He recalled the Cheshire grin of Sanford Hotchkiss and shuddered. So much of what he recalled was apocryphal – crazy ideas sowed by Hanni, his mother, Błaszczyk, or whoever else implanted microphones inside his temple. Those microphones were now mute, but the menacing grin was real. Hotchkiss was real. *Was* real, Wallace reminded himself. The grin lived on in the emails.

Wallace detested admitting anything, but the anti-psychotic and mood-stabilizing medications helped. He tapered down but still reached for them when he felt stressed. Right now, he did not feel stressed. He had a mission – to reconstruct his past and why the government confined him. Hotchkiss' email helped fill some of the gaps but did not explain why the arresting officer mentioned espionage, or, indeed, whether that too was hallucinated. There was nothing about his arrest in the newspaper. Twenty people watched government agents escort him in handcuffs to the service elevator, yet none of the news wires mentioned it. The online registry of arrest records was also mysterious. It listed "Wallace, George (M/A) of New York, reported on 06/28/2011 in New York County, for Drunk" with no record of a court appearance or conviction. And then the listing disappeared, evidently expunged. Wallace dissociated his emotions from the problem. He attacked a seemingly intricate, impersonal puzzle.

The government searched his apartment and equipment thoroughly. They confiscated everything electronic, including the flash media card of his Dictaphone recordings of Sanford Hotchkiss. What the government returned was so obviously tampered with that Wallace considered its continued use foolish. He was sure his apartment was bugged, and every keystroke monitored, even after taking a full dose of Zyprexa. He wondered how the government would react if he began typing in Cyrillic. Would they detain him again, shifting focus away from Iran? Wallace dropped Russian after his third year of college, but it served him when he returned to Birmingham; did they even know? The idea humored him but he resisted the temptation. He had no interest in justifying another lockup.

Wallace bought a commercial bug detector, stud detector and camera for taking infrared photography, then scoured the walls and furniture for eavesdropping devices. He marveled at the one overlooking the toilet. Was that really necessary? He located a reasonably safe place to operate and drew the curtains.

Wallace restored data files as needed from the disguised and encrypted remote servers. He broke the files into millions of noncontiguous jigsaw puzzle pieces when he archived them, sending the parts to dozens of remote servers, so that it took access to a large number of the servers, not just one or two, to archive a simple Microsoft Excel file. There were duplicate puzzle pieces, of course, so no file was imperiled by the failure of one or even several servers, but the pieces for any given file were widely distributed. A specific BitTorrent implementation could reassemble them, and Wallace was pretty confident he possessed the only copy. He programmed it.

The first files he retrieved were from Hanni's wacky electronic home security system. The Feds switched the surveillance feature off after their first entry, presumably pursuant to a lawful search warrant (Wallace's recollection was vague), but they overlooked the back-up devices. Wallace believed in redundancy. They searched the apartment thoroughly and left with almost all his electronics. A smaller unit returned several months later to return the equipment and, as a courtesy, wire the apartment further. Wally sat as a result of this courtesy with his laptop and new hard drive in the crawl space under his piano. He would go deaf if someone pounded *Chopsticks* on the keyboard. But there was no one left to pound *Chopsticks*. Wallace set down the computer and cradled his head in his hands.

Wallace was decidedly more adept at hiding and securing databases than the legal department of NYL Health Systems. He was the one-time IT chief of a regional bank. And he was an unheralded computer voyeur, a hacker, with a penchant for observing third-party financial transactions. Wallace's talent was detecting and leaking information to the IRS about American citizens' holdings in undisclosed and otherwise-taxable overseas accounts. White American citizens. White American citizens whose racial insensitivity got on his nerve. The popular media and financial press were full of them.

Wallace spent fourteen years in Birmingham after college, working the last eight for a regional bank. At night, he perfected his IT skills. The hacking community derided him. His activities brought him to the doorstep of wealth — elaborately concealed wealth — but left him with just a snapshot. Their activities, by contrast, paid for ever-better electronics and corporate contracts.

Wallace realized he was wrong. The microdots weren't labeling devices at all ... not all the dots, at least. At first blush, the microdots were bibliographical — the same information one found in a card catalog, except no one today used a card catalog. They were designed to look innocent, although a simple QR code would have been more so. It was the random collection of extraneous dots that were meaningful — not individually, of course, but reassembled in a BitTorrent-like algorithm from thousands of files transferred to Europe and then reassembled in a bunker outside Tehran. The last assertion was conjecture. The bunker could as easily have been in Skopje, Bucharest, Sofia or Basra – anywhere southeast of Hungary – but Wallace wagered Tehran.

If he possessed all the pieces, he could reconstruct the source code or "How To" manual for any number of forbidden US exports. But the resulting code was meaningless. He leaned back against the post housing the grand piano's pedals and reexamined the endless list of files – the seemingly infinite jumble of medical articles and trade publications and random collection of amateurish pornography. He decided to examine the sets separately.

☙❧

Hanni regarded the man sleeping in the waiting area. She knew she would not be admitted to see Susan until morning, not if the patient's own husband were exiled to the waiting area. She exhaled. She did not especially like the guy. He was cold, aloof, caught up in his own, what, brilliance? No, that wasn't it. Superiority. He oozed the arrogance of New York's white-shoe professional establishment – men who populated the upper echelon of law firms, consulting firms and financial institutions, men who had nothing to prove to or learn from lesser mortals. Jack quite obviously regarded Susan, Hanni, perhaps even Wallace (a chief technology officer!) as lesser mortals. They didn't matriculate from the Ivy League. They didn't attend a top-five graduate school. They couldn't trace their lineage to the Mayflower. Hanni decided to let the man sleep. She pulled out a copy of *The Economist*.

☙❧

Dr. Weinstein scrubbed for the third operation on the patient's leg. The open thigh fracture caused substantial blood loss. Circulation to the calf and feet were constricted during the airlift. She did not want to reprise the fate of Matthias Lanzinger, a gifted Austrian racer who suffered a similar open break during a World Cup race in Kvitfjell, Norway in 2008. Lanzinger was rushed to the base in a sled then airlifted to Lillehammer for surgery on the leg and then to Oslo for surgery on the circulatory system. He had two operations in succession, both to restore circulation. Both eventually failed. The lower half of his leg was amputated.

Weinstein botched the first IVC filter ("Damn you, Lester!"), but the second one was fine. Actually, it was tilted, but would still prevent a clot from migrating. The patient wore compression socks which inflated and deflated regularly. Weinstein did not have to airlift the patient twice. And the patient's time until surgery was shorter. But they still had to operate a third time – one arterial bypass after another. The other injuries, some of them severe, seemed minor by comparison. Weinstein was sure she could have saved Lanzinger's leg. She was sure she could rescue the patient's. Judas Iscariot would have to sit this one out. He was attending a patient who arrived the previous afternoon from Northstar, plus the usual parade of 3 am knifings.

৵৽

"Her vital signs are stable. I think she'll regain use of her legs. Two hours ago, I wasn't as sure." The husband and the woman's friend both nodded. "She's in a medically-induced coma. There are still a number of operations we need to perform. Besides, her body has suffered too much trauma. No amount of painkillers would make her comfortable. We prefer for now that she remain asleep." The man and the woman again nodded.

"May we see her?" inquired the woman.

The man answered first, "It's not pretty."

"No, I'm afraid it's not," agreed Dr. Weinstein, "but I think she'll recover – not 100 percent, but enough to enjoy life. If all goes well, you'll not only be able to see her, but perhaps converse with her in four or five days. Until then, we're letting her rest."

"And her head?" the man inquired.

"It was pretty shaken. Look, we'll know more about neurological damage when she wakes. There's no question the goggles and helmet saved her life. They remained with her for most of the descent."

The man and woman sat at the patient's side for an hour. The man turned to the woman and said, "You haven't had breakfast yet, have you?" She shook her head slowly. "I'll buy you breakfast in Tahoe. I need to return Susan's rental car and retrieve her clothes. Can you give me a lift?"

"You don't … you don't want to stay here with her?" Another selfish bastard, the woman thought. Any excuse whatsoever to get away. His shoulders slumped.

"If it made even the slightest difference to the outcome, Hanni, I would. I'm just trying to be practical. My understanding is she rented a Miata. I have to either return it and replace it with something more, well, practical, or impose on you for God knows how long. If I deal with the car now, I can return in a day and camp out here until she's discharged." Hanni was unconvinced.

Jack tried again. "Melissa and my sister Eleanor are flying in on Monday. I need a roomier car. A two-seater won't do." Hanni seemed dubious. At last Jack blurted out, "How's this? I can't drive a stick shift. I might as well have inherited an airplane."

Hanni burst into laughter then shushed herself. Even she knew when to remain solemn. "So what you *really* want is for me to drive you to San Francisco in Susan's car so you can pick out something a little boy can drive?"

Jack shrugged. "Something like that. Would you do that for me, please?"

Susan's husband no longer seemed superior. He was a pathetic little boy in knickers. "Come on, Mario Andretti, let's go. You drive the first leg, back to Tahoe. The SUV's got automatic transmission." She hesitated a moment, then added, "You can buy me dinner, too."

ॐ

"How do you survive flights?" inquired Jack. They left the hospital parking lot thirty minutes earlier. Hanni reclined in the passenger seat and lit her second cigarette.

"Nicotine patch. The smoking's new," she asserted. "I started up again when I began working with the hospital. They all smoked."

Jack was surprised. "The doctors?"

"Who else? They pop pills too – Oxycontin, Celebrex, Dexedrine – whatever relieves the stress. They reach for antibiotics whenever they feel a draft."

"I used to smoke constantly, not just now and then."

Jack did not consider three cigarettes per hour 'now and then'.

"Back in Europe and during my first few years in the US, before I moved in with Wally. He made me scale back, especially during the winter. It was frigid cold on the balcony."

Jack smiled. The Adirondacks in the winter were frigid cold. New York City winters were balmy, especially during the previous two decades. "Then I got pregnant," Hanni added. "I quit entirely for two years, and afterward smoked only sporadically, usually after sex. Wally still made me smoke outside. So, I'd make him lay me on the balcony – on our marvelous Brookstone chaise. Or should I say a love seat?" Hanni chuckled. "The Athletic Club's ballroom is on the eleventh floor. Its terrace overlooks our apartment. During the summer, the guests would hang over the balcony railing, dressed in their gowns and tuxedos, wondering what I cooked up for Alya and Wally." Jack wondered too. Wally said they always ordered take-out. Poetic license, he supposed.

Hanni continued, "The ones who hung over the balcony – I could tell they wanted to trade places with us. That's why they were outside. They spent the entire evening at the railing. They stationed themselves there when they arrived, retreated for brief interludes inside, but always scurried back, dreaming about life in the city or a happy household or someone they'd never meet." Hanna smiled sadly. "We didn't use candles when we made love, only when we dined, but we must have been visible. The city never gets really dark, not like eastern Turkey, not unless there's a blackout."

Hanni changed the subject. "You're a lawyer. What do you think? Can the government really revoke my citizenship?"

The question caught Jack by surprise. "For seducing your husband on a balcony?"

"No, silly, who said I seduced *him*? Anyway, that's not what I meant. I meant for smoking cigarettes on an airplane. You asked me how I survived the long flights."

"You said you used a patch? Did I miss something?" Jack was not surprised Hanni flouted the rules. Lots of passengers tried, especially during the early 1990s – before the rest of the world caught up.

"I use a patch now. They didn't exist when I came to this country. Or maybe I hadn't heard of them. Actually, I didn't think the airlines were serious. I figured it was a game of cat and mouse – like speeding. I never dreamt they would arrest me."

Jack's foot slipped onto the brake. The Honda lurched and shook then regained its composure. The needle climbed back to 65 miles per hour. "Sorry about that. You were arrested?"

"Convicted. I paid a fine and received a year's probation. The woman from Legal Aid said it was a good deal. But now I'm not so sure."

Jack could not restrain his incredulity. "What happened?"

"Oh, you know, new to the country. My English professor assigned us *On the Road* during spring break. Have you heard of it? A French Canadian wrote it, Jack Kerouac."

Jack smiled. He'd "heard of it."

"It was something I had to do myself – rough it across America. So I bought a duffle bag and made my way west – Amtrak to Philadelphia, Greyhound to Pittsburgh, hitchhiked to Chicago. I made it all the way to San Francisco." Jack could not imagine Hanni in her designer wardrobe thumbing across America. He could not imagine her "roughing it" but said nothing.

"That's how I discovered Lake Tahoe. My route followed Interstate 80. I saved enough money here and there to fly back – a direct flight to JFK but late at night. The airplane had five seats in the center section. I changed seats after we took off and moved to the back. A lot of passengers did. If you found an empty row, you could lift the armrests and make a bed. That's what I did. Only someone reported smelling smoke from under my blanket. I tried to stub it out but couldn't fool the stewardess. She scolded me and said she would be watching. She did, you know. I remember her stern face with its hawk-like beak. It was dark, kind of spooky. I expected her at any moment to seize a broom from the galley, open the rear hatch, and fly away cackling to her next connection. But she did not. She hovered around me, her bat-like senses trained on my lighter. I couldn't take it any longer. I snuck into the lavatory and disconnected the smoke detector. The worst thing was, they didn't even let me smoke when I got off the plane. They just bundled me out, paraded me in handcuffs to a squad car, and took me to some precinct in Queens. The lawyer said they could send me to prison for a year. I didn't care, I said, 'I just want a fucking cigarette!' I totally forgot about my duffle, the one I left on the plane, or the novel I scrawled on a roll of toilet tissue. I never saw them again."

"Okay," thought Jack, "This is more in character."

"Did she give you one? A cigarette, I mean."

"Yeah, I suppose she did. Then there was this pissing match with the assistant prosecutor. She wanted to make an example of me. Can you believe it? 2,245 people murdered in New York City in 1990, 18 percent more than in 1989, and this clown wanted to make me the poster child of everything awful in America. Marcia Fucking Wasserman, I still remember her name." Jack did too but said nothing.

"The judge, I think his name was Dinardo, slapped her down, but I was still stuck with a felony conviction. Now there's a guy who says he can invalidate my citizenship because I left it off my H-1B and green card applications."

Wally would never do that, thought Jack. Would he? "Look, I don't know what the rules are. I'm just a securities lawyer. Who helped you with your original filings?"

"He retired years ago. I'm not even sure he's alive. But I suppose I should hire someone. I just thought you might know about this stuff."

Jack was flummoxed. Who would hate this woman so much as to threaten her with exposing a conviction – a conviction that was laughable if it weren't for the Patriot Act. Jack refrained from offering a legal opinion but was confident tampering with a smoke detector was neither an "aggravated felony" nor the kind of violent crime Congress had in mind when it enacted wider grounds for deportation. But that was not the issue. The issue was whether lying about a criminal record rendered her visa and subsequent citizenship applications invalid. He didn't know.

Americans were funny about lying. You could con the country into war with falsified evidence of taboo weaponry and retire from office with impunity. But if your predecessor tried to play down his feeble infidelities with an intern, that was grounds for impeachment. Or you could surgically remake your entire body to get ahead in politics and show business, but if you so much as dallied with performance-enhancing drugs, your career as an athlete was over. And some Congressman would want you thrown in jail for exercising your Constitutional right to plead innocent.

"How is it possible," he asked himself, "that an obviously-guilty hardened felon is entitled without prejudice to plead innocent during arraignment ('Not guilty, your honor!'), but an athlete is guilty of perjury if he pleads innocent to something that has never, ever been a crime?" There wasn't even a statute of limitations. Was there one for Hanni?

Jack answered Hanni the only way he could. "Who's doing this to you and why?"

Hanni remained silent. "Do you always obey the speed limit?" she finally asked.

"Only when I can," he answered. "Most of the time, there's too much traffic. Then I have to speed like everyone else. It's crowd pressure. I don't want anyone to rear-end me."

"Wally didn't want anyone to rear-end me either, my car, I suppose. He told me to leave the hazard lights on when I ran out of gas."

Out of gas? Jack arched his eyebrows but was not especially surprised. The gas station was their first stop upon exiting the hospital. Jack noticed the dial near empty. Someone must have siphoned off enough for her to reach Reno.

"He was right," answered Jack. "There have been some pretty awful accidents." He thought of the woman lying in a coma. They skied at Squaw Valley, what, sixteen years ago. They stopped in Tahoe City for coffee, at the same shop he and his brother frequented. Jack pointed out Tamara McKinney but not the owner's older brother, Steve – the fastest man on skis. He set the all-time record for speed skiing of 200 kilometers per hour. He set the record in 1978. It took snowboarding 22 years to catch up; that's how fast he was. His weather-beaten Volkswagen was not as fast. It broke down somewhere near Sacramento in late 1990 and Steve climbed into the back to sleep. He could hail help or fix it himself when the sun rose. He did not get the chance. A car swerved into the shoulder and crushed him. He was buried five years when Jack sat at Cafe O' Lake with his future fiancée.

"It's not like New York," he added. "There is no ambient light. You don't see anyone until you're on top of them." Jack thought about the man who hang-glided off Mt. Everest – not just climbed it; but hang-glided down. He survived a hundred-foot fall off a rock face at Donner Summit but could not survive a weary driver who swerved momentarily out of his lane.

"Don't you like to drive fast?" persisted Hanni. She sounded like Susan. Jack resisted the urge to be petulant.

"I love to, but only on a track," was his answer.

"Susan picked the wrong analogy." It was Jack's turn to change the subject. Hanni glanced over in confusion.

"She had a run-in with someone at her birthday party – a newswoman who was killing time between stories. She decided to invite herself to our soiree."

"I heard about it," Hanni volunteered, "the PED fracas."

"Cosmetic surgery," Jack clarified, "about how politicians and newscasters wring their hands over the terrible example athletes set by taking drugs to get an edge, when they themselves routinely risk disfigurement to look a tad younger than their competitors."

"She's right, you know. It's worse than anything the doping agencies have come up with. There isn't a girl in ten who doesn't have an image complex. Her breasts aren't firm enough; her waistline isn't thin enough; her face isn't Heidi Klum-enough. It gnaws at her self-confidence. Every time she loses a date, loses a boyfriend, doesn't get a job, she thinks it has something to do with her boobs or her nose or her chin. So, she spends $10,000 because she's unsure. Or she reexamines her lips and spends $5,000 more. And so it goes. But she'll never get the boy or the job of her dreams because they don't exist. The only dream dates and dream jobs are between the sheets, after you close your eyes – and I don't mean what you're thinking." She glanced seductively at the driver. "If I had the money, I'd get surgery too."

Jack suppressed a cough. He assumed Hanni had. No one's body was that perfect. Was it? "I'm sorry. I meant Susan could have singled out something nearer and dearer to the fat, ugly men who judge the athletes – on television, in Congress and at the various anti-doping agencies. They can work themselves into a lather about PEDs and, if anyone cared, unnecessary cosmetic surgery because the chances are slim they abuse either. But what if it was something that was illegal, incredibly dangerous to themselves and society, yet easy to root out, and every single one of them was guilty? I mean really, really guilty. Would that be compelling?"

Hanni smiled quizzically. "It might be? What did you have in mind, child molestation?"

Jack chuckled. "That would be nice, wouldn't it, but I don't have the evidence. I mean something more pedestrian. Actually, I mean automotive. You asked me if I like to drive fast. Well I think a stack of speeding tickets should disqualify you from holding higher office, should be a legitimate character consideration in determining whether you're competent to hold a job, especially in government or media, and that ticketing should be handed over to EZ-Pass."

Hanni laughed. "What are you, a Nazi?"

"No, just objective … and a New Yorker." Hanni knew what "I'm a New Yorker" meant. New Yorkers shunned driving. No one owned a car unless they had to. They despised suburbanites who refused to take public transit, didn't car-pool, and clogged the pedestrian walkways. Two points on the license and a $200 fine were the appropriate penalty, but they were only imposed during the height of holiday season, and then only in the shopping district. Hanni was like every other New Yorker in considering passenger cars a toxic nuisance in the city. But out here? On the highway?

"Accidents kill, Hanni. PEDs and cosmetic surgery almost never do. It is one of the most studied phenomena in government regulation. There are dozens of studies proving mortality rates rise, often dramatically, when traffic flows at 70 rather than, say 62 or 63 in a 55-mile-per-hour zone, or at 75 when the speed limit is 65. Collisions increase too, but because of heightened variance — a couple biddies clinging to the speed limit while everyone careens around them and jockeys for pole position. That's why we're all pressured to 'go with the flow,' even if we want to obey the law, because variance is dangerous. It's peer pressure, Hanni, peer bullying to make otherwise law-abiding drivers dangerous, yet the majority of Americans view speeding the way they view gun ownership – a sacred right – protected by some undocumented Bill of Rights amendment. 'Speeding doesn't kill,' they say. 'Bad drivers do.'" Hanni regarded Jack with amusement.

"WADA can drone all it wants about PEDs and you and Susan can bemoan unnecessary plastic surgery, but the aggregate death counts are puny. Speeding costs us thousands and thousands of lives each year, more than alcohol and texting and our multiple wars against terror, but it will never cease because politicians don't have the balls to do the obvious: randomly ticket drivers whose EZ-Pass records prove they were speeding. To think they call themselves patriots! They speed because they are too fat, lazy and intellectually stunted to run, ski, skate, bike, hike, swim or do anything requiring genuine physical effort. Instead, they climb into their monstrous SUVs and sneer at the speedometer because it's the only way their spent, impotent libidos can pawn themselves off as virile – that and by humiliating genuine athletes."

"Think about it, Hanni, we've been collecting the data on hundreds of highways for decades. It used to be time-stamped slips of paper – when and where you entered the toll road, when and where you exited. Now the data is collected electronically. We know when a car passes point A and point B; we know the distance from A to B. In short, we know the average velocity from A to B. We should randomly ticket every hundredth or thousandth speeder. Speeding would drop overnight. It would be so much cheaper than our antiquated 'Smokey and the Bandit' approach. Lawmakers wouldn't be able to flash their smiles and drive away and EZ-Pass wouldn't single you out just because you were a black man driving a sports car. In addition, you couldn't ignore your tickets. EZ-Pass would debit your account automatically."

Hanni rolled her eyes. "And what if no one buys EZ-Pass?"

"Let them wait in line at the tolls. The price of zipping through is driving responsibly. It might take a while, but behavior would change for the better. We could save fifteen to twenty thousand lives each year."

What did Susan see in this guy? No wonder she's so unhappy.

"I agree with Susan," he continued. "I don't give a damn whether Roger Clemens used PEDs. He's not a role model for my figure skating daughter and never will be. But when I'm forced to accelerate to seventy to avoid choking the freeway each time we drive to a practice in Monsey, my daughter notices. *I* am her role model, and my actions instruct her to abide by laws which are convenient and disregard those which aren't. We as a nation bend over backward to teach our children hypocrisy. Alex Rodriguez's occasional PED infractions are despicable but daddy's *daily* contribution to the national death toll is just fine. You want to teach our children something useful? Teach them that illegally risking other people's lives is expensive, not to some cartoon character in a sportscast, but to daddy. And teach them over and over until daddy learns. Then they won't grow up with hypocrisy wired into their DNA."

Hanni sighed audibly. The conversation was boring. Jack Roberts was boring. She reached into her purse for a cigarette.

Jack turned right off 267 onto North Lake Boulevard. "Ten minutes, Hanni."

"Two," she corrected him. "It comes up really quickly."

"I meant the time lost by letting me drive. We lost ten minutes driving 65 miles per hour instead of 80. We left the hospital 55 minutes ago." They pulled into the driveway next to the "For Sale" sign. Hanni would have driven 90 to be spared Jack's harangue.

❧❦

Wally pried the back off the flat-screen television and DVD player in his daughter's bedroom and slipped the hard drive and pocket modem inside. The puzzles were more sensible when the pornographic data was separated. He could visualize the missing pieces but not resurrect them. Where were they? And why were seemingly random and occasionally misleading pieces substituted in their place? Had he overlooked a hidden server? Or did the server collude with other servers off-site? Why hadn't he detected their interaction?

The pornographic files were bizarre. They were so banal, so grainy, so amateurish. There was no drama, no story. They didn't even show faces – just body parts and long snippets of copulation, always from an uncomfortably close angle. Wallace couldn't watch. They made him nauseous. He wondered how many he would have to endure to fathom their connection to the data-smuggling.

Wallace decided he'd fulfilled his quota of nausea for the day. He flipped on the DVD still inserted in the unit, a romance about vampires and werewolves. He watched it from beginning to end, ruminating about the missing and substituted files. The plot seemed a caricature of Shakespeare. He was unsure whether he heard Volturi or Verona. They were both apparently in Italy. Wallace sighed. He could not ask his daughter to explain it.

Jeff found the woman from the Bureau attractive – not young but neither was he. She was not like the women at Langley. She did not consciously hide everything, least of all her personality. She spoke what she thought, more like a district attorney than a field agent. And her hair was hypnotic. It was dyed, of course, the Julianne Moore reddish brown that was the rage nowadays, but it had this wild, impossibly tangled sensuality about it. She pulled it back in a loose ponytail but as many strands wiggled free as were bound. They sprang up and down as she walked, and swayed side to side as she spoke. Every now and then she smiled, a broad radiant smile, as if she possessed not a care in the world, which of course she could not. She could retire any time she wanted, and the government would pay for everything. Her employer always paid its bills. It owned the Mint. It never defaulted. Mother would like her, he thought. He did not mean the Big Chief at Langley. He meant his real mother in New York City –

the one who wrote romances for young women a third his age. Why didn't she write romances for him? He could use some sage, debonair advice. He ventured onto a limb.

"That was pretty clever of her, programming the server to randomly replace encrypted files with media files from his iPhone."

"They were rapes, Jeff – rapes of our informant, tacitly or expressly countenanced by you and your pals at the Agency. Maybe she wants you to see how much you debased her." Jeff winced at the awkward start. He forgot it was his agent's vagina and uterus that were dismaying scientists in a hidden bunker outside Tehran.

"Well, the important thing is she injected gibberish into the code and let us insert malicious code of our own."

Trade secrets, wire transfers, counterfeit securities; the operation was astonishingly efficient. The securities were the most valuable part. Hotchkiss, Erdoğan and their as-yet unidentified accomplices allowed the government to circumvent financial sanctions. They could transmit almost any information undetected. Inserting Kaplan into the equation was genius. She furnished Erdoğan with two prime suspects in the event the trail got hot – a clueless IT administrator with digital fingerprints all over the incriminating evidence and a wife with a hot body and obviously divided national loyalties. Błaszczyk trained his agent well.

"Did we really have to let him go?" It was the eighth time she asked, "Erdoğan, I mean."

"You don't get it, Jill, do you? The objective is national security, not some publicized affirmation that bad guys were apprehended, and justice was served. We got what we needed, and our assets are secure. What we don't need is publicity."

"He won't last six months," she countered.

"We gave him a choice – protection and a cell at Gitmo, a trial in the distant, indefinite future before an undefined tribunal, followed by a lengthy prison sentence in some God-forsaken extraterritorial prison and eventual deportation back to a land that would execute him for treason. The man chose freedom."

Special Agent Kroll was dissatisfied. The case was closed, the records sealed, but there was no sense of closure – of a jury verdict, a sentence, or even an elementary exchange of pleadings. Where were the defense attorneys, the prosecutors, the Congressional inquests, the press?

The Department of Homeland Security saw the situation differently. The spigot of misappropriated data was destroyed, the transferred information useless, the recipient computer systems sabotaged, the perpetrators dead or defanged, and every detail copiously documented and explained. DHS possessed what it needed, behind closed doors, to assuage the White House and Senate Committee on Homeland Security and Governmental Affairs. Turning the investigation into a media circus would endanger assets in the field and divulge proprietary investigative techniques.

DHS slapped Jill's wrist more than once for arresting Wallace on charges of computer fraud and espionage. It did not help that he was so quickly exonerated. Still, the seeming ambivalence to due process made her uneasy.

"Ends over means, Jill." The speaker could have been Osama bin Laden or Kim Jong Un or Bashar Hafez al-Assad but it was CIA operative Geoffrey Błaszczyk. "Sometimes you have to bend the rules a bit, like we did when we let Sanford Hotchkiss observe George Wallace's interrogation. You objected vehemently but Hotchkiss and Erdoğan took the bait. He bought us time, Jill. They would have cut and run."

"So you let a hit man assassinate Lyden and Hotchkiss instead."

"We don't know that, Jill, not for a fact. Besides, it made the situation clearer for Gürhan Erdoğan. He talked." It did not seem to bother Błaszczyk that the hit man was still at large, and that the elusive leader, Marja, was still just a hazy silhouette. Detective Kroll paused a moment before continuing.

"You don't think it was cruel using George Wallace the way we did. I mean, his daughter was dying, and his life is ruined. And his wife? My God, she was just a child when you recruited her."

Jeff held up his hands in mock surrender. "Guilty as charged, Jill. Guilty as charged. I would love to say war is hell and recite all sorts of patriotic bullshit. But I won't insult your intelligence. I did what was expedient. Believe me; I did not expect their daughter to get sick. No one did. It was horrible timing for everyone. I am going to try to make it up to them."

Jill nodded but said nothing. No power on earth could make it up to them.

Part IV:

The Co-opted

Chapter 24

WALK. In letters. Wallace thought for a moment he'd been transported back to 1990 but acknowledged time travel was confined to his dreams. At least today.

Andrew descended the stairs to the service entrance, slipped through the open door, and glimpsed the morning bustle of the laundry room. A wall of dryers chugged and groaned epithets at the washers. The wall of washers clanked and rasped churlish rebukes. A crowd of women chatted comfortably, some seated with tabloids on cheap plastic benches, others congregated about an inexpensive Formica island with four protruding piers. An iron moved on one of those piers, making firm, sweeping strokes across a draped linen surface. A fleet of wire laundry bins navigated the channel between the ironing boards and dryer portals and two monstrous front-loading washers. A skirmish broke out over who was entitled to use the triple loaders next. Two flotillas of laundry bins mobilized into position, a defensive perimeter and an offensive blockade. Naked fluorescent bulbs glared and blew harsh ripples on the warped linoleum tiles. The cadence, sultry heat, soft lilt of Jamaican accents, and riot of tossed, folded and ironed colors were tropical – a bric-a-brac, subterranean Kingston Town. Andrew surmised none of the women lived upstairs. He doubted the residents could describe the place – no inlaid marble, no burled paneling, and no soft, recessed lighting. He turned down the corridor and located the managing agent's office. He knocked unannounced on the door frame.

Randall gazed up from an oversized desk. Andrew wondered how they maneuvered it through the doorway. He presumed it belonged once to a tenant – no point letting it go to waste. He had to move the green plastic deck chair into the doorway to seat himself opposite the building manager. He could not imagine working in this cramped, windowless cabin – a makeshift office in the bowels of an aging, 35-story steamship.

Andrew savored the analogy. The co-op was indeed a steamship, as were most residential and commercial structures in Manhattan. 100,000 buildings consumed 13.6 megatons of steam annually from pipes under the streets of Manhattan. It was the only system like it in the world. The steam heated the water, ran the heating units, fueled the washer-dryers, vented eerie clouds of vapor from manholes, and ignited occasionally spectacular sidewalk explosions. The most memorable occurred July 18, 2007, just off 41st Street and Lexington Avenue. Andrew had a bird's eye view from his mother's office. The eruption reached the fortieth floor. It showered scalding mud, debris and asbestos from the underground pipes onto pedestrians and commuters congregating around Grand Central station and the Chrysler Building. The timing was inopportune – 6 pm, the height of rush hour. The city cowered, thinking it was under terrorist attack, but it was just the cantankerous belch of an archaic and distinctive power distribution system that needed a makeover after 119 years of service.

Andrew regarded his occasional partner. He needed a makeover too. His tie was nondescript and dark – as dark as the rings under his eyes. His skin was pallid, sallow – the color of his cheap button-down shirt. An inexpensive H&M blazer lay folded on the wall of recycled metal file cabinets packed tightly behind him. He picked at an "everything" bagel with cream cheese on a wax paper wrapper. Randall pushed it to the side in embarrassment.

"Uh, hello Andrew," he stammered, surprised by the visitor's appearance. Tenants and building staff poked their heads in all the time. That's why he kept the door ajar, but a visit from Andrew was special. He doubted Andrew had ever been there, or ever entered the building. A ray of hope infused him. The repair of the N line, his apartment included, was a crushing headache. The tenants were impatient and increasingly hostile. The old men on the board were worse, pestering him constantly about work schedules, as if he had control over anything. His LinkedIn account said "resident manager" but his mind said "designated pincushion." Was Andrew here with an olive branch, perhaps even to propose a date?

Randall had never been courted at his office. His heart swelled with sheepish joy. He felt as he did when he was sixteen, when Alex reached down and gripped his hand. Neither said a word. They were always afraid to, afraid the other would take mortal offense, brand the other publicly as a faggot. But Alex did not. He reached for his hand and just held it, tightly, as if it was the most natural gesture in the world. Randall felt the color return to his cheeks.

"This is such a … surprise," he managed. "I wish you called. I could have met you somewhere … somewhere nicer." He glanced apologetically at the surroundings. He wondered whether there was a way to make Andrew more comfortable. "Would you like to go for a walk," he offered, "in the park?" Perhaps they could hold hands, just as he did so long ago with Alex.

"That won't be necessary," answered Andrew abruptly. "I'm actually here on business."

Randall's heart sank. He had a premonition. Andrew wanted him to remove his belongings – the few bibelots and articles of clothing he kept at Andrew's apartment. He could taste the bile rising in his throat. He reached instinctively for the Vitamin Water that stood on his desk. Andrew continued.

"I'm doing some legwork for Allison Pfouts. She lives in your building."

Randall knew Mrs. Pfouts. She was the old lady who lived in 14P, next door to the disaster in 14N. She wore her hearing aid when she had visitors or used the phone. Otherwise, she was as deaf as a post. It took two days before she discovered the parade of workmen outside her door. Now she was a constant presence, so concerned about her "dear neighbor, Shelly," but unable to tear herself from the drama in 14N. The superintendent chased her out three times. She never had carte blanche to her neighbor's apartment before nor, Randall presumed, his past life. Truman found her poring through photo albums in the large walnut sideboard the first time. It was a big, hulking piece of 1920s furniture. Randall could not imagine how they fit it into the service elevator. Truman found her bouncing on the bed the second time, testing the springs on the late wife's side. Truman could tell whose side was whose in an instant. There was a black-and-white photograph of a glamorous young woman on Mr. Vogel's side, and a black-and-white photograph of a dashing young man on the other. The third time, Mrs. Pfouts was discovered rearranging items in the refrigerator.

"Yes, she lives in 14P; a bit eccentric, but very sweet." Randall surprised himself. He expected to insult her, as he secretly insulted all the tenants, but could not, not when he considered her interest in dear old Shelly. She was daft and nosy but a decidedly sweet old lady, not unlike his mother. "She spends a lot of time traveling – makes two or three trips a year. What's going on?"

"Sorry, Randall, attorney-client privilege." Andrew waited his entire life to say that. He felt grown up and important. Randall slumped in his chair. "What can you tell me about Mrs. Pfouts' neighbor, Sheldon Vogel?"

"Oh God," panicked Randall. "The lawsuits have begun. How on earth was 14P damaged? It didn't share the bathroom wet wall with 14N, did it?" He suppressed the impulse to roll out the master floor plan on his desk. "Privileged information," he thought. Let Andrew subpoena him.

Randall answered, "Not much – a quiet, polite, dapper old man, widowed like Mrs. Pfouts. It's a pity about the accident." Randall realized he liked Mr. Vogel, too. He was a bit like his dad.

"What accident?" It was Andrew's turn to be curious.

"The one I told you about two days ago," Randall gloated. "The one I told you about when you weren't listening," he repeated silently, "the reason I have to work on Saturday."

Andrew struggled to remember. At last he blurted out, "Damn it, Randall, this is an important case to me. Mother is all over my ass about drumming up work. Help me out this once, will you? I'll make it up to you, I promise."

"Damn," thought Andrew, "That's how I got suckered into sharing my apartment the first time. Well, I'm not going to allow it this time. I'm going to get what I need and dump him. I'm sick and tired of being used. Stupid Dyke-man."

Randall sighed. "Sheldon Vogel stepped in front of a bus. He almost died. The superintendent found him unconscious in the bath after it spilled over and flooded the N line. He's been at Roosevelt Hospital since Tuesday."

Suicide, thought Andrew. Vogel must have been overcome by guilt. The "accident" was tantamount to a confession. But what if he died? Then he'd have to establish mental state without proof.

"How bad is he?" Andrew asked. He meant physical condition, not character. Randall evidently understood.

"Serious. Truman says he has pneumonia and a bunch of tubes jutting out of his body. He spent the first couple days in a coma. Evidently, they had to operate." Andrew did not like the sounds of this.

"Has anyone else been to see him?"

"Not me," replied Randall. "I'm too busy managing the cleanup. You should speak with his lawyer, John Roberts. I hear he's been at his side the entire time; won't leave the poor fellow alone."

Andrew's ears pricked up. "Lawyer?"

"Yeah, John Roberts. He lives in the building. The doorman says he was with Mr. Vogel during the accident. It seems like they know each other quite well."

Andrew was suddenly intrigued. "Do you know how long they've known each other?"

"Years, I imagine," came the answer. It was Randall's seventh week at the building. "At least that is what everyone else says." Randall recalled the call from the attending physician at Roosevelt Hospital, the one who asked him to rummage through Mr. Vogel's Rolodex. The memory made Randall angry. He was pressured from all sides to bend the rules, forgetting (or knowing) he would take the blame if something went wrong. He did not cave in. He stood his ground. "Yes," he said, "You'll have to deal with Mr. Roberts if Mrs. Pfouts wants to sue Mr. Vogel for water damage. Mr. Roberts is the old man's consigliere." Randall added the last word for drama. It pleased him that Andrew paid attention.

Andrew's mind raced. He no longer wished to see Mrs. Pfouts. He excused himself from Randall's office. "This has been really helpful, Randall. You say Mr. Vogel is at Roosevelt Hospital, on Tenth Avenue, right?" The building agent nodded. "I want to get over there before the other visitors arrive. I'll call you later this week. I promise." He rose from the chair and strode past the laundry room to the service exit. The concierge watched his movements on the monitor upstairs. Randall sat back and scratched his head. He doubted whether Andrew would keep his promise. He pulled a dog-eared yearbook from his desk and opened it to page forty-six. A kind face peered up from the third row of photographs. Where was he now, Randall wondered, and did he ever open his copy to page forty-one?

ȣ∵

"So you are a lawyer, too?" remarked Dr. Martinez sourly. "At least you have the decency to say so." Andrew raised his eyebrows quizzically. Martinez explained, "Your colleague, Mr. Roberts, he's a number."

Andrew resisted the impulse to correct Martinez's misimpression. "I'm so sorry to hear that," he offered. "In what way, may I ask?"

"Oh, by being so mysterious. First, he says he hardly knows the guy but he's at his bedside day and night until he wakes. Then he's the first one to speak with him. Doesn't notify a nurse that the patient has awoken for an hour. Then, all of a sudden, he's been the patient's lawyer for years. The patient says so. And now he's vanished. Not a trace. Some lawyer! Some friend!" Dr. Martinez omitted mention of banishing him from the hospital. The legal department decided it was not the most prudent response.

"Well, that's why I'm here," improvised Andrew. "Would it be all right with you if I spent some time with Mr. Vogel? You see, there has been substantial water damage to his neighbors' apartments. We are trying to sort matters out with the insurers. There are so many of them – different carriers for each apartment. It's enough to drive you crazy. I am sure Mr. Roberts is stressed. So that is why I'm here, to help relieve some of the burden. I promise not to agitate Mr. Vogel. We just want to make sure he returns to a habitable and perfectly-restored apartment." Dr. Martinez smiled. There was hope for the legal profession after all. Old men like John Roberts gave the profession a bad rap. This younger generation was not as shady.

"Of course, you may," he replied, "and come see me afterward if you want to discuss his treatment." He shook Mr. Fallis's hand cordially and offered his card. Andrew reached for his wallet, thought twice, then apologized for forgetting his cards at the office. He inquired at the nursing station where he could find Mr. Vogel.

❧❧

The patient was apoplectic. "What do you mean, the money has not been restored? I saw the documents myself. Mrs. Pfouts signed them. So did Cathy, your mother, and Jack Roberts."

"But you were not there in person?"

"Well, I thought I was, but how could I be? I've been here. No, Jack Roberts took care of everything. He sold the gold, restored Mrs. Pfouts' account, secured her written waiver, rebated my annual advisory fee as gratitude to Mrs. Pfouts, and put the

346 • PATRICK FINEGAN

rest of the proceeds in my own account. I don't know what I'd do without him."

Andrew reflected a moment then inquired, "You are confident my mother attested the waiver agreement, that you saw her notarized signature?"

Sheldon was pretty sure. He was so groggy. Well, of course he was sure. Who else would have signed in her place?

Who indeed, thought Andrew? "I am sure it is just a matter of timing, the Jewish holidays, perhaps. The bank probably didn't update its records until this morning. Would you mind going over the gold part one more time? You see, I'm covering for my mother, who's out of town until next week, and don't want to interrupt her meetings. Could you do that for me?"

"Such a considerate young man," thought Sheldon. "Pity Helen never met someone like him before she died. She was always with Diana. The two were inseparable – like twins. I bet it was awkward for the guys, having to butt in like that. They were probably so put off they gave up." Marian would have a word with her, he decided. He turned back to the nice young man in the gray silk suit with narrow lapels. "So you see, Mr. Fallis, Mr. Roberts took care of everything. Now would you forgive an old man for being tired? I would like to rest. Will I see you tomorrow?" Andrew promised he would. He raced back to his office, passing over the paved-in crater from the 2007 Grand Central geyser.

❧

"No, of course I did not notarize a waiver. I'm in Philadelphia. You are sure Mr. Vogel saw my signature?"

"Yes, Mother. I think he's been defrauded by this Mr. Roberts, his lawyer."

Catherine Fallis could not imagine her friend, Shelly, hiring a lawyer, or doing so without asking her for a referral. She agreed silently the man sounded suspicious. "What firm does he work for, this Mr. Roberts?" She expected Fitzsimmons & Fitzsimmons or any of a dozen other firms that advertised brazenly in the subways.

"He doesn't. As far as I can tell, he's been unemployed since May. Martindale-Hubbell says he was a partner at Dewey & LeBoeuf before it crashed. Before that he was a partner in the New York offices of Brobeck Phleger and Harrison, which also collapsed. He started at Brown & Wood and was at Drexel Burnham & Lambert when it tanked – one failed enterprise after another. I bet he and his family are strapped financially," ventured Andrew. "The maintenance on the front apartments is three or four thousand dollars a month, plus I understand he still has a mortgage. I bet they're burning through sixteen or seventeen grand a month."

"Or more," reflected Catherine. She knew what it cost to raise a family on Central Park South. Andrew had no idea. "Look," she said, "I agree there is something fishy going on. Have you frozen the account?"

Andrew did not reply.

"It's okay, Andrew. You've done a fine job. Mr. Vogel sounds like he made an honest mistake but was duped by this Mr. Roberts in trying to fix it. Roberts has probably absconded with all of Mrs. Vogel's gold jewelry and appeased him with a bunch of phony documents. But we can't rule out his siphoning money from Mrs. Pfouts' account. Let's prevent that from occurring or notify the authorities to monitor the account and perhaps catch him in the act."

Andrew admitted this was a prudent course of action. He kept his mother on the phone while he powered up his aging Dell computer.

"I'm proud of you, Andrew," she offered, "for showing initiative. This is a nice piece of detective work. Just make sure Mrs. Pfouts knows we are tracking down a 'discrepancy' in her monthly balances – nothing that will interfere with her travel plans. Sheldon Vogel is such a dear friend to both of us. I am sure he'll make good on the $90,000. Right now, we have to concentrate on the real pirate, this Captain Jack Roberts." That sounded almost as good as Captain Jack Sparrow, she thought. There must have been a Captain Roberts in the history books, she decided. Andrew accepted the praise but ignored the witticism. He was already in law school when *Pirates of the Caribbean* was released. He found the reference to children's movies condescending.

Andrew refreshed the browser two more times. He verified the account number against the printouts on his desk. He consulted the transaction history for a full minute in dazed astonishment before responding to his mother. "He's emptied the account, Mother. Captain Jack Roberts has emptied the account."

Chapter 25

The figure winked at his counterpart across the street. His counterpart winked back. Thus began their conspiracy.

This can't be true." She threw the report on the desk. "It can't be!"

She slammed the door shut for privacy then continued pacing her small windowless office. Her unit investigated computer fraud. Large thefts, small thefts, it scarcely mattered. One day she assisted the CIA in throttling funding sources for international terrorism, the next day she cased a wayward lawyer with outsized spending habits and limited resources. Exhibit A was John B. Roberts, her unwitting former heartthrob and suspected $1.4 million embezzler. The victim was an 81-year-old widow in his apartment complex. A befuddled money manager was his stooge or his dupe; she was unsure which. The Fallis law firm described the players plainly – with one important omission. The biggest victim was Jill Fitzgerald Kroll, cat's paw to a pathetic and absurd saccharine fantasy. The guy was a fraud, a grifter. He insinuated himself into a woman's mind, held it hostage for, what, twenty-five years and then smashed it against the rocks with one cold dose of reality. How many suitors had she rejected? Five? Six? Roberts was the impossibly high standard. No one else considered Todd English, Sarah Caldwell, or calla lilies. No one else penned and then scratched out obscure references to Shakespeare. And now there were no more suitors, just a file and some clipped photos of a fallen lawyer, one who stooped to robbing defenseless widows.

She ran a cursory trace of the money. The perpetrator liquidated the estate's securities, transferred the proceeds to an individual account set up under a phony alias at the same institution, then wired all but a few thousand dollars to a secure account in

Cyprus – secure, that is, from the intruding eyes of the authorities. The account could as easily have been in the Cayman Islands or Panama. Tax haven sounded so benign, but it hid and laundered the swindled life savings of a helpless widow. Heaven knew whether the money was still in the account and, if so, whether it could be frozen or recovered. She would certainly try.

≈

Wallace sat on the edge of Alya's bed. He stared at the signed concert poster of Lady Gaga. How had Hanni managed to procure it? The poster of Justin Bieber was also signed. Were they counterfeit? No, the movie poster from *Yellow Submarine* was unsigned. Hanni could get in to see anyone, anyone numbering among the living. He buried his head in his hands and whispered his daughter's name. He moved nothing since returning from confinement – a time capsule. But she no longer numbered among the living. He re-entered the capsule in anticipation of the move. Hanni said she found a buyer, this time for real, this time for cash. She called him personally to say so. She sounded excited, radiant, eager to turn another chapter. The reticence he felt he felt alone. He had long since packed up the other rooms – dozens of moving boxes stacked and labeled in the dining area and master bedroom. Some were for Hanni but most would be stored in the garage of his childhood home in Alabama, the one abutting the cemetery. The furniture and desk items were all that remained. He sat in Alya's room and said good-bye.

≈

Wallace entered Melissa Roberts' bedroom with two airline rollers. He pulled the signed posters of Lady Gaga and Justin Bieber out of a cardboard tube and presented them to Mrs. Roberts. "I'm sure Brierley could sell them at auction if you don't want them." He knew about private school fundraisers. Hanni handled the ones for Alya's school. She arranged better celebrity dates than the Democratic Party. Wallace felt ashamed offering the Roberts signed celebrity posters, but Susan accepted them graciously. She even managed to rise from her wheelchair, totter a few steps and embrace him. Her right leg was noticeably shorter than her left. She would probably insert a platform in her right shoe when she went out. She would need a thick one. The luggage contained American Girl outfits, skating gear and a wardrobe of children's haute couture – most of it with tags. He knew none of the items fit Melissa but was confident Brierley could auction some of them. A commotion drew Melissa and Wallace into the foyer. Susan followed in her wheelchair. Two policemen and a plainclothes detective stood in the doorway. The detective wore a navy-blue skirt suit and a white, collared dress shirt. She resembled the assistant district attorney on *Law & Order*.

"Mr. Roberts? Mr. John Roberts? We'd like you to accompany us to the eighteenth precinct. We have some questions to ask you in connection with your work?"

Work? Jack hadn't worked in five months. He stood dazed but regained his composure, "Yes, officer. May I ask whether I am suspected of criminal activity?" Susan felt suddenly lightheaded. She gripped the wheels of the chair to keep from fainting. Her hands somehow slipped, and the chair lurched forward. It rammed Wallace and he stumbled forward awkwardly then righted himself. He gazed directly into the eyes of Jill Kroll, the woman from the FBI, the woman who helped conduct his interrogation.

Jill stepped back in shock. Her head spun but she managed three words, "Yes, him too."

৯৯৯

Jill excused herself from the police detail and hastened to the office. She left instructions for the men to be detained until she returned. If either insisted on calling a lawyer, they should allow it. She did not expect them to waive their rights. Roberts was the most elusive man in America. The important thing is she knew who he was. Now at least they could track him.

Jill rummaged through her file drawer and extricated the top secret file on Gürhan Erdoğan and NYL Health Systems. She was not supposed to retain a copy. "Screw Błaszczyk," she muttered. "He never followed the rules." Wallace and his wife were citizens, for Christ's sake. He treated them like Sudanese Al-Qaeda. The poor guy would be moldering in Guantanamo if I hadn't made a stink about the recordings, the recordings that plainly implicated Hotchkiss. Now, she almost regretted it. Still, she was not going to call CIA until she was sure. It could all be one crazy coincidence. John Roberts, the embezzler, and George Wallace, the confused ex-husband of a CIA informant, could just be neighbors.

Slowly and painfully, Agent Kroll connected the dots. There were too many dots for coincidence – crazy or otherwise. She had stumbled across the biggest prize of all: the most wanted man in America. She would arrest Roberts on charges of embezzlement, conduct a thorough search of his files and equipment, interrogate him herself, then place a call to Langley. She cursed herself for not seeing the connection earlier; her mind was too clouded by emotion. "Damn it, girl. You meant nothing to him. He doesn't even recognize you!"

☙❧

Bail was set at $3.5 million. The apartment and investments were secured as collateral. His attorney shook his head at the alleged alibi. "It never happened? How do you explain the disappearance of $1.4 million? Or the fact that half New York says you are his lawyer? Believe me, you need to do better than that to avoid jail time. Let's start again, from the beginning…"

☙❧

"Your client understands he has the right to remain silent?"

"Yes."

"And that anything he says can and will be used against him in a court of law?"

"Yes."

"And that you are his attorney?"

"Yes."

"Then let's begin…"

The defendant stated his name, date of birth, address, marital status, and former places of employment.

"Mr. George Wallace visited your apartment this morning with two large suitcases? Do you know where he was traveling?" Mr. Williams stared at the woman in disbelief.

"Who said Mr. Wallace was going anywhere?" the attorney objected.

"The question is for Mr. Roberts. Mr. Roberts, do you have any idea why Mr. Wallace visited you with two large suitcases?"

"Who said he visited Mr. Roberts? My understanding was he was in the child's bedroom with Mrs. Roberts and her daughter, and that the cases were full of his late daughter's clothes, skating equipment and doll accessories."

"None of which suited or fitted the Roberts daughter. What else was in the case, Mr. Roberts?" Roberts and his attorney sat speechless.

"I'll make it simpler. What did Mr. Wallace say to you?"

Jack leaned forward and motioned his attorney to remain silent. "We exchanged pleasantries. He asked to see my wife and Melissa, my daughter. He brought items that might be of interest to the auction committee at my daughter's school."

"And he brought nothing more?" Jack appraised whether the question was a trap. Could he possibly be contradicted at trial? He risked being forthright – no need to antagonize the FBI unduly.

"I am not aware of what was in the cases, just what he asserted they contained. My wife and daughter were the only ones who inspected the contents."

"I see. We arrived too soon. Tell me, what did you and Mr. Wallace discuss Saturday mornings in the park – in the winter, I mean, before your trip to Alabama?"

Mr. Williams was annoyed. His client disavowed everything to him yet here was an identified co-conspirator. If Wallace squawked first, Roberts could go to prison for years. Williams planned a blunt conversation with his client. He was inclined to request a recess right now.

"We discussed our daughters' respective interests, including figure skating."

"Anything else?"

"Our wives' respective interests."

"I see, and by wives you mean to include Mr. Wallace's *ex*-wife, Hanife Kaplan?"

"They were married then, but yes, I mean *Mrs.* Hanife Kaplan Wallace."

"Did you discuss her business?"

"I'm not sure. My impression is that she was an event planner."

"Indeed … fitting title. And did you discuss your respective lines of work?"

"Past work, mainly, our work in the 1980s. The stories were more interesting and easier to relate to. I suspect we both thought our current lines of work rather boring."

"I see. And what exactly is your current line of work?"

"I am an unemployed securities lawyer. I worked for law firms that helped clients raise money in the capital markets."

"And you consider yourself an expert in that field – helping clients raise money from nameless investors, I mean?"

"I object!" interrupted Williams. "You're distorting his answer." Where the hell was this leading?

"Noted. How about Mr. Wallace? What is his area of expertise?"

"My understanding was he was CTO, that's Chief Technology Officer, of NYL Health Systems, a respected hospital management company."

"Foundation, you mean, with no public SEC disclosures. Isn't that right?"

"I don't know. We never discussed its organizational form."

"Let me repeat the question: What would you consider his area of expertise?"

Mr. Williams interrupted. "Are you asking my client to aver facts or issue a naked opinion?"

"An informed opinion, if you will, together with the factual basis for that opinion."

"He said his biggest priority was to improve data security at the hospitals. He said there was a large gap between the level of data protection at NYL and at his previous employer, a regional bank."

"Good, hacking. Now …"

Williams objected. "My client said Wallace expressed interest in improving data protection. He said nothing about the converse, breaking into data systems."

"Noted. You spent a long weekend with Mr. and Mrs. Wallace in Birmingham, Alabama. Did you have any private conversations with either of them?"

"Yes, I suppose I did."

"And what did you discuss?"

"My sorrow at their loss. We were there to bury their only daughter."

"Very neighborly of you." Williams was furious at the tone. Why didn't his client seem angry? His client remained composed, suspiciously so. What was he hiding? "Can you recall discussing anything else?"

"No, although my wife and I helped Mr. Wallace return home. He was pretty distraught."

"I see. So you sat with him on the flight from Birmingham to Atlanta, the flight from Atlanta to New York, and the car service back to your building?"

"Yes I did."

"And you can't recall discussing anything other than the funeral that entire time?'

"No, I can't. We were all rather shaken. I don't suppose you've lost an only child, Ms. Kroll?" Ms. Kroll ignored the question.

"Tell me, Mr. Roberts. Why does Mr. Wallace call you Captain? Did you serve in the military together?" Jack was suddenly unnerved. Eavesdropping? Wallace or his conversations had evidently been bugged, but for how long? The interrogation had precious little to do with Sheldon Vogel or his portfolio.

"I did not serve in the military. I have no idea whether Mr. Wallace did."

"Yet he calls you Captain."

"Yes, it is a joke. I call him Governor George Wallace, and he calls me Captain Jack Roberts."

Ms. Kroll shook her head. "That doesn't fly, Mr. Roberts. Your surname isn't Sparrow. I repeat, why does he call you Captain?"

Jack gave up. "Ms. Kroll, my middle name is Bartholomew. You will discover that John Bartholomew Roberts was indeed a genuine eighteenth-century buccaneer, not your fictitious Disney character, and that this line of questioning will only lead the prosecuting attorney to public ridicule."

The agent huffed. "Good, a pirate and a racist – apt monikers for a pair of suspected criminals."

"What?" demanded Williams, pounding on the table. "This is preposterous!" Kroll ignored him.

"Let's talk about your flight to Chicago, the one you took in early April." Jack and his attorney exchanged quizzical glances. Jack motioned for him to again remain silent. "What did you discuss with Gürhan Erdoğan?" Blank comprehension. "Come, come. You sat directly behind him. I saw you exit the plane together." Jack's attorney wondered what possible connection this had to embezzlement. He read an article about Erdoğan in *Forbes*. Or was that the prime minister of Turkey? Mr. Williams wondered whether he read the wrong indictment. Jack wondered why he had not recognized her earlier.

"Jill," he gushed suddenly. "Jill Kroll!" A smile brightened his face.

"Yes, that's my name. Must I repeat the question?" Jack's face darkened. He glanced down sheepishly. His attorney reached over but Jack gave him a reassuring nod.

"I'm sorry. It was just a random thought, a memory actually, but I'm back now. I am pretty confident the man seated in front of me and I exchanged no words whatsoever during the flight. I suspect the passengers seated around me can confirm that."

"I see. You then traveled to Reno, Nevada, where you met with Mrs. Hanife Kaplan Wallace, did you not?"

Jack's representative could no longer contain himself. "I'm sorry for being obtuse, Mrs. Kroll, but could you explain what relevance this has to the alleged charges? I will not countenance random fishing."

"I am *Ms.* Kroll, Mr. Williams, not missus. The connection will become clear as we progress. Will your client answer the question or not?"

"My wife Susan lay in Renown Regional Medical Center in a coma after a skiing accident at Squaw Valley. She shared a cabin with a girlfriend, *Ms.* Hanife Kaplan Wallace. We sat vigil together during my wife's recovery."

"And what did you talk about during your time together?"

"About Susan."

"Nothing else?"

"Not that I remember."

"Did you know Ms. Kaplan worked for Gürhan Erdoğan, the man you sat behind on the plane?"

"The plane to Chicago-O'Hare International Airport? No, I did not."

"Did she mention him?"

"Not that I recall."

"Do you recall dining at the restaurant, Trattoria Dell'Arte, on March 29th of this year?"

March 29th was Susan's fortieth birthday. "Yes." Boy, did he remember!

"What did Ms. Kaplan discuss with you when she arrived?" The question puzzled Jack. Hanni promised to come but never showed. Was she standing in one of the corners?

"I'm sorry, Ms. Kroll, there were so many guests. I somehow missed her."

"I find that difficult to believe, Mr. Roberts. Our detectives say the back room was nearly empty when she arrived – just an old lady and her nurse, a young girl, *and you*. Are you challenging our detective's account?"

"You must mean later," surmised Jack. "The maître d' will confirm we had dozens of guests until the guest of honor, my wife, stormed out. I must have missed Hanni in the commotion."

"We'll check that. Did she leave anything for you or you for her?"

"Not that I recall."

"What about in Reno? Or Lake Tahoe? I understand you spent the night with her?" Mr. Williams raised his eyebrows. Jack shook his head.

"I retrieved my wife's belongings and rental car. I rested at the motel before returning the car to San Francisco."

"Yet returned to the motel for an evening before continuing on to Reno … and did not sleep on the couch."

"Christ," thought Jack. "Do they have eyes everywhere?"

"We skied for a day. I needed a break from the tension. I think Hanni did too."

"And that included consorting during the evening?"

Jack swallowed the temptation to protest. This was the only charge that would stick. It wasn't criminal, Jack conceded; it was worse. "Yes," he said matter-of-factly, "It did."

"So, you felt sleeping with your close friend's wife while your own wife lay in a coma would somehow relieve the tension?"

Jack crept onto the offensive. "I am curious, Ms. Kroll, how Mr. Wallace became my *close* friend and how his re-marriage to the *ex*-Mrs. Wallace escaped my attention. My wife was dying and an unmarried woman offered me solace. I accepted it."

Ms. Kroll continued coldly, "And what did you offer her in exchange?" Jack stared at her blankly. "Come now, Mr. Roberts, you're a big boy. Mr. Erdoğan offered her emoluments, gave her husband a plush job, ensured her event planning business was brimming with activity. Surely she demanded something from you."

Jack furrowed his brow, thought for a moment, then shook his head. "I'm sorry to hear about her affair with Gürhan Erdoğan. I would like to believe he coerced her. You'll have to ask Ms. Kaplan, though. I just don't know."

"Why did you use the word affair rather than relationship? You said yourself Ms. Kaplan was divorced."

"She divorced her husband after the funeral. I assumed, evidently falsely, that the *relationship* preceded her divorce. That was un-chivalrous of me and I owe Ms. Kaplan an apology. I have no idea as to the marital status of Gürhan Erdoğan – either then or now."

Mr. Williams was no closer to seeing a connection than Jack was. He was prepared to adjourn the interrogation. Jill decided to lay her suspicions on the table. The man had nowhere to run. His real employer would publicly disavow him, then secretly dispose of him and his family, just as it had with Hotchkiss and Lyden. Car accident? Poison? It scarcely mattered. Roberts' only hope was to cooperate. She switched off the recorder.

"We are on to you, Mr. Roberts, you and your entire covert operation. Let me spell this out for you and your consigliere, although I doubt he or anyone else can help you."

"First, your alias is Marja. The CIA has been after you for years. You arranged the financing and enforcement of the data flow to Iran." Jack blinked. Mr. Willams' jaw dropped. Jack's ex-wife's name was Marcia. Jack wondered whether Kroll somehow got them confused. What in heaven's name was Marcia up to?

"Erdoğan and Hotchkiss set up the data mill at NYL South but you and Wallace were the masterminds. Only a junk bond specialist and mentally imbalanced Internet hacker could have formulated a BitTorrent implementation that transferred the digital signature for billions of dollars of corporate securities, allowing the Iranian government to circumvent trade sanctions. The trade secrets were gravy, but you were pretty generous with them too. A pirate and a racist, I like that – cartoon agents of the jihad." Jack liked the imagery too, except he missed the part about Bit-Torrent and Iran and trade sanctions. What was Wally doing, piping pirated MTV videos into Tehran? And why the hell would that implicate him? Jack listened to Cole Porter … on vinyl. Did MTV even still exist?

"Erdoğan's individual payments and instructions were channeled through the Warwick Hotel on Sixth Avenue, just a stone's throw from your office at Dewey & LeBoeuf. That's why you stuck around until the end. Everyone bailed except you. You went down with the ship, didn't you? It's because you needed inconspicuous access to the rendezvous spot. How many times this spring did you stop there? Ten? Twenty?"

Jack did not respond. He realized by this point the questions were rhetorical. Jack did in fact lunch at the Warwick bar with Susan, colleagues, and occasionally alone, but never with Gürhan Erdoğan. His closest contact was with the gelled follicles of his comb-over on a cramped flight to Chicago. He remained with Dewey & LeBoeuf until the end because he was too busy attending Susan and his daughter to worry about anything else. Besides, he was lamed by lost confidence and indecision. The legal profession was in ruins. He was a lumbering dinosaur. He was no longer agile and there was no place to jump to if he could.

"Tell me, who is your contact in Turkey?" Jack just stared. "Come now, you prepared quite a dossier – 420 pages, all neatly annotated and organized. Times, dates, places – you only omitted the contacts. That was careless, don't you think, leaving the folder on your desk like that. You were so meticulous with electronic files; distributing them in encrypted pieces to servers all over the planet, yet your paper file was right there in plain view. I'm disappointed in you, Mr. Roberts."

Jack suppressed the desire to respond. Kroll was editorializing – about what he was not sure. Hurling aspersions was her prerogative. There was no productive way to respond. She repeated the question. "So who was he, your contact?" Jack wracked his brain. He could not remember whether the tour operator mentioned one. He booked the trip so long ago. He remembered Kroll shut off the recorder. It would be foolish to respond. He just shrugged.

"It's okay, you'll tell us eventually. You'll have to. Besides, we have your tickets. That's incriminating enough. You and your family planned to skedaddle – a one-way cruise to the Greek Islands and Asia Minor … except the CIA caught wind of your operation before you could wind it down. So you and Kaplan set Erdoğan up for the fall. You held back critical pieces of the puzzle." Williams' eyes widened. Ms. Kroll's discourse was fascinating. He never represented a terrorist before.

"How embarrassing for Dr. Erdoğan – images of Ms. Kaplan's vagina instead of vital code sequences. If we didn't silence him, the Iranians would. You made it look like his accomplice, Sanford Hotchkiss, double-crossed him – tried to extort more than he was promised. How convenient he was your neighbor! I bet you wept bitterly during news reports of his murder, especially the part about his lover committing suicide. You were at Trattoria Dell'Arte, weren't you, but Wallace? We'll get to that faker later." Jack remembered the newscasts. The camera crews were out front for days. He took Melissa to school via the garage. So did his sister Eleanor. The Hotchkiss family eventually moved back to Iowa. They could not take the publicity or the shame.

"So what was the plan, Jack, sail into the sunset with Mata Hari after packing her dribbling cuckold in the loony bin and your wife six feet under? It's fickle of you, flitting between women like that. It's a wonder they fall for you at all." Jill Kroll glared at her quarry.

Jack wasn't following any of this, but the last part angered him intensely. He suppressed his indignation a bit longer. That is what he trained his entire life to do, suppress emotional outbursts. He knew his Fifth Amendment rights, and he knew how easily they could be waived. He let his attorney express outrage on his behalf, except Williams was scribbling notes furiously – grist perhaps for a memoir. Jack began to wonder whether Williams was the right person for this assignment. Jack wondered whether anyone was; it was all so preposterous.

"It didn't work out, did it? No more cash machine at NYL, no more pocket change from Dewey & LeBoeuf. But you inherited a girlfriend with higher maintenance than you imagined. A Seminoles hoodie wasn't good enough, was it? This chick likes Givenchy and Jean Paul Gaultier. She only wears haute couture. And what about the conversion of those life insurance policies? Guilt trip because your wife survived? I understand the renewals are expensive. I'd say nigh unaffordable and not much sense unless you were planning, what, to stage your own funeral? Too bad Hotchkiss wasn't as clever as you." Williams scribbled like mad. This case was extraordinary. It heightened his respect for his client.

"So, you went back to earning money the old-fashioned way, the 1980s vulture-fund way, by stealing. It's a wretched shame, Mr. Roberts. You should have stuck to international espionage. You had Geoffrey Błaszczyk and the CIA eating out of your hands." Williams could not agree more. Dumb move, Jack, he thought. But I love the espionage part.

Messrs. Williams and Roberts sat in silence. Roberts raised his hand to allay Williams' urge to earn his fee. He concluded the interrogation. "Thank you, Ms. Kroll, for your exposition. Mr. Williams and I now have a better understanding of the charges against me. We look forward to answering them in the appropriate forum. Please make sure Mr. Williams receives a copy of the tape. I presume, Ms. Kroll, we are through." He uttered the presumption more forcefully than intended.

"We are," she confirmed as forcefully. "Do not try anything foolish, Jack. The CIA won't handle you like I do."

"Jack," he marveled. "She called me Jack." He strained to remember what else she said.

"What do you mean by that – 'the CIA won't handle [him] like [you] do'?" demanded Williams indignantly.

"As a citizen," answered Ms. Kroll. She gathered her files and left without ceremony. The two men exchanged awkward glances. An office shredder chewed a yellowed letter and postcard. A bud vase shattered against the wall, and a mango-tinged calla lily crumpled to the floor.

☙❧

Andrew paced the lobby. The case was not evolving the way he planned. He planned to take action against the Roberts family estate. But the estate was encumbered by a bail bond and several million dollars in debt and expenses. Plus, there was a media circus in front of the building. Someone leaked the story. Everyone wanted to speak with his client, an elderly widow who lost everything. She could not even foot his bill. It was increasingly clear that neither Mrs. Pfouts nor Fallis *et Fis* would recover anything. He decided to salvage something from the fiasco.

"Ladies and gentlemen, my name is Andrew Fallis. I am the attorney for Allison Pfouts and the Ezra Pfouts Estate. My client is an 81-year-old widow, a frail woman who has just lost every penny of her late husband's hard-earned savings. You can imagine her physical and mental state is, at this moment, quite fragile, and she will not be able to answer your questions in person. She was swindled by a neighbor, a lawyer so shameless that he preys on defenseless widows."

"John B. Roberts is the reason, ladies and gentlemen, why America is fed up with lawyers. He is a blight on society, on my client in fact, who lost everything and will now most likely wind up destitute in a shelter and on welfare. I am appealing to you, the press and the public, to come forward with anything that might aid our investigation of Mr. Roberts' and his accomplice, George Wallace, and their nefarious, respective financial dealings. This is not just a criminal case to put two unscrupulous scam artists behind bars, but a civil case to restore vital funds to an impoverished widow." Andrew did not know what information the public could possibly provide, but he was determined to wrest something positive from his exertions. Televised publicity was a start. He counted down the minutes until other defrauded widows called him for assistance.

∽∾

Morton Williams gathered his legal team. This was the biggest case in his career. The reputed ringleader, the "most elusive man in America," was his personal client. The firm would work 24/7 to check every thread of the conspiracy and interview each of the named witnesses. He feared the government's case was bullet proof, but there was no way in hell his client would plead guilty to lesser charges. A full public trial would generate staggering amounts of prime-time, televised coverage for his growing practice. Some cases were larger than life, larger than a client's right to zealous representation. Besides, he planned to be zealous, overzealous in fact, just not zealous about cutting deals. Williams reasoned further. The right to counsel was a right of citizens, not enemy combatants. From what he knew, Roberts and Wallace forfeited their citizenship the moment they pledged allegiance to an Islamic nation. Williams slipped out of his office, bought a prepaid cellular phone at the corner, and placed a call to Fox 5 News New York.

ॐॐ

Meryl Scott Rupert distanced herself from the rambling, platitudinous discourse of the attorney on the corner and listened more intently to her cell phone.

"Give me that again, from the beginning. I want to make sure I've got it straight." She listened to her assistant's notes from the anonymous phone call. If even a fraction of what she heard was true, it was the biggest scoop of her career. "Call the team together. I'll be back in twenty minutes. Gerry, I could kiss you!" Gerry mouthed "Eew!" and hung up the phone.

ॐॐ

"I'm sorry, Mrs. Fallis. I should have told you earlier. My student visa expires next week. I have to return to Greece tomorrow."

"I'm disappointed, Denise. You should have told me earlier. I planned to sponsor your application for an H-1B visa. You're practically indispensable to us. I thought for sure we had you another six months."

"I'm sorry, Mrs. Fallis, really I am. I would love to stay, but my immigration lawyer says the H-1B process is a lottery, and that I'm not the kind of skilled worker the INS has in mind. I hope if I go back to graduate school in Athens, I'll have a better chance when I re-enter. I want to become a lawyer, just like you, fighting for the rights of female workers. You are ... you are my inspiration."

Catherine Fallis choked back tears and hugged Denise closely. She wanted to adopt the girl and raise her as her own. But the government had outmoded ideas about protecting American jobs. She had churned through one American employee after another. She could not find a single one who worked tirelessly, amiably and proficiently for $28,000 per year. But Denise? Denise was a godsend. Thank God for student visas. Mrs. Fallis reached into her purse and withdrew a checkbook. She scribbled furiously, tore off the top check and folded it, then handed it without ceremony to her prized acolyte. "We will miss you terribly. I think this will pay for your first year of studies." Denise glanced at it in embarrassment. It was a tax-free gift of three months' wages.

Sheldon gazed up at the television monitor in astonishment. Cathy's handsome son, Andrew, had just addressed the camera. "What have I done?" he stammered. "If I had just confessed to Cathy and Allison the moment I discovered the mistake, everything would have been fine."

It wasn't fine. He tried to buy time by covering his tracks. He tried and failed. He involved a perfect stranger, a person he knew only in passing, and allowed him to appropriate everything. Mrs. Pfouts' estate was gone. Marian's gold was gone. As far as he was concerned, his life was gone. Sheldon felt miserable and ashamed.

He wanted to pick up the phone and berate the scoundrel, even if he only reached voice mail. Rich enough to post $3.5 million bail, yet too poor to let a widow keep her life savings. Predatory bastard! He picked up the phone and began to dial but hesitated. "That's peculiar," he thought. "I can't remember his number." He recalled speaking with the man dozens of times during their negotiations but could no longer remember his number. He considered rummaging about the bed for his business card but decided a call would serve no purpose. The man had no scruples. He would just laugh – a contemptuous, carnivorous sneer.

Was the whole world this way? He was sickened when Equity Funding defrauded its policyholders – policyholders Sheldon solicited. And sickened when his neighbors lost their savings to Bernie Madoff. But this? This was a thousand times worse. Sheldon saved Susan Roberts' life. The maggot admitted it. This was personal.

Sheldon remembered the revolver ensconced in the rear of his bureau, behind the itchy woolen sweaters, near where he stuffed the cigarette pack after he quit smoking. It belonged to his great, great grandfather – an officer in the American Civil War. It was an heirloom, a family treasure. Sheldon resolved to put it to use before he died. "Forgive me, Marian," he said, "You'll have to wait a week longer." For the first time in three days, Sheldon was determined to exit the hospital alive. He pressed the call button and asked the nurse to summon his occupational therapist.

❧

The woman in the wheelchair practically shouted. "Dr. Martinez. I'd like a word with you!"

She slipped out of the apartment building through the garage. She arranged to have a stretch limousine descend to meet her. Stretch limousines featured dark tinted windows. Regular sedans did not. Susan no longer took chances.

The limousine negotiated the steep narrow driveway up to 58th Street then circled right onto 57th Street before heading west to St. Luke's-Roosevelt Hospital. Susan promised the driver a hundred dollars if he waited and another hundred dollars to protect her privacy. The driver assured her he would. He handled a call the previous evening from Alec Baldwin. "Nuttin' in de tabloids dis moyning, Mrs. Roberts, not one woyd." Mrs. Roberts was sufficiently reassured. She and her daughter ascended the elevator to Mr. Vogel's floor.

"I'm Susan McDonald. I learned from the news that you work here. You saved my life, remember?"

The doctor struggled for a moment then beamed. "The Squaw Valley airlift, right?" He was sure she was the woman, not some imposter sent by that serpent, John Roberts, to entrap him. "What are you doing here?" The woman was surprisingly attractive. At the hospital she was a heap of crushed bones and torn flesh, practically a corpse.

"I'm here with my daughter, Melissa, to thank you for repairing me. I live just a few blocks from here."

Melissa was rehearsed, "Thank you, Dr. Martinez, for saving my mother's life." She rushed forward and hugged him tightly. "You are my hero!" She stretched the last word for effect.

Dr. Martinez blushed but was inwardly proud. He extricated himself carefully then grinned at Miss McDonald. "You look fantastic. I mean, there wasn't much left of you when they brought you in, yet here you are looking … well … splendid. Tell me, are you walking yet?"

Susan rose carefully from the chair and did her best impersonation of a runway walk, back and forth in front of the elevators. She had fashioned pieces of corrugated cardboard into a lift. The limp was almost imperceptible. Melissa placed two fingers to her lips and wolf whistled. Even Susan was impressed by the intensity. Nurses cringed and put down their clipboards. An old woman near the elevator glowered. Susan lowered herself into the chair and exhaled. "It's still a challenge, but it's a lot better than a month ago."

"I think you are doing marvelously. I am really glad you looked me up. You say you heard my name on the news?" He frowned slightly. The doctor hoped the woman from Fox 5 News had kept it confidential.

"I'm afraid so. Isn't it remarkable? It's such a small world. I know Sheldon Vogel too."

Martinez started. "You do?"

"Oh yes," Melissa interjected. "Mr. Vogel saved Mommy's life, didn't he, Mommy?"

Melissa was again rehearsed. "Try to sound like you are nine again, pumpkin, okay? A perfect princess. We have to save Daddy. If we don't, no one else will."

Susan addressed Dr. Martinez. "I'm afraid I tried to outrace a bus – not very intelligent. Mr. Vogel gave me the boost I needed to succeed. We're here to see how he's doing. The bus swiped him rather hard."

"He's my second hero!" Melissa exclaimed. "I baked him cookies!" She reached into the bag that stood by the elevator and pulled out a small box with a ribbon. The box and ribbon were identical to the wrapped box Dr. Martinez saw before – the one he tossed in the trash.

Lester Martinez braced himself against the reception desk. He felt suddenly lightheaded. He tried to regain his composure but could not think of anything to say. Susan thought of something for him.

"I wonder, Dr. Martinez, how Mr. Vogel is doing emotionally. I mean I dreamt all sorts of things when I was in a coma. So much of it seemed real – more real than the hospital that greeted me when I finally woke. I am really grateful you and Dr. Weinstein arranged for me to see a psychiatrist. That helped a lot. By the way, how is Dr. Weinstein? You and she were such a fabulous team."

Dr. Martinez felt nauseous. His stomach convulsed and he swallowed back the sour remains of his lunch. Melissa took the cue.

"Would you like a cookie, Dr. Martinez? They're superhero cookies. I decorated them myself. Let's see … I think I'll give you Thor because … because he wields the hammer of God, just like you do. Don't you like the way, at the beginning of the movie, he can't tell good people from bad, so he smites them all down? With his mighty hammer, I mean? Because he thinks he's God and can do as he pleases." Dr. Martinez struggled to remain standing. His knees wanted to wobble and buckle. It took all his concentration to command them to obey.

"And Mr. Vogel reminds me of … of the Hulk. He's only superhuman some of the time, when it's really necessary, but then he forgets everyone and everything around him. It's like he drifts into another universe. That's like Mr. Vogel, isn't it, Dr. Martinez? It's a shame the Hulk and Thor hurt innocent people when they're confused, but if they didn't, we wouldn't know they had feelings, would we? They have to make mistakes to show they're human, not just superhuman – sometimes really big mistakes. Don't you agree? Dr. Martinez?"

Susan adjusted the small ball of glass beneath her left brow. Melissa aligned it perfectly in the elevator. Now Susan moved it out of kilter, just slightly. She tilted her head and smiled ingratiatingly at Dr. Martinez.

Dr. Martinez hoisted himself to a standing position, covered his mouth with his sleeve, and brushed past the crowd exiting the elevator to a bathroom at the corner. He had no time to acknowledge the Hulk or Thor. He was too busy disgorging cookies of his own.

Melissa pushed the down button for the elevator. She and her mother decided it was premature to visit Mr. Vogel.

ॐ✑

"Uh, Hi Wally. This is awkward. Aren't you in jail?" Stuart was incorrigibly direct.

"I was until my aunt posted bail. She and my cousins mortgaged everything. How are you doing?"

Stuart knew Wallace's call was not social. Stuart did not feel especially sociable. Shit, NYL was falling apart at the seams. The organization was still reeling from the fucking Hotchkiss-Lyden murder-suicide and the Feds spent four months thrashing about the organization's files. He was sure the microdots were just a feint, Wally's way of keeping Stuart from sniffing where it mattered. Rumor slipped back about the interrogation. They tried everything short of waterboarding. "Thank God Wally left me out of it. They could have fucking nailed me for insider trading."

Everyone at NYL was sworn to secrecy. It was a Department of Homeland Security affair. Anyone who leaked anything would be considered an accomplice and hauled away like Wally. No one saw or heard from him for months. After the initial interrogations, the ones Hotchkiss boasted about, Wally just vanished. Hotchkiss said he was an incoherent, babbling infant by the end; he didn't even heed the call of nature. Hotchkiss left notes from the interrogation in plain sight. Stuart wondered whether Homeland Security asked him to do that – to intimidate anyone on the executive floor from speaking out. Days, weeks and months after Wally's perp walk there was nothing in the paper. It seemed like science fiction.

But now NYL Health Systems was in disarray. Employees were too worried about their jobs to gossip about Wally's peculiar arrest. Besides, he was back at his apartment. Everyone said so. And yesterday the evening news confirmed it. Whatever his situation, the situation at NYL was awful.

The organization was awash in red ink. The new auditors certified it, the ones appointed under pressure from the New York State Attorney General. The old accounting firm was apparently too creative in how it established and managed reserves. Existing board members were encouraged to retire. The CFO was holed up with the white-collar defense group of Kramer Levin Naftalis & Frankel LLP, anticipating criminal indictment. And Gürhan Erdoğan, the suave commanding voice of the organization, was nowhere to be found. It was a good bet he was not returning. He disappeared before a conference in Chicago. Some said he skipped town. Others said he was abducted. Still others said he was murdered. Hospital Corporation of America and a number of other conglomerates sniffed around with their M&A teams. They would dismiss everyone in administration; probably even some of the doctors. Stuart was polishing his résumé when Wallace called. He could always return to banking.

"Trying to plug a fucking volcano. How about yourself?"

"Trying to clear my neighbor's name. I need your help."

That was blunt, thought Stuart. "Why shouldn't I report every fucking word you say to the police?" he inquired. "Why aren't you trying to clear your own name?" he secretly wondered.

"I hope you do report everything – for your sake – but as you're doing so you can do me a favor. Hear me out."

৯৯৯

"You are absolutely sure? … And you have the actual recordings? … And you say you have a physical copy of the police interrogation? … Don't worry. You'll receive the usual remunera-
tion and then some – enough to take that lovely wife of yours to
Tahiti... Ciao. I've got a story to break."

"God, I love this business," she effused. "God I love News
Corp.!" Meryl Scott Rupert confirmed every important aspect of
her assistant's notes, plus some interesting angles of her own.
Frants was a treasure. He captured the voicemail recordings of
9/11 victims and their families in 2001 but this was better. Frants
successfully intercepted telephone conversations between Morton Williams, the attorney for John B. Roberts, and his staff of
attorneys, plus an electronic transcript of the FBI's preliminary
interrogation of Mr. Roberts. Meryl would nail the creep and, if
possible, cut that wife of his down to size. No one made a fool
of Meryl Scott Rupert.

Frants was awesome, she extolled, better than any of the
hackers at *News of the World*. "It's a shame they weren't as good
as you," she thought. "The news from England might still be interesting."

Chapter 26

"Run!" the mother shouted, tugging at his hand. The walkmen tittered. They'd randomized the crossing duration but in perfect synchronization. Last time, they trotted on- and offstage in 3.8 seconds. The hacker chuckled. He loved fucking with municipal networks.

The story broke at 8:30 pm, an exclusive from Fox 5 News New York. Regular prime-time programming was cancelled. The United States government had just arrested the mastermind of the most insidious money laundering and data smuggling ring in US history – one with documented links to Iranian authorities and known Islamic extremists. Ms. Rupert did not think it necessary to distinguish between "Iranian authorities" and "known Islamic extremists" but the network insisted on playing it safe. The best part was the bombshell about Roberts' wife, *nee* Susan *"Susie Mac"* McDonald, or *Poison Sue* as she was known to her track-team rivals.

present day

It was Meryl's idea, connecting her to the conspiracy. The self-admitted PED abuser and her brother, an imprisoned Muslim drug dealer, played a seminal role ("Seminole role", Meryl inflected, congratulating herself on the pun) in turning 1990s track and field into a sport defined by illegal doping. Years later, McDonald would support her husband's global criminal enterprise. An enterprise of this scale required seed capital. Where else did it come from but the collapsed veins of thousands of young PED addicts – adolescents who dreamed of escaping poverty through sports, but were conned by McDonald and her co-conspirators into risking bulging muscles, shrunken testicles and a lifetime of persecution just so they could enjoy a shortcut? "Take that, Miss *'Holier Than Thou'* Tummy-Tuck Despiser!" Meryl snickered.

"Authorities have not stated definitively whether funding for the Roberts-Wallace conspiracy came from the proceeds of illegal steroid injections, but neither have they denied it. Several prominent legislators, including Senators McNally Hornochs of Kentucky and Archer Locke of Lousiana, have called for an independent investigation of the matter. White House Press Secretary Jay Carney said it was too early for the President to comment."

"Were Barry Bonds, Mark McGwire and Roger Clemens unwitting financiers of Islamic militants – militants who waged attacks on our soil and embroiled us in two costly wars? The President refuses to say. The implications are as chilling as they are shameful." Meryl fought with the network over describing the wars as "costly." The network thought costly sounded pejorative. Its defense industry advertisers and Mr. Murdoch might object. In the end, Meryl Scott Rupert prevailed. She painted the Iraqi and Afghan missions as "Obama's wars."

Meryl added a tragic personal twist. The young Susan McDonald and her brother brainwashed their mother, a docile and loving housewife, into becoming a fire-breathing religious zealot who railed against the sins of white men and other Americans, however few there might be. Personally, Rupert felt everyone else should produce their long-form birth certificate, but that was another story. A Fox affiliate in Fort Lauderdale tracked down the father – a town drunkard in a small village in Broward County. He admitted, "I was scared, scared [beep]less, scared for my life. Ain't never seen a woman turn evil so fast."

A panel of self-appointed experts heaped forth their conclusions. Third from the left was Andrew Fallis, "respected trial attorney and international expert on computer fraud." The panel agreed that habeas corpus had outlived its usefulness, drug use among athletes was a pressing national security concern, and today's developments were the plainly foreseeable result of

Obamacare. "Why else would they have chosen a hospital foundation as their locus of operation?" One panelist stressed the not-for-profit angle – a failed vestige of socialism. He expounded five minutes on the depravity of Moscow on the Hudson before the moderator prodded him back on topic.

The panel closed by agreeing the two women in the story were hotties. The eldest commentator reconsidered a moment then demurred, "Please, gentlemen, we have a mixed audience. I believe the appropriate word is 'babes.'" They chortled agreement. Sarah Palin and Michelle Bachman never objected. Andrew joined the levity – no need to divulge his sexual orientation. Few gay Republican commentators ever did. Andrew suppressed a sudden rush of paranoia. He decided to prove his allegiance to the network's intellectually challenged, straight-white-male, Christian-conservative demographic. "I look forward, gentlemen, to the day when the Supreme Court curtails its expansive view of unreasonable search and seizure, so I can chip in and do my part, especially with that Kaplan-Wallace woman." The moderator tittered nervously. Even he was not sure that was appropriate. Off-screen the producer guffawed. The kid was perfect. Maligning suspected traitors for their looks was good fun – no worse than deriding Hitler for his mustache. The kid had a future at Fox 5 News New York.

ஒ•ஒ

An orderly switched off the television. It was curfew for the patients at a small nursing home outside Atlanta, Georgia. Before shuffling out of the recreation area, the patients regarded the thin old woman who shook, sipped Ensure with a straw, and muttered verse from the Bible. They regarded the women with newfound interest. They broke into spontaneous applause. She gazed up, strained to discern the cause of the commotion, then resettled her gaze on the straw. "You have no excuse," she mumbled at the television, "every one of you who judges. For in passing judgment on another you condemn yourself, because you, the judge, practice the very same things. Romans 2:1." An orderly wheeled her to her room. He asked a nurse to snap a photograph of himself with the woman and uploaded it to Facebook. He counted 13,647 likes when he woke the next morning.

❦

The broker at Halstead received a late-night call from the buyer. There was no way in Hell he and his wife were going to subsidize terrorism. The deal was off.

"You should specify 'traitors' or 'anti-Semites only' in the listing. I can't believe you wasted our fucking time!" The man hung up in a huff.

❦

Jack's ex-wife Marcia rolled out from underneath Stanley and wondered who would support her frugal lifestyle. Certainly not Stanley. Becky could not afford to divorce him. Even if she did, he would never marry Marcia. He would hunt younger game, teenagers perhaps. He serviced her for pocket change – something to jangle alongside his other jewels – his only assets, really. Suavity and learned conversation were not his strong suits.

The last thing Marcia desired was to find a job. Work was so … well … tedious. How could Jack do this to her? He was the most reliable man she knew, a total bore, never late with the check, yet he jilted her now, threw his lot in with the penal crowd. "Cheap bastard. You would do anything to get even with me, even make me call Father, wouldn't you?"

Father could indeed assist Marcia, but she would have to thaw relations. She dreaded that, more than seeking a job. She was waiting for him to die. That was so much easier. He was 86, wealthy, and utterly alone. Marcia planned to hold out until he keeled over but Jack ruined everything. She had to find work or patch relations with Father.

"Screw you, Jack, for making me choose!" Jack wasn't there, but Stanley sensed the command and obliged. He had pride. His clients were always satisfied. Besides, this was more productive than sneaking into the New York Athletic Club. Marcia could not play squash worth shit. She could play with his other balls just fine. Moreover, Marcia's bathroom was nicer. He could shower there after his workout in privacy. He did not have to share a locker room with the Athletic Club's token diversity members. The club wasn't worth belonging to anymore, he decided. He was glad they revoked his membership.

The producer of CBS News called an emergency meeting and decided to yank the biopic about Bo, President Obama's Portuguese water dog. Wolf Blitzer revamped his agenda for the following afternoon's *Situation Room*. NBC decided it could compress live coverage of the Skate America Figure Skating Championships in Kent, Washington down to a twenty-minute, mixed-doubles mash-up of the competition's biggest spins, jumps and falls – digitally synchronized to the music of Queen. ESPN caught wind of the tape and decided to make mixed-doubles figure skating the cornerstone of its upcoming *Winter X Games*. They faxed letters to Tonya Harding, Nancy Kerrigan, Chris Bowman and Johnny Weir beseeching them to participate. Bowman's executor faxed back his regrets. Meanwhile, Geraldo Rivera's panel discussion of whether hoodie buyers should sign assumption of risk waivers was, by stroke of coincidence, postponed. Rivera was embroiled in a public relations spat with his eldest son, Gabriel, over how to make the discussion politically acceptable. The working title, "Killed by Fashion?" did not help matters. ABC affiliates breathed a sigh of relief.

Every news bureau in the United States and Europe assigned teams to cover the charges. Phones rang incessantly at Langley, and advertisers begged Fox to air their ads during the next Meryl Scott Rupert news blast. Geoffrey Błaszczyk excused himself from a meeting in Cairo and watched the taped segment on his iPhone. "That wasn't nice, Jill," he murmured to no one, "reopening the Erdoğan file without me, thinking you could handle this the 'open and transparent' way, the 'due process' way. Now you can deal with the fallout."

Błaszczyk still bristled at the FBI's insistence on arresting George *"Wally"* Wallace publicly before having a chance to interrogate him "the company way." Thank goodness Kroll was so transparent. She telescoped her plan to him a month in advance. His team got to Wallace first, reduced him to a babbling psychotic infant. Kroll was of course suspicious, but the blood tests turned up clean. She had no choice but to institutionalize him and withdraw him from the normal judicial process.

Błaszczyk doubted from the outset whether Wallace was involved with Erdoğan. Good grief! Kroll didn't need to know it, but Błaszczyk recruited him. Besides, the data transfers coincided too neatly with his term of employment at NYL. Did he write the program overnight? Kroll was fixated on his extracurricular hacking, the hacking he did twenty years ago. "For Christ's sake, Jill, the guy is a patriot. He did what the IRS can't – bust tax cheats who make you and I pave the roads so they can clog them with their BMWs." Kroll didn't buy it. Wallace's digital fingerprints were all over the data. He was the logical tech support guy. He was so much more qualified than their other leads, Stuart Chu and Andrea Lyden.

Błaszczyk consented to bringing him in but doubted they could pressure him to turn state's evidence even if he was guilty. No one double-crossed Marja openly, not if they had relatives they cared for. Wallace cared deeply for his wife and his cousins in Houston, Texas and Norfolk, Virginia. If Wallace knew anything, it could only be extricated off the record, in an undocumented time and place.

Alas, Wallace was not Gürhan Erdoğan. He was a United States citizen, the son of a World War II veteran. His brothers served and died in Vietnam. He could not just disappear, not as long as the process police from 935 Pennsylvania Avenue called the shots. It was so much easier in his father's day, back when he spied on the Transit Workers Union for J. Edgar Hoover. His mother never knew. But Geoffrey did. Geoffrey had access to his file. The CIA kept dossiers on all the FBI operatives. You didn't trust anyone in his business, especially not the Feds, not with the information they possessed.

Błaszczyk diffused the Wallace situation with help from San Francisco, the fertile crescent of psychotropic enhancers. "PEDs: performance-enhancing drugs." He savored every syllable. His contact was a man who turned tripping into science – round tripping, that is. The introduction was casual, a shared park bench on the lagoon facing the Palace of Fine Arts. "What is hip?" inquired Błaszczyk nonchalantly, gazing at the enormous faux Greek rotunda. It was one of the few surviving structures from the 1915 Panama-Pacific Exposition, the exposition's outdoor art gallery and promenade.

"Hipness is what it is," murmured the man.

"Apropos," thought Błaszczyk, "but five words are easy to remember … or random coincidence. He tried another stanza. "Seen in all the right places, seen with just the right faces, you should be satisfied, but it ain't quite right."

The man with the receding hairline and thin Carlos Santana mustache smiled. "There's one thing you should know, 'What's hip today, might become passé.'" Błaszczyk returned the smile. He found his pharmacological guru.

The guys at Bay Area Laboratory Co-Operative were amazing. Victor Conte and his team could make anything undetectable, especially what they themselves imbibed during their heyday as musicians with Tower of Power. That stuff was performance-enhancing too, but in a different way. Just ask Jimi Hendrix or Janis Joplin or Ron Pigpen McKernan. Błaszczyk corrected himself. He could not ask them. They each tripped one San Francisco beat too many.

Błaszczyk kept his cache of BALCO elixirs in reserve. Magic mushrooms? LSD? He wasn't sure what they started with and did not care. He just knew it could drive a man insane and blood tests came back normal. God bless the catering guy in front of NYL South, the one who never forgot a face or an order, and God bless BALCO! It was a titan of American innovation. Too bad the FBI and United States Anti-Doping Agency shut it down. He tried dissuading Victor from entering sports medicine – too much witch hunting – but he didn't listen. Błaszczyk's budget could not compete with Barry Bonds'. "Such a waste!" Błaszczyk sighed. There was nowhere left to turn. The guys at Biogenesis were buffoons.

Błaszczyk watched the Fox News segment again on his cell phone. "No, Jill, circumventing us was not nice." John B. Roberts was a United States citizen. Kroll went after him the proper way, the Constitutional way, with all the pomp and pageantry of due process. Kroll supplied the pomp. Błaszczyk supplied the pageantry. He enlisted Frants to feed Fox News the story. Błaszczyk let Frants off the hook a year before during the 9/11 flap by making all the phone records disappear. Błaszczyk recognized and appreciated special talent. Frants repaid the favor. Special Agent Kroll could feel the weight of due process … and the magnificent Fourth Estate. Błaszczyk congratulated himself on his handiwork.

☙❧

Stuart watched the Fox News segment in stunned silence as he followed Wallace's step-by-step instructions. 300,000 attempted viral attacks a day. Wallace not only catalogued them, he dissected them. He actually reverse-engineered how the most insidious of them worked. And now he asked Stuart to release one.

Stuart was not sure whether to laugh or cry at the broadcast. The conspiracy was as plausible as Meryl Scott Rupert's re-imagining of the Kennedy assassination. "What really happened those fateful moments on the grassy knoll?" she intoned, before insinuating a massive CIA-orchestrated conspiracy to silence the President. "I'm just saying," she persisted. Stuart did not think journalists were permitted to use the phrase. That was seven years ago. Now of course it was *de rigueur* – proof a commentator's unsupported allegations were beyond reproach. Stuart decided to reserve judgment on the story until *The New York Times* and the other news sources concurred, which might in fact happen tomorrow. Wallace tipped Stuart off that the special segment would be airing. Was he prescient or just well-connected? Wallace knew a lot more than he let on.

∂∞⑤

Wallace fretted whether Jack Roberts was an embezzler but was positive he had nothing to do with NYL Health Systems, Gürhan Erdoğan, or international espionage. The truth was, Wallace knew Jack wasn't an embezzler. The man lacked the moxie.

Wallace's neighbor was like every aging lawyer he'd met – manifestly computer illiterate. The Wallaces learned during family dates that the folks in 8B were hopeless clods when it came to data processing, Internet security, or even basic mathematics. Wallace could see the man counting secretly on his fingers as they played penny-a-point rummy. The family turned to Wallace when their PC conked out, which happened frequently because they neither updated their software nor understood how. Pop-ups and adware infected the unit habitually, and Wallace's inbox was stuffed with spam originating from Susan, Melissa and Jack Roberts' hacked individual email accounts. Alya and Melissa were close friends, but even Alya knew better than to plug a flash drive from the Roberts family computer into one of hers (she had two), or to download an attachment from the Roberts family without first inspecting it for viruses.

Two years earlier, when Wallace started at NYL, Jack sheepishly forwarded him his résumé. He said he was weary of working for a big law firm and the legal market was swiftly contracting. Perhaps there was a general counsel position at NYL or the bank. He had advised many such organizations.

Wallace doubted there were openings but promised to forward his résumé to the respective CEOs and endorse his candidacy if opportunity arose. That was Jack's idea of networking, of broadcasting his experience and availability. Wallace suggested networking via the social website, LinkedIn, but Jack feared creating an account. It could be interpreted by Dewey & LeBoeuf as job dissatisfaction. It could prejudice his annual distribution, perhaps even trigger his "retirement." Wallace shrugged. Older bankers behaved the same way.

He opened the Microsoft Word document in curiosity. Jack should have saved it in Adobe Portable Document Format (PDF) so it could not be modified and reposted elsewhere by practical jokers. The possibility evidently escaped Jack's attention, yet Jack was a seasoned corporate lawyer. Wallace was scarcely surprised.

Wallace glimpsed the document's properties in Microsoft Word. The creation date was August 12, 1989, and the author was "DBL." Wallace filled in the blanks: Jack Roberts pecked out the first draft of his résumé in 1989 in Windows 2.0 or 2.1 on an IBM XT 286 desktop personal computer at an office in Drexel, Burham & Lambert, saved the file to a floppy disk, then updated it periodically as one employer after another filed for bankruptcy. Wallace marveled at the formatting. Jack used space characters in place of tabs – dozens of them. The few tabs he employed were each left-justified and spaced one half inch apart. He used them to indent paragraphs, breaking lines mid-sentence with carriage returns and tabs to make sure the text aligned properly. Jack also used a series of tabs, together with a string of space characters, to right-justify dates. Customizing the justification and distance between tabs was neither part of Jack's legal education nor later job training. Jack entered the workforce during the age of secretaries and did what was minimally sufficient to survive beyond it.

No, Jack did not have the moxie to be an embezzler, not on the Pfouts estate's scale. Someone else tapped into Allison Pfouts' account. Wallace considered the computers of Mrs. Pfouts, Sheldon Vogel, Jack Roberts and Catherine and Andrew Fallis. By now, neither Mr. Vogel nor Mr. Roberts possessed a thing. The FBI would have taken their equipment, just as they re-expropriated most of his. But Stuart could still trace activity on the Fallis and Pfouts computers. He hoped he gauged Stuart correctly.

ഒൟ

Geoffrey Błaszczyk woke Agent Kroll around 4 am. The line crackled, probably long distance. He said he was calling from the Middle East. Jill dreaded what would come next.

"That wasn't nice, Jill – informing Fox News before us. We have an interest in this too; some might say a bigger one."

"It wasn't supposed to blow up like this, Jeff. Roberts or his attorney must have spoken to the press, although I cannot imagine Roberts skewering his wife like that. What purpose would it serve him? I'm not even sure we have the right man. It could all be a series of wild coincidences."

"Meryl Scott Rupert sounded certain enough. I'm sure some of her material comes from, how shall I put it, verified accounts of actual conversations." Kroll regretfully concurred. Direct criminal evidence eluded her, but she could not help believing Rupert was involved in the 9/11 voicemail hacking scandal. In addition, a number of suspected *News of the World* operatives resurfaced in the "New World" after the British tabloid ceased publication. Four thousand mobile phone and voicemail accounts were hacked in Great Britain alone just to fill the tabloid's headlines and society pages. Fifteen months later, Parliament and Scotland Yard were still handing down indictments. Jill was positive Rupert Murdoch's organization employed similar practices in the United States. It was just a matter of gathering the evidence.

"I'll be in New York in three days. I think we should have a chat – the two of us." He terminated the call abruptly.

෨෴

The Theatre Musicians Association reacted to the Fox News broadcast later that morning. It sent notice via personal courier to St. Luke's-Roosevelt Hospital advising its patient, Sheldon Vogel, that his services were no longer required. He would be paid his customary advisory fee for the month but was instructed forthwith to remit custody of the investment account to TMA. The letter cited Sheldon's somewhat dubious relationship to a federally indicted lawyer, John B. Roberts, as sufficient grounds for their decision. Given the connection, it was impossible for Mr. Vogel to furnish adequate assurance that the life savings of TMA's member musicians were secure. The letter thanked him for his many years of dedicated service.

The notice arrived during Sheldon's interview with Dr. Simmons, a staff psychiatrist. Dr. Simmons wanted to ensure Mr. Vogel's mental faculties were unimpaired by the accident. Sheldon assured him they were fine. It was not as if the bus struck his head, although his neck ached terribly.

The notice brought the interview to an immediate close. The hospital was kind enough to wheel Sheldon to an administrative workstation, so he could relinquish control of the Theatre Musician Association's account to its legal counsel and confirm that transfer by voice and email. He returned to the workstation an hour later, after receiving a similar notice from Actor's Equity. The exercise steeled his resolve. If he was well enough to sit in front of a workstation and relinquish his last reliable source of income, he was well enough to settle matters with John B. Roberts.

෨෴

Nelson Foster was incensed. He stayed up practically the entire evening. He reviewed the bylaws and house rules carefully. He was in favor of due process and the presumption of innocence but enough was enough. The Roberts and Wallace families had to go. The other board members would take his lead. If he had colorable grounds for eviction, he would invoke them. He was not going to wait around, as he did with the Hotchkiss family, waiting for shame to drive them away. Roberts and Wallace knew no shame. They could sue him afterward for all he cared.

"When hell freezes over," he murmured. "They are as guilty as Osama Bin Laden and the Shoe Bomber." Roberts' wife was black, presumably Muslim, as Muslim as the President. That's what Fox 5 said, even if no other station corroborated it. So was Wallace. Why on earth did the previous board let them into the building? What were they thinking? That the co-op was a social experiment, a college campus? It was a privately held enterprise, for Heaven's sake. It was no place for affirmative action. My God, the Athletic Club across the street was blatantly exclusive. Why couldn't we be just a little? And what about his ex-wife, the one no one could locate, the Arab? She had jihad written all over her perfectly shaped body. Nelson remembered ogling it in the lobby. He wondered whether it was kosher to fantasize about a Muslim. He shrugged off the question. It was time the board gave the building back to the tenants, not some confederation of extremists and thieves.

Nelson Foster moved into the E line twelve years earlier and led an insurrection against the sponsor-controlled board. The number of sponsor-held units declined, and Foster eventually wrested majority control. There were now three "independent" shareholder directors, in contrast to the sponsor's two. Foster and the independent directors were closely allied. They campaigned together and allotted proxies evenly among themselves so each of them always won reelection. Foster guarded his power tightly, some said viciously. His word was law – among the tenants, the employees and the building's vendors. Outwardly, he was a civic-minded philanthropist to the acting community, a former dentist, as liberal-minded as the city he adopted. Inwardly, he was a despotic egomaniac from a conservative stronghold in central California who trampled anything or anyone who interfered with his agenda for the building. Right now, the Roberts and Wallace families interfered with that agenda.

Foster consulted the house rules on noise and construction: "No tenant shall make or permit any disturbing noises in the Building or permit anything to be done therein which will interfere with the rights, comfort or convenience of other tenants." He convened an emergency telephone meeting of the cooperative's board. Messrs. Green, White, Black, Brown and Foster agreed by unanimous voice vote to amend the noise rule. Henceforth, no tenant could make, permit or "be the proximate cause of" disturbing noises in the Building ... whether arising inside or outside the Building, so long as such noise arose on the premises. In addition, fines were modified to account for each day of infraction, not month. The amended rules were slipped under everyone's door by 4 pm. The board could begin fining the Wallace and Roberts families in the morning. In three days, their collective fines would total $2,000 per day. The two families would either close the building's yawning budget deficit or vacate promptly. The board congratulated itself on, once again, championing the rights of tenant-shareholders. Foster reckoned it would figure prominently in his perfunctory reelection appeal, the one printed and mailed at the co-op's expense.

Foster wished all board resolutions were as easy. Most board meetings degenerated into shouting matches: the three independent directors against the two sponsors. Interest rates were low, incredibly low, and Foster wanted to borrow $15 million more to spruce the building up – to help make square-foot pricing more competitive with newer structures erected all around them. But borrowing meant raising monthly maintenance fees, something the sponsors, who depended on fixed rental income, desperately opposed. A lot of tenants opposed higher common charges too, but they learnt to keep their mouths shut. Maintenance fees had doubled in just twelve years. For the vast majority of tenant-shareholders, pensioners in their seventies and eighties, common charges exceeded monthly income, inclusive of Social Security. They ate into savings, which was precisely what Foster intended. Personally, he intended to bequeath his children an apartment at the highest imaginable stepped-up basis, which his children could then flip tax-free to a rich foreign buyer. He held no illusion that his children could afford on an extended basis the common charges he'd foisted on the building. He believed the majority of elderly tenants felt as he did. They did not want to pass an abode on to their children. Their children were middle-aged men and women. They wanted to pass on the proceeds.

Jack shook his head whenever he received one of Nelson Foster's quarterly reports. "Wouldn't it be simpler and more profitable to just sell the building? Let some developer raze it to the ground and erect an eighty-story eyesore. We could get four or five hundred million dollars for the property tomorrow, probably more. Why double and redouble everyone's living expense if the end game is to sell out?" Nothing the board did made communal economic sense. It only made sense to owners who were sure of their imminent demise, and too lazy or selfish to consider renting an apartment for their last one, two or five years of life.

Nelson Foster smiled in satisfaction as he telephoned legal counsel for the co-op. Longstanding younger tenants were a nuisance. Thank goodness there were so few of them. Governance would be so much simpler when all the tenants either had one foot in the grave or were recent foreign investors outbidding one another to wager their savings in dollar-denominated luxury real estate. The new house rules were a step in that direction. Applied judiciously, Foster could rid the building of more than just the Roberts and Wallace families. There were a dozen or more tenants who routinely threw their votes behind the sponsors. Foster reflected on the television crews out front. They were not so bad, after all. They helped secure leverage he should have obtained a decade ago.

❧

Hanni rolled over and flipped on the news. The apartment in SoHo was tiny but Błaszczyk warned her against being picky. He had no obligation whatsoever to help her pay the bills, nor provide her with a new identity. He admitted only grudgingly that Hotchkiss and Lyden's murder-suicide might have been staged, and the assailant, if indeed there was one, might still pose a threat to Hanife Kaplan Wallace – Gürhan Erdoğan's consort and witting or unwitting accomplice.

"You're kidding, right?" she remembered asking. "Diana Prince, as in Princess Diana of Themyscira?"

"As beautiful as Aphrodite, wise as Athena, strong as Hercules, and swift as Hermes," replied Błaszczyk. "Look, it's the best I could come up with. You should be flattered." Hanni rolled her eyes. Henceforth she was known among comic book aficionados as her alter ego, Wonder Woman. Superhero comics were apparently popular among the agents at Langley.

William Moulton Marston, famed psychologist and co-inventor of the polygraph, was convinced by his lie detection research that women worked more efficiently, reliably and truthfully than men and therefore deserved a superhero of their own. Diana Prince, *aka* Wonder Woman, was his answer. Geoffrey Błaszczyk either shared Marston's high opinion of the female gender or daydreamed about his prize informant donning scarlet boots, a tiara, and a scant, one-piece swimsuit while shackling him to a bed with her magic lasso. Hanni was not sure which. What she was sure of was that his organization shared little in common with the Justice League of America. Chivalry was not among its virtues.

❧

At first, Hanni thought she was dreaming. She switched to MSNBC and then CNN and then Fox. She ran downstairs and bought the paper. She flipped on her Sony Vaio and read more. There were photos and family videos of her splayed across the networks. And, of course, there were photos and videos of Wally and the Roberts family. Unless she took precautions, her new identity would vaporize in a New York minute. Raven black hair and tortoise-shell glasses would be a start. An inexpensive jumpsuit from the I-Ching boutique downstairs might also help. "No more haute couture. Hanife Kaplan, I'd like you to meet Diana Prince, *circa* 1968." She picked up her phone and dialed Geoffrey Błaszczyk.

"Damn it, Wally," she steamed, as the iPhone rang. "Why do you always have to be in the wrong place at the wrong time?" She knew Wally had absolutely nothing to do with Gürhan Erdoğan's vile former enterprise or even Jack Roberts' family. The Roberts were bystanders to a divorce. They chose sides like everyone else and Wally was the loser. He was always the loser. It was precisely what Jack asserted. Wallace emptied Alya's room so his ex-wife could sell the apartment.

"You had no right," she fumed, "she was my daughter too!" She wanted the signed Lady Gaga poster back, even the poster of Justin Bieber. Alya was hers, damn it, hers! She clicked off the phone and wept inconsolably. Błaszczyk noticed the missed call and resolved to call the Princess of Themyscira when he retired for the evening. The voice and images he kept on his iPhone would help him sleep.

❧◈❧

"Say, aren't you the lady on the news, the one whose bank account was hacked by a neighbor?'

The woman glanced about furtively and asked the man to lower his voice. Actually, the man was a pimply-faced teenager with a pallid, greasy complexion. He wore a cheap polyester vest over his white poly-blend shirt and brown polyester tie. The woman stared down at the small display case. It was lined with cheap gray felt. A velour box held thirty or forty rings, some with stones, the majority fashioned from gold. There was another box displaying simple gold necklaces and a third with twenty or thirty sets of earrings, again set in or fashioned from gold. Most looked old, worn and tacky. There was a hodgepodge of hues – brassy 10 karat to rich yellow 24 karat. Most of the items clustered near the brassy end. There was not an item on display that Mrs. Pfouts considered worthy of Van Cleef & Arpels or Bulgari. She wondered whether she read the card correctly. She wondered, in fact, what she was doing here.

Allison Pfouts avoided 48th Street between Fifth and Sixth Avenues like the plague. The noise and congestion irritated her. The gauntlet of shop owners vying to hustle her inside, vying to part her from her money, unnerved her. The throng of long-bearded jewelers in black overcoats and black flat-brimmed fedoras crisscrossing between shops, oblivious of the cars and rules of traffic, intimidated her. And the gang of youths loitering nonchalantly mid-block, scoping their next easy mark, absolutely terrified her. She regarded the display windows, with their endless rows of brilliantly illuminated, densely packed gems, pearls and bargain-basement price stickers, as sordid, crass and banal.

The Diamond District was another world, more alien and bustling than Stanley Market, yet considerably more sinister. A merchant in Stanley Market could cheat her out of, what, twenty dollars? And a pickpocket could snatch her purse but would do so gently, completely unnoticed. He would never knock her down. Here a merchant could cheat her out of four or five thousand dollars in one small sale. How could she, a non-expert, possibly match wits with an unscrupulous dealer? How could she, a defenseless octogenarian, defend herself against thugs in a crowd so thick they could disappear without a trace in an instant?

The Diamond District was a place for seasoned dealers and thieves. There were bargains to be found, but not at street level. The bargains were in the vaulted offices upstairs, where experienced middlemen haggled over how much of the mark-up to Cartier the merchant and middleman would share. Why for goodness sake did she bring the jewelry back to its place of origin?

Allison knew the answer. She could not demean herself at Van Cleef & Arpels or even Tiffany's. She could not admit in public she needed desperately to pawn the jewelry. And she lacked the courage to visit any booth Shelly had not tacitly endorsed by frequenting time and time again.

The boy could not contain himself. "Hey Pop, look who's in front. It's the woman from the news – the one who got fleeced by her neighbor, you know, the Iranian dude, the spy, Jackie Robinson."

"Roberts," a voice bellowed. "Number 42 was a Brooklynite like you, a hero. The Iranian dude is John Roberts, although, who knows, maybe his friends call him Jackie." A man stepped out from behind a curtain. Allison saw a narrow cubby where the man evidently enjoyed some privacy. The space was no wider than her toilet. Paul Giordano and Sons occupied a small stall on the first floor of 50 West 48th Street. There were two entrances, spaced twelve to fifteen feet apart. A narrow corridor reached back into the building, turned, then swerved back to the front, patterning itself into a horseshoe. Dimly-lit stalls lined the horseshoe, each stall inhabited by a different jeweler. Giordano was the only Italian name she recalled seeing. The man wore neither a black overcoat nor a flat-brimmed fedora. His face was shaven, although perhaps not recently. He wore a poly-blend shirt and inexpensive silk tie. He grinned solicitously and said, "Welcome, Mrs. Pfouts, my son and I have been riveted by the details of, what are they calling it, Wallygate? It must be devastating, just devastating. I imagine you're looking for something to console yourself?"

Watergate this was not and Irangate was preempted. Fox 5 settled on Wallygate. Meryl Scott Rupert was not thrilled by the selection but knew the drill. If you want to sell a conspiracy, elevate its importance by assigning a "gate". In this case, Wallygate sounded better than Embezzlegate, Robertgates (the recently retired Secretary of Defense) and Central Park Southgate (a restaurant abutting the art deco lounge of the Essex House). The network knew that each of the park entrances was also a gate. The Seventh Avenue entrance was Artisans' Gate. Ms. Rupert tried various inflections but there was no way to make it sound sinister. She rifled through the catalog: Artists' Gate, Merchants' Gate, Warriors' Gate, Farmers' Gate, Hunters' Gate, Explorers' Gate, Children's Gate, Scholars' Gate. Damn! Not one of Central Park's famed entrances served Fox News' purpose. Wallygate was deemed the best selection.

"I actually need to sell jewelry, not buy it," she confided. "You see, it's all I have to live on. Are you Paul Giordano?"

"Uh, no," answered the man, straining to hide his disappointment. "Dad retired several years ago. My name is Richie. Richard Giordano."

"Oh dear," replied Allison, secretly pleased. She feigned being flustered. "I was hoping you'd recognize the pieces, that you'd appreciate their value."

"Well look, Mrs. Pfouts. Let's see what you have. You're welcome to compare appraisals. There are twelve merchants on this floor alone. My dad made great stuff, some of it really intricate. A few of his pieces sold at Bulgari. Another made it into the catalog from Cartier." He pointed to a faded magazine advertisement taped to the wall.

Allison paused a second, opened her handbag then pulled out three massive charm bracelets, six sets of large gold earrings, two solid gold bracelets, four gold pendants, several gold brooches, twenty gold chains, and an elegant gold watch. Richie Giordano suppressed a gasp. His son blurted, "Holy shit, Pop, that's five pounds at least. It's all 24 karat." Pop glared icily, reminding his still-pubescent son that salesmanship was a game of poker. Never show your cards. Still, neither Giordano nor son had any problem with the math. They were staring at $120,000 to $150,000 in gold. Who cared whether the old man was an artist, a master of filigree. Even if they treated the woman fairly, they could net $30,000 in ten minutes. And Richie was in no mood to treat the woman fairly. He sensed desperation and could exploit it.

"It's exactly five pounds, six point three ounces," she interjected. "I verified the weight on my scale against your father's signed appraisals." She thrust the stack of yellowed slips on the display case. "At today's bid price, according to the nice man at Fidelity, you should be willing to offer $148,000, give or take a couple thousand." Allison knew better than to quote the ask price. "Still, I think some of the pieces are worth more as jewelry than as ingots, don't you agree, especially the brooch in the Cartier ad? And these ones here, I think they're the ones from Bulgari."

Richie was speechless. How the devil was this woman swindled out of a million dollars? She was a hawk. He decided against instinct to be honest. "Look, Mrs. Pfouts, I think you're right, but we don't deal in this kind of volume ... or quality. Our business has," he glanced sheepishly at the contents of the display case, "changed. I can't offer you seventeen-fifteen an ounce because the guys upstairs won't offer me seventeen-thirty or anywhere close. I'd be lucky to get sixteen-fifty. And you won't get them to budge above fifteen. Plus, you're right, some of these pieces are collectibles. Why, this one here might be worth three times its weight," he elaborated, motioning to one of the bracelets. "They should be sold at auction." Richie's son stared at his father in blank amazement. This was not how Pop taught him to play poker.

Allison regarded the man carefully. She decided she liked him. He was a bit like Ezra. No, she thought. He's a bit like Shelly. "I see ... What do you suggest?"

"First, let me order a car service to take you home. You should not be on the street, least of all *this* street, with eighty-six ounces of 24-karat gold jewelry. Next, let me photograph some of the pieces and Dad's appraisals. I want his opinion."

Allison interrupted. "Are you sure that's necessary? I mean, he's retired."

"Think, Allie, think!" she urged herself. "Why for heaven's sake didn't you plan for this?" She decided to prevaricate. That sounded so much better than lying. Besides, she was defending her economic interests. She had every right to be here. Andrew Fallis said Shelly intended to give her the proceeds. How was he supposed to know the gold was still in Shelly's closet?

"Well," she relented, "if you think he's up to it. Shelly would be here in person if he weren't so badly injured. It tears him up inside to part with his wife's keepsakes, but he has no other way to repay my loss. He feels so responsible. It tears me up, too. I feel like such a traitor to his wife. She was an absolute doll." Allison scarcely remembered Marian. They exchanged pleasantries in the hallway and at the trash chute. But then she was bedridden and Allison seldom saw her. When she did, the woman in the wheelchair was a lifeless, emaciated shell, nothing like the glamorous beauty at Shelly's bedside.

Richie Giordano blinked back a tear, a genuine one. "I hope they put that creep away for a thousand years, Mrs. Pfouts, I really do. Don't you worry; Dad and I will make sure you get every penny possible. Let's agree here and now that we'll retain no more than six percent of what this grosses, just like in real estate. You won't find anyone on the planet willing to match that for you. And besides, you know the value in weight. You can always walk away." Richie paused a moment. He worried whether even that entreaty sounded pushy. His son worried whether his father would hand over keys to the shop and say, "It's all yours, Mrs. Pfouts, because, well, we're saps."

Mrs. Pfouts interrupted the son's digression. She reached over the counter and pulled his father close. "Thank you," she wept into his shoulder, "Thank you for being so kind to a woman in distress. You have no idea what this means to me, after everything that's happened, discovering there's still chivalry and integrity and class in this world." She dabbed her eyes with a silk, monogrammed handkerchief but continued to sniffle.

Richard Giordano stood erect, chest held high, proud of his decision, blinking back the tears welling in his eyes. When was the last time he did anything that exuded integrity, chivalry or class? So what if he did not win the jackpot. She could as easily have walked into someone else's booth. He held no monopoly on her possessions. He was a Good Samaritan, a white knight, a decent human being. He lost nothing by helping her. He was solvent yesterday. He would be solvent tomorrow. But in St. Peter's ledger, he would be a very wealthy man. He addressed Mrs. Pfouts gently, "Promise me not to do anything for twenty-four hours. If it is all right, my dad and I will visit you. You can invite a neighbor or your attorney or your friend from Fidelity if you're frightened, need a witness, or want another expert. I'm familiar with your building. It's all over the news. May we have your number?"

Allison regarded the man carefully. She definitely liked him. "He must take after his father. I can see why Shelly kept coming back to him." She had a momentary pang of apprehension.

"You've both been wonderfully kind. Remember, there is no need to inconvenience your father, none whatsoever. Let him enjoy his retirement. But I do look forward to seeing you again tomorrow. I hope you'll give him Sheldon Vogel's warmest regards."

The elder Giordano dialed a local car service, photographed the jewelry and appraisal certificates, then placed Mrs. Pfouts in the sedan. "Boy, will Dad be surprised to hear about this!" he whistled, sweeping past his still-bewildered son.

Chapter 27

Steam wafted up from the vent, partially obscuring the signal. The fingers appeared and dissolved, one by one, until there was nothing remaining but a fist. Hanni crossed reluctantly.

Andrew wished Meryl Scott Rupert were more discreet. There were less conspicuous ways to help each other. He was still nominally in Mrs. Pfouts' employ.

The PDF attachment would not open. He cursed Adobe. They released too many updates, sometimes two or three per week. iPhone could not keep pace. Andrew huffed. He stopped at his office before continuing south to Christopher Street. He enjoyed being a celebrity. Even the cleaning lady showed respect. He could be a lot more selective in choosing friends. To think he once settled for Randall Dykeman ... or even Norbert.

Andrew Fallis, television pundit and outspoken defender of widows' rights, deserved better than Norbert Axelrod. He signed retainer agreements with three elderly women during the afternoon alone and could not keep pace with his voicemail. "Good grief, Mother, why didn't you tell me Denise quit?" He had no choice but to foist two inquiries on the office matriarch, the firm's senior partner.

"What goes around, comes around," gloated Andrew. "Now who's boss?" The self-anointed new boss at Fallis *et Madre* flipped off the computer, gathered the sheets from the printer, and shut the door behind him. He rushed downstairs to the waiting car service. Stuart watched Andrew switch off the computer from the browser window in his cluttered office at NYL South. The aging Dell seemed to power down but did not, and its video camera still worked beautifully.

Stuart glanced up from his screen. He regarded the collection of cartons, some destined for storage, some for destruction, and two small boxes to take home. "I'm sorry, Wally," he murmured. "We've all been sacked. I can't fucking risk this from home." Stuart substituted a comma for a hyphen in his LinkedIn profile, indicating the nag had breached Troy. He hoped Wally would brief him on what followed. "You were an okay boss, Wally, as bosses go. I learned a lot of cool stuff." Enriching stuff. Stuart closed the ESPN window, logged off LinkedIn, powered down his notebook, and left it cable-locked to the desk. It was hereafter the property of Hospital Corporation of America.

∂∞∂

Mildred Whiting wrestled with the repair work. The contractors were booked for weeks. There was no assurance they could match the gilded claret, damask silk wall covering in her bathroom. The pattern would almost certainly vary from the pattern in the bedroom and the parlor. Worse, they were unlikely to repair the hand-painted Sherle Wagner Floral Chinoiserie toilet, sink and bath without visible imperfections in the cloisonné-style enamel.

Mildred slumped. The apartment was scarcely habitable. The tub, toilet and sink functioned adequately, but the ceiling required painting. The carpet was ruined. Mildred regarded the bathroom and adjoining hallway as a canker, a scourge, a trammel to her literary concentration. She fretted over the inevitably discordant wall coverings, the lasting stain in the corridor and the visible imperfections in $17,000 hand-painted vitreous china. She was inclined to redecorate the entire apartment but no longer owned a *pied a terre* in London or Zurich. Living elsewhere for several months was impractical. She could not afford more evenings at the Jumeirah Essex House, not unless she produced a bestseller.

The evening news jarred her attention. There was yet another broadcast about her neighbors, John B. Roberts, George C. Wallace and Sheldon Vogel. Mildred mulled why the networks never mentioned Vogel's middle initial, as they did with John B. Roberts and George C. Wallace. Was it because his middle name was Uriah or Umberto and SUV sounded confusing, or because he was not an alleged accomplice and therefore worthy of such appellation? "Politician, mogul or master criminal," she decided. "You must be one of these to merit a middle initial." Fitting triumvirate, she reflected. They held so much in common. A freshly dusted terrier eyed her curiously.

Its gaze implanted a thought. "My God, Ruby, you're absolutely right! Why am I so dense? The story of a lifetime is upstairs and I'm sitting here moping about Sherle Wagner. I could write an exposé that makes Woodward and Bernstein look like yearlings. I've got the inside track in this building. Everyone knows me. Everyone talks to me. Who says I can't write solid journalism? I went to journalism school, didn't I? The best school in the country. I graduated too!" which was indeed an accomplishment. Many of her contemporaries did not.

"I worked for a newspaper, Ruby, a real one. I didn't make stories up ... at least not when it mattered." Mildred could scarcely contain herself. "Revelations and insights that only an accomplished romance writer could detect; that rare human touch. I bet they double my advance. I have millions of devoted readers. They'll turn out in droves at the book readings. I'll be on all the talk shows. 'Tell me, Mrs. Whiting, what inspired you to apply your literary talent to such a riveting contemporary drama? How were you able to humanize the story, infuse it with so many sympathetic, believable and yet horribly insidious characters?'"

"They'll have to hire someone to handle all the Tweets," she exalted. "You are an amateur, Ms. Rupert. The next Edward R. Murrow is about to hit the bookstores." She wondered whether the book should be bylined Mildred B. Whiting instead of the usual Mildred Whiting, forgetting she was neither President nor corporate mogul nor master criminal. She recalled the final scene from *A Star is Born*, where the singing idol Vicki Lester (*nee* Esther Blodgett) introduces herself on stage as Mrs. Norman Maine after the suicide of her once-famous husband. The scene brought Mildred to tears. It brought millions of theatergoers to tears. She and Gerald sat through the movie three times. They skipped class. Even Gerald cried. "I've decided, Ruby: Mildred Whiting *Błaszczyk*!"

஛

The report did not look good. Roberts had not logged onto his computer for days. The browser history hadn't been cleared in months, perhaps years. It was badly infected by adware. And there were no cookies indicating traffic on bankofamerica.com. They found an unopened letter to Sheldon Vogel in the daughter's room, but it was an invoice from Verizon. That hardly constituted a smoking gun. The concierge at the building said it was a clerical mistake. What on earth was the concierge doing sorting US mail?

George Wallace's computer was clean, very clean, as if he performed no substantive activity except browsing, budgeting and elementary correspondence following his release from confinement. He was scrupulous about deleting cookies and expunging deleted files. He was an IT specialist, after all, a hacker. Special Agent Kroll was sure he and Błaszczyk were hiding something. The mental collapse was too convenient, too perfectly timed, and, based on her subsequent observations, too contrived. He was no less balanced than she was. He was wittingly or unwittingly drugged, she decided, and Błaszczyk was using or protecting him, just like he used and protected the ex-wife, Hanife Kaplan, who somehow remained at large. "Thank you for being so helpful, Jeff!" she steamed. She knew he was hiding her somewhere – Jeff's idea of witness protection, Jill's idea of obstructing justice. The FBI had Wallace, she consoled herself. He was the IT wizard. Her agents watched him like a hawk.

managed to sneak onto the floor, menace the staff and other patients, and attempt to out-scoop their comrades. The newscasts
were a blur – nonstop coverage of the defenseless widow bereft
of fortune, the befuddled old man who left the vault wide open,
and the solicitous neighbor and accomplice who defrauded not
only them but his nation.

Sheldon felt weary. He felt mortal. He felt ashamed. He no
longer possessed the strength and resolve for vengeance. Yesterday's oaths were memories – dimmed by the weight of crushing
physical anguish, relentless media ridicule, and oppressive personal remorse. He should have double-checked Allison's trades.
He should have confessed his mistake the following morning. He
should have handled matters personally. He should not have
trusted a stranger – an *unemployed* stranger. He should have saved
his daughter. Instead, he killed her … at this very same hospital.
Marian said nothing. Neither did Diana, yet Marian somehow forgave him. Diana never did. Careless, careless, careless – it seemed
like such a trivial matter, as simple as entering an electronic sell
order. Yet he bollixed that too. His daughter lay under a head-
stone in Woodlawn Cemetery, his neighbor was fated to be a pau-
per, and he was the latest late-night punch line.

Sheldon resolved to make amends, to stop blaming the hospitals and doctors and hucksters and conmen in his life. It was
time to take responsibility for his own foolish misjudgments so
that he merited a chance, however remote, of joining Marian Willis Vogel on some untroubled Elysian plain. He had no use for
Heckscher, the Great Lawn, North Meadow, or any other field
outside his apartment. Neither did he plan a bench next to Marian's. The only future he could afford was in Oneonta, on a small
hillock under an Elm.

He instructed Catherine Fallis to reimburse Mrs. Pfouts from
the proceeds of a reverse mortgage on his apartment, surrender-
ing title to the lender. If he rented the unit out, he could cover
mortgage payments and interest. He was certain the board would

approve a sublet. They might even extend the maximum duration – anything to rid themselves of a troublesome tenant. The apartment would pass tax-free to the bank when he died, whereupon it would be auctioned to repay the mortgage. Any excess proceeds would be returned to his estate. Sheldon estimated half a million – enough to satisfy the eventual water damage settlements with his neighbors and buy Allie Pfouts a spectacular vacation. He did not expect his property insurance carrier to mount a vigorous defense. The policy limits were paltry. It was on the hook for $20,000 under every conceivable scenario. So he asked Cathy to manage the apartment litigation too. It was in Mrs. Pfouts' best interest to fight the damage claims zealously. Sheldon sighed. He could rent a shack in Oneonta and survive on social security – one of Mitt Romney's wretched 47 percenters. He did not expect to rent long. He possessed his great, great grandfather's revolver.

Sheldon thanked his old friend, Cathy, put the handset back in its cradle, and rested his head against the pillow. He begged off another visit by Dr. Simmons. Dr. Simmons could speak with him in the morning. Right now Sheldon Vogel needed to rest.

Catherine Fallis massaged her scalp and sighed. So much waste, so much ruin, and to such a good man! She wished he had shown interest in her after Marian died – just one flirtatious glance or knowing smile. God knows she tried to evoke one. Then he would not have to live out his years on food stamps in a dilapidated shack in Upstate Nowhere. He could share a classic seven on Fifth Avenue and make a lonely woman very happy. Catherine fired up her computer and began drafting.

☙❧

Paul Giordano was silent. Of course, he recognized the items. They were his finest works. Some were museum pieces. Almost all were labors of love. And now they were for sale. Paul listened absently to his son's account. How many years had it been? Thirty?

Forty? He clung to these memories for three decades, reconstructed them moment by moment, embraced them, watched them flutter sweetly to the ground, then gathered them up again.

"Marian Willis was a fine woman," he at last ventured, "truly fine. And Shelly is a good man, tireless. He would have sawn off his limbs for her." Paul Giordano did not have to. He sold the pieces to Shelly at one fifth their value. Marian knew, of course. She always knew. They were his gifts, too.

Their weekly trysts were at the Monkey Bar in the Hotel Elysee on East 54th Street. The management was discreet. The two came and left separately. No one ever recognized them. But their brief hours upstairs were bliss, enough to sustain him for a week, a month, even a lifetime. They were childhood sweethearts in Oneonta – nothing more. And that is how they would have remained. But the Giordanos moved to Brooklyn and the United States was swept into another war. Sheldon befriended Paul during basic training. Sheldon was kind – the most loyal, honest and reliable man Paul knew. He wasn't the brightest galoot in the platoon, but he was the one you wanted behind you.

They crossed paths again in the early 1960s. Sheldon needed an engagement ring, then a wedding band. He invited Paul to the wedding, but Saturday was an important business day. The Jewish merchants observed the Sabbath. He and the handful of remaining merchants held monopoly over the trade on 48th Street. They only opened during the morning, but it was the most profitable session of the week.

Sheldon brought his wife to the shop a year later. She was struck speechless. Paul Giordano stammered something about Oneonta. And Shelly chattered obliviously – thrilled to introduce at last his wife to his longtime buddy from the Service. He treated everyone to lunch at Sardi's, then asked Paul to design something really special for their first anniversary that was, in confidence, also affordable. Paul got the first part right and insulated Shelly from the second. For a couple hours each week, Marian and Paul stole into paradise. Sheldon's clumsy attempts at chivalry were a source of conspiratorial merriment and Paul's irascible wife and whiny son became tolerable, ill-defined shadows.

Their halcyon equilibrium continued for nineteen years. But Marian took ill, deathly ill, and for a long while thought only of her Maker. Silently, without ceremony, she ceased wearing furs and jewelry. She stowed Paul's soul in a closet and endured the rest of her life with her husband – tender and caring as always, but less vivacious and carefree. Her thoughts were often distant, tinged with melancholy. Sheldon ascribed the change to the demands of chemotherapy and an adolescent child. Paul ascribed it to a frozen heart. Sheldon loved her all the more deeply.

"I'd like to see Shelly again," Paul decided, "before you meet with Mrs. Pfouts. I'd like to see him *alone*."

૱৵

Wallace waited for night to fall then closed the drapes and extricated the hard drive and wireless pocket modem from Alya's television. He seated himself under the piano, flipped to Stuart's profile on LinkedIn, then redirected the browser to ESPN. He clicked on the link for ESPN Radio *& More*. For Wallace, "& More" was a pike character in the ESPN page footer. Wallace entered a 24-character alphanumeric string in the page's Search box and pressed the customized "& More" link. The sections entitled "Latest from Podcenter," "Today on ESPN Radio" and "ESPN Radio on Facebook" dissolved into an electronic workspace. Wallace called up the computer network map of Fallis & Associates. The virus had propagated to units FALLISC and ADMIN02. It began at FALLISA. The units were dormant. He flipped on the video cameras of the two FALLIS units as a precaution. The administrative unit did not possess one.

Wallace perused the directory of FALLISC. There were several current documents relating to Sheldon Vogel. His chest heaved as he read them. The man's life and reputation were ruined. He checked for activity on the browser. The browsing history listed just three financial institutions during the previous twenty-four hours, Fidelity, Citigroup and Bank of America. The report from Fox 5 said Bank of America. He opened the page link on the off chance Internet Explorer saved her logon and password. It did not. No one was that foolish, not even Jack Roberts. He did not peruse her Microsoft Outlook folder. He did not feel he had the right to. He would leave that up to someone at News Corp.

Wallace repeated the exercise on Andrew Fallis' computer. It was only used intermittently. The man was evidently too busy schmoozing with the media. But there were several recent page hits at Bank of America. He opened one that said login and shook his head. There were indeed people foolish enough to let Internet Explorer store financial account IDs and passwords. Wallace copied the information to an electronic post-it but did not enter the account. He was sure the account was frozen and monitored. On an impulse, he reviewed the browsing history of ADMIN02.

"Bingo," he exclaimed. Someone entered the identical Bank of America account three evenings earlier but applied a different password, a password Fallis & Associates obviously changed because they learned the account had been hacked. Who sat at this computer? He reviewed the folder names in the "Documents and Settings" subdirectory: Administrator, All Users, Currie, Default User, Frazier, Guest, Jacobson, Reed, Stojanovska, Temple, Turner. He thought a moment then researched Stojanovska's etymological country of origin.

"Macedonia." Wallace opened the "My Documents" directory and searched for documents containing Stojanovska and its Cyrillic equivalent, Стојановска. There were dozens. The last one was dated one day earlier. The administrator's name was Denise. She worked at the Fallis law firm for approximately four months, presumably as receptionist or paralegal. He searched "immigration" and discovered documents and letters to her immigration attorney. She still had seven months remaining on her F-1 student visa. Wallace reached for his Blackberry and dialed the law firm's switchboard. The call diverted to a recording.

"You have reached the law offices of Fallis and Associates. If you know the last name of the party you would like to reach, begin typing it now." Wallace typed STO.

"Hi. You've reached the desk of Janice Currie. I am unable to take your call right now, but if you leave your name, number and a brief message, I will …"

Wallace terminated the call. He searched the local drive for Janice Currie's name. There were two documents, both dated today. Janice was Denise's temporary or permanent replacement – presumably permanent. Otherwise she would have logged in as Guest.

Wallace was satisfied. He had enough to stir the pot. There was suddenly activity on the video camera. The overhead lights flickered on. Wallace stopped searching the administrator's hard drive. He heard a door shut quietly and saw a figure brush past Mrs. Fallis' screen. "Just the cleaning lady," he shrugged. He was about to close the ESPN window but hesitated. "Hanni?"

Wallace gaped. He watched in blank astonishment as his ex-wife rifled through the documents on Catherine Fallis' desk, tried to pry open her drawers, then reappeared moments later seated at the desk of her son, Andrew. She reached down to switch on the computer. Moments passed and the machine appeared to boot. The Windows login screen arose and Hanni sat there thinking. Wallace watched the keystrokes and shook his head.

"Good guess, Hanni. Try again." The second guess was further from the mark. She tried again. This time, Wallace substituted the correct keystrokes, B-A-D-P-I-G-G-I-E-S, and she pressed Enter. Immense satisfaction registered on her face. Wallace wanted to reach through the browser and kiss her. Instead, he noticed movement in Catherine Fallis' office. A skirt tail flashed past the screen. A clear plastic trash bag slid into view and an arm reached down to empty the wastebasket.

Wallace's fingers flew. "IT'S ME, WALLY. HIDE!!!!" The image appeared as a flashing, 48-point pop-up. He then darkened Andrew Fallis' monitor. His wife stared at the screen, dazed, and then dove under the desk. Wallace watched the empty desk helplessly as the desk chair closed in tightly. Wallace hoped she pushed the waste basket into plain view.

On impulse, he opened Microsoft Word on Mrs. Fallis' PC and maximized the speaker volume. He searched clipart for an alarm and chose 00388265.wav, a ten-second piercingly shrill air raid siren. He previewed the siren over and over. The maid appeared in front of the desk and darkened screen, squeezed her hands over her ears, and dragged her bag of trash outside the office. The door shut with a thud. He immediately did the same to Andrew Fallis' computer and Janice Currie's. The office lights dimmed abruptly, and a door slammed. Hanni illuminated her face with her iPhone. "Thank you, honey" she mouthed, before blowing a kiss to the camera. Her figure faded in the darkness.

Defense attorney Morton Williams' team made headway with their investigation, but his client remained stubbornly uncooperative. Jack Roberts continued to insist that Sheldon Vogel conjured Jack's crime in his head – not the embezzlement of $1.43 million or theft of an as-yet undetermined amount of jewelry; those actually happened – but the retention of and alleged association with George C. Wallace? For all Roberts knew, Vogel retained another attorney or stole the money himself.

Pathetic. There wasn't a juror alive who would believe that. And the data-smuggling charges? Williams did not know where to begin. His client offered no alternative explanation, just that it was not him. "Thank you, Jack. Thank you very much." Williams wondered how effectively he could grandstand without a scintilla of exculpatory evidence. This wasn't about DNA or ill-fitting gloves or Bruno Magli loafers. This was about direct positive IDs by a bevy of qualified witnesses. He did not look forward to impeaching each and every one of them on the stand.

"Ladies and gentlemen of the jury, the defense will show that the victim, Mrs. Allison Pfouts, and the prosecuting attorney's main witnesses – Mrs. Pfouts' attorney, her building staff, her longtime money manager, Mr. Sheldon Vogel, and Mr. Vogel's doctor – are each shameless habitual liars, united by one singular purpose, to bring hardship and ignominy on the residential co-operative's only multiethnic families. Yes, ladies and gentlemen. This trial has nothing to do with embezzlement or international espionage and everything to do with that nefarious staple of American indecency: racism." Williams paused.

"Damn it, Jack, you could at least be black!" Williams threw up his hands in frustration. The case was driving him crazy. The one consolation was it paid the rent. His team was billing fifty hours per day, $100,000 per week. "The client won't miss it," he assured himself. "He'll spend the rest of his life in taxpayer-subsidized housing – just another moocher, part of Mitt Romney's 47 percent."

☙❧

jeffblazik@hotmail.com? Jill Kroll gazed at her inbox in amazement. Since when did Geoffrey Błaszczyk use Hotmail? And why doesn't he spell his name correctly? She was leery of viruses, but the email contained no links, attachments, or HTML formatting. It was also very short.

"Don't overlook Denise Stojanovska, an F-1 student visa holder who works in Catherine Fallis' office. Her Greek passport number is AE5160943. I suspect she accessed Allison Pfouts' account the evening the funds disappeared."

Agent Kroll smiled. "Thank you, Jeff. I don't know where you dig this stuff up but thank you." She would call INS and Mrs. Fallis in the morning.

❧

"Well, of course we'd like to tell our side of the story, Mrs. Whiting. But you see, our hands are tied. We can't say anything until after the trial."

"I understand, Mrs. Roberts. I do hope we will get that chance. In the meantime, you don't perhaps know how I can get in touch with Mr. Wallace's ex-wife, Hanife Kaplan. I understand you were once quite close."

Still are, thought Susan. "No, but I'd be delighted to mention you if I see her. It's such an honor receiving a call from a famous author." Susan wracked her brain to remember any of her titles. There were so many – row after row of them on the magazine racks at the airport. The long-haul flight attendants all read them, even Susan McDonald. Except today she could not remember a single one. They all fused together. She asked the author to keep her posted and hung up.

"Ugh!" she announced. "Now they're hounding us on the house phone." She disconnected the landline and changed her cell phone number, but they still found a way to get through. One reporter went so far as to rappel down from the roof, trying to reach her balcony. His line snagged on the fifteenth floor and he had to be rescued. Now they stationed a porter on the roof deck to make sure no one tried again.

Susan had mixed feelings about the daily $1,000 fine from the board. She could see why they were upset, and how the media circus cost the building money in additional security. But $1,000? She hoped Jack was right – that he could contest it successfully in court. That would also cost money, but Jack could point to genuine regulations and case law. He sounded for once like a real lawyer, not at all like the guy helping Morton Williams with his defense. Susan sighed. Jack would go to prison for life, and Susan and Melissa would be vilified by their neighbors, but John B. Roberts would not pay a dime for violating the new house rule against excessive noise. "Great priorities, Jack. That's sticking it to the Man!"

He had not yet returned home with Melissa. She crept outside to run an errand.

❧❦

"Dr. Martinez, I'd like to talk with you about Sheldon Vogel."

"Of course, Dr. Simmons, what is it?" Dr. Martinez drew the hospital psychiatrist into an unoccupied patient room and shut the door.

"It is impossible to conduct a proper examination. He is bombarded at all times by distractions, even with a policeman stationed outside his door. I don't know whether his answers are influenced by the commotion around him, the nonstop interrogation, or the story that's spoon-fed to him on television, but I cannot say with confidence he isn't fabulating."

"Fabulating?" inquired Martinez.

"Making things up. Filling in the narrative gaps with whatever seems plausible, given what he's heard from everyone else."

Martinez protested. "But everything he's said has been corroborated by others, sometimes two or three times."

"That's just it. He's bombarded. He's heard so much about embezzlement and gold and international conspiracy that he can't separate what he said, saw or did from what others assert he said, saw or did."

This was not what Dr. Martinez wanted to hear. "I'm sorry, Dr. Simmons. I'm just a surgeon. Do you have an example, an instance where you suspect fabrication?"

"Fabulation. Sure: this whole notion of retaining John Roberts as his attorney. The only representations I'm confident of are that he injured himself saving Roberts' wife and Roberts was at his bedside when he emerged from a coma. I've asked him to describe those episodes four or five times now. Each time he uses different words, begins and ends in different places, and stresses different things, but the gist of the story is identical. For the negotiations, it's always the same words, the same imagery, as if his response is programmed."

"Isn't that good, consistency, I mean?"

"Not really, it's more likely he's afraid to trip up or contradict himself. Or he lacks sufficient recollection to describe the events with additional clarity. Look, it may all be subconscious. I doubt he intentionally contrived anything, but I do think it's possible he hallucinated during his coma, and that those hallucinations are now unshakable memories because others heard about them, thought they sounded plausible, and repeated them. Word got back to the patient, and now everyone seems to be on the same page – except no one can supply rich, contextual detail. Instead, the story gets thinner and more focused with each retelling."

Dr. Martinez stared down and said nothing. Dr. Simmons was also silent. Dr. Martinez eventually broke the silence. "Thank you, Dr. Simmons. Thank you for your insight."

❧

Catherine Fallis returned to her office and her emails. She had accomplished what she promised but was emotionally drained. She worked twenty-four hours straight. She hadn't worked that feverishly in years. Ordinarily she would be exultant. How many reverse mortgages were negotiated and closed in a single day, with no advance notice? Plus the conflict waivers, the powers of attorney, and the signed and attested will?

Catherine Fallis was distraught. She was as old, tired and weak as the man whose real estate interests she now represented. She worked tirelessly and zealously but had no stomach for this kind of work – not if success meant grinding a good man into mulch.

She slumped in her chair, turned on the computer and opened her email. She had an interoffice message from Janice Currie, the new administrative assistant. Oh yes, that too. She interviewed and hired a new administrative assistant, prepared her tax and insurance records, and set up her workstation – all within the space of twenty-four hours. Where was Andrew, her hotshot son, the new talking head at Fox News? She shook her head in confused disgust. The boy did no constructive work, just bleated inanities to a camera crew outside her longtime client's apartment building, and within minutes was a pundit on national television.

"International expert on computer fraud? Experienced trial lawyer? He can't even reconcile a checkbook. Where is the justice in that?"

"At least he's out of my hair," she consoled herself. "It won't take long before he opens his own shop for hundreds of desperate widows who think they've been swindled. Heaven knows how he'll help them. He certainly hasn't helped Allie Pfouts."

"Damn it, Janice, why didn't you text me?" She made a mental note to speak with her assistant in the morning. An email that Special Agent Kroll of the FBI called should have been escalated as urgent. Cathy dialed the number on the message. She hoped the delay in calling back wasn't noticed. She did not want to upset the FBI.

∂∽∾

"Why no, Detective Kroll. Denise Stojanovska left our employ two days ago. Yes, of course we have her contact information, but I believe she returned home to Athens."

"My God," she added silently, "What have we done?" She hung up with Agent Kroll and dialed Andrew's voicemail.

"Call me, Andrew. It's urgent." She repeated the plea as a text message then pulled out the file containing her malpractice insurance policy. She wondered what the dividing line was between protected negligence and unprotected gross negligence. "Please, Andrew, don't let this be a case of gross negligence."

∂∽∾

"Good morning, soldier. I heard you were hiding here. Why don't you come see me anymore?" Paul Giordano slipped into Sheldon Vogel's room. He was so frail and stooped that the staff and police officer mistook him for a patient. His voice, however, was still smooth and reassuring. Sheldon lifted his head and squinted.

"Paul? Paul Giordano?"

"Hello Sheldon." He shuffled to the patient's side and gripped Sheldon's shoulder. "You're all over the news. Even my boys are talking about you. How are you holding up?"

Sheldon regarded the stooped figure standing over him. "Barely surviving," he replied. "Same as you."

Paul started at the remark but laughed. "Time hasn't been kind, Shelly, has it? At least we're both alive." He laughed again. "Remember how we used to fret about surviving the war? We slipped through, you and me, discharged without ever seeing a day of battle. Now here we are joking about the infirmities of old age. What's it been? 55 years? 56?"

Sheldon smiled ruefully and shrugged. He remembered Paul as tall, rugged and dashing, a ladies' man, a real Lothario. He wondered what his own impression was on someone who hadn't seen him for years, hadn't accustomed his eyes to his gradual, ir-retrievable decline. "A long time."

"Allison Pfouts came to my son, Richie. I guess you gave her Marian's jewelry."

Sheldon was confused. "Allie Pfouts?"

"Yes, your neighbor, the one who was swindled. You said she should sell the jewelry to help recover her losses. It tears me up to see you do this. I know how much Marian meant to you. I stopped by to make sure it was what you wanted."

Sheldon fumbled for words. "You say Allie has it all … the jewelry?"

"I assume so. I don't have an inventory of what I sold you, but I think so." Actually, Paul Giordano recalled exactly what he gave Marian. All but three pieces were there: an engagement ring; a wedding band; and a daughter. The first two were buried with Marian in Oneonta. The third was buried at Woodlawn Cemetery in the Bronx, next to Sheldon's sister and his parents. Helen called them Aunty and Grandma, but Marian knew they were not.

Helen bore a striking resemblance to her father, her real father. He and Marian were mortified Sheldon would figure that out. They never risked unprotected sex again. Heaven forbid she should bear a son. Even Sheldon would have identified the connection. The years passed and Marian bore no more children, yet not for lack of trying. It was God's way, Paul and Marian consoled each other, of sanctifying the real exchange of vows.

Paul stooped over Sheldon and smiled sheepishly. He knew he would die soon. In fact, he was certain. Pancreatic cancer was unforgiving. He wondered whether he would be reunited with his daughter, the one who learned of her parentage the month she died, and with the woman who bore her. No matter. He could tolerate Gladys for eternity, but Marian? That would be Elysian.

Sheldon struggled to remember. Was he unclear? Did Jack misunderstand the instructions? Or did Jack give Allison carte blanche to the jewelry while he depleted the brokerage account, just to keep her from getting nosy? What about the litigation waiver? Andrew Fallis said there wasn't one. Sheldon was suddenly impatient. He needed to clarify matters with Cathy Fallis.

"Yes, of course, Paul. It's exactly as Allie says. I am so grateful you dropped by to see me. Will you be here in an hour? I'm scheduled in five minutes for occupational therapy."

Paul shook his head. "I promised to meet Richie at Mrs. Pfouts apartment. I'll return for a few minutes in the evening."

"I'd like that," Sheldon replied.

Paul Giordano once studied to become a priest. He was steered in that direction by his father. But Gladys Rizzo got pregnant and he married her. He became a jeweler like his father. Paul was the closest Sheldon came to befriending a Catholic priest. There was something he needed desperately to confess.

⤜⤛

Susan ducked into the subway at the Time Warner Center and made her way to SoHo. She was pretty sure she wasn't followed, but it was dark. She climbed the steps to the High Line, paused a moment to take in the view, then descended back to street level. Hanni greeted her in a gray hooded jumpsuit. They headed west to the waterfront edging Chelsea Piers. Susan noticed she wasn't smoking.

"You can take the cross-town M23 to Broadway, then transfer uptown to the N or R." Susan nodded. Her daughter's test sessions were upstairs on the East Rink, 7 am before school. The last one was two Wednesdays ago. It seemed like two centuries.

"This is driving me nuts, Hanni. I've decided to leave Jack."

They stood at the rail, gazing at the thin red glow above Jersey City. The pier to their left buzzed as the yacht prepared for a dinner cruise.

"The easiest thing would be to spend some time in Rye with Jack's sister, Eleanor, but I'm thinking far away."

Hanni bit her tongue. She never understood Jack's attraction, but was unsure criminal indictment was the right reason to desert him. She was pretty sure Jack was telling the truth, and that Susan believed him. But she could also detect panic – the rapidly evaporating bank account, the nonstop media pressure, and the oppressive and intrusive hand of law enforcement. Still, Jack stayed with Susan night and day for three-and-a-half weeks during the spring. He bathed, clothed and fed her for two more months, helped her onto the toilet, cleaned the bedpan each morning, washed the sheets. He didn't have to. Jack knew Susan flew to Tahoe with little intention of returning. Even Melissa knew. Hanni knew only one other man in the world who would have done that. She shivered.

"Why don't you start with Eleanor," she suggested. "Then you won't burn any bridges." Hanni burnt plenty of bridges, seldom with regret, but not always, certainly not the most recent one. She hoped she could repair it. She changed the subject.

"Any developments I should know about?"

"Not really, although the romance writer, Mildred Whiting, expressed keen interest in interviewing you. I think she wants to write a book."

"She and five hundred others. How did she find you? I thought you changed all your numbers."

"House phone. She's our neighbor."

Hanni chuckled. "No thanks, Susan. My story stays with me to my grave. You hungry? I have frozen pizza and a chilled bottle of Pinot Grigio at the apartment."

Susan remembered the hot tub and Southern Comfort and yip of a dozen coyotes. She remembered the crescent moon and smell of musk and cigarettes oozing from her pores. She remembered the crushing headache and moaning figure under the blanket. And she remembered her anger at a resort that caved in to money and to dabblers. She had no patience for dabblers.

"I'm sorry, Hanni, another time. I have a lot to think about." She reached forward, kissed Hanni longingly on the lips, then thrust her back. She tottered away as quickly as her crutches would carry her.

Chapter 28

The walkman glistened, scrubbed clean for the momentous weekend. The pedestrian fencing, the partially erected grandstands. Even the hand seemed to smile. For naught. At last moment the marathon was cancelled.

THURSDAY, NOVEMBER 1, 2012

Melissa regarded her skates. Wollman Rink opened the previous Saturday – the day after the camera crews arrived, the day after her apartment building's entrance became impassable. She hoped the skaters and instructors would treat her kindly, not judge her by the sins of her father. He assured her the charges were a mistake, but that's not what she heard at school, not what she heard on the news, not what she saw on his ankle, and not what she read on the Internet during the limited time she had access. The government confiscated the family computer. She crept into a public library on York Avenue after school to type her homework. Her father milled around Agata & Valentina, trying to remain inconspicuous, sipping coffee and purchasing the next day's groceries. Melissa notified him by text message when she was finished, although she lingered considerably longer than necessary. She had mixed feelings about returning to her family.

Her father met her at the corner. It was late enough to board the M31 bus unnoticed, although they still had to stand. Her father wore a Yankees cap low over his forehead and dark sunglasses to be safe – sunglasses at six in the evening. He had not shaved since the arraignment. No one exchanged a word. They arrived home after seven-thirty.

"All right," he relented. "Let's risk it." There were still three mornings left before Eastern Standard Time. They could exit the apartment in complete darkness.

Melissa outgrew afterschool skating the previous season. She graduated to the skating school's Elite Academy, which scheduled its sessions early in the morning, shortly after the rink opened. The rink opened most mornings at six-thirty.

Thursday mornings were quiet – a few individual lessons and the Adult Academy at seven-thirty. If Melissa stowed her belongings outside and departed by seven-thirty, she could avoid a barrage of chance encounters. Most such encounters were unpleasant. Strangers stopped and spat at her father, told him to rot in hell, and marveled why a judge granted him bail, notwithstanding the ungainly, ever-visible ankle bracelet. They cursed Melissa too. Longtime neighbors brushed past, fearful of being associated. Melissa and her father paced themselves half a block apart. She paused in a doorway unnoticed whenever he was accosted. She wondered whether she would continue hiding after he rotted in hell or in prison (the judge hadn't decided which), and whether her mother would also have to wheel herself twenty paces behind her.

Susan reminded Jack there was a testing session Thursday morning for upper classmen at the school. Melissa would not be admitted before noon.

"Wonderful," thought Jack. "I get to sneak in and out of the building six times – one roundtrip to the rink and twice to school." He went to bed early but could not sleep. He had fallen out of practice. He checked on Melissa during one of his trips to the bathroom. There were so many of them.

Melissa slept soundly. Susan sat on the sofa, examining the checkbook and a stack of bills. She wished she had not been insistent about the whole life insurance policy conversions. They could have used the $19,000. Jack knew better than to intrude. He lay awake in bed until two-thirty. How had he come to this? He no longer bothered with the Levitra. Susan knew he was spent. Her injuries were just an excuse. She bought him a bottle of Herradura Blanco. Don Julio was too expensive.

The alarm peeped at 4:45. Jack showered, shaved for the first time in days, and roused Melissa. They exited through the garage at 6:05. It was a moonless morning – still seventy-four minutes before sunrise. The windows in the hotels and high-rises along Central Park South were dark. A lone taxicab slowed beside them, hoping for a fare, then moved on. The news vans slept. They crossed unnoticed into the park.

The gate was chained but the padlock was open. Jack slipped the chain off the bars, let his daughter in, then reproduced the locked-gate illusion. They nodded to the guard stationed inside the door, but the man was absorbed in his Sudoku. Melissa was the first skater to arrive. They bypassed the benches and lockers and pushed open the heavy doors to step outside. They seated themselves on a bench along the back wall and Melissa reached in the bag for her skates. She stepped on the ice at six-twenty, immediately after the Zamboni finished resurfacing. Jack sat huddled and groggy against the wall, his chin nestled deep in his jacket. A baseball cap and sunglasses completed his disguise. He entered the building briefly to sign his daughter in, but otherwise avoided personal contact. The parents and instructors seemed grateful. Melissa came off the ice at seven-thirty and begged to skate an hour longer.

～∽

Jill Kroll called George Wallace and his attorney at seven-thirty. She was holding a press conference at 8 am, clearing him of charges. There was a new suspect in the Pfouts embezzlement case, another suspect in the theft of Sheldon Vogel's gold jewelry, and insufficient evidence to pursue charges against anyone for international espionage. The Pfouts and espionage cases seemed unrelated. She apologized curtly for his inconvenience. She was convinced Wallace was involved but lacked proof.

She tried reaching John Roberts, but he already left for the morning. His cell phone lay near his bed, an aging clamshell LG. He returned the Blackberry to Dewey & LeBoeuf when it folded. It was not unusual for him to leave the LG behind when he ran errands or biked around the park. No one called him anymore.

Kroll spoke with Morton Williams and Susan Roberts instead. Mrs. Roberts was delighted by the news and couldn't wait for Jack to come home. She would remind Jack to call Kroll and Williams immediately. Williams hastily arranged his own press conference.

⁊✺⁊

Meryl Scott Rupert was beside herself. "Andrew Fallis' *secretary?*" The girl's brother already confessed. It wasn't often that a Greek Cypriot bank analyst arrived at work in a Lamborghini. Interpol had not yet located the mother or sister or 1.3 million dollars, but it was clear John B. Roberts, husband of Susan *Spoiled Sport* McDonald, was falsely accused by none other than Fox 5's newest talk show sensation, Andrew Thomas Fallis. "ATF," she snarled, "Bureau of Alcohol, Tobacco, Firearms *and Explosives.*" Right now, Meryl Scott Rupert wanted to detonate an explosive under Fallis' tight gay ass.

The next insight concerned the jewelry. It was an inside job, all right, but the gold was stolen by the schlemiel's client, not his attorney, which apparently, he never had. He, Fallis and the jokers at the building and the hospital made that part up. Rupert did not consider such extensive fabrication possible, by seasoned Fox journalists perhaps, but not by ordinary New Yorkers. Yet the special FBI agent in charge of the investigation just said so. She strove to clear any 'media misunderstanding' about this issue several times.

"Cover-up," Meryl concluded. "The government is concealing something." But at the moment the world only saw egg, lots of it, smeared in ugly streaks across Meryl Scott Rupert's perfectly re-sculpted face. She was furious. No one made a fool of Meryl Scott Rupert. No one! She resolved then and there to aim her journalistic gun sight at Special Agent Jill Fitzgerald Kroll of the Federal Bureau of Investigation. Although the rebuke at Trattoria Dell'Arte still burned, Susan McDonald and the Roberts family were minutiae.

Agent Kroll had no comment on the asserted data-smuggling ring between employees and affiliates of NYL Health Systems and Iran. "Neither the FBI, CIA nor Department of Homeland Security has ever commented on the possibility of such a ring, nor announced any related closed or pending investigation. Any statements you have heard relating to such alleged criminal activity arose from non-governmental private sources. We have no comment on their credibility or accuracy."

Kroll concluded with a special nod to Fox 5 News New York. "I am unaware of any closed or pending local, state or federal investigation of Susan McDonald Roberts in connection with distributing performance-enhancing drugs or financing domestic terrorism." She took questions but surrendered no ground.

Meryl texted Gerry her conclusions. $1.43 million was embezzled by a Greek national from a helpless, United States widow. The Greek national, in conspiracy with other Greek nationals, channeled the funds to a known banking center for Russian and Middle Eastern organized crime. $1.3 million was still missing, as were the asserted perpetrators. Meanwhile, five witnesses to John Roberts' role as counsel to Sheldon Vogel – witnesses who, with one exception, were unacquainted with each other before Roberts' arraignment – changed their testimony, presumably under pressure from Iranian and/or US government authorities. Finally, the government refuses to comment on the alleged international data-smuggling and security counterfeiting connection. She asked Gerry to draft quickly. "No comment" meant *nolo contendre* in her lexicon, no different than *mea culpa*. She raced to rejoin the camera crew outside Susie PED-Mac's apartment building.

૱૰

Wallace donned green khaki pants and a blue denim work shirt. He hoisted his luggage up the stairs from the service entrance onto the sidewalk. He considered wearing a jacket but thought it would jeopardize the illusion. He stood by the mountain of densely packed trash bags – clear ones for recycling, black ones for waste. Network crews clamored in front of the building and at the garage entrances. They were on to John Roberts' means of egress. For the first time in his life, Wallace did not mind being confused with a janitor. He reached down, clutched one of the bags of trash, and tugged it down the sidewalk, together with his luggage, until he reached the entrance to the subway. He left the bag in the heap in front of P.J. Carney's and descended into the station. He took the N train to Astoria Boulevard, walked downstairs to Hoyt Avenue, and hailed the Q31 bus to LaGuardia. He stood by for a Jet Blue flight to Atlanta and purchased a ticket at Hartsfield International Airport to Birmingham, Alabama. He directed the cab to his childhood home near Oakland Cemetery.

∾∽

Hanni was overjoyed by the news. She did not care whether Wally's phone was tapped. She dialed him immediately but received voicemail. She terminated the call. Instead, she scrolled through her emails. She stopped blocking his account after Tuesday evening's video cam encounter. There was more to Wally than met the eye, even if he wore Spiderman pajamas. Their exchanges had been brief.

"Thank you, sweets."

"Any time."

"Get what you wanted?"

"And how!" Actually, she left the office in fright. She wanted to blackmail the lawyer, make him pay like those other bastards, Gürhan Erdoğan and Sanford Hotchkiss. She was sick and tired of being dragged into other people's crap. She had nothing to do with Jack Roberts' desperate financial misdeeds and neither did Wally. Her answer had to do with Wally, but she did not elaborate. Any further exchange would be imprudent. Not really, but she had to maintain the pretense. When it came to Geoffrey Błaszczyk, it was always about maintaining pretense.

This morning's email was more substantial.

"Dear Hanni, The cartons are stacked and labeled. The moving company will arrive Monday morning at 10 am. Truman has the key card. I've arranged for your boxes and furniture to go to Manhattan Mini Storage in Chelsea – the West 21st Street location. Susan says you live near there and it's convenient. You're prepaid through March but must change your address on the registration before the apartment closing. I'm going home. I will save on expenses and someday repay my defense attorney for his services and my aunt for the bail bond. Your support payments will come first. I promise. I am storing the remaining boxes and furniture in the garage until I figure out what to do with them. Stay out of trouble. Wally."

Hanni crawled under the covers. She forgot to tell him the buyer cancelled. He (maybe also she?) could remain in that wonderful apartment. She was only thirty-seven. She did not have to take the pill. Beril had a child at forty-two and Hanni was much more fit. She could resume being Hanife Kaplan *Wallace*, and, in Błaszczyk's mind, become bait to capture Marja. Błaszczyk would express dismay and outwardly protest but inwardly endorse it. He would burst with pride; his best acolyte – willing to sacrifice everything for her country. Another fucking pipe dream! Wally was gone. She clenched the blankets in her hands and sobbed. "Damn, you, Geoffrey Błaszczyk. Damn you!"

�❧

The voice from downstairs was uncommonly chipper. "Good morning, Mrs. Roberts. Doctor Martinez is here from Roosevelt Hospital. I checked his identification. May I send him up?"

So the building staff heard the news. Thank goodness! Susan was at wit's end – ready to move to Tallahassee. But Doctor Martinez, Dr. Lester Martinez? What on earth did he want?

"Sure, John, send him up." Susan threw on a robe and checked her appearance in the mirror. She shrugged. What difference did it make? The man meant nothing to her. She hobbled on crutches to the door.

"Uh, hello Mrs. Roberts. May I come in?" Susan motioned toward the ottoman.

"I wanted to apologize to you and your husband. Is he home?"

Susan wasn't especially interested but resolved to hear him out. An apology was better than indifference. "No, I'm afraid he's at the rink with my daughter. I expect him back shortly. Would you like to wait?"

Dr. Martinez called at 8:45 am, as early as he considered decent. He had to be at the hospital by 9:30. They were moving Sheldon Vogel to the psychiatric ward, perhaps temporarily, perhaps longer. The shouting match the previous evening between the patient and his Army buddy did not help. They had to be restrained. The visitor suffered an aneurism, lost consciousness, and was now in ICU. Sheldon Vogel fared only slightly better. His speech was slurred and had difficulty digesting the morning news. He spent the morning muttering gibberish about his wife, daughter and the devil. Dr. Martinez felt miserable.

"Look, I can only stay a few minutes. I'll be brief. I was wrong about your husband. I got caught up somehow in my patient's narrative – it seemed so real – and then everyone else started parroting and corroborating him. But we were wrong. We were all wrong. I am really, really sorry." Susan reclined in the couch and stretched her legs. She wished she recorded the apology so she could replay it later and judge whether the man was sincere, whether he would approach the next hallucinating patient somewhat differently.

"Mr. Vogel saved my life. I can't blame him for things he said. I don't have the right. But the accusations have made our life … well, uncomfortable. It was not nice of you to repeat them, and to repeat them to the press. What were you thinking?"

Martinez dreaded that question. He was not proud of the answer. "I want to say the reporter was pushy. She was insanely pushy." Susan knew. Boy she knew. "But I could have retreated down a locked corridor. I could have ended it there. But I didn't.

I was mad. I was so sure your husband deceived me, made a fool of me. Male pride? Machismo? I don't know. I just snapped. I am really, really sorry."

Susan smiled faintly and nodded.

Martinez continued. "I wish your husband were here. He has every right to deck me."

Susan laughed. "I hate to disillusion you, but I do the decking around here." She could not imagine Jack decking anyone. "When do you have to be at the hospital?"

"Now, unfortunately," he replied, "but before I go, would you give these to your daughter? I baked them myself. Tell her they are 'Tollpatsch Cookies' – direct from the world's biggest Tollpatsch."

Susan accepted the small box with the narrow pink ribbon. "You mean Tollhouse Cookies, don't you?" She was amused the great doctor was so ignorant.

"No, I mean Tollpatsch. You can look them up online. Only certain people get to make them."

~❦~

Abby sipped her morning coffee. She was able to escape the hospital the previous evening to her cottage in Zephyr Cove. She drew back the drapes and opened the sliding door. She leaned against its frame, entranced by the view. Minutes passed. The sun chased the roof's shadow off the patio. It retreated to a narrowing band near her feet. The light came from behind but was blinding. It defined every boulder, shrub and stump on the distant mountains and bathed the wide lake in a crisp, shimmering glow. Abby toasted a croissant, peeled a banana, and brought them outside with the previous weekend's *San Francisco Chronicle*. The air was scented with cedar and pine. Birds chirped in the hedges partitioning her plot from the neighbor's. Abby settled into a recliner, luxuriated in the sun's warmth, and scanned the paper's headline: "Iranian Spy Ring Foiled, Wave of Indictments in New York."

"Boring," she thought, "another world," and turned to the pages in *Lifestyle*. She put the paper down. It took so little these days to upset her; the mention of New York did it every time. She wanted to firebomb the city for luring Lester away from her, for harboring the ungrateful thief. She wanted to firebomb Lester. Lester earned his transfer to a prestigious New York hospital because of her. She trained him, tutored him, made up for all the time he wasted in medical school. That is how he wound up in Reno. He was at UCLA, for heaven's sake. The only reason he interned at Renown is because no urban hospital would accept him. Others saw questionable talent; she saw potential. She roused him off his butt, instilled him with confidence, motivated him to study, made him a man. She'd castrate the jerk if she saw him again. She'd select the sharpest scalpel and cast his genitals to the sturgeon. Some fisherman would haul the ancient fish onto the dock, carve free its precious sack of caviar, and marvel at the size and quantity. Only Abby would know the reason; it was nourished and paid for by Dr. Lester Martinez's precious gonads.

Bobby Hatfield interrupted her thoughts of vivisection. He hungered for her touch. Her iPhone said so. Abby waited a long, lonely time, deliberating whether to answer. She was not on call. This was a genuine day off. But she was always on call. There was always someone who was overwhelmed. She put down her coffee and stepped inside. She answered the call before it switched to Voicemail.

"Abby Weinstein." She inherited the habit from her father. He never answered the telephone, "Hello?" He announced his name instead. It spared having to respond, "Speaking." It encouraged callers to get to the point. But it did not work. Callers still said, "Hello, may I speak with Morris Weinstein?" Her father still wound up answering, "Speaking." Abby inherited the identical burden from her father. She waited impatiently for the doltish question, "Hello? Is this Abigail Weinstein?"

"Abby, it's me, Les." The brevity caught Abby by surprise. Her mind was wired to answer a different question.

"Hello? This is Abigail Weinstein. May I ask who's calling?"

"Abby, honey, it's me, Les. Lester Martinez." This time Abby comprehended. Thirty seconds earlier she would have screamed at him.

"Hello, Les!" she gushed. She felt her pulse quicken and heart thump. "How *are* you?" She squeezed her legs together. "Oh God, why?" she pleaded silently. "Why do I have to urinate *now*?" She pressed the phone close to her ear and wracked her brain, "How do I mute this? How do I mute this?" and rushed to the bathroom.

"I'm okay. I'm … okay." The voice was strained, awkward. What do you say after six months' silence? Complete silence: no phone calls, messages, texts or Facebook exchanges. They weren't even Facebook friends.

"Listen," he continued, "I'm rushing to the hospital, but I have just one question for you, a really important question." Abby was perplexed.

"Will you take me back?" Neither of them seemed to hear the loud whoosh in the background.

∂∞∂

Williams paced back and forth in front of the building. He grew impatient and marched toward the rink. If he walked quickly, he could intercept them. He was advised at the rink's entrance that he just missed them. There was a celebratory mood among the parents and instructors. A couple parents rushed forward to congratulate him and thank him for rescuing a member of their "family." Others seemed less certain, as if Roberts had pulled off an OJ. Either way, they regarded Morton Williams with newfound respect. Williams excused himself. He had no time to bask in adulation. Televised adulation awaited him on Central Park South.

ॐॐ

Jack and Melissa returned the long way, west under Driprock Arch, then south past the entrance to the playground. They followed the path around to the small meadow where they played badminton and up the hill to the park drive. They waited for the line of taxis to drain south down Seventh Avenue, crossed the drive, and strode along the bench-lined path to Artisans' Gate, the exit to the park. Jack paused for a moment at Sheldon Vogel's bench, the one he dedicated to Marian. Jack decided to visit him at the hospital, to mend broken fences, provided he could sneak past Dr. Martinez. He decided to send a note first, after he took Melissa to school.

He saw the crowd in front of the building and shuddered. He was unsure which was worse – a mob of angry journalists or a throng of adoring ones. "It will soon be over," he consoled himself, "yesterday's news. No one cares long about the exonerated, just the charged, unless of course you are OJ Simpson." He grasped Melissa's hand tightly and strode to the corner. Melissa beamed.

Someone pointed and a dozen cameras aimed their lenses in his direction. Reporters edged onto the street, but the cars and buses brushed them back. The light changed but a large red tractor-trailer blocked the crosswalk. It was the height of rush hour. Jack picked his way around the Papa John's semi to the median but was swarmed by cameramen and reporters. Microphones banged against his chin and lenses bumped against his nose. He answered the cacophony with the same four words, repeated until he was hoarse. "At the corner, please!"

Cars honked and honked. The street was impassable. The mob inched slowly to the curb. When at last everyone was assembled on the sidewalk, Jack held up his free hand for attention. The crowd pressed against him, his back to the street, his left side protected by the metal lamp post supporting the traffic signal. A familiar voice screamed from behind, "Jack!"

Jack glanced over his left shoulder to see his attorney, Morton Williams, picking his way diagonally across the intersection. Meryl Rupert used the opportunity to push herself forward. Her heel dug into a pair of Converse Chuck Taylor All Stars and the cameraman recoiled in pain. Jack lost his footing and stepped backward into the turn lane. A Toyota 4Runner swerved right to avoid the man crossing the street against the light but had no time to avert clipping the sidewalk. Jack's body was dragged over the curb and onto Seventh Avenue.

আ৵

Susan picked her way on crutches to the terrace. She expected a throng of people and plenty of honking but not the sirens. Perhaps the mayor attended Jack's media circus – hopefully the last in a long, long while. She maneuvered around the planters and chairs and peered over the railing.

Policemen diverted traffic away from Seventh Avenue. A man stood next to a black SUV, shaking. A child in black leggings and a Lululemon training jacket lay sprawled on the sidewalk, streaked with blood, cradling an old man in a rumpled windbreaker. She rocked back and forth, wailing inconsolably, until a police officer and woman on crutches helped her back into the building.

Chapter 29

Darkness.

Susan picked through Jack's belongings, deciding what to discard, what to donate, what to preserve. The suits were boxy and old-fashioned but well-maintained. The Salvation Army could resell them. To think she once thought he was hand-some. Even lying in repose, the best she could say was he looked avuncular. His files were submitted to storage, in case there should be further litigation. There had been so much already – against the building, insurers, government, and assorted individual witnesses, yet it was practically for naught.

Thank heaven Jack had life insurance, but even that was a battle. One of the carriers insinuated the driver of the Toyota 4Runner, a Lebanese national, was an organized crime enforcer, hired to take out a terrorist co-conspirator. It did not help that his name appeared on the TSA watch list and that his H-1B visa had expired. Somehow or other, the insurance agent paired Jack with the only life insurance carrier in North America that still inserted a policy exclusion for terrorism and acts of war. "Thank you, Stanley Hochstabler," she fumed. She had to beg Agent Kroll at the FBI to intervene – itself a battle. Agent Kroll took an extensive leave of absence to deal with personal issues. It took three months before the carrier relented. Then there was the carrier that insisted the whole life conversion, taken just days before Jack died, was in actuality the issuance of a new policy, and therefore subject to a two-year moratorium on claims. Jill used the proceeds from the two carriers that paid to fight the two that did not.

Meanwhile, she paid Morton Williams $238,240.63 for doing nothing, Empire Bail Bonds $350,000 for its $3.5 million two-week loan (2,600 percent interest), $23,000 a month for living expenses, plus $50,000 in ongoing lawsuits.

Jack was a seasoned lawyer but detested litigation. Susan began to understand why. The cooperative retracted her $3,750 fine for violating the house rules on noise, but it cost her $12,000 in legal fees to persuade them. Wally just paid the fine. He was like Jack. He did not have the stomach for litigation. The only definitive outcome was that Nelson Foster redoubled his efforts to evict them – inconspicuously, of course. Susan hobbled to Home Depot on Third Avenue and 58th Street when Melissa's toilet clogged. "I'm sorry, Mrs. Roberts. The building staff's plungers are not for individual use." Printer cartridges were removed from the recycling receptacle and returned to her apartment. "I'm sorry, Mrs. Roberts, we are not permitted to dispose of these in the normal trash."

"How the hell do they know they were mine?" she fumed, "And why now, after disposing of them there for fifteen years?"

"I'm sorry, Mrs. Roberts, but scooters are not allowed in the lobby or elevators."

"It's a knee walker," she protested, "for resting my leg while I run errands."

"The house rules are clear, Mrs. Roberts. You'll have to use a wheelchair or the service elevator."

"Like the rest of our kind," she muttered.

Robert fidgeted uncomfortably. He hated fighting Nelson Foster's wars. The device was obviously not a plaything. But he did not want to be assigned night duty either. Mrs. Roberts dragged the walker to the stairwell and summoned the service elevator.

The lawsuit for false arrest settled quickly, but modestly. She recovered enough to settle the fees of the bail bondsman and Mr. Williams, but not enough for the lawsuit itself. The libel and slander claims were hopeless. Everyone asserted good faith reliance on what they heard from someone else. Except for the assertions of Sheldon Vogel, the government's case was hearsay. The hospital and Catherine Fallis settled for modest sums, enough to put matters behind them, but the board of the cooperative stonewalled. It would defend the testimony of the managing agent, superintendent, doorman, concierge and handyman until the building's reserve fund was exhausted, and if necessary, use financial necessity as an excuse to replenish the fund with a $15 million low-interest, non-amortizing 10-year loan, to be paid off by whoever still held shares after the existing directors were deceased. Susan placed a monthly lid on litigation expense and the law firm reluctantly acceded. Approached judiciously, the engagement could still become a lucrative annuity.

Susan did not bother suing the networks. Morton Williams was gung-ho in favor, but not one of Jack's former colleagues endorsed Mr. Williams' recommendation. This wasn't London or Canada. For better or worse, the Wallace and Roberts families were public figures. They had to prove actual malice – actual knowledge of falsity or reckless disregard for the truth – to sue the networks for libel. Susan was positive at least one network rose to that standard, but few thought she could prove it. Endless lampooning by Jon Stewart and Rachel Maddow were her only consolation.

Jack's books were the easiest effects to sort. She and Melissa carried bag after bag to Strand, the world's largest second-hand bookstore. It had been a fixture near Union Square since 1927. Susan and her daughter stood in line each day with students, the homeless, elderly widows – anyone who wanted to dispose of rare or used books for a profit. The profit was typically measured in pennies, although first editions of classics commanded higher prices. Jack possessed many such first-edition classics, but most of them were professional – outdated and of little use to anyone. Jack spent fewer and fewer hours with his books as he aged. He seemed to regard them as a mirror.

Susan didn't care about the profit but could not just fling them in the dumpster. She could not do that to Jack, not even posthumously. Someone at Strand would have to, not her. She gave the proceeds to Melissa.

Susan leafed through a small leather-bound volume entitled *Roberts' Rules of Order*. "Cute," she thought. She wondered why she never noticed it. She checked the back of the cover page, 1951, sixth edition – practically worthless. So what if it was a special seventy-fifth anniversary edition? A slip of paper dropped from the book as she flung it into the tote bag. She reached down with the 32-inch grabber Jack bought her when she returned from the hospital. Squatting was impossible. It was a faded dry-cleaning voucher, issued by TWA, with a name and number scrawled on the back. Her heart skipped a beat as she fished the small book from the tote bag.

"Keepsakes? Jack had keepsakes?" She seated herself at his desk and removed a page from *The Wall Street Journal* – a map of sports activities in Central Park. Her shrug betrayed disappointment. Jack hoarded the oddest things. At least the next items were sensible – a snapshot of the two of them in Napa Valley and one under the tram at Snowbird. There was a photograph of the three of them – Melissa was just an infant – smiling in front of the Widder Hotel in Zurich. There were photographs of his brother, Steven. She recognized him from the family portrait on the fireplace mantelpiece in Rye. There was also a badly yellowed photograph of a man, woman and two tiny children – a boy and a girl.

Susan assumed they were Steven, Eleanor and Jack's parents, but they did not resemble the figures on the mantelpiece – not Steven, not Eleanor, and not the parents. The boy resembled Jack. However, the family looked poor, like homesteaders, not much different from her mother's family photos. She surmised the boy and girl were Jack's grandparents. There was another photograph of the boy and girl, also yellowed and badly faded. Her facial features were barely discernible but his were clear. It was the spitting image of Jack as a young man. She'd seen photographs from his law school graduation. Susan often wondered about his grandparents. He looked nothing like his sister or brother. He was shorter, his complexion darker, his hair swarthier. He didn't share his brother's freckles or ginger hair. And Jack rarely sunburned. Here at last was the answer. Jack resembled his grandfather. She would ask Eleanor about the grandparents when she saw her.

She came to the last page of the book. Scotch-taped inside the cover was a short letter in a woman's hand – the only letter he preserved. Susan presumed it was a letter from Marcia. Susan never wrote Jack any letters. She texted him or used email. It was a "Dear John" letter dated April 27, 1988. Susan smiled at the irony, but then frowned. She cast the book down and the room spun. The author wasn't Marcia Wasserman. It was Special Agent Jill Fitzgerald Kroll.

✤✥✤

Hanni sat with Mildred Whiting and several other guests in a small living room overlooking the base of Trump International Hotel, the front doors of the Time Warner Center, and the Merchants' Gate entrance to Central Park. The centerpiece of the room was Gaetano Russo's 13-foot-tall marble statue of Christopher Columbus. The statue was dedicated to New York City in 1892. It commemorated the 400th anniversary of Columbus' first voyage to America. The statue stood atop a 75-foot marble column at the convergence of Broadway, Central Park West, Eighth Avenue and Central Park South. It was a block west from Mildred Whiting's apartment. Hanife Kaplan Wallace was the last of many sources Mildred sought to interview. She spent countless hours with Susan Roberts, Sheldon Vogel and the convicted burglar Allison Pfouts, presently released on probation. She liked Mrs. Pfouts. The two shared a fondness for travel and adventure, although Allie seemed more inclined to action than Mildred. Mildred regarded life from a distance. Mrs. Pfouts dove in, even if that meant a berth on a cruise ship, or, in the case of the late Marian Vogel's jewelry, tiptoeing around her neighbor's apartment.

Mildred also interviewed surgeon Dr. Lester Martinez, psychiatrist Dr. Hubert Simmons and retired attorney, Catherine Fallis. The latter called it quits. The last case was too much for her. She retired to the seclusion of her pre-war classic seven on Fifth Avenue and mumbled incoherently about writing her memoir. Mildred listened patiently but decided there was nothing to tell. She regarded her conversations with Catherine's son and with the late Jack Roberts' lawyer as complete wastes of time. The two were now partners – guardians of the conservative and liberal downtrodden. Williams became a star guest on MSNBC and Fallis remained popular on Fox News. Dissolution of the case had not visibly dimmed his popularity. There was always appetite for conspiracy.

Before meeting with Hanni, Mildred tracked down and interviewed current and former employees of NYL Health Systems. She found a nice young man, Stuart Chu, to explain what Bit-Torrent meant and how data could be encrypted and smuggled using the program. She found administrators who, in strictest confidence, described how their chief technology officer was escorted from the building in cuffs, and how the witnesses were 'advised' by federal government agents to remain silent. They described the frequent sexual overtures of their chief counsel and CEO, and how, together with the board of trustees and CFO, they doctored financial statements to appear profitable. Mildred tried vainly to procure interviews with Special Agent Jill Kroll of the FBI and to learn the identity of her counterpart at the CIA. No one seemed to know. No matter. She had plenty to compose a gripping and meticulously detailed account of the various criminal enterprises and political chicanery surrounding their investigation. She was convinced she could produce a bestseller.

Procuring the interview with Hanife was a windfall. She had long before given up hope. On impulse, she slipped one last missive in the woman's mail cubby, including her business card – the new one embossed on taupe parchment, the one with her newest penname, Mildred Whiting *Błaszczyk*. The woman called the next day.

Mildred climbed the seventy-foot catacomb of scaffolding leading to *Discovering Columbus*, the Japanese artist Tatzu Nishi's up-close unveiling of the 120-year-old statue in the context of a modern-day living room. Hanni arrived seconds after Mildred. She had considerably less difficulty managing the stairs. She wore a dark navy jumpsuit and track shoes. Mildred wore pumps.

Mildred admired the choice of locale. This Kaplan woman was shrewd. Visitors were allotted thirty minutes before they had to descend. Kaplan intended to keep the interview public and short. Kaplan took the initiative.

"Błaszczyk. That's an unusual name."

"My late husband's. There aren't many of them in Chicago."

Hanni digested the information. "Children?"

"Just one. Former naval officer, like my husband. He works in law enforcement."

"Here in New York, I suppose."

"No, I'm all alone here. Well, I have Ruby with me, of course, but no, Geoffrey is in Washington, DC." Hanni wondered which one of the exhibition guests was Ruby but did not inquire. She had the information she came for.

"Mildred? May I call you that? You can call me Hanni. I would love to assist you with your research. But you must promise to keep my assistance private. Would you do that for me?" Mildred was taken by surprise. She had not expected so much cooperation.

"Of course, Miss … Hanni. I'm a professional journalist. I always protect my sources."

"Good. Let's go back to your building. I'll show you my old apartment. Have you ever seen a surveillance device? The kind used by the CIA? There are several there, not to mention a few nifty gadgets of my own. I think I can fill some gaps in your story, pick up where the network coverage ends." The two women rose and circled to the stairs. "Is Ruby coming?" inquired Hanni, curious who the mystery companion was.

"Always," smiled Mildred, "Always." She gazed lovingly at the brilliant jeweled ring on her right ring finger. "The one on my left hand is from Gerald, of course, but this one here is Ruby, my prince." His cremated ashes were now a gemstone. She no longer obsessed about keeping him dusted.

৵৽

Geoffrey Błaszczyk met Agent Kroll for a final debriefing. She'd made a fool of herself and the Bureau and was forced to take two months off for personal reasons. Personally, Błaszczyk thought she should retire. She could, of course. She put in twenty-five years of service. She was entitled to full pension, the same as he was.

Błaszczyk could have weighed into her but was shocked by her appearance. Her face was leaner, more pallid. Perhaps it was the make-up. He reminded himself neither of them was young. They only appeared youthful because they worked at it. Jill probably worked wonders with cosmetics. Today she must have been lazy.

She looked gaunt and her hair was different. That was it. It wasn't wild and springy. It was matted down, impossibly smooth – the same Juliane Moore reddish brown but considerably more demure. There weren't thousands of untamed strands. Perhaps that was it, why she suddenly looked old.

"You win some, you lose some, Jill. It's the way life works," he consoled her. He could not believe he was comforting her. He should have been excoriating her, reminding her to respect his superior judgment. But someone beat him to the punch. She nodded dumbly at his counsel. She sat slouched in her chair and remained detached. Nothing he said elicited a rise out of her.

The meeting did not last long. Błaszczyk doubted they would assign her another high-profile case. She lost the drive. She was no longer a hunter. She looked like roadkill.

Błaszczyk rose to leave but Kroll interrupted him. "Listen, Jeff. You were right about everything. Thank you for tipping me off about Fallis' secretary, Denise Stojanovska. I was digging a deeper and deeper hole. I wanted to crucify John Roberts. I let him get to me personally, let him cloud my judgment. Thank you for helping me see the situation clearly."

"Uh, sure, Jill, any time." Błaszczyk slipped into the corridor and shut the door. "She's cracked. I never said anything about Denise Stojanovska." Back then, Błaszczyk wanted to crush her. It was personal. Now he just wanted to get away — her old age and lethargy could be contagious.

☙◦❧

Denise reclined on a chaise lounge, sipping a piña colada. The man beside her was droning about his problems. Late fifties, perhaps, with a close-trimmed gray mustache and beard, chiseled arms, and obligatory white muscle shirt and swim trunks. He sipped something with rum.

The man was hiding. The authorities in Belize wanted to question him in connection with the shooting death of his neighbor. So now he was across the border in Guatemala, insisting he was framed, insisting he invented anti-viral software, as if anyone could be that old. Even Denise's mother remembered computers, and she was a lot older than he was.

Phonies! The world was full of phonies. Denise was a phony, too. She had an alias, false passport, and bank account with nearly $1.1 million. Plus, a coterie of neighbors who each insisted they were wrongfully persecuted and pursued. Denise was the only one who openly admitted ripping anyone off; she just refused to elaborate how or whom.

"Poor Dmitri," she thought. She advised him to be more careful. But careful was not in his vocabulary. He was a rascal, always was. He only drove the car for a day. Now he would spend six, perhaps seven years in prison and be released into an economy where sixty percent of young adults were unemployed. "Stupid, stupid, stupid," she thought. He should have caught the same flight she took to Madrid and Buenos Aires. Her mother was down the beach procuring vegetables. They could live comfortably among former hedge fund managers, arbitrageurs and software executives for years. Most days, they picked up her dinner and bar tabs. There were plenty of men like John McAfee – outcast American expatriates, desperate to share their 'unique' personal tale of injustice and woe. Sometimes she slept with them. Sometimes she did not. It scarcely mattered. They wanted a sympathetic ear, someone who understood their distinctive travails. Denise's only travail was that damned Lamborghini. It could have bought a lot of jet skis.

∂∽∾

Stuart debated erasing NYL from his résumé. CTO of a company whose top executives were either dead, on the lam, or indicted for accounting fraud was not helping him procure future employment. And his sideline business was on hold; he no longer possessed the inside scoop.

Stuart idled away his savings in his small studio apartment on the Lower East Side, marveling at the tools Wallace bequeathed him. Some of them were brilliant. Wallace had this penchant for being, well, fucking retentive. Everything was meticulously documented, like a fucking cookbook. Wallace wrote the unpublished authoritative textbook on hacking – apparently for defensive purposes. He was a man on a mission, to infiltrate and understand enemy invaders so he could protect his own clients against intrusion. Stuart could not fucking believe Wallace let him see this stuff.

The message was discreet, a small change in Stuart's LinkedIn profile. It took a while for him to detect the changes. Fortunately, he saved a copy of his original profile in Microsoft Word, where he performed most of his text editing. Wallace ... presumably Wallace, Stuart corrected himself, had inserted words intermittently through the profile that, taken together, left the meaning unchanged. Some of the sentences were wordier, but outwardly the changes were unremarkable. He added a numeric string to the end of the biography, a seeming typo. Stuart copied down the added words and reordered them per the numeric string. He was directed to a previously unnoticed program on the special ESPN Radio & More workspace.

The program gave him direct access to the account of Danielle Stojko, Argentinean expatriate living in Puerto Barrios, Guatemala with her aging aunt. The account was in a small bank in neighboring Belize. He included a photograph of the passport photos used to establish the account. They bore striking resemblance, hairstyle and hair color notwithstanding, to the photograph of fugitive Denise Stojanovska on the evening news.

"What's your favorite charity?" queried a spontaneous chat box.

Stuart smiled before responding, "Me."

"Besides yourself," the chat box insisted.

Stuart thought about his former boss and mentor, the one who taught him to fuck politics and consider what was best for the client. He thought about the man's daughter, clinging to life at NYL North, and how her death destroyed him.

"Shit, the Leukemia and Lymphoma Society?" he at last volunteered.

"Thank you," came the response. "Click Enter."

Stuart did as instructed. The chat box disappeared, and his browser opened to Danielle Stojko's transaction history. She wired one million dollars to the Leukemia and Lymphoma Society's childhood disease fund. Stuart shredded his résumé. He identified a more satisfying calling … charity fundraising! A face in Alabama smiled. That was his specialty once. He was glad someone else succeeded him.

ഔൟ

Eleanor helped Susan empty the trunk. Susan was indecisive, unsure whether to dispose of the items or save them. Perhaps Eleanor would want them, just as she wanted mementos from Steven. She selected very little – photographs mostly. The rest could go to Goodwill or the trash heap. Susan brought forth the yellowed photograph of Jack's grandfather, great aunt, and great grandparents, the grandfather who resembled him so much as a young man.

"That's not Jack's grandfather," Eleanor laughed. "That's Jack!"

"Huh?" stammered Susan, "then … then who are the others?" Eleanor read her mind.

"That's his birth family, the Bartholomews."

Susan's eyes widened. "*Birth* family?"

"He never told you?" It was Eleanor's turn to exhibit surprise. "Weren't you ever curious? I mean, he didn't look anything like us."

Susan did not know where to begin. Who was this man, this John Bartholomew, the man she married and shared a bed with for sixteen years, the man who preserved a love letter from Jill Fitzgerald Kroll? Susan needed to sit down. Eleanor fetched a tea cup from the pantry, hesitated, then selected two brandy snifters instead. She returned with the snifters and a bottle of Jack Daniels.

"So…" she began. "What can I tell you?"

ഔൟ

Sheldon arrived home to a floor party. Allie Pfouts and Mildred Błaszczyk arranged it. Many of the older tenants were in attendance, together with several of the board members. Nelson

Foster was conspicuous in his absence. He asserted a Broadway-related conflict. There were a smattering of younger faces, neighbors along the hall, and a woman on crutches. The other tenants gave her room.

The two measured each other shyly, then Susan rushed forward and embraced him. She held him so tightly he thought he would suffocate, but then she released him, kissed him warmly on the cheek, and clasped both his hands.

"Welcome back, Sheldon. We missed you."

His emotions were confused. They were confused since that evening in the hospital, the evening he discovered his best friend fathered his baby, his only child, and that Marian and he were never lovers – spouses, perhaps, and then only by legislative fiat – but never lovers. At first, he wanted Helen's grave exhumed, cast out of the family plot. He wanted to murder her father with his great, great grandfather's service revolver and then himself. He did not care where he was buried. There was no plot beckoning him in Oneonta, no bench of repose in Central Park, no hallowed ground at Woodlawn Cemetery, and no Elysian Field in heaven. Above all, there was no Roman Catholic god. Marian Willis and Paul Giordano were instruments of the devil.

It began so innocently. He inquired whether Paul would take his confession. Paul laughed.

"You're not going to die. Save it for the padre."

"But I've screwed up so many lives. And I've always been able to blame the circumstances. But this time I can't."

Paul thought he meant leaving the vault unlocked. He decided to play along. "What's eating you, son?" Paul had an unorthodox approach to church vernacular.

"It's about Helen. I've never told anyone, except of course Mildred and Diana, but they were there. I didn't need to tell them." Paul's ears perked up. His mind raced. He remembered her last month. She had a huge argument with her father, her legal father, the father she grew up with. Marian called him about it. They hadn't spoken in years. Coming out of the closet, she called it. Helen and Diana came out of the closet, only Sheldon didn't like that. He flew into a rage and banished her from the household.

"I might have done the same, Sheldon. Attitudes were different then. She was your only child. Heck, I might do that today." Paul considered homosexuality a sin against God, something he could no longer express openly, not even to his own family. He suspected Sheldon and he shared many old-fashioned views.

"That's not what I mean, Paul. She stormed out of the apartment and walked straight into an oncoming taxi. I don't know whether it was intentional or an accident. I don't think I'll ever know. But she didn't die. She was just broken. The doorman called an ambulance and they rushed her here, to Roosevelt Hospital. They set her bones and placed her in ICU. Marian wouldn't look at me. Diana kept vigil in the waiting room, waiting for a moment when she could sneak in. Even a tyrannical old man needs a bathroom break."

Paul waited. He heard the account before, differently of course, but only mildly. How was Sheldon to know she would dash in front of a car? Paul wanted to bring the confession to a close. The memory upset him. Sure, he had two sons, but only one child with Marian. He was just as grief-stricken as Sheldon was. "Her heart gave out," he offered. "Marian wrote me."

Sheldon paused. "She did?" He had no idea they corresponded.

Paul thought quickly. "She invited me to the funeral, because you and I were buddies."

"Oh, of course," mumbled Sheldon. "I knew that. I just forgot. No, she only wrote that to protect me. Helen was bedridden, lots of broken bones. They pumped her full of saline and painkillers, the same ones they're giving me now, only she was out of it, out cold. But she bled all over the bed sheets. Marian said it was just that time of month. She inserted a pad and said to ignore it. Only I couldn't. It kept oozing and flowing and soon enough, the sheets were drenched again. It was harrowing, Paul. I saw her life draining away because I didn't approve her lifestyle, because I threw her out of the apartment. Well, I marched to the corner, bought the most absorbent tampons I could find, waited for a moment when we were alone, inserted one then covered it with that useless pad. Well, she didn't bleed anymore. She just died. The doctors said it was toxic shock syndrome. Diana began shrieking at me, demanded I be prosecuted for murder. 'Everyone knows about tampons and TSS,' she screamed, except that I did not know a thing. I thought I was saving her." Sheldon hung his head. Paul sat in stunned silence. He spoke first.

"You dumb fuck. You dumb miserable fuck! Don't you read the paper? Don't you listen to the news? Everyone in America knows superabsorbent tampons are dangerous. And you inserted one in an unconscious patient who couldn't even know she was suffering sepsis. You dumb miserable fuck!" Sheldon was taken aback. Catholic confession was not much different than confessing to his father. His father would beat him with his shaving strap. Paul just reached forward and strangled him. A nurse heard the commotion and tried to separate them. She called for reinforcements – in this case, the police officer absorbed in his Sudoku.

"This fucking idiot killed my daughter, this stupid fucking idiot!" Sheldon thought Paul lost his marbles. "You don't get it, peanut brain, do you?" Paul persisted, arms locked behind him by Officer Jacobs. "She's my daughter, not yours. Marian and I slept together weekly for nineteen years. We were lovers. Why do you think the jewelry was so cheap? That I was a fool? You're the fool, Sheldon, you. Look in the mirror. Who did she look like, you or me?" The last words pierced Sheldon's cortex. A synapse flashed and white-hot anger registered on his brow.

"No!" he roared, trying to break free from the nurse's hold. "No!"

Paul was ushered brusquely from the room but did not make it to the elevator. A gurney rushed the collapsed patient to emergency. Sheldon continued roaring for twenty minutes, until the sedative knocked him unconscious. It was unclear whether his last raving words were slurred. The ones uttered incoherently the next morning certainly were.

Susan placed Sheldon's arm in hers and guided him from the elevator to his apartment. He was sure they had the wrong floor. Mildred Błaszczyk and Allison Pfouts beamed. They were sure the renovation would please him. Mildred's book was selling like hotcakes. It outsold Nora Roberts, Danielle Steel and James Patterson combined. She had guest appearances on all the major talk shows plus invitations all over Canada and Europe. She and Allie decided to let Shelly manage their money, or at least a portion of it. Mildred knew better than to place all her eggs in one basket, but what she assigned him more than compensated for what he lost. He would still have to live frugally, of course, because of the water damage to his neighbors' apartments, but the lion's share of the loss was borne by Mildred Whiting. She instructed her insurer to settle low. She was planning to redecorate anyway.

Susan gave the three of them her airline and cruise ship tickets to the Greek Islands and Asia Minor. Melissa transferred two weeks earlier to a boarding school in Connecticut, and Susan had no interest in traveling alone. Melissa and Susan hardly spoke anymore. The two needed time to themselves.

There was a small cabin on the cruise ship, originally for Melissa, and a spacious one with two beds for Jack and Susan. She assumed Mildred, Allison and Sheldon could arrange something sensible.

Susan sought to distance herself from Jack and his gifts. She was still recoiling from her conversation with Eleanor. Jack was a foster child, adopted by Reverend and Mrs. Julius Roberts after Mrs. Bartholomew died. Mr. Bartholomew was a logger, a dying breed even then. They lived in a three-room shack on the outskirts of North Creek.

"Most days he was just a drinker," Eleanor inserted. "The wife struggled to protect Jack and his sister from abuse, but she was tiny. That's why Jack was so short. Barto – everyone called him Barto – just got meaner and angrier. The sheriff, my uncle, finally ran him out of the county. We never heard from him again. Some say he headed west, where they still had logging."

"The three of them were really close. They'd been through hell together. Jack and his sister, they were inseparable – almost like twins. I think he was a year older. That's the way they would have remained, dirt poor but scraping by. Her mother gave piano and dance lessons. She taught for free at the local elementary school, just to advertise her services. Did Jack ever play for you? He was quite gifted, you know." Susan knew. She suspected the mother liked Cole Porter and the foxtrot.

"And then she died. They found her one morning in bed, lifeless and stiff as a board. The town didn't know what to do. Jack was fourteen. Barto's sister offered to take in the girl. She and her family lived in Syracuse. My parents offered to take in Jack. Steven was older, but the two of them played together – you know, rafting, skiing, hiking, that sort of thing. Steven was a natural born mountain man."

"Well, the separation devastated him. He tried to be a good foster son but he was always running away, hitching rides south and west toward Syracuse. She was just as bad. The difference was, she was more athletic. She could outrun anyone. She actually made it. She must have been sixteen at the time. Mom and dad let her stay with us for a while. What harm could it do? But we all knew she'd have to go back eventually. You could see the two of them, truant from school, down at the river, reminiscing about their makeshift river launch and swimming hole."

"It was Saturday morning, mid- or late April. Barto's sister was driving in from Syracuse the next day to drag the poor girl home. We were depressed. No one wanted to be around when that happened. We each made plans. Well, the two just disappeared. We assumed they were out for another walk. They broke into the shed with the big rubber rafts and dragged one down to the river. The water was still icy cold. Walls of ice six feet thick protruded out across the river, leaving a jagged gap in the middle. The snow melt off the Adirondacks made the current swell. It's some of the roughest whitewater in the East, and back then we didn't have wet suits. We had vests, of course, and makeshift helmets, but it was primitive. They picked a really open section, strong current, but wide open. She popped out where the gorge narrows. Jack searched around desperately, but the raft kept dragging him downstream. She surfaced a couple days later, caught beneath the ice. Jack spent the rest of high school in psychiatric care, working with a shrink. He never forgave himself."

"She made him do it, you know. She was too young to raft when they sent her to Syracuse. She wasn't going back without trying it just once. Jack would never admit it, but I don't think he ever had a choice."

Susan drained the glass of Jack Daniels and poured herself another. She tried to digest what Eleanor told her. She pointed to the photograph. Her next question was random. It meant nothing, really. She just did not know what else to say.

"What did she look like?"

"Back then, you mean?" Eleanor asked.

"Of course, back then," she nearly blurted. Instead she just nodded. Eleanor was as bad as Jack. What else could she mean?

Eleanor thought for a moment, raised herself from her chair, and went to the bedroom. She returned with a small album. She opened to page three and said, "There."

Susan wondered why Eleanor was playing games with her. "That's me, in my wedding gown." Page one was a photograph of the couple; page two was a photograph of the wedding party.

"I'm sorry, Susan. It's the best I can do. I don't have any photos of her, not as a teenager, but I can assure you, she looked exactly like you. The first time I saw you I gasped. I thought she returned from the dead."

Susan did not believe her. "I'm black, Eleanor. How could she possibly look like me?"

"Because she was black too ... like her mother. No darker than Lena Horne, almost exactly like you. Jack of course looked like his father."

Susan thought about her daughter, whose skin was so light most parents thought Susan was the nanny. She knew she would regret the answer but asked anyway.

"You haven't told me her name."

"I don't have to, child. You already know." Eleanor closed the wedding album, returned it to the bedroom, then poured herself another Jack Daniels.

ॐॐ

Mildred's book was a media and government sensation. She was called before the House Judiciary Committee to divulge her sources. The book was chock-full of poignant and at times embarrassing revelations about the NYL investigation, especially in its use of paid informants and unorthodox counterintelligence procedures. The Committee declared the information was classified and therefore leaked.

Mildred's fan base of young, unmarried women filled the chambers and spilled onto the steps of Congress. Journalists had difficulty muscling for seat space.

Mildred stood her ground. She was pressed repeatedly to reveal her sources but insisted they were protected, and that none of them, not one, was a government employee who had ever been privy to or leaked classified information. If anyone was in possession of classified information, it was someone else's fault, which, of course, was the purpose of the investigation – to pinpoint, silence and punish the leaker. Secretly everyone knew. She would not say it and they could not prove it. So, they stripped him of his security clearance and gave him a desk job in accounting. He wanted to complain to his mother, but that would have made matters worse. Hanni flipped off live CNN coverage in satisfaction. She had a plane to catch.

৵৵

A day's-long drizzle finally ended. The field glowed orange in the afternoon sun. It was the fourth week of April, yet the temperature hovered around forty. Jill lay the shopping bag down and inspected the gravesite. She shivered and leaned against it as she paused for breath. She pulled a trowel from the bag and sank to her knees. She dug three hundred small holes, each spaced twelve inches apart. The holes formed a seventeen-by-seventeen-foot canvas. She filled and closed each hole carefully. She rocked on her aching knees and coughed. She stepped back to regard the handiwork. There was a single bulb in each of the holes – one mango-tinged calla lily for each month she rued not answering her door. She flew back to Boston to keep her appointment at Brigham & Women's Hospital but returned once more in late June when the lilies were in bloom. The fragrance was light, barely discernible, but the blazing forest of trumpets was gorgeous. She taped a small pink ribbon, barely discernible, to the side of the gravestone. On it were inscribed the words, "Such as we are made of, such we be." Like the warm-weather flowers scenting the gravesite, she knew she would not survive the coming winter. Such an odd case, she thought, the last of her career. The elusive Marja, the cast of hackers, lawyers and informants who drifted on and off her stage – she never asked Błaszczyk what became of the files that were swapped out of Gürhan Erdoğan's database. "Destroyed, I suppose, like everyone remotely connected with this comedy."

৵৵

Susan sat at the bar of the Gar Woods restaurant in Carnelian Bay, Lake Tahoe. She sipped a white wine spritzer. The Happy

Hour crowd cavorted with their Wet Woody's. Susan kept to herself. She considered adjusting the glass eye to appear more diffident. Off kilter even slightly, it was maddeningly disconcerting. A man smiled at her from across the bar. The face was familiar. Handsome, she thought. He rose slowly and maneuvered around the crowd.

"A year ago, at the intersection of 267 and North Lake Boulevard, a bashed powder blue Miata – I pulled over to see if I could help. May I join you?"

Susan started. The boy? He was scarcely twenty. It couldn't be.

"They're married now. Can you believe it? I'm pretty sure Officer Dierich checks in on them, just to make sure everything's okay."

Susan was still marveling at the transformation. The boy was at least twenty-eight, maybe thirty.

"I'm a resident at Tahoe Forest Hospital in Truckee. I heard about your accident from a friend, your surgeon, actually. I couldn't believe you were the same person. But how many single women drive around Tahoe in a fender-smashed blue Miata. I put two and two together."

Susan opened her mouth but said nothing. Instead, she reached for her spritzer.

"I checked in on you several times, in part to observe the surgery – in case I inherit a case like yours. You're lucky to have both legs. How do they feel?"

"Pretty good," Susan managed. "I'm trying them out tomorrow at Squaw Valley."

The man chuckled. "I thought you'd say that. Alone again, I suppose?"

Susan nodded sheepishly.

"Tell you what. I'm volunteer ski patrol and off from the hospital tomorrow. Why don't you let me escort you around the mountain, just to make sure everything's stable?" Susan regarded him skeptically. "Really, I mean it. Here's my ski patrol ID and my doctor's badge at Tahoe Forest." Susan did not have her reading glasses but inspected them anyway. She was convinced. Besides, he was handsome and at least, what, thirty?

"And you say you're a surgeon in residency?"

"Yes, ma'am, finishing my sixth and final year. I plan to hang my own shingle in August." The man laughed. It was a breezy, comfortable laugh. He regarded Susan for a moment, then blushed.

"What?" she asked. She reached impulsively for her eye. The doctor reached up and gently pulled the hand away. He lingered a moment before letting go.

"I was just going to say, well, your face is beautiful."

Susan smiled. He meant it. "I would love to go skiing with you tomorrow. Where shall we meet?"

"How about Syd's Bagelry in Tahoe City. It's just before the turnoff for 89. Know it?"

"Tamara McKinney's old place," she remarked. "Yeah, I know it."

The man started in surprise. McKinney was a legend in Tahoe, but back east? This woman must once have been a racer. He adjusted his game plan.

"Fantastic! 7:30 am. Stick with me and you can skip the lift lines. I'll show you my favorite fall lines. There's a real killer off KT-22," Susan's heart sank, "that we can tackle in the afternoon … after the sun softens it."

Her outlook brightened and she smiled broadly. Susan raised her glass. "To tomorrow then, and a gnarly schuss down KT-22!" The doctor clinked the spritzer with his beer mug.

"Tell me, what shall I call you?" The man looked at her quizzically. She had just inspected his identification.

"How about Bart? That's what my friends call me in Oregon. Down here they just call me by my real name, Tom Bartholomew. But I can see what you mean. Bartholomew is a mouthful."

☙❧

"No, please don't go. My parents want you to stay. Alya misses you terribly."

Hanni wanted to scream, "She's dead, you fool! So are your parents!" But she did not. She was here, too, calculating where they might squeeze her in when the time came.

"I don't usually come at this hour," he volunteered. "The mosquitoes swarm something fierce." Wallace cringed in embarrassment at how that sounded. His mother would not have condoned the construction – too much time spent in Birmingham. He tried again, "I don't like the smell of Cutter and Off. It irritates me as much as the mosquitoes. And I've read it hurts the central nervous system. So I stay away from here at dusk. I kid myself that if I live clean and eat clean, I won't wind up like my father and daughter, as if that matters much. Pretty pathetic, don't you think?"

"Um-hmm," she replied noncommittally. She regarded him silently. He shed fifteen, perhaps twenty pounds since she last saw him, but not from exercise. He looked stooped and old. She wondered what he was eating. "I don't suppose you could lend me some ... some DEET. The smell doesn't bother me and I don't think I can return during the day." She wanted to add, "and crop dusters overshot the orchard regularly when I was a kid. They bombarded our yard. Beril and I pretended the insecticide was snow," but she decided not to add that. Wallace was sensitive. There was no cause to berate him.

"Walk with me to the house?" he inquired.

"Yeah, sure. My meter isn't running, not since I left that rat hole. They treated you rough there, too, I suppose?"

"Your lawyer? Yeah, I suppose he did, but he was just doing his job. He told me at least twice to retain my own. That's what his letters said. He even typed the recommendation in bold. I just wasn't thinking clearly during the ... during the turmoil. By the way, I should have thanked you for letting me stay at the apartment. It was temporary, of course, but so was the ... the ... the confinement." He still did not know what to call it. "I could never have sorted things out inside that ... that hospital." Hanni stepped back. She did not expect him to speak casually about the breakdown. He was such a mess after the interrogation they recommended admitting him to Belleview. But suddenly he improved. It was just a matter of medication. The report said so.

"Not my lawyer, silly, the Feds. The Feds charged you with espionage when Alya died and again when Jack Roberts was indicted."

"Yeah, they did," he agreed slowly, "Only I don't think I understood what they were saying. They handcuffed me, pushed me through a crowd of onlookers, locked me in a cell, and then started barraging me with questions about plutonium and Iranian reactors. All I could think about was you and Alya and the hospital and that stupid divorce. I kept asking them to define 'constructive abandonment' and the best salvage therapy for a dead person and the parameters of a streaming-media price-fixing litigation hold. When I realized they were testing thermodynamics and molecular physics, I began pleading for my notes. The textbooks told me nothing. The exam would cover what Professor Clark talked about in class. Only I could not remember a thing. It was so long ago. I could only remember the mole on the left side of his nose. It bobbed up and down as he strutted in front of the chalk board and when his nostrils flared to make a point. I was terrified I would fail and they would send me home, the one Cornwallis to avoid the draft, survive the war, and make it to college, dishonorably discharged for paying too much attention to a mole. They kept me awake for four or five days in a row, shrieking at me the whole time. And then they switched on the regular lights, handed me my Dictaphone, and said, 'Mr. Wallace, we're so sorry. This has all been a terrible mistake.' Only it wasn't a mistake. I was still guilty of constructive abandonment, just as the divorce decree said. I still lost my child and my job and my savings and my apartment and my ... and my everything, and I was still babbling on and on about thermodynamics for weeks and weeks and weeks." He stubbed his toe into the soft earth and glanced up sheepishly. Tears streamed down his cheeks and he jerked his head away to hide them. Hanni did not react. She was thinking about what he said – about "paying too much attention to a mole."

"I hated you so much after that," he injected. "I hated you so, so much." His voice tapered into a dying whisper.

"It was mutual," she assured him matter-of-factly. "I hated you too."

"The other time was nothing. I even got to go home, work on my own defense. Well, you know." Hanni knew. She remembered hiding under Andrew Fallis' desk. Somehow, she was sure it was Wallace who cleared John Roberts and thus himself.

They stood in the driveway several minutes, saying nothing, watching grave markers cast long shadows in the opposite direction. Shad flies swarmed but still they said nothing. At last she broke the silence.

"Do you suppose I could spend some time here with you? Until I find a place of my own, I mean? The sublet in New York ... It expired."

"I don't know," Wallace stammered. "You see, it's like this." He could hear his mother scolding him again, "'You see, it's like this' is not fit talk for a college graduate." Wallace tried again, "I'm just scraping by at the moment. I work two jobs to make ends meet. You deserve much better."

"I know, baby. That's why I receive alimony, which I might add has always been on time." She kissed him gently on the cheek. He blushed – a fifty-seven-year-old man and he blushed. Hanni could tell him about the offer from Langley in the morning. Then they could work for the same company – different departments of course, and lower pay than at the hospital, but for the same team. "Suppose I pitch in a bit?"

"Would you?" He sounded like the dopey adolescent she met sixteen years earlier. But he suddenly reflected, "You don't still throw your clothes everywhere, do you?"

"If I'm in a good mood. Why, does it matter?"

"I suppose not," he replied, not entirely persuaded by his answer, or by hers. He wondered whether he could fit all his clothing in a plastic container under the bed. There was a Bed, Bath & Beyond on Summit Boulevard. He could race over there tomorrow between shifts. Hanni did not tell him about the two-bedroom apartment in Arlington, Virginia – the one with his-and-her walk-in closets, both with her name on them. Or about the electronic surveillance system and door lock.

Hanni nestled closer to Wallace and clutched his hand, just as she had so many years before. She checked her FSH fertility level before boarding the plane. The tests said she was ovulating. She led him back to the house, declined the DEET, but made sure the mosquito netting sealed them in tightly. She rose several hours later, powered on her tablet, and filed the missing data with Tehran.

AFTERWORD

Cooperative Lives sat on my OneDrive for seven years. I completed the first draft May 11, 2013 after seven furious months of head-scratching, typing, deleting and re-typing. I sat despondently as friends deleted the attachment from their inbox or let it molder on their hard drives. I let it molder on mine.

Four months ago, I revisited the manuscript. I'd hung up my job and my skates and had time to invest. The manuscript needed work but the story felt genuine. The emotions it evoked were still raw and they were mine. I promised myself publication before my sixtieth birthday, even if that meant self-publishing it for random passersby.

To all such random passersby, I hope you enjoyed my story. Thank you for giving it a chance. I hope you tell your friends about it and mention it online. Also, please consider writing a review. It will help others find the work and encourage this full-of-doubt, first-time author to continue writing. Mahalo!

ACKNOWLEDGMENTS

I am indebted to my wife, Dorene, for permitting me to scribble away as our savings waned and my job search withered. It wasn't until month six that she realized I was writing a novel. She'd assumed it was just another professional publication, a manifesto on performance-based pay or risk management. Perhaps it should have been; it might have paid the bills. Thank you, nevertheless, for being so patient. And thank you, Kealani, for being so supportive of Dorene.

I am also indebted to my friend and former law school classmate, Aaron Iverson, whose insights as playwright and author helped reshape the final manuscript and helped validate that the first draft, although rough, had literary potential.

I'd like to thank Denise Beaumont for the many marvelous conversations we had as we schlepped our daughters to practices in Monsey, Stamford and White Plains. We logged hundreds of hours conversing – hours devoted to, among other topics, our favorite books. It was your admiration of Elizabeth Strout's Olive Kitteridge (Random House 2008) that inspired me to weave together a collection of otherwise independent fictionalized stories about my neighbors.

Last, I am indebted to my long-time pen pals in Cologne and Graz, Ulrike Gemein and Elisabeth Unger, for reading the first draft cover-to-cover and actually enjoying it. Or saying so. If this book makes it to press, you will receive the first signed copies. Danke!

ABOUT THE AUTHOR

Patrick Finegan was born during the latter half of the Eisenhower Administration and graduated during the Carter and Reagan Administrations from Northwestern University and the University of Chicago Law School and Graduate School of Business. He worked more than thirty years in law, corporate finance, management consulting and risk management. He has a wife and grown daughter and has lived in the New York metropolitan area his entire professional life.

Mr. Finegan began writing fiction in 2013. *Cooperative Lives* is his first published work. It has won more than twenty literary awards and generated considerable editorial praise. You can contact Mr. Finegan or learn more about his work at www.twoskates.com.

Made in the USA
Middletown, DE
07 July 2020